The Forbidden

F. R. Tallis is a writer and clinical psychologist. He has written self-help manuals, non-fiction for the general reader, academic text books, over thirty academic papers in international journals and several novels. Between 1999 and 2012 he received or was shortlisted for numerous awards, including the New London Writers' Award, the Ellis Peters Historical Dagger, the Elle Prix de Letrice, and two Edgars. His critically acclaimed Liebermann series (written as Frank Tallis) has been translated into fourteen languages and optioned for TV adaptation. His latest novels include *The Forbidden*, *The Sleep Room*, *The Voices* and *The Passenger*.

For more on F. R. Tallis, visit his website
www.franktallis.com
or follow him on Twitter @FrankTallis

By F. R. Tallis

The Forbidden
The Sleep Room
The Voices
The Passenger

Writing as Frank Tallis

FICTION

Killing Time
Sensing Others
Mortal Mischief
Vienna Blood
Fatal Lies
Darkness Rising
Deadly Communion
Death and the Maiden

NON-FICTION

Changing Minds
Hidden Minds
Love Sick

F. R. TALLIS

The Forbidden

PICADOR

First published 2012 by Macmillan

This edition published 2016 by Picador
an imprint of Pan Macmillan
20 New Wharf Road, London N1 9RR
Associated companies throughout the world
www.panmacmillan.com

ISBN 978-1-4472-0498-5

1 3 5 7 9 8 6 4 2

A CIP catalogue record for this book is available from the British Library.

Typeset by Ellipsis Digital Limited, Glasgow.
Printed and bound by CPI Group (UK) Ltd, Croydon, CR0 4YY

Visit **www.picador.com** to read more about all our books
and to buy them. You will also find features, author interviews and
news of any author events, and you can sign up for e-newsletters
so that you're always first to hear about our new releases.

Acknowledgements

I would like to thank Wayne Brookes, Catherine Richards, Clare Alexander, Sally Riley, Steve Matthews and Nicola Fox for their valuable comments on the first and subsequent drafts of *The Forbidden*. I would also like to thank Brendan King for answering questions about J.-K. Huysmans's characters in *Là-Bas*, Owen Davies for answering questions on magic books and the capture of demons in glass, and Dr Yves Steppler for alerting me to the existence of TTX.

PROLOGUE

1872

Saint-Sébastien,
an island in the French Antilles

During the great siege of Paris I had worked alongside one of the Poor Sisters of the Precious Blood. Her name was Sister Florentina and it was she who had written to me, advising of a vacancy that had arisen for a junior doctor at the mission hospital on Saint-Sébastien. Perhaps it was because of the dismal autumn weather and the heavy rain that lashed against my windows, but I immediately fell into a reverie of sunshine and exotic landscapes. Throughout the day, these images played on my mind and I began to take the prospect of Saint-Sébastien more seriously. I envisaged learning about rare diseases, visiting leper colonies and embarking on a kind of medical adventure. That evening, sitting in a shabby restaurant with sticky floorboards and frayed tablecloths, I looked around at my glum companions and noticed that, like me, they were all regulars: two dowdy seam-stresses, a music teacher in a badly fitting dress and a moribund accountant with greasy hair. By the time I had finished my first course, I was already composing my letter of application and, two weeks later, I was standing on the deck of the paddle steamer *Amerique*, a vessel of the General Transatlantic Company, bound for Havana.

The Saint-Sébastien mission hospital consisted of a low, whitewashed building in which the patients were cared for by nuns under the general direction of a senior medical officer, Georges Tavernier. Outpatients were seen in a wooden cabin just removed from the hospital, and next to this was a tiny church. Every Sunday, a priest arrived in an open carriage to celebrate Mass.

My new superior, Tavernier, was an easy-going fellow and dispensed with formalities as soon as we met. When I addressed him with the customary terms of respect, he laughed and said, 'There's no need for that here, Paul. You're not in Paris now.' He was a bachelor in his middle years, of world-weary appearance, with sagging pouches beneath his eyes and curly, greying hair. In repose, his features suggested tiredness, fatigue, even melancholy, but as soon as he spoke his expression became animated. He was a skilled surgeon, and during his ten-year residency on Saint-Sébastien he had acquired a thorough under-standing of tropical diseases and their treatment. Indeed, he was the author of several important papers on the subject and had invented a very effective anaesthetic oint-ment that could be used as an alternative to morphine.

The hospital was situated some distance from the capital, on the edge of a forest which descended by way of gentle undulations to a mangrove swamp. Our only neighbours occupied a hinterland of scattered, primitive villages, so it was fortunate that Tavernier and I enjoyed each other's company. He often invited me to dine at his villa, which was perched high on the slopes above the hospital, an old plantation owner's residence that had seen better days – an edifice of faded stucco, crumbling pillars and cracked bas-relief. We would sit on the terrace, smoking and drinking aperitifs. The view was spectacular: a solitary road winding its way through lush vegetation down to Port Basieux, the busy harbour, boats swaying at anchor, the glittering expanse of the sea. As the sun sank, a mulatto girl would light hurricane lamps and bring us plates piled high with giant lobster and crab, mangos, pineapples, sapodillas and yams. The air was scented with hibiscus and magnolia and sometimes we were visited by armies of brightly coloured frogs or a curious iguana.

Tavernier was keen to hear about my experiences during the Paris siege, and he listened attentively.

'The winter was merciless. People in the poor districts – driven mad through starvation – were breaking into cemeteries, digging up corpses and making gruel with pulverized bones.' I paused to light a cigar. 'One evening, while walking back from the hospital to my lodgings, I came across a shocking scene. A building had been shelled and the road was obstructed by fallen masonry.

Through the smoke, I could see men rushing about, trying to put out fires. I climbed up the bank of rubble and, on reaching the top, saw a pale arm sticking out from the wreckage below. I scrambled down and began removing the bricks that were piled around it. The skin was smooth and it was obvious from the delicacy of the elongated fingers that they belonged to a woman. "Madame!" I shouted, "Can you hear me?" I took her hand in mine and pulled a little. To my great horror the entire arm came away. It had been detached from its owner by the blast and the lady to whom it belonged was nowhere to be seen.'

Tavernier shook his head and lamented the folly of war; however, his mood could change quite suddenly. The siege had exposed profound social inequalities and I was illustrating this point with a revealing anecdote. 'Along the boulevards, the best restaurants remained open and when the meat ran out, they simply replenished their stock with zoo animals. Patrons were offered elephant steak, stewed beaver and camel fricassée.'

Tavernier slapped his thighs and roared with laughter, as if the horrors I had only just described were quite forgotten. I came to realize that, although his clinical judgement was sound, in other respects Tavernier could be quite wayward.

Naturally, I had wondered why it was that such a talented individual was content to languish in relative obscurity. He was not devout and his specialist knowledge would have made him a valuable asset in any of the better universities. I began to suspect that there might be a story attached to his self-imposed exile and indeed, this proved to be the case.

One night, we were sitting on Tavernier's terrace, beneath a blue-black sky and the softly glowing phosphorescence of the Milky Way. A moist heat necessitated the constant application of a handkerchief to the brow. Again, much of our conversation concerned Paris, but our talk petered out and we sat for a while, listening to the strange chirrups and calls that emanated from the trees. Tavernier finished his rum and said, 'I can never go back.'

'Oh?' I said. 'Why not?'

'My departure was . . .' he paused, considering whether to proceed. 'Undignified.' I did not press him and waited. 'A matter of honour, you see. I was indiscreet and the offended husband demanded satisfaction. Twenty-five paces – one shot, the pistol to be brought up on command.'

'You killed someone?'

Tavernier shook his head. 'He didn't look like a duellist. In fact, he looked like a tax inspector, quite portly, with a ruddy complexion. After agreeing to his conditions, I learned that he had once been a soldier. You can imagine what effect this information had on me.'

I nodded sympathetically.

'The night before,' continued Tavernier, 'I couldn't sleep and drank far too much brandy. When dawn broke, I looked in the shaving mirror and hardly recognized

5

myself: bloodshot eyes, sunken cheeks, my hands were trembling. A thought occurred to me: *This time tomorrow you will be dead*. My seconds arrived at seven o'clock. "Are you all right?" they asked.

'"Yes," I replied, "quite calm."

'"Have you had breakfast?"

'"No," I replied. "I'm not hungry." Another gentleman, the doctor, was waiting in the landau. I shook his hand and thanked him for coming. When we got to the Bois du Vésinet, the other carriage was already there. I looked out of the window and saw four men in fur coats, stamping their feet and blowing into their hands to keep them warm. My seconds got out first, and then the doctor, but I found that I couldn't move. The doctor came back and said, "What's the matter?"

'I was paralysed. It was obvious that I wouldn't be able to fulfil my obligation. "I'm sorry," I said. "I'm not feeling very well – a fever, I think. I'm afraid we'll have to call it off." I was taken back to my apartment, where I spent the rest of the day in bed. In the morning I made arrangements to leave and have not been back since.' Tavernier gazed up at the zenith. A shooting star fell and instantly vanished. 'I disgraced myself. But at least I'm alive.'

'Honour is less important these days,' I said, 'now that the whole country has been disgraced. You could return, if you really wanted. And who would remember you? Ten years is a long time.'

'No,' said Tavernier. 'This is my home now. Besides, there are other things that keep me here.'

I didn't ask him what these 'other things' were, but I was soon to find out.

That year, the carnival season began late, and I was aware of a growing atmosphere of excitement. Preparations were being made in the villages and some of the patients were eager to be discharged for the festivities. I paid little attention to all of this activity, assuming that the season would pass without my involvement. Then, to my great surprise, I received an invitation to attend a ball.

'Oh, yes,' said Tavernier. 'The de Fonteneys always invite us.'

'The de Fonteneys?'

'They're local gentry,' he pointed towards the volcanic uplands. 'Piton-Noir.'

'Are you going?'

'Of course I'm going. I go every year. I wouldn't miss it for the world!'

It had been a long time since I had attended a social function and I felt increasingly nervous as the date approached. The de Fonteneys were a very old family, having settled in the Caribbean during the reign of Louis XIV. I was not accustomed to mixing with such people and thought that I would appear gauche or unmannered. Tavernier told me to stop being ridiculous. When the day of the ball finally arrived, we were allowed to use the mother superior's chaise, so at least we were spared the indignity of arriving on foot. We took the Port Basieux road and, on reaching the coast, began a steep ascent. A large, conical mountain loomed up ahead, rising high above the cultivated terraces. This striking landmark was La Cheminée; its sporadic eruptions, over a period of many thousands of years, had created the Saint-Sébastien archipelago. A ribbon of twisting grey smoke rose from its summit.

We reached a crossroads, at which point the chaise came to a juddering halt.

'Straight on, Pompée,' said Tavernier.

Our driver seemed uncomfortable. He began to jabber in a patois which I found difficult to follow. Something was disturbing him and he was refusing to proceed. He pointed at the road and jumped down from his box.

'For heaven's sake, man,' Tavernier called out. 'Get back up there and drive!'

More fulminating had no effect, so Tavernier and I alighted to see what Pompée was looking at. A primitive design had been made on the ground with flour. It consisted of a crucifix, wavy lines and what appeared to be a row of phallic symbols.

'What is it?' I asked.

'A vèvè,' said Tavernier. 'A bokor – a native priest – has put it here to invoke certain spirits. Pompée thinks we will offend them if we pass it.'

'Is there an alternative route?'

'No. This is the only road to Piton-Noir.'

Tavernier and his servant continued to argue and as they did so I heard the faint sound of a drum. Pompée stopped gesticulating and looked off in the direction from where the slow beat was coming. The sun had dipped below the horizon and the looming volcano made me feel uneasy.

'Are we in danger?' I asked.

'No,' Tavernier replied. 'It's just superstitious nonsense.'

He stomped over to the vèvè and scraped his heel through its centre. The effect on Pompée was immediate and melodramatic. He cowered and his eyes widened in terror. Tavernier kicked at the ground, producing a cloud of flour and red dust, and when the vèvè was utterly destroyed he turned and said, 'See? It's gone.' I had expected Pompée to respond with anger, but instead, he now seemed anxious for his master's safety. He removed an amulet from his pocket, an ugly thing of beads and hair, and insisted that Tavernier take it. Tavernier accepted the charm with an ironic smile and we returned to the chaise. Pompée leaped up onto his box and struck the horse's rump. He was eager to get away, and for some obscure reason so was I. When the steady pulse of the drumbeat faded, I was much relieved.

We entered the de Fonteney estate through an iron gate and joined a train of carriages. An avenue of torches guided us to an impressive facade of high windows and scalloped recesses, and as we drew closer, the strains of a chamber orchestra wafted over the balustrade. We were announced by a liveried servant and welcomed by the Comte de Fonteney, who addressed us with the slow finesse of an aristocrat. With brisk efficiency, we were then ushered into a dazzling ballroom full of mirrors, gilt embellishments and the portraits of bewigged ancestors. The dancing was already under way. I proceeded to the other end of the ballroom and stood on my own, watching the revellers. In due course, a young woman appeared at my side and we began to exchange pleasantries. She was small and strangely artificial, like a doll. Her eyelashes were long and her ox-bow lips were the purple-red of a ripe cherry. I asked her to dance and she offered me her hand. Her name was Apollonie. Afterwards, she introduced me to her cousins, all of whom were of a similar age and dressed in lustrous silks. They surrounded me, like exotic birds, with open, quivering fans and asked me many questions about Paris: what were the society ladies wearing, where did they shop and which operettas were most popular? I allowed myself a little inventive licence in order to retain their attention. At midnight, the ball ended and I went outside with Tavernier to wait for our chaise. I had enjoyed myself and was reluctant to leave.

'Ah,' said Tavernier. 'You are thinking of that coquette I saw you dancing with. And why wouldn't you: she was very pretty. But I'm afraid it can't go any further. We are only welcome here once a year and, if I'm not mistaken, your little friend was the governor's daughter.' I sighed and he gripped my arm. 'Don't be downhearted. Look, there's Pompée. Might I suggest that we stop off in Port Basieux. I know some places there that I'm sure will cheer you up.'

We drove down to the harbour and kept going until we came to the docks. Behind the warehouses were some narrow streets. Tavernier ordered Pompée to stop outside a crudely painted shack and tossed him a coin. I could hear the muffled sound of carousing from inside. 'Wait here,' said Tavernier to the driver, 'and don't drink too much.' I followed Tavernier into the shadows, traipsing down alleys and passageways until we came to a shabby building with shuttered windows. We walked around to a side entrance, where, hanging from a post, was a candle burning in a red paper lantern. Tavernier knocked and we were admitted into the hallway by a plump middle-aged woman, wearing an orange silk turban and paste jewellery. She greeted Tavernier warmly and led us up a staircase to a small room containing only some wicker chairs and a small card table. We sat down, lit cigars and five minutes later two women entered, one a negress, the other a mulatto. They were carrying bottles of rum and wore no shoes or stockings on their feet. Tavernier reached into his pocket, took out Pompée's amulet and handed it to me with a wide smile. 'Here, take this.'

'Why are you giving that to me?' I asked.

'The last thing I want right now,' he said, 'is protection from wickedness.'

The following night, I found myself dining again with Tavernier. Nothing was said about the brothel: it was as though we had never been there. The heat was oppressive and I was being eaten alive by mosquitoes. After we had finished our meal, my companion leaned across the

table and said, 'Why did you become a doctor, Paul?'
He had been drinking excessively and his speech was
slurred.

'My father was a doctor, as was his father before him.
It was always assumed that I would uphold the family
tradition.' I was not being entirely candid and Tavernier
sensed this. His eyes narrowed and he made a gesture,
inviting me to continue. 'When I was a child, perhaps no
more than eight or nine, my father took me to an old
church. It must have been situated somewhere in Brittany, which was where we usually went for our summer
holidays. The nave was long and empty. On both sides
were arches and, above these, high, plastered walls that
had been decorated with some kind of painting. At first,
all that I could see was a procession of pale figures,
hands joined, against a background of ochre. It reminded
me of that nursery entertainment. You must have seen it
done: whereby artfully cut, folded paper can be pulled
apart to reveal a chain of connected people. As my eyes
adapted to the poor light, I became aware that every
other figure was a skeleton. My father told me that the
mural was called a Dance of Death. He crouched down,
so that his head was next to mine, and identified the
different characters: friar, bishop, soldier, constable, poor
man, moneylender. "Everyone must die," said my father.
"From the most powerful king, down to the lowliest
peasant, Death comes for everyone." I was beginning
to feel frightened and experienced a strong desire to run
back to the porch. "But look at that fellow there," my

father continued, pointing his finger, "the fellow wearing long robes, do you see him?" His voice had become warmer. "How is he different from the rest?" Where my father was pointing, I saw a figure, flanked, not by two skeletons, but by a man and a woman. He was the only human participant in the dance who was untouched by Death. "Do you know who he is?" my father asked. I had no idea. "He is the doctor. Only the doctor can persuade Death to leave and come back another day; only the doctor has such power." From that moment onwards, my destiny was set.'

Tavernier's expression was enigmatic. 'What a peculiar child you must have been, to have found the idea of vanquishing death appealing: such vanity in one so young!'

I had never thought of myself as a proud person and was quite offended by the remark. 'You are being unfair, Georges,' I protested. 'I merely wanted to help others, to save lives.'

Tavernier smiled and said, 'Paul, you are such a romantic!' Then, taking a swig of rum straight from the bottle, he added, 'No good will come of it!'

Most Sundays, Tavernier and I made an effort to attend Mass – it was judicious to keep up appearances. One week, as the nuns were departing with their charges, we noticed that the priest had been delayed by one of the villagers, a short, wiry man, who was becoming increasingly agitated. Tavernier loitered and tilted his head. 'That's interesting,' he muttered.

'What is?' I asked.

Tavernier silenced me with a gesture and continued to eavesdrop. The exchange we observed was short-lived and ended when the priest issued a severe reprimand. He then climbed onto the open carriage, made the sign of the cross and set off down the Port Basieux road. Tavernier went over to the villager and struck up a conversation. I tried to follow the patois, but, as usual, found it incomprehensible. When Tavernier returned, he said, 'A young man passed away last week, his name was Aristide, do you remember?' It was custom for the recently bereaved to walk the local byways, proclaiming their loss like a town crier, and I did indeed remember a woman calling out that name. 'Well,' continued Tavernier, 'that fellow there,' he pointed to the receding figure, 'is Aristide's father. He came to ask Father Baubigny to pray for the release of his son's spirit.'

'I'm not sure I understand.'

'He believes that Aristide's soul is still trapped in his body. His son has become one of the living dead.'

'I'm sorry?'

'A spell was put on the boy and the day after his funeral, he was spotted in the forests below Piton-Noir.'

'How absurd,' I said. 'No wonder Father Baubigny was angry.'

'I'm afraid I must disagree,' said Tavernier. 'The people of this island believe many stupid things; however, the existence of the living dead is something that I would not dispute. Father Baubigny was wrong to castigate Aristide's father, who will now have to seek another solution – not that Baubigny's prayers would have done any good. Funeral rites, as practised by the villagers, consist almost entirely of efforts to make death real and lasting. In my opinion, they have good reason.'

I assumed, of course, that Tavernier was joking, but there was no light of humour in his eyes. Indeed, he spoke with uncharacteristic gravity. One of the nuns reappeared and called out to us. A patient had collapsed. Tavernier and I ran to assist, and our conversation was brought to a premature close.

The following evening, Tavernier returned to the subject while we were eating. 'That man who came to see Baubigny yesterday – Aristide's father – he's been down to Port Basieux. He consulted a bokor, who has agreed to lead a search party tomorrow night. They're going to find the boy and release his soul.'

'How do you know all this?' I asked.

'Pompée told me. He's related to the family and intends to join them. They're meeting in the village at sunset.'

'Why don't they just look in the grave?'

'They have. The coffin was empty.'

'Then the body has been stolen?'

'Yes, in a manner of speaking.'

'In which case, the family should inform the police. If a crime has been committed, then the perpetrator should be identified and arrested.'

'Someone removed the soil and opened the coffin. But that was the full extent of their grave-robbing: the thing that Aristide has become emerged from the ground without further assistance.'

'Come now, Georges,' I said. 'This joke is wearing thin.'

Tavernier looked at me in earnest. 'I know that there is nothing I can say that will persuade you. I was sceptical too, once.' He paused to light a cigar. 'But you don't have to accept my word. We could join the search party.' He blew a smoke ring which expanded to encircle his face. 'Then you could see for yourself.'

I was beginning to wonder whether he was not merely eccentric, but slightly mad. Even so, the intensity of his expression made me enquire: 'You're being serious?'

'Yes,' said Tavernier. His eyes glittered.

Removing a handkerchief from my pocket, I wiped the perspiration from the back of my neck. 'All right,' I said. 'I'll go.'

Something like a smile played around Tavernier's lips. He flicked some ash from his cigar and nodded once.

The next day, I began to have second thoughts. Tavernier had not, on reflection, been a very good influence. Although he had taught me a great deal about tropical medicine, he had also introduced me to the brothels of Port Basieux and now I too shared his proclivities: his appetite for dusky flesh and depravity. I did not like to degrade women in this way, to use them as objects of pleasure, and I frequently resolved never to return. But

I discovered that I was weak and the prospect of gratification was a siren call that I could not resist. Thus it seemed to me that I was about to take another step down a headlong path. Even so, as the hours passed, I did not make my excuses. Instead, I met Tavernier at the appointed time, and as the sun was setting, we accompanied Pompée to the nearest village. On our arrival, I saw men carrying torches, mothers and children huddled in doorways and a nimble man wearing a straw hat, cravat and ragged trousers posturing as he danced around a green and red pole. He was rattling something in his hand and anointing the points of the compass with water. I noticed the carcasses of two chickens at his feet.

Tavernier leaned towards me and whispered, 'The bokor from Port Basieux.'

Pompée marched over to the village elders, among whom stood Aristide's father. When Pompée spoke, they all turned at once and looked in our direction. Their expressions were not hostile exactly, but neither were they welcoming. Tavernier responded by raising his arm.

'Are you sure we should be here?' I asked.

'I took Pompée in as a child,' said Tavernier. 'He was only eleven years old. The people of this village know that I can be trusted.' His allusion to 'trust' made me feel uneasy and I wondered what confidences I would be expected to keep. The burden of complicity would weigh heavily on my conscience. I regretted not having acted on my earlier misgivings. Pompée returned and spoke a few words to Tavernier, who then said: 'We'll walk a short distance behind the party. We are guests and must show respect.' The bokor picked up a bamboo trumpet and honked out three notes, the last being extended until his breath failed. This signalled his readiness to begin the search, and when all the men were assembled, he led them down the road. Pompée, Tavernier and I fell in at the rear. A hulking, muscular giant stopped walking and stared back at us. There was something about his general attitude that I did not like, and I was not surprised when he spat on the ground. Pompée said something to Tavernier.

'Georges?' I asked, anxiously.

'Keep walking,' Tavernier replied.

As we drew closer, the man spat again.

'Georges? Why is he doing this?'

'Just keep walking!' said Tavernier, impatiently. The giant shook his great head, turned on his heels and loped away, quickly catching up with the other villagers. 'There, you see?' Tavernier added, forcing a laugh. 'Nothing to worry about.'

I was not convinced.

After travelling only a short distance, the bokor took a pathway which branched off into a forest. Our noisy arrival disturbed the sleeping birds. There was squawking, the beat of wings and a general impression of flight overhead. When the fluttering died down, the night filled with other sounds: frogs, insects and the rustle of larger animals in the undergrowth. We seemed to be heading across country in the direction of Piton-Noir, and in due course, when we finally emerged from the trees, we were presented with an awesome spectacle. The summit of La Cheminée was emitting a baleful red light, which rose up to illuminate the underside of some low-lying clouds. A sparkling fountain erupted into the sky, climbing to a great height before dropping back into the wide vent: at once both beautiful and terrible.

The bokor was not distracted by the eruption. He sniffed the sulphurous air and led us into another forest, so dense with convolvulus and wild vine that the men had to hack their way through with cutlasses. The heat was intolerable and my clothes were drenched with per-spiration. Eventually, we came to a clearing. The bokor signalled that we were to be quiet and, crouching low, he crept across to the other side. I could hear what I imagined was a beast making noises, but as the sound continued I realized that the source was human. It reminded me of the glottal grunts and groans of a cretin. The bokor let out a shrill cry and the men sprang for-ward. We chased after them, through a line of trees, and then out into a second, smaller clearing, where we dis-covered a young man, not much older than sixteen, chained to a stake. He was naked but for a soiled loin-cloth, and his eyes were opaque – like pieces of pink coral. He held his arms out, horizontally, and began to walk. His legs did not bend at the knee and he achieved locomotion by swinging his upper body from one side to the other. After he had taken only a few steps, the chain was stretched to its limit and he was prevented from proceeding any further. His head rotated and he seemed to register each member of the search party. When his gaze found me, his body became rigid. I will never forget that face, those hideous, clouded eyes and the fiendish smile that suddenly appeared. It was as if he had recognized an old friend. I willed him to look away, but his fixed stare was unyielding. A low muttering started up and quickly spread around the clearing. There was something in its sonorous tremor that suggested unease.

'Why is he looking at me like that?' I said to Tavernier through clenched teeth.

'I have no idea.'

The bokor shouted, waved his hands and succeeded in capturing the young man's attention. His head swivelled round and I sighed with relief. The bokor then began to chant and shake his rattle while performing a ballet comprising of sudden leaps and awkward pirouettes. While he was doing this, I heard him say the name 'Aristide' several times. There seemed to be no question as to who this captive creature was. The boy bellowed like a bullock and, as he did so, his father fell to the ground, releasing a plangent cry of his own. My intellect recoiled, unable to reconcile the evidence of my senses with what I understood to be impossible. I was overcome by a feeling of vertigo and feared that I might pass out.

When the bokor had completed his ritual he was given a cutlass. I saw reflected fire on the curved blade. There was a sudden silence, a flash of light and the sound of steel slicing through air. Aristide's head dropped to the ground and his open arteries produced a shower of blood that fell around us like heavy rain. The decapitated body remained erect for a few seconds before toppling over and hitting the ground with a dull thud. I watched in dumb amazement as a gleaming black pool formed around the truncated neck. The men descended on the remains of Aristide like vultures. There was more chopping as the body was cut up into parts small enough to bundle into hemp sacks. When the butchering was complete, the men began to disperse, leaving no evidence of their handiwork, except for an oval stain.

'My God!' I exclaimed, grabbing Tavernier's arm. 'They've killed him.'

'No. He was already dead, or as good as.'

'But he was breathing, standing up – walking!'

'I can assure you, he wasn't alive in any meaningful sense of the word.'

'Georges, what have we been party to!'

Tavernier grabbed my sopping jacket and gave me a firm shake. 'Pull yourself together, Paul. Now isn't the time to lose your nerve.'

I was about to say more but he shook me again, this time more violently. His expression was threatening. I spluttered an apology and struggling to regain my composure, said, 'Let's get away from here!'

We set off at a quick pace, stumbling through the undergrowth. I had not taken the trouble to get my bearings, and assumed that Pompée would negotiate our safe return. Eventually, we came to the location overlooked by

La Cheminée, and once again our progress was arrested by its infernal magnificence. The low-lying cloud was now fretted with purple and gold, and a thin rivulet of fire trickled down the mountain's steep slope. There was a sound, like the crump of distant artillery, and a halo of orange light flickered around the summit. Some burning rocks rolled down the leeward slope and a column of billowing ash climbed into the sky.

There was some movement in the vegetation and, when I turned, I found myself looking into the crazed face of the bokor. He jumped forward, brandishing a knife, and at that same moment I was seized from behind.

'Georges?' I cried out.

Tavernier raised his finger to his mouth. 'Be quiet. And whatever you do, don't try to escape.'

I could sense the size of the man standing behind me, and guessed that it was the giant who had demonstrated his contempt for us by spitting on the ground as we were leaving the village. The bokor rose up on his toes and pressed his nose against mine. His stinking breath made me want to retch. Out of the corner of my eye I saw glinting metal and was fully expecting to be stabbed. But instead I felt a sharp pain on my scalp as the bokor grabbed a tuft of my hair. He then brought the blade up and deftly cut it off. Still keeping his face close to mine, he hissed something incomprehensible and then barked at Tavernier.

'He wants you to know,' said Tavernier, 'that if you tell anyone what transpired tonight, you will die.'

'Yes,' I nodded vigorously. 'Yes, I understand. I won't tell anyone.'

'He wants you to swear,' Tavernier continued. 'I would suggest that you invoke the Saviour and name some familiar saints.'

'I swear. I swear in the name of Our Lord, Jesus Christ, Saint Peter and Saint John, and the Blessed Virgin Mary. I swear, I will tell no one.'

The bokor withdrew, taking a few steps backwards, then, pointing a wrinkled, thick-boned finger at my chest, he suddenly screamed. His cry was so loud, and chilling, that even the giant flinched. The bokor's eyes rolled upwards until only the discoloured whites were exposed, and he began muttering the same phrase, over and over again.

'What is he saying?' I asked Tavernier.

Tavernier sighed. 'He's says that if you break your oath, you will be damned – and that you will go to hell.'

The muttering abated and the bokor fell silent. His irises reappeared and he drew his hand across his mouth in order to remove some foamy saliva. For a few seconds, he seemed disorientated, but he quickly took possession of himself and signed to his accomplice. The powerful arms that were restraining me relaxed, and a few seconds later the bokor and the giant were gone.

Anger welled up in me. 'What in God's name . . . ?'

'I'm sorry,' said Tavernier.

'"Sorry"? You said that there was nothing to worry about! You could have got us both killed tonight!'

'No,' said Tavernier shaking his head. 'I don't think so. You are not known to these people, and what happened back there . . .' Tavernier gestured into the trees and then shrugged. 'The bokor was simply anxious to be assured of your discretion. Please, my friend, I have no wish to argue. We are both tired and the sooner we get back, the better.' He then instructed Pompée to proceed, and reluctantly I followed. When we reached the church, Tavernier said, 'You look like you could do with a drink.' His face was flecked with dried blood. 'You'd better come with me.' I wanted to storm off into the night, but I also felt a pressing need to make some sense of what I had witnessed, and Tavernier was the only person I could talk to.

'Yes,' I replied, swallowing my pride. 'I think you're right.'

Seated on Tavernier's terrace we gazed out over the balustrade at a swarm of fireflies. The trembling points of lights were strangely calming. Even so, it took several glasses of rum to restore my customary disposition.

'Well,' said Tavernier. 'You can't say I didn't warn you. I did tell you that such things existed.'

'I don't understand. You have always said that their religion was nonsense.'

'Gibberish! Of course it is.'

'Then how . . . ?'

'Allow me to explain.' Tavernier handed me a cigar, and then, after lighting one for himself, he leaned back in his chair and exhaled a cloud of smoke. 'A feud has existed for many years between Pompée's relations and another family who live in one of the Piton-Noir villages. Aristide was accused of stealing one of their goats and, shortly after, he became very ill. A rumour quickly spread that he had been bewitched by the Piton-Noir bokor and, sure enough, the boy became very ill and died. But his death was – how can I put this? – an imposture. In fact, he had been given a poison which paralyses the diaphragm and retards respiration. Under its influence, the heart slows and the pulse cannot be detected.'

'An asphyxiant?'

'Indeed. It can be derived from many sources: the skin of the puffer fish, certain lizards and toads, the venom of the small octopus, and it is many times more potent than cyanide.' Tavernier poured himself another glass of rum. 'The anaesthetic ointment I invented uses the same substance. In very small quantities, applied topically, it has a numbing effect. The bokors have been using it to engender a death-like state in their victims for nearly two centuries. Of course, they pretend that they have achieved their ends by sorcery, that they can kill by sticking pins into effigies and that they can raise the dead, but the truth is more commonplace. Their magic is chemical, not supernatural. Needless to say, more often than not, they miscalculate dosages and when they open a coffin they find only a rotting corpse inside; however, very occasionally they meet with success. The victim has survived and the poison has begun to wear off. The bokor can then command the occupant to climb out and he, or she, will obey. Living dead are remarkably docile, having suffered significant brain damage due to lack of oxygen.'

As Tavernier was speaking, a question arose in my mind. 'If the bokors are anxious to maintain the illusion of their possessing magical powers, then I must suppose that they also guard their secrets closely. How is it, then, that these mysteries were revealed to you?'

'I introduced one of them to morphine and when he was addicted, I told him that I wouldn't supply him with any more unless he explained how the deception was accomplished.' Tavernier produced a wide grin. 'It was child's play!'

'Why were you so interested?'

'Soon after my arrival here, a young woman with whom I was acquainted died, and the following week I saw her stumbling around behind the brothel where she formerly plied her trade.' He adopted a frozen attitude, raising his eyebrows theatrically. 'It gave me quite a shock, I can tell you, but I'm a sceptic by nature. I knew there would be a rational explanation and immediately began to make enquiries.'

I was unnerved by Tavernier's matter-of-fact manner. Unwanted images kept on invading my mind: the rain of blood, the decapitation, the mob dismembering the fallen body, the fitful orange light around the summit of La Cheminée.

'What's the matter? asked Tavernier.

'We have just witnessed a murder,' I said, flatly.

'No, Paul, you are quite mistaken. We have just witnessed the liberation of a soul. Aristide had become the slave of a bokor. Can't you see what that means to the villagers? For them, there is nothing worse than slavery. It is a fate worse than death.' A drum began to sound and its jaunty rhythm was almost immediately supplemented by another. 'See?' Tavernier continued. 'They're celebrating. Aristide is free now. He can join the ancestral spirits.'

I stubbed out my cigar and said, 'Perhaps we should report what we saw to the authorities.'

Tavernier laughed. 'The authorities? Go on then, go down to Port Basieux and tell them what happened. Do you honestly think that they'll be the slightest bit interested? Now, if a horse had been stolen from one of the plantations, that would be a different matter . . .' He waved a languid hand in the direction of the drums, leaving a trail of cigar smoke. 'The life of a villager has no monetary value. It is of little consequence to the authorities.' He stood up and strolled over to the balustrade. 'Anyway,' he continued, gazing out into the darkness. 'It wouldn't be such a good idea for you, having made a promise to the bokor. You promised to say nothing. If you break that promise, you'll go to hell. That's what he warned. Remember?' When Tavernier turned round, he was grinning like a maniac and his head was surrounded by darting points of light. Unsurprisingly, I did not find his irony amusing.

PART ONE

Damnation

1

Autumn 1873

Paris

I returned from Saint-Sébastien to a Paris that, although not quite recovered from its humiliating defeat, was starting to show signs of restored confidence. As soon as I had found somewhere to lodge, I wrote to my father, and we met shortly after to discuss my prospects. I was becoming increasingly fascinated by the nervous system and was keen to learn more from an expert. Indeed, ever since that fateful night when I had witnessed the murder of Aristide, I had become preoccupied with the brain and its workings. I wondered to what extent consciousness was preserved in the living dead? What – if anything – did they experience? These sober reflections prompted broader philosophical inquiries, concerning the mind and its relation to the body.

'Duchenne,' said my father. 'That is who you should work with.'

This seemed an absurd suggestion. Guillaume Duchenne de Boulogne was the leading authority on nervous diseases. He had been an early advocate of electrical treatments, had made advances in the field of experimental physiology and was the first doctor to use photography as a means of recording laboratory and clinical phenomena.

'Why should he employ me?' I asked.

My father then explained that we were distantly related. A letter was written, and a week later I received an invitation to visit Duchenne's laboratory. He was of sage appearance, possessing a bald, flattish head, thick eyebrows, strong nose and long, bushy side whiskers that stopped just short of meeting beneath his chin. I learned during the course of our conversation that his son, Émile, had died during the Paris siege after contracting typhoid. Émile had been Duchenne's assistant and the old man had made no attempt to find a replacement. Perhaps he was feeling lonely, or maybe our distant kinship influenced his thinking; whatever the cause, Duchenne was disposed to offer me the position formerly occupied by his son, and I accepted without hesitation.

Shortly after commencing my work with Duchenne, I read his handbook on batteries, pathology and therapeutics. Needless to say, I was already aware that electrical devices were routinely employed to treat a variety of medical conditions, but had never before come across examples of their use to resuscitate. I was surprised to learn that Duchenne had been conducting experiments in this area for almost twenty years. One of his earliest case reports concerned a pastry cook's boy, a fifteen-year-old who – because of some imaginary trouble – had imbibed a large quantity of alcohol before climbing into his master's oven, where he fell asleep and became asphyxiated. He was found the following morning and his apparently lifeless body dragged out. As luck would have it, the doctor lodging above the bakery happened to be Duchenne. The boy had stopped breathing and no pulse could be felt with the hand, although a feeble murmur was heard through the stethoscope. A battery was swiftly brought down from Duchenne's rooms and an electrical charge was delivered to the boy's heart. After a few seconds, slow and weak respiratory movements appeared and in due course he gave a loud cry and began to kick. His circulation and respiration were re-established, his colour returned and he was soon able to answer questions.

Other attempts to resuscitate are recorded in Duchenne's handbook, but he was careful not to exaggerate his achievements. He offered a balanced review. Most of the cases he reported were only partial successes: temporary recovery, followed by the final and complete loss of vital signs. Even so, I was fascinated by these findings and wanted to learn more. Duchenne was an obliging mentor and demonstrated his method using rats as experimental subjects. Each animal was chloroformed until it stopped breathing and general movements ceased. Then, electrodes were touched to the mouth and rectum, until convulsive movements and twitching provided the first evidence of reanimation. As with human subjects, outcomes varied. Most of the animals did not respond at all to electrical stimulation, some enjoyed a brief recovery which lasted a few minutes, but one or two rats from each basket were successfully brought back to life.

In his middle years, Duchenne had become interested in the physical mechanisms underlying the expression of human feelings. He had shown that, by applying electrodes to the face, it was possible to stimulate muscular contractions and manufacture emotion. His photographic record of these experiments was reproduced in a landmark publication, *The Mechanisms of Human Facial Expression*. It is a masterpiece of medical portraiture. For the work of a man of science, Duchenne's preface begins with a surprisingly unscientific assertion. He states that the human face is animated by the spirit, and I suspected that, although he had ostensibly been engaged in identifying the muscle groups that excite the appearance of emotion, the true nature of his project was somewhat deeper. For Duchenne, there was no tension between religion and Enlightenment values. The presence of God could be felt as strongly in the laboratory as in a cathedral. He was not really studying facial expression, he was studying the soul.

Duchenne's notebooks were filled with observations and ideas which were worthy of more extended treatment. I suggested that some of this material might be incorporated into academic articles that I was willing to draft. He did not object and we worked together on several papers that were eventually published. One of them took the form of a comprehensive review of the literature on resuscitation.

At that time, I made no connection between Duchenne's pioneering attempts at resuscitation, which began in the 1850s, and his subsequent book on facial expression, which appeared some ten years later. Had I been more astute, I would have discerned a natural progression. There was a reason why Duchenne wanted to study the soul, but I would not discover that reason for several years, and then only on the night that he died.

I chose to work late and when my labours were completed, Duchenne would invite me into his parlour, where we would sit and talk until the street sounds diminished and there was silence outside. On one such occasion, we were discussing a rare form of palsy, when Duchenne suddenly said, 'There's a fine example just admitted into the Hôpital de la Charité. Let's see how the poor fellow's getting on.' He rose from his seat and went to fetch his coat.

'What?' I replied, 'Now?'

Duchenne looked at me askance. 'Yes. Why not?'

And so it was that I discovered my mentor's peculiar habit of visiting hospitals at irregular hours. He did this so often that his appearance on wards at two or three in the morning was usually greeted with indifference by the nurses. On arriving, he would usually check up on his patients and then look for interesting cases. He was permitted such liberty, not only because of his considerable reputation, but also because of his impressive virtue. If he discovered an impoverished patient with a painful condition who could not afford to continue treatment, Duchenne invariably offered his services without charge. I remember him moving between the beds on the wards, a gaunt figure, passing in front of the faintly glowing gaslights, head bowed as if in prayer, administering drugs with the gentle authority of a priest giving Communion.

We were particularly welcome at the Salpêtrière, because the chief of services and recently appointed chair of pathological anatomy, Jean-Martin Charcot, was a former pupil of Duchenne. Under his canny stewardship the Salpêtrière, previously an insignificant hospice, was already on the way to becoming a neurological school of international renown. More like a city within a city than a medical institution, the Salpêtrière consisted of over forty buildings arranged around squares, markets and gardens. It even had its own church, a baroque edifice with an octagonal cupola, large enough to accommodate over a thousand congregants. Although Charcot was a proud man, whenever we encountered him he always treated Duchenne with the utmost respect, and if accompanied by an entourage of students, he would introduce his old teacher (a little too theatrically, perhaps) as 'the master'.

After a year as Duchenne's assistant, I had settled into a very comfortable routine. The possibility of finding employment elsewhere had never occurred to me. However, one day, Duchenne informed me that Charcot was looking for someone young to fill a post at the Salpêtrière and he advised me to apply. I protested, but Duchenne was insistent. 'I cannot be responsible,' he said, 'for holding you back. This is a splendid opportunity and I will be mortified if you do not take it.' He sent a letter of recommendation to Charcot and, such was his influence that news of my official appointment, when it arrived, was a mere formality.

As a junior doctor, I was obliged to attend Charcot's Friday morning lectures, which at the time of my appointment were still relatively modest affairs. Long before his arrival, the auditorium would begin to fill, not only with physicians, but also with curious members of the public: writers, artists or journalists. The platform was littered with posters mounted on stands, showing enlargements of microscopic slides, family trees and different categories of neurological illness. Brain parts floated in jars of preservative next to dangling skeletons with deformed joints. The doors would fly open, revealing Charcot, accompanied by an illustrious foreign visitor and a troop of assistants. He would ascend to the podium, pause, allow the silence to thicken and then start his address in sombre tones. Occasionally, he would stop and illustrate his observations with skilful drawings on a blackboard, or ask one of his assistants to man the projector, and images would suddenly materialize on a hitherto empty screen. Charcot was never a great orator, yet he knew how to manage a performance and compensated for his deficiencies with solid, reliable stagecraft.

I was never entirely comfortable in Charcot's presence. I found him too self-conscious, too obviously the author of his own legend. He was humane, told jokes, and abhorred cruelty to animals, but essentially he was an authoritarian. None of his interns dared to question his theories. It was common knowledge that some of our predecessors had been dismissed for voicing imprudent objections. Irrespective of my reservations concerning his character, our professional relationship was friendly and collegiate. He was favourably disposed towards me, probably because of Duchenne's letter of recommendation, and our meetings were always agreeable. I was accepted into Charcot's inner circle and began to receive invitations to his soirées; these became, like his Friday lectures, an obligatory fixture in my diary.

Charcot lived in a cul-de-sac adjoining the busy Rue Saint-Lazare, situated between the train station and the Church of the Trinity. It was a substantial if not particularly striking residence, which belied his prosperity. He had married a young widow who, in addition to inheriting her deceased husband's fortune, was also (being the daughter of a highly successful clothier) independently wealthy. This shrewd connection ensured Charcot's complete financial security and guaranteed his admission into the upper echelons of society.

The Salpêtrière was an energetic hospital and its corridors reverberated with academic debate. There was a kind of fervour in the air, fuelled by the constant thrill of discovery. Although my feelings towards Charcot were mixed, it would be churlish to deny that he was an inspiration. Because of his patronage, I was introduced into a talented fellowship and profited greatly from the lively conversation of my peers. When I was sufficiently established, I accepted more clinical responsibilities and the additional remuneration I received enabled me to secure better rooms. Life was good, but for one sad event: the death of my old teacher, Duchenne de Boulogne.

When I received news of Duchenne's illness, I immediately sent a message, informing him that I was at his disposal. He declined my offer of assistance but requested that I visit him at my earliest convenience. This note of urgency filled me with apprehension. He had obviously determined that his remaining days were few in number. An arrangement was made for me to call on him the following evening, which – as Duchenne had suspected – proved to be his last.

A storm broke as I travelled to his apartment. Thunderclaps preceded a downpour of exceptional ferocity. My driver had to stop twice: once to don his oilskins, and a second time in order to calm the horses. When we arrived at our destination, I thanked him for persevering. A maid escorted me to Duchenne's bedroom, and when I entered I was shocked by his appearance. He was sitting up in bed, his back supported by pillows, a frail, desiccated creature, with grizzled side whiskers. As I closed the door, he began to stir.

'Paul, is that you?' His voice was barely a croak.

'Yes, it's me.'

I crossed the room, sat at his bedside and noticed that he was clutching a wooden crucifix. He released the object from his grip and reached towards me, whereupon I took his hand in mine and squeezed it gently.

'Thank you so much for coming,' he said. 'It's a terrible night. Listen to that rain.' Then, twisting his neck so he could see me better, he added: 'How are you? Are you keeping well?'

His solicitous remark brought me close to tears.

'I am very well.'

'Good. I wish I could say the same. But, as you can see, I am very weak. Indeed, I fear that I have little chance of making a recovery. Still . . .' He left his sentence unfinished, and shrugged, suggesting that he was confronting the prospect of death with equanimity. He did not dwell on his predicament, but instead made some polite enquiries about my duties at the Salpêtrière. When I had finished answering his questions he closed his eyes and became very still. It seemed that he was no longer breathing: a flash of lightning transformed his face into a collection of hollows and cavities. My anxiety subsided when his eyes opened again and he whispered, 'Lately, I have been troubled by certain matters that I now wish to talk to you about.' He paused and seemed a little uncomfortable, even embarrassed. 'The first of these concerns my son, Émile. I am sorry to say that I misled you. He did not die during the siege. He became ill . . . mentally ill. It was necessary to have him interned at the asylum of Saint Anne in Boulogne-sur-Mer. He is still there today.'

'Do you want me to visit him?' I asked, 'Check that he is being properly looked after?'

'No, no. Provision has been made for his care. Besides, I would not dream of burdening you with such a commitment. You understand, I hope, that I do not wish to die with a lie on my conscience.'

'It is perfectly understandable that you should—'

'That is the first matter,' Duchenne interjected, raising his hand to silence my protest. 'There is also a second.' He swallowed and moistened his dry lips with his tongue. Another flash of lightning was followed by a colossal thunderclap. 'Paul, you were always interested in resuscitation.'

'Indeed.'

'It is regrettable that resuscitation by electrical stimulation is rarely attempted. The field has hardly progressed since the publication of my early reports, yet I still believe that this is a branch of medicine that promises to be of the greatest benefit to mankind. I can envisage applications beyond the remit of clinical practice. Batteries might prove to be a kind of philosophical tool.'

I supposed that he wanted to hear that I intended to continue his work, and I offered him some bland promise, to the effect that, if the opportunity arose, I would certainly resume a programme of laboratory experiments. As I spoke, he seemed to become impatient and he interrupted me again. 'No, Paul. There is more. Please, allow me to finish.' He sighed and added, 'I have struggled, not knowing whether it is right or wrong to . . . God created a lawful universe. If science lifts the veil . . . it is revelation, and revelation is divine.' His speech became incoherent and I wondered if he was slipping away, but another clap of thunder seemed to bring him back. 'Paul?'

'Yes, I am still here.'

'Do you remember case number six in my book on therapeutic applications?'

'The woman asphyxiated by carbonic oxide?'

'I lost her, but when stimulated, her respiration was restored. In my summary, I stated that she regained her intelligence and that she was able to give me information about what had happened to her. A few hours later she sank into a coma again and died.' He pointed at a jug on the table and I poured him a drink. He took a few sips from the glass and then continued. 'My summary is incomplete. When she regained her intelligence, it is true that she gave me information about what had happened to her, but it was not information about her symptoms. In fact, she spoke of an experience.' A faint smile appeared on his face, and retrieving the wooden crucifix, he pressed it against his heart. 'A remarkable experience.'

I was unsure what he meant by this. 'What? She recollected something from her past?'

'No. Between going and returning she saw things.'

He seemed to be making such an extraordinary claim that I thought it prudent to seek clarification. 'Between going and returning? You are referring to the time that elapsed between the woman's death and her being revived?'

'Precisely!' He found some last reserve of energy and beat the blanket with his clenched fist. 'Yet she saw things.'

'Some kind of hallucination?'

'No. What she saw was no hallucination. She was entirely lucid and the very specific terms she employed to describe her experience persuaded me of its authenticity.'

As he spoke, I felt as if the world outside was receding; the cascade that tumbled from the gutter, the keening wind that rattled the window panes, all of these sounds became a distant murmur. Even now, I can remember his lips moving, the sense of being drawn in – a tremor of excitement passing through my body, scepticism becoming interest, and interest becoming wonder. That night, my life was changed forever.

2

Duchenne's death had made me more contemplative, more inward-looking. Instead of dining with friends, I preferred to go for solitary walks by the river. I would steal into empty churches and sit, deep in thought, until the light faded and the gloom intensified. I sought out booksellers who stocked works of theology, and found myself buying copies of Augustine and Aquinas. What I had previously dismissed as sterile debate, pointless sophistry, I now approached with interest.

It was about this time that I first encountered Édouard Bazile. The circumstances of our meeting were unremarkable and I did not suspect that one day we would become close friends. He had engaged me to treat his wife, who was suffering from progressive loss of hearing. Prior to seeing me, she had consulted a number of doctors, none of whom had been able to improve her condition. I had been recommended to the Baziles by one of my former patients, a librarian with peripheral nerve disease. After examining Madame Bazile, I decided to use one of Duchenne's electrical therapies – a risky undertaking because the tympanic membrane is very delicate and stimulation with strong currents can cause total deafness. I advised Madame Bazile of the dangers, but she was insistent that we should proceed, and, after six administrations, her hearing was fully restored. Needless to say, I did not expect to see the couple again.

Several months passed, during which I moved to pleasant rooms on the ground floor of an apartment block in Saint-Germain. The great church of Saint-Sulpice was only a few streets away, and this remarkable building, magnificent and austere, became my habitual refuge. I familiarized myself with its interior, the Corinthian columns, grand arches, carved dome and chapels, the gilded pulpit, the exquisite statue of Mary as the Mother of Sorrows and its trove of curiosities.

One evening, as I was leaving Saint-Sulpice, I heard someone call my name, and when I looked up I saw a short, stocky man, with longish black hair and an untrimmed beard and moustache. He removed his hat and I immediately recognized Édouard Bazile. We shook hands and I enquired after his wife. There had been no recurrent problems and he thanked me again for my help. Our exchanges were cordial and I mentioned, in passing, that I had just moved to the area and was fond of visiting the church.

'Well,' he said, 'you must let me show you around the north tower.' I had a dim recollection of his occupation having had some connection with ecclesiastical life, but its exact nature escaped my memory. Indeed, it is possible that he had never been very precise. He detected my confusion and added, 'That is where Madame Bazile and I live. I am the bell-ringer.' We arranged to meet by the chapel of Saint Francis Xavier the following afternoon.

Bazile was already waiting when I arrived at the appointed time. Removing a key from his waistcoat pocket, he unlocked the door, invited me through, and we commenced our ascent up a winding staircase. Eventually, we came out onto a narrow wooden ledge. I was suddenly overcome by anxiety. I felt disorientated, unsteady, and feared that I would fall.

'We're a long way up.'

'About halfway.'

Shafts of light entered the tower through tilted panels. I looked down, and saw a complex arrangement of joists and beams that descended into darkness. Among the lattice of timbers was an array of enormous bells. They were oddly fascinating. Bazile directed my attention upwards, where I saw yet more bells, floating magically. I noticed bright patches on the inside of each one, where the surface had been repeatedly struck by the clapper.

'Glorious, aren't they?' said Bazile. 'For me, they are much more than pieces of metal. They are like people; each bell has its own personality.' He smiled and added, 'Did you know that they are baptized? It is a Church tradition. And as they grow older, their voices change, mellowing with age.'

I felt the air move, a ghostly caress on my cheek. The woodwork creaked and the bells began to rock.

'In the Middle Ages,' Bazile continued, 'bells were cast

by itinerant founders who would travel all over France. Villagers would throw their valuables into the boiling bronze, their jewellery, candlesticks and family heirlooms – the things that they loved most – thus creating a unique alloy which gave the bell its individual voice. The bell embodied the virtue, the generosity of the people, and its chime was supposed to comfort the sick and repel evil spirits. It is no coincidence that when we think of home, the place where we were born and raised, more often than not, we think of an area which corresponds roughly with the sounding of a particular church bell.' He brushed a cobweb from his sleeve and added, 'There is more to see.'

Another climb brought us to the stone arches beneath the roof of the tower. We were in a rotunda, the floor of which was perforated by a circular hole surrounded by rusty iron railings.

'You can lean over, monsieur. It's quite safe.' I peered into the abyss. 'Would you like to go all the way to the top?' Bazile pointed at another staircase.

'Not today. Thank you.' I was still feeling a little unnerved by my attack of vertigo.

Bazile was an erudite man. As we talked, it became apparent that – at least with respect to the church and its history – he was extremely knowledgeable. I asked him how it was that he knew so much, and he replied, 'When I was younger I wanted to be a priest. I was admitted into a seminary, but left after only a few years. I suppose I had a . . .' he hesitated before adding, 'crisis.' I was tempted to press him for more information but resisted the urge. Bazile's eyes widened and I thought he was about to disclose more, but suddenly he turned away and spoke over the void. 'I came to Paris and became the assistant of a scholarly priest at Notre-Dame. He was a very wise man and taught me a great deal. Indeed, I learned more about Church history and theology from him, than I'd ever learned at the seminary.' He paused again and stroked the rusty rail, dislodging a few red flakes. 'Although I had decided against taking Holy Orders, I still wanted to maintain a connection with the Church, to serve God daily, but I wasn't at all sure how I would achieve this. Then, quite by chance, I came across several works on campanology in the priest's library – *De Campanis Commentarius* by Rocca and *De Tintinnabulo* by Pacichellius, wonderful books – and it occurred to me that bell-ringing might be just the solution to my predicament. I served an apprenticeship, right here, in Saint-Sulpice, and when the old bell-ringer died, I took his place.'

The gentle breeze outside was now gathering strength, and an eerie wailing filled the rotunda. I raised the collar of my coat. 'Ah,' said Bazile. 'You are cold, monsieur. On our way down – if you are not in a hurry – we could, perhaps, visit my rooms. I'm afraid I can't offer you a brandy, but I have some very good cider.'

Bazile's lodgings were located directly beneath the bells. We entered a spacious parlour with rough stone walls, semi-circular windows, and a vaulted ceiling. The floor tiles were partly covered with a faded rug and the furniture was rustic in appearance. A stove stood in the corner. Its thick pipe crossed the ceiling and disappeared through a canvas sheet that had been used to replace a broken pane of glass. Next to the stove was a bookcase packed with volumes. The air smelled of cooking: not a stale smell, but homely and pleasant.

Madame Bazile appeared, and, to my great mortification, delivered a lengthy eulogy. The term 'miracle worker' was used. I objected, but she would not be contradicted. When her stock of superlatives was finally exhausted, she produced a ceramic pitcher full of cider and two tankards. Bazile and I sat at the table, where we smoked, drank and continued our conversation. It was to be the first of many, for we were, in a sense, kindred spirits, and soon recognized in each other a common sensibility. There are those who discern in felicitous meetings the hand of Providence, and, I must admit, the timely entry of Édouard Bazile into my life did feel as if it had been arranged for my benefit. I had become preoccupied, isolated, and needed to unburden myself. I needed someone to talk to about theology, mysticism and the meaning of existence, a believer, but a believer for whom faith did not also mean the disavowal of reason. Bazile was such a man. He embodied these qualities and possessed many more that I would learn to appreciate as our friendship deepened.

From that day forward, whenever Bazile discovered me, either seated at the back of the nave, or pacing the aisles of Saint-Sulpice, he would greet me and we would start a conversation that could only be satisfactorily concluded several hours later, seated at his table in the north tower. We agreed to meet on a more regular basis. I would arrive with a leg of lamb for Madame Bazile to cook, and she would prepare it beautifully with a purée of turnips and caper sauce. After dinner, Bazile would light his pipe and we would talk until the candles had burned down and the sconces were overflowing with wax.

For many months, I remained silent on the subject that I needed to speak of most and when finally I confided in Bazile, I did so almost by accident. We were discussing, as I recall, logical proofs for the existence of God.

'What could be more convincing,' said Bazile, 'than the moon, the sun and the stars? Or this room, with me and you sitting in it? There is something here,' he struck the table with a rigid forefinger to emphasize his point, 'when, so easily, there might have been nothing. Aristotle informs us that all effects have their causes. It is a universal principle and utterly irrefutable. God's effects are the proof of his existence. There must have been a first cause, and that first cause was God. Of course, some would say that logic has no place in theology. It is not a view I subscribe to, but one must recognize that the human mind has its limits. We cannot expect reason to supply answers to all of our questions.'

'My teacher, Duchenne de Boulogne, would never have accepted such a position. He was a scientist, but also deeply religious. He studied facial anatomy, because he believed that our expressions are animated by the soul, and he believed in the soul because—' I stopped myself mid-sentence.

'Yes?'

'Because he knew that something of us survives death: he had no doubt about this, and his unshakeable conviction was based on strong evidence.'

'He dabbled in spiritualism?'

I shook my head. 'Do you remember the machine I used to treat Madame Bazile – the battery? It can also be used to resuscitate.'

'What?'

'It can be used to bring patients back to life after they have died.'

Bazile took his pipe from his mouth and looked at me in disbelief.

'If the heart fails,' I continued, 'a jolt of electricity can sometimes start it beating again.'

'I did not realize medical science was so advanced.'

'The method is far from reliable and most patients are afforded only a temporary reprieve. Typically, those who have undergone the procedure report nothing. Death is experienced as a loss of consciousness, like dreamless sleep; however, there was one exception, a woman who claimed to have had what might best be described as an encounter.'

Bazile could see that I was hesitant, and poured me another drink. I thanked him, sipped the sweet liquid and said: 'She told Duchenne that her soul had risen up from her body, and that she had found herself floating just beneath the ceiling. Looking down at the lifeless person below, she registered the closed eyes and bluish pallor – the right arm hanging limp off the side of the bed. She observed Duchenne, dashing out of the room and returning with a battery. The woman was not frightened. On the contrary, she felt very calm and pitied the doctors and nurses, who appeared agitated and distressed. She wanted to say to them, "Do not worry, there is no need, I am perfectly comfortable and happy." The hospital melted away and the mouth of a tunnel materialized in front of her. She glided, without effort, into the opening and coasted towards a light that was emanating from the other end. Her speed increased, she was drawn rapidly through space and expelled into an expanse of uniform brilliance. It was not light as we understand it, but rather something far more wondrous and pure. She said it was like being irradiated with love. This experience was utterly overwhelming: rapturous, ecstatic. She sensed an immanence in the light and presumed that she must be in the presence of a higher being, an emissary.'

Bazile frowned. 'An emissary? What did she mean by that?'

'The woman remained in this state of blissful suspension for an indeterminate period of time. Then, quite suddenly, she was pulled by a powerful force back into her body. Duchenne was standing over her, removing the electrodes from her chest. She felt no joy, only a terrible, crushing sadness. She wanted to return to the light. When her condition had stabilized, she told Duchenne what she had experienced. Two hours later, she became comatose and died; however, at the moment of death, Duchenne observed something very strange. She smiled. And her smile seemed to be directed at someone, or something, quite invisible.'

The creases on Bazile's forehead deepened. 'Extraordinary, a fascinating account, but . . .' He hesitated before adding, 'Deathbed visions are not so uncommon. Ask any parish priest and he will tell you such stories. How the blacksmith's wife claimed to see the Virgin Mary or the baker's daughter heard a heavenly choir. They might, or might not be, authentic. We can never know. Is it not possible that Duchenne's patient was simply hallucinating?'

'Édouard, dead people do not hallucinate. Her heart had stopped and there was no blood circulating through the arteries of her brain. There was no breath in her lungs. Only a living brain is capable of dreams and hallucinations. Moreover, her observations of Duchenne's activities, made while she was unconscious, were entirely accurate.'

'Ah,' said Bazile. Removing the now-extinct pipe from his mouth, he tapped it against the table leg in order to dislodge a plug of tobacco and fell into a troubled reverie, during which he worried the tangled mass of his beard with restless fingers. After a very considerable interval, he said, 'If I am not mistaken, you have just recounted the most compelling evidence for life after bodily death ever reported. Would it not be appropriate, therefore, to inform the scientific community of Duchenne's remarkable discovery?'

'It was Duchenne's dying wish that I should continue his work and offer the world irrefutable proof of the life hereafter. He hoped that the provision of such evidence would change the hearts of men: that if people knew, with absolute certainty, that they would one day be judged by their Maker, they would not stray so easily from the path of righteousness.'

'And did you agree to do as he asked?'

'I did.'

Bazile pressed his palms together. 'A grave responsibility.'

'Indeed. And thus far, I have done nothing.'

3

1876

I began my programme of research using animals: rats, initially, and then stray cats. There was no shortage of equipment at the Salpêtrière and I had use of the very latest chloride of silver batteries. Death was 'administered' by means of chloroform intoxication. A particularly successful trial resulted in one of my cats being revived after an unprecedented four minutes. She was very weak, but over the next two days she regained her strength and was able to chase a ball of paper tied to a piece of string. As far as I could tell, she had retained all of her feline faculties. On the morning of the third day I gave her a dish of milk and a sardine that I had saved from my breakfast, and released her into the hospital grounds. She scampered off and soon disappeared from view.

Only two opportunities arose where I could attempt the electrical resuscitation of humans. Both were patients with epilepsy whose vital functions ceased during particularly violent seizures. The first of these, a middle-aged man, never regained consciousness; the second, a young woman, 'awoke' in a delirium that lasted for thirty minutes before she fell into a coma and passed away. Even so, I was not discouraged. The results of my experiments on animals were very promising, and I had in mind some procedural modifications that I was eager to test on human subjects.

I continued to visit Bazile, and my research was a frequent topic of conversation. He was usually excited by news of any developments, however, one evening, his reaction was somewhat muted.

He chewed the stem of his pipe and seemed ill at ease. 'It is not possible to know the mind of God and I would not presume to do so. Be that as it may, it seems to me that the finality of death communicates something of His purpose. If He had meant there to be traffic between this world and the next, then would He have troubled to erect so great a partition?'

'That is a problematic argument,' I replied, 'because if you apply it consistently to all natural phenomena, you arrive in great difficulty. Take illness, for example. If God had meant us to be in good health, then he wouldn't have permitted diseases. It follows, therefore, that the practice of medicine must be irreligious. No one, however, would endorse such a view. Indeed, healing the sick was fundamental to Christ's ministry.'

'But death seems so . . .' Bazile paused, searching for an appropriate word, 'decisive! To reanimate a dead body, to snatch a departed soul back from eternal rest, might seem to many Christians to be something,' he winced before adding, 'unnatural.'

'When holy men perform miracles they are made into saints. What is a miracle, if not unnatural? The Church has always rewarded the violation of natural laws!'

'Resuscitation is indeed miraculous, but it may not be miraculous in quite the same way, as, let us say, the feeding of the five thousand.'

I smiled mischievously. 'Perhaps not, though surely it bears comparison with the raising of Lazarus. And are we not told, even as children, to learn from Christ's example?'

Bazile conceded the point, but I could see that he was still uneasy.

Months passed, autumn became winter, and I received a letter from a surgeon at the Hôtel Dieu (at that time, this the oldest hospital in Paris was being rebuilt, and the new building – situated next to the cathedral – was nearing completion). He had recently read my review of the literature on electrical resuscitation – the one I had co-authored with Duchenne – and there were several technical matters that he wished to discuss with me. These were too numerous to be addressed by post, so I agreed to meet Monsieur Soulignac at a private dining room above a restaurant on the Boulevard Saint-Germain.

The man who greeted me was in his mid-forties and immaculately dressed. He had blond hair which glistened with a generous application of pomade, blue eyes and a neatly trimmed beard and moustache. His questions were not difficult to answer and the next few hours passed agreeably. By the time the brandy and cigars arrived, we were in our shirtsleeves and feeling very much at ease.

Soulignac spoke candidly: 'Surgeons have been slow to take advantage of electrical devices. The old methods of resuscitation are still favoured by nearly all of my colleagues. Inflate the lungs, apply pressure to the abdomen, and then start praying!' He exhaled a cloud of yellow smoke and shook his head. 'I have been using batteries for nearly a year now, and without doubt, more of my patients survive crises as a consequence. I have been able to revive patients whose hearts were barely beating and would otherwise almost certainly have died. But I have yet to save a single patient whose heart was already stopped. And I have tried on many occasions.'

'Perhaps you should acquire a more powerful battery,' I suggested. 'Duchenne used to swear by his volta-faradic apparatus. It was heavy and cumbersome, but could still be carried in an emergency, and its graduating tubes could measure the weakest doses as exactly as the strongest.' I told Soulignac about my animal experiments and the cat I had returned to life after four minutes. He declared the result 'extraordinary'.

The atmosphere in the room became hazy with cigar smoke, almost conspiratorial, and I found myself talking about my father and that long ago day in Brittany when he showed me the Dance of Death and I had resolved to become a doctor. It transpired that Soulignac had had a similar epiphany when he was much the same age, coinciding with the tragic and horribly premature death of his mother.

'One of my patients told me something. . .' said Soulignac. He seemed to become lost in deep introspection.

'Oh?' I responded, reminding him of my presence.

'A civil servant . . . I really thought there was no hope. He wasn't breathing, but I detected a faint beat – not even that, a murmur – an undertone. I stimulated his heart, his pulse returned, and, remarkably, he regained consciousness a few minutes later. He was very feeble, but he reached out, gripped my arm and was insistent that I listen to him. "It's all true," he said, "all true," and he proceeded to describe a visionary experience.'

The account that followed corresponded exactly with the testimony of Duchenne's case number six. As Soulignac described the tunnel, the light and the sublime being, I was, at once, both excited and disturbed.

'Now, I do realize,' Soulignac continued, 'that the whole thing could have been the product of a brain starved of oxygen and nutrients, but I can't bring myself to believe that. Perhaps you will consider me foolish, but I think there was more to it. You see, this gentleman, he was a down-to-earth fellow. During his convalescence, I visited him many times, and we discussed his vision in minute detail. He said that what he had experienced was nothing like a dream. Indeed, he maintained that it was the very opposite – a more immediate and vital reality. He confessed that prior to his resuscitation he had been a lifelong atheist. Yet, when he was discharged, he went directly to a monastery with the intention of dedicating his life to Christ.'

I did not respond and Soulignac mistook my silence for disapproval.

'You will say it was a hallucination,' he added, somewhat embarrassed.

'Not at all,' I said plainly. 'One of Duchenne's patients, a woman resuscitated after carbonic oxide asphyxia, reported something very similar.' I told him of my mentor's deathbed confession. When the waiter appeared, more to impress upon us the lateness of the hour than to be of service, we ignored his dyspeptic expression and ordered more cigars.

It became clear to me, as the night wore on, that Soulignac's interest in electrical resuscitation was as much motivated by spiritual curiosity as a desire to advance medicine, and that our ultimate purpose was identical: the provision of scientific evidence for the existence of the soul and its survival after bodily death. We both recognized that, by combining our resources, this objective could be realized more readily. I, a neurologist and erstwhile assistant of the great Duchenne, had access to a variety of batteries and was already embarked upon an impressive programme of animal experiments. Soulignac, a surgeon habituated to the frequent loss of patients in the operating theatre, had ample opportunity to test the new procedures I was developing. Those successfully brought back to life could be asked about their experiences, and we might, over time, collect their testimonies together for publication. The appearance of such an article in a respected professional journal would cause a sensation. When we finally made our way downstairs and out onto the deserted street, we did so flushed with alcohol and exhilarated by the audacity of our ambition.

Three months after our initial meeting, an amputee whose heart had stopped for almost a minute was resuscitated by Soulignac using the chloride of silver battery I had been using on my stray cats. The man awoke from his temporary extinction and informed Soulignac that he had been to a world of brilliant light and while there he had conversed with his dead wife. The man died two days later, but not without having first provided his surgeon with a comprehensive account of an astounding voyage to the frontier of eternity.

The first time I saw Thérèse Courbertin was at one of Charcot's soirées. We were introduced and exchanged only a few words before Henri Courbertin, an associate professor, swept her away, keen to show off his pretty new wife to the other guests. His behaviour occasioned some mischievous comments the following day. Courbertin was a decent man – artless, amiable, with a cheery bedside manner – but he was ageing badly. Thin strands of hair, raked across his crown and fixed by unguents, did little to disguise the fact that he was almost bald, and his bulging waistcoat struggled to contain a hefty paunch.

Courbertin had returned to his home town in order to find a wife, and, I imagine, by backwater standards, he must have cut an impressive figure: the distinguished and prosperous physician from the big city. One could appreciate how his reputation, generosity and solid virtues might appeal to a certain type of woman, eager to escape the tedium of provincial life.

After an initial burst of social activity, Thérèse Courbertin was seen less and less, and once the Courbertins' son Philippe was born she wasn't seen at all. When questioned about his wife's health, Courbertin replied that she was well and enjoying motherhood. In fact, she was suffering from depression, but this – I would later discover – was something that Courbertin found difficult to come to terms with. I suspect that he blamed himself (rather than a post-partum disturbance of metabolism) for his wife's unhappiness. Doctors are notoriously bad at coping with illness when it arises in their own homes.

Several years passed before Thérèse Courbertin started to appear in public again. The Charcots had crossed the Seine and now occupied a wing of the Hôtel de Chimay, a mansion on the Quai Malaquais. I can remember watching Madame Charcot as she guided a tall, elegant woman around the parlour, drawing her attention to particular pieces of art, and suddenly realizing that this fine lady was none other than Thérèse Courbertin. It was remarkable how much she had changed.

On a subsequent visit to the Hôtel de Chimay, somewhat bored by the company, I excused myself and found a solitary spot by one of the full-length windows where I could look out and enjoy a view of the river. I became absorbed by the play of light on the water and was startled when I heard a female voice say, 'It's beautiful, isn't it?' I turned, and there was Thérèse Courbertin, standing right next to me. We began a conversation but I have only the vaguest recollection of what was said. I can only recall the smoothness of her skin and the luminosity of her eyes.

We tended to seek each other out at Charcot's soirées, and if we found ourselves standing apart from the others, our talk soon became peculiarly intense. She had become interested in spiritualism and frequently referred to the seances she had attended. I was sceptical, but curious, and always encouraged her to tell me more. She spoke of ectoplasm, objects materializing out of thin air, and messages from the dead. We were once overheard by Courbertin, who moved closer and said, with strained affection, 'Thérèse, my darling, Monsieur Clément isn't interested in such things.'

'Oh, but I am,' I protested. 'The great questions of life and death are endlessly fascinating.'

Courbertin laughed, slapped me on the back and said,

'I hope she hasn't made a convert of you!' He steered me away and whispered in my ear, 'Thank you for humouring her, Clément, you're a good chap.' He then urged me towards an imposing gentleman surrounded by a group of bespectacled young doctors. 'Now,' he continued, pausing to catch his breath. 'Let me introduce you to Monsieur Braudel. His recent article on hereditary ataxia is set to cause quite a stir – a man worth knowing.' It was Courbertin's way of showing gratitude. He was relieved that someone was willing to keep his wife 'amused'.

One sunny afternoon, I saw Thérèse Courbertin in the Luxembourg Gardens. She was sitting on a bench and little Philippe was playing at her feet. I approached, and when she saw me, she stood and waved.

'Where is the professor?' I asked, looking around.

'At his club,' she replied, a note of irritation sounding in her voice.

We began a conversation which became increasingly intimate. She spoke of feeling dissatisfied, unfulfilled and, although these remarks arose in the context of some broader point she was making concerning the human condition, it was obvious to me that she was really talking about her marriage. When we parted, she offered me her hand and allowed my lips to linger.

At the next Charcot soirée, I thought that it would be wise to avoid Thérèse Courbertin. I feared that if we spoke, our mutual attraction would be so obvious that others would notice. It is ironic, therefore, that as I was preparing to leave, Courbertin approached me with Thérèse on his arm.

'What, going already?' he said jovially. 'We've hardly had a chance to speak.'

I can't remember how it came about, but a few minutes later we were talking about music. The Courbertins were supposed to be going to a concert the following evening, a rather refined affair at the home of Le Coupey, a professor at the conservatoire. The performer was a young woman called Cécile Chaminade and the programme was to include a selection of her own piano works and songs. Courbertin was lamenting the fact that he could no longer go, on account of Charcot, who had just informed him of an impromptu committee meeting which he was obliged to attend. Then, all of a sudden, his eyes widened and he exclaimed, 'Just a minute! If you're fond of music, why don't you take my place?'

'Oh, I couldn't,' I replied.

'Of course you could.' He turned to face Thérèse. 'There you are, my darling. That is the solution. Clément will be your chaperone.'

'We cannot impose on Monsieur Clément in this way,' said Thérèse.

'Nonsense,' said Courbertin. 'He wants to go. Don't you, Clément?'

I made a submissive gesture. 'You are too kind.'

'There. You see?' Courbertin chuckled. 'That's settled then.'

The concert was delightful. Chaminade – who was

much younger than I expected, barely in her twenties, in fact – had short curly hair and soft, rounded features. She looked a little like a milkmaid, albeit a very serious one. When her hands touched the keyboard, she produced enchanting music, although its spell was never powerful enough to make me forget Thérèse Courbertin, whose closeness had become a kind of torment. She was wearing a tight-fitting dress of black silk, striped with satin and faille. At one point, she changed position and her hem rose up, revealing a sparkling stocking of peacock blue and a petticoat trimmed with cream lace.

After the concert, I hailed a cab and we sat, side by side, talking mostly about Chaminade, with whom Thérèse was well acquainted. They had met at a seance and had since become friends. I was informed that the young composer was a strict vegetarian, preferred to work at nights and was much more interested in music than suitors. As Thérèse told me these things I began to feel light-headed with desire. I seemed to enter some altered state of being in which every detail of the world was magnified: a dewy reflection on her lips, the powder on her cheeks, flecks embedded in the green transparency of her eyes; suddenly, restraint was no longer possible, and she was in my arms, submitting to my kisses.

That was the start of it: the secret notes, the deep-laid plots and 'accidental' meetings in the Luxembourg Gardens, the play-acting, the lies and deceit, all leading to a shabby little hotel in Montmartre, where we finally consummated our passion.

As I watched a droplet of perspiration evaporating from her body, I said, 'I want you to leave him.'

She sighed. 'I can't.'

'Because of Philippe?' I enfolded her in my arms and she nestled into my chest. 'Then what are we to do?'

'I don't know,' she replied. After a lengthy, thoughtful pause, she was only able to repeat the same, disappointing words.

Soulignac and I continued to question patients who had survived resuscitation. After a year, we had collected five accounts similar to the one given to Duchenne by his case number six. Of our five cases, I was responsible for resuscitating only one, a stable boy who had sustained a serious head injury. He was surprisingly eloquent and his description of communing with the infinite was deeply affecting. Sadly, his recovery was fragile and he died later from a brain haemorrhage. There were other patients, returned to consciousness from serious illness, whose breathing had slowed and whose hearts had almost – but not quite – fallen silent; however, none of this group said anything about tunnels or light. Most reported nothing, and a few described vivid dreams. Some of these dreams were religious in nature and featured radiant angelic beings, but Soulignac and I were never tempted to confuse them with what we now recognized as authentic contact with the numinous. A simple rule was emerging: the greater the loss of vital signs, and the longer the duration of their absence, the more likely it was that a resuscitated patient would subsequently report a spiritual experience.

Shortly after Thérèse and I became lovers, I told her about the research I was undertaking with Soulignac. She was amazed. 'Why didn't you tell me before?'

'There was never the opportunity.'

'But we have always discussed matters of the spirit.'

'Yes, at the Hôtel de Chimay, where anyone might have overheard what I was saying.'

'And what if they had?'

'As far as my colleagues are concerned, I am trying to refine electrical resuscitation techniques and nothing more. If Charcot knew what I was really embarked upon I would probably be dismissed. He is a staunch anti-cleric, a low materialist.'

'But isn't your project scientific? I thought that was its purpose: to prove, beyond doubt, that death is not the end.'

'I need evidence.'

'You already have it.'

'Yes, but not enough. And in the meantime I have my reputation to consider. '

She raised herself up on an elbow, stroked my forehead, and said in a hushed half-whisper, 'You will be famous.'

The seed was planted. Ambition fed on the compost of my vanity.

I imagined myself eclipsing Charcot, installed in a

mansion on the Rue du Faubourg-Saint-Honoré, feted, entertained by ambassadors, kings and potentates, lauded in the society pages – the modern Odysseus – and in this fantasy, always, Thérèse Courbertin was by my side.

An idea arose in my mind that floated, kite-like, above my everyday thoughts. At first it seemed too fanciful a notion to be taken seriously, but the more I reflected on it the more I persuaded myself that a favourable outcome was not unlikely.

'Interesting,' said Soulignac, 'but what you are proposing could never be accomplished. The risks are too great.'

'When I was working at the Saint-Sébastien mission hospital, I learned of a poison that paralyses the diaphragm and slows the heart. It is found most abundantly in the skin of the puffer fish.' I explained how the poison had been exploited for centuries by the native priests of the Antilles. 'A precise quantity – determined through experiments on animals - might produce a temporary suspension of vital functions in a human subject. And then, such a subject could be returned to life in the usual manner.'

Soulignac pulled at his beard. He looked sceptical.

'I know this poison is effective,' I continued, 'I once saw . . .' It had been a long time since I had thought of Aristide's murder. Images of blood and fire tumbled into my mind. 'I once saw a village boy who had been declared dead, risen from his grave – breathing and walking.'

'What were the circumstances?' asked Soulignac.

I hesitated. The bokor had made me swear never to reveal what I had witnessed. I remembered his bony finger poking my chest, his chilling cry and the discoloured whites of his eyes.

Soulignac was still frowning at me. 'Well?'

Tavernier had said that the magic of the bokors was chemical, not supernatural, and that their religion was nonsense, gibberish. What was there to fear?

I lit a cigar and began to describe the events of that terrible night: the meeting in the village, the journey into the jungle and Aristide's decapitation. Recollecting the rain of blood still sent a shiver down my spine. When I had finished, Soulignac produced a lengthy exhalation and said, 'That is a very remarkable tale.'

'And every word of it is true.'

My companion tapped his fingers on the table and said, 'Where would you get this poison from? We are a long way from the Antilles now!'

'Indeed,' I replied. 'But we are not so very far away from a zoo.'

The head keeper was most obliging. He was a widower whose wife had suffered a painful death. When I told him that I was trying to develop a new anaesthetic compound, he was eager to assist. There were puffer fish in the aquarium, and in the reptile house I found a tank of frogs from the Saint-Sébastien archipelago. It was relatively easy to isolate the poison by filtration, and I soon had enough to begin experiments on animals. The poison had several interesting properties. It was consistent in its action, making it easy to establish a clear relationship between dosage and effect. Moreover, the arrest of functioning it produced was more easily reversed by electrical stimulation than the arrest of functioning produced by chloroform. Thus, I achieved a higher number of successful resuscitations, particularly after extended periods of lifelessness.

'Think of it,' I said to Soulignac. 'For millennia, men have dreamed of voyaging to the other side, and returning. And now it is possible. Indisputable proof of an existence beyond the grave: not the makeshift proof of the theologian with his unconvincing arguments and dusty authorities, or the groundless proof of the priest exhorting us to pray for the gift of faith, but the strong, unshakeable proof of direct experience. It has fallen upon us – you and I – to penetrate the mystery.' Then, trembling with excitement I added, 'I want to go.'

When I told Bazile of my intentions, he was silent for a very long time. Then, removing his pipe from his mouth, he said, 'The Lord forbids self-slaughter.'

'I won't be committing suicide,' I responded, 'just submitting my body to a state of temporary suspension.'

'But at the moment when you stop breathing and your heart stops, you will be dead.'

'Yes, but only for a minute or so. Then, I will be brought back to life.'

As I said these words, I realized that I had become like a bokor; I now exercised fearful powers.

'Dear God,' said Bazile. 'What you are about to do is so very extraordinary.'

Before entering the Hôtel Dieu, where Soulignac had prepared an operating theatre, I paused to look up at the great towers of Notre-Dame. Clouds were racing across the sky and the light was just beginning to fade. 'Father,' I whispered, 'into thy hands I commit my spirit.'

4

I lay on the operating table, stripped to the waist, my bare feet pressed up against a metal footplate. A trolley was positioned next to the table and on the trolley were two batteries: a new chloride of silver, and beneath it, an older, volta-faradic apparatus. Soulignac produced a syringe and injected me with morphine. Its purpose was to ease the distress caused by the poison, which was already coursing through my veins and causing my lungs to labour. A pleasant warmth spread through my body and I began to feel detached from the world. I heard Soulignac say, 'Good luck, my friend.' His voice sounded distant. The hiss of the gas jets and buzzing of the batteries seemed to get louder and when I closed my eyes, I started to feel sleepy. I was aware of pain in my chest, the inflexibility of my ribcage, and the effortful exertion of my weakening heart, but all the time, my consciousness was dimming, until at last, all that remained was a flickering sense of self, trembling at the very edge of oblivion, and then, non-being, nullity, absence.

There was no slow awakening, no gentle return of intelligence, but a sudden and disorientating jolt. I did not, as I had expected, find myself floating beneath the ceiling, looking down at my body. Instead, I was hovering in the air, high above the hospital. Beyond the river, I could see the rooftops of the Latin Quarter and the dome of the Panthéon. I drifted out, over the parvis, turning in space until I was facing the cathedral. Its Gothic detail was bathed in a soft red light emanating from above. Veils of luminescence circled above the central spire, blushing and shimmering, dissolving into points of slowly descending brilliance: the phenomenon was in a constant state of flux, the dissolution of one veil presaging the appearance of another. Delicate tendrils of crimson lightning spread through the entire system, defining its awesome height and circumference. I was so entranced by this wondrous sight, so entirely emptied of thought by its hypnotic beauty that it was only when I passed between the blunt towers of the cathedral that I realized I was being drawn towards its core. Below, I could see a row of gargoyles. Winged, devilish creatures, staring balefully over the city.

I rose up through a crackling mist and halted directly above the spire. The copper statues, ascending the slope where the nave and south transept connected, looked as if they had been sculpted from blocks of ruby. I began to rotate in synchrony with the clockwise motion of the cloud, and through glittering sheets observed every compass point of the horizon. Suddenly, awe became fear and I screamed, and the scream was so all-consuming that I was, for a moment, nothing but the medium for its raw expression. I was no longer a person, recognizably human, but a scrap of terror, confronted by forces beyond my comprehension. And then I plummeted into darkness.

It seemed that I was falling down a shaft, sunk deep into the earth. This impression was reinforced by the appearance of an oval aperture, faintly glowing at some abysmal remove. The aperture expanded, and, dropping through its centre, I found myself disgorged above a pit of astounding immensity: a funnel of concentric tiers that shrank, step by step, towards its lowest point. It would have been impossible to discern the geography of this benighted landscape were it not for various incendiary events: conflagrations, eruptions, winking fires and thin reticulations of scarlet.

My descent continued. I saw jagged mountains, lakes of filth, blasted forests and plains of ash, and when I descended further still, sufficient to discriminate the motion of figures on a human scale, what I saw next made my soul convulse with horror: a stampede of naked men and women, stumbling, slipping and scrambling, pursued by winged, reptilian creatures – hopelessly attempting to evade capture. Those at the rear of the herd were lashed with chains, flayed and beaten until their bodies were reduced to a bloody pulp. From my elevated vantage I could see demons in flight, hunting prey, swooping down to impale their quarry on pitchforks. Victims were tossed into the air, mercilessly butchered and eviscerated with indifference.

The beat of leathery wings alerted me to two devils rising up from below, a struggling woman in their clutches. I glimpsed her contorted face as the fiends took hold of her arms and legs and began to draw apart, until all four limbs popped out of their sockets and what remained of her fell back to the ground. I watched the head and torso shatter, producing a burgundy sunburst.

My trajectory changed and I came to a desolate place, of narrow ravines and volcanic dust. It seemed to me that I had arrived in some dismal hinterland, set apart from the principal thoroughfares of damnation. The cries receded and the ground came up to meet me. My long descent ended when, with the natural precision of a snowflake, I landed on an expanse of black and magenta pumice. I had, until that instant, seemed discarnate, but now I was embodied. I could feel heat on my skin, smell foul vapours rising from vents in the earth and taste the bitter iron of fear in my mouth. My whole person was shaking and I was seized by an animal instinct to seek safety and find cover. I ran towards a fissure in a basalt outcrop and entered a narrow channel that proceeded between two smooth, glassy walls. I had not gone very far when I heard someone groaning, and looking up, saw an old man, hanging from the rock face, arms outstretched. Nails had been driven through his hands and feet. A bird-like creature was sitting on his shoulder, pecking at one of his eyes. It inserted its long beak into the socket and pulled out a grey-pink floret of brain tissue. I gasped: the bird swivelled its head around, fixing me with a curiously intelligent gaze. I ran the length of the channel and out onto a charred wasteland littered with boulders. This bleak arena was illuminated by pools of magma that coughed molten pellets into the air.

I had not been there for more than a few seconds when I heard a woman shrieking, and as the noise became louder, I also heard other voices. These were low, guttural and punctuated by rough barks. I crouched behind one of the boulders and peered around its edge. A troop of demons appeared over the nearest ridge, one of them carrying a young woman slung over his shoulder like a sack of coals. Her pale buttocks made a lunar circle next to the demon's hideous, leering face. As they advanced, I drew back and waited for them to pass, but they halted before reaching my hiding place. I heard them, close by, yawping and growling, while the woman continued to shriek. Occasionally, the demons made a sound which was like laughter, a rasping cackle. There were hammer blows, rock splintered and the woman's shriek became a howl of pain.

When I peered around the side of the boulder again, I saw that she had been nailed to a flat rock and her legs were hanging over the edge. There were five demons, all of them holding pitchforks. Their wings, when folded, arced elegantly from hooked prominences above the shoulders to tapering points beside their ankles. When spread out, they resembled the ribbed and scalloped wings of a bat. The demons were standing in a loose group, jeering and making lewd gestures while the woman writhed in agony.

One of their number parted the woman's legs and positioned itself between her thighs. I saw it lunge forward, the woman juddered and she let out a piercing scream. The demon began to rut, its haunches moving backwards and forwards as its tail thrashed the ground, raising columns of grey dust. Its body was scaly and powerfully built, and each brutal thrust made me wince. The other demons stamped their feet, shook their forks, and flapped their wings, producing a ghastly parody of human applause.

The rutting demon raised its arm, revealing three great talons. It drew them across the woman's belly, opened her up, and dragged out a length of colon. Looping the entrails around its neck, it looked to its audience for approval. The phosphorescence of the magma pools was reflected in the blood which splashed around the demon's feet. Another demon vaulted over the woman's body, leaving its pitchfork behind in her smashed ribcage, but she did not stop howling. There was no end to this torment, no release – because, of course – she was already dead. Moving with the slow grace of a python, the loop of colon was already beginning to free itself from the rutting demon's shoulders. It climbed over the demon's head, dropped onto the woman's thighs, and insinuated itself back between the ragged lips of her abdominal rupture. I saw the woman's blood defying gravity and flowing slowly back into her torn arteries.

She was being reconstituted, renewed, so that her suffering could be sustained in perpetuity.

It was then that one of the demons, a fierce-looking monster with prominent forward-projecting horns, broke away from the group and sniffed the air. I saw its wide nostrils flaring. Its malevolent expression changed, and insofar as I could interpret its significance, confusion turned to surprise. It grunted and started towards my boulder. I drew back and cowered, naked, vulnerable, my bowels loosening, and terror – indescribable terror – rendered me insensible. I stood, jabbering, wringing my hands together, as I listened to the pumice breaking beneath its heavy tread.

Its eyes were yellow – evoking something putrid – and broken by thin, vertical ellipses. The retraction of its lips produced a smile of cruel intent, made more sinister by the length of its fangs and the slithering of its forked tongue. There was still something like disbelief lingering in its expression as its wings rose up and it positioned itself in readiness to pounce.

There was a mighty pull, as if I was being yanked backwards. The demon's eyes seemed to stay with me for a moment, then they vanished; such was the magnitude of the impact that followed that I might have been hit by a steam train.

Soulignac was shouting: 'Breathe, Clément, for God's sake, breathe!' He pressed electrodes against my bare chest and I felt a painful electric shock. My back arched and fell back heavily on the operating table. 'Speak to me, Clément! Can you hear me? Say something!' My torso felt as if it had been wrapped in metal hoops. 'Come on, take a breath.' I gasped, and my lungs seemed to fill with fire. 'That's it, and again.' Soulignac's expression was wild and his forehead glistened with perspiration. I opened my mouth and sucked at the air. 'Well done, Clément. Keep going.' Gradually, my breathing became regular and Soulignac gripped my hand, 'You've been gone for three minutes. I thought I'd lost you.' He wiped his brow. 'You're not out of danger yet. I'm going to stimulate the phrenic nerve.' I nodded, and closed my eyes, submitting to his ministrations. 'No, Clément. Keep your eyes open. Stay awake.' Several minutes passed before he removed the electrodes and helped me to sit up. 'Well,' said Soulignac, 'what did you see?'

I shook my head and replied: 'Nothing.'

PART TWO

Possession

5

For the next two weeks I was confined to my bed. Soulignac, who nursed me through the initial stages of the sickness, wanted to consult a specialist in respiratory disorders.

'Don't do that,' I said. 'It's unnecessary.'

'But I am concerned,' Soulignac implored. 'The poison may have caused some bronchial damage.'

'A few more days,' I responded. 'I'm sure I'll be better in a few more days.'

Bazile came to see me and was obviously disturbed by my appearance. He rearranged my pillows and set a vase of flowers by my bedside. 'A present from my wife,' he said, pulling the curtains apart.

'No,' I called out, covering my eyes. 'The light gives me headaches.'

'I'm sorry,' said Bazile, quickly drawing the curtains again. He sat down and lit his pipe. 'Well, my friend, what happened?'

'Nothing,' I replied. 'I lost consciousness – died – and was brought back to life. I saw nothing, only darkness. It was like going to sleep.'

Bazile stroked his beard and after a lengthy silence said, 'We know already that not all patients who are resuscitated are granted a preview of eternity. One must assume, therefore, that such experiences – the tunnel, the light, encounters with divine presences – do not follow automatically from death, but are afforded only to those who are in some sense ready.'

For a while, he elaborated on this theme, but thereafter our conversation was rather stilted. I was too tired to talk, and realizing this, Bazile stood to leave. 'You are exhausted, poor fellow. If you need anything, anything at all, let me know and I'll return as soon as I can.' I thanked him and he left the room.

Turning my head to one side, I gazed at Madame Bazile's flowers: white amaryllis, chrysanthemums and sea lavender. I felt curiously numb, incomplete, as if my resuscitation had been only partially successful, and that a part of me, perhaps the most significant part, was still dead. Reaching out, I took a petal between my thumb and forefinger. The sensation was pleasurable and familiar, but strangely deficient, as if I were observing someone else performing the action, rather than feeling the velvety softness directly for myself.

I dozed off and was beset by bad dreams. I saw demons rolling rocks over a heap of squirming bodies, cavorting with prodigies that crawled from fissures in the earth; I saw a great vortex made of wailing humanity, spinning across a boundless flatland and leaving in its wake a trail of gore. I saw myself standing behind a boulder, naked, incontinent, shaking uncontrollably, knees knocking together, hands clasped protectively over my genitals, mouthing gibberish. And then I awoke, still yammering, the bedclothes soaked in perspiration, the awful vision of my utter helplessness still impressed on the darkness, persisting until its gradual dissolution released me from a suffocating terror.

Night had fallen and my head was throbbing. I heard the bells of Saint-Sulpice and thought of Bazile pulling on the ropes in the north tower, performing his sacred duty. The sound had a soothing quality, and with each chime the pain became less severe. When the ringing stopped, I felt oddly restored. A question arose in my mind: *Why did you lie to Soulignac and Bazile?* But I could not give myself an answer.

I spent the next two hours tossing and turning, unable to get back to sleep. Dawn was breaking and a gap in the curtains admitted a strip of light that fell in disjointed sections across the rumpled bed sheets. There was enough illumination to see that Madame Bazile's flowers had wilted. Many of the petals had dropped off and were now scattered around the vase. Scooping up a handful I inspected them closely. They were shrivelled and brown at the edges.

Soulignac was puzzled by my swift recovery. I was soon walking every day, down to the river and as far as the cathedral. A few of my symptoms were tenacious, particularly my excessive sensitivity to sunlight, but the solution to this problem proved simple enough. I was able to obtain some 'eye-preservers' (pince-nez with blue-tinted lenses) from an optical instrument shop on the Rue de Tournon, and, subsequently, morning and afternoon excursions were relatively painless. Returning from one of my walks, I found a letter from Thérèse Courbertin. She had learned from her husband that I was recovering from a chest infection (a plausible fiction supplied to Charcot in order to explain my absence) and her brief missive was sympathetic and tender. It was obvious that she wanted to see me and the desire was mutual. Employing one of our usual devices, we arranged to meet at 'our hotel' in Montmartre.

I had never disclosed my intentions to Thérèse Courbertin. She knew nothing of the experiment. By withholding the truth, I was not seeking to prevent her from worrying about my safety, but rather indulging in a childish conceit. I had wanted to succeed first, so that I could then surprise her with the astonishing revelation, that I, Paul Clément, physician and neurologist, had made the ultimate voyage, and had now returned to change the world. In my vainglorious fantasy, I imagined her overwhelmed by the magnitude of my achievement. Of course, this dramatic scene would no longer play out as I had planned. However, my disappointment was moderated by a consoling thought: Thérèse would not be asking me any difficult questions.

When I entered the hotel room I found her already

waiting. She took off her hat, which was adorned with a fresh orchid, and allowed her sable wrap to slip from her shoulders. I closed the door, advanced and encircled her supple waist with my arms. We kissed, and when we parted I began to undress her. I loosened her fastenings, unlaced her corset and, when she was naked but for a pair of stockings, she fell back onto the eiderdown. Her arms were thrown back above her head and her luxurious writhing communicated readiness. I removed my own clothing with clumsy haste and flung the garments aside.

There was something about her scent, a fragrance of extraordinary sweetness, that seemed to create in me a state of unbearable excitement. With every inhalation my want of her increased, until I was possessed by a furious urgency. She tried to calm my agitation by touching my face and whispering the word 'gently' in my ear, but her scent was maddening and I could not stop myself.

Afterwards, as we lay together, our limbs still entangled, she said, 'I thought you were supposed to be ill?'

'I'm feeling much better now.'

'Obviously,' she retorted. Her hand travelled over my chest and stomach. 'You've lost weight.' Before I could respond, she added, 'I've missed you.'

'Yes. I've missed you too.' She turned away and I curled to accommodate the curve of her spine. 'You're wearing a new perfume.'

'No I'm not.'

'It smells stronger. Sweeter.'

87

'Don't you like it?'

'I like it very much.' I kissed the nape of her neck. 'I want to see you more often.'

She sighed. 'Paul . . .'

'I was thinking of renting a room for us – in Saint-Germain – somewhere discreet.'

'That would be too close.'

'Not necessarily. Not if we're careful. It would make things easier.'

'Would it really?'

'Yes. I think it would.'

When we were dressed and getting ready to leave, Thérèse picked up her hat and wrinkled her nose.

'What's the matter?' I asked.

'My orchid.' She plucked the flower from the brim and held it out to show me. 'It's dying. And I only bought it this morning.' I had put on my eye-preservers. 'What are those?'

'Spectacles made with coloured glass.' Thérèse's expression became quizzical. 'To soften the light. I'm still getting headaches.'

'They make you look . . .' she hesitated and smiled coyly. 'Rather interesting.'

I resumed my clinical duties at the Salpêtrière and was immediately given new responsibilities. Charcot was becoming increasingly interested in hysteria, a condition that had mystified physicians since ancient times, and he was determined to systematize its study. To that end, many junior doctors, including myself, were instructed to collate various measurements. These included thermometry, respiration and pulse. Tables were compiled, graphs plotted and the effects of different treatments meticulously recorded.

Dramatic presentations of hysterical illness are frequently connected with some religious idea or the symbolism of the Church, and one of our patients, a humble washerwoman, had contractures that resulted in a form of muscular crucifixion. Her arms would extend and gradually become rigid, her ankles would cross and she would maintain this position for hours. She was completely unresponsive and could be lifted or leaned up against a wall like a statue – a spectacle that Charcot delighted in demonstrating to visiting professors.

Bazile was always fascinated to hear accounts of such phenomena: 'When the contractures ceased, what did she say?'

'She described a blissful transport. Ecstasy, rapture.'

'Hallucinations?'

'Yes.'

'But how do you know that? How can you be sure this woman did not commune with the infinite?'

'She responded to Charcot's treatment. Compression of the ovaries released her from the fixed attitude she had adopted.'

Bazile was sceptical. 'I once saw a stigmatic in a religious retreat, a kind, devout man who had about him an air of profound spirituality. I saw for myself the wounds of Christ in the palms of his hands, and I do not believe, cannot believe, that he was, in fact, a species of lunatic suffering from psychosomatic haemorrhaging, and that baths, electricity or applying pressure to his body would have caused those divine injuries to heal over. I fear that if Monsieur Charcot had encountered the great stigmatics, Saint Francis of Assisi, Saint Catherine of Sienna or Saint John of God, he would have locked them away and subjected them to all manner of indignities. The faculty of reason is God-given and sets us apart from the rest of creation. But we must use it wisely. It seems to me that the ruthless logic of scientists frequently takes us further from, rather than closer to, some of the essential truths.'

In addition to religious visionaries, there were also demoniacs at the Salpêtrière, and these, too, Charcot counted as hysterics. The wretched individuals complained of sharp pains, clawed at their throats, grimaced and leered, spat, cursed and shouted blasphemies. Although they ate little and had wasted physiques (some were almost like skeletons), they were also extraordinarily strong and had to be kept in restraints, for fear that they might damage themselves or cause harm to others.

One morning I was conducting hourly examinations – taking and noting temperatures – when I heard, coming from an adjacent ward, a crashing sound followed by a scream. This in itself was hardly unusual, but the scream was interrupted by pleas for mercy and as I listened I thought I recognized the voice. It belonged to Mademoiselle Brenard, a young nurse admired for her cheery manner and tireless industry. I dashed to her assistance and found a chaotic scene. A bed and trolley had been tipped over and the floor was covered with tablets and spilled syrups. Some of the patients had hidden themselves under their bed sheets while others were cowering in corners and crying out, 'God help us, he'll kill us all.' One of my colleagues, Valdestin, was standing in front of Mademoiselle Brenard, who was being held captive by Lambert, a demoniac who had apparently managed to remove his straitjacket. Lambert was holding a scalpel against the nurse's throat and grinning. His other hand cupped one of her breasts.

'That's enough, Lambert,' said my colleague. 'Let her go.'

'No, monsieur. She's mine now, mine to enjoy.' Lambert bumped his crotch against Mademoiselle Brenard's rear and produced a hideous cackle. 'All mine. Come any closer and I'll open her up.' He licked the nurse's face. 'I like them this fresh. Don't you, monsieur?' I saw the poor girl flinch when the maniac whispered some unspeakable obscenity into her ear. 'Isn't she a peach? Ripe and succulent, I'd like to peel her, taste her pulp, her lovely, delicious sugary pulp.'

'Please let me go,' whimpered the nurse. 'I beg you.'

'I must insist,' Valdestin commanded, taking a step forward, 'that you release Nurse Brenard at once!'

The demoniac nicked the nurse's throat, causing her to scream.

'Shut up!' he shouted, grabbing a handful of her hair. He then pulled her head back to expose a bead of blood that grew slowly before trickling down to the collar of her uniform. Valdestin froze. The demoniac studied the red trail, which was particularly vivid against the paleness of Mademoiselle Brenard's skin, and traced its length with the tip of his finger. Sucking the blood off, he said, 'As sweet as they come.'

Valdestin turned to me and asked: 'What on earth are we going to do, Clément?'

It was then that Lambert noticed me. He fell silent and his head began to jerk – a series of nervous, bird-like movements. His expression was still typical of derangement, wild staring eyes and hair standing on end, but his brow seemed to compress under a weight of anxiety. Something seemed to have shaken his confidence.

'Ah,' said Lambert. 'Forgive me. I did not realize. Please, take her – a token of my respect.' Releasing Mademoiselle Brenard, he pushed her in my direction. She stumbled and fell to the floor. Lambert waved the scalpel magnanimously. 'She's all yours. I meant no disrespect, all yours.'

I quickly interposed myself between the sobbing nurse and the demoniac. Fear had made my mouth dry and I was barely able to utter, 'Put the knife down, Lambert.' These words sounded thin and he immediately sensed the unsteadiness of my resolve. Whatever it was about me that had made him give up his prisoner could not be relied upon for sustained effect. He was clearly having second thoughts concerning his impulsive act of surrender. Not wishing to lose my advantage, I advanced and repeated my order, this time, more firmly. 'Put the knife down!'

Lambert studied the glinting blade and then transferred his attention back to me. I was expecting him to lunge at any moment, and was preparing to leap out of the way, when he smiled, obsequiously, and whined, 'Of course, of course. Anything you say.'

He dropped to his knees and, making a great show of his willingness to comply, placed the scalpel on the floor just in front of my feet. I kicked it out of his reach and he squealed, 'Please, don't punish me.' Then, lowering his head, he began to kiss my shoes while imploring me to take pity on him. I stepped back, disgusted, and as I did so, he started to retch. The position he assumed made him look like a huge insect: sharp elbows, bent and pointing upwards, plates of bone and vertebrae clearly visible beneath taught, grey-green skin. He rocked backwards and forwards until the contents of his stomach gushed out of his mouth and splashed on the tiles before forming a wide pool. The stench was appalling. My disgust was amplified when he pushed his hands through the steaming vomit and picked up something which he held up for my inspection. His expression communicated that he was eager for me to take it. At that point, some stocky porters arrived, accompanied by an associate professor. They dragged Lambert to his feet, and twisting his arms behind his back, frog-marched him off the ward with the professor in attendance. I remember how Lambert kept turning his head to look back at me. He was still looking when I lost sight of him.

Valdestin was already dressing Mademoiselle Brenard's wound.

'That was strange,' he said. 'The way Lambert suddenly changed his mind.'

'Yes,' I said. 'We were lucky.'

Mademoiselle Brenard's injury was more serious than I had realized and a significant amount of blood was seeping through the bandage. The poor girl was distraught, tears streaked her face and her chest was heaving.

'Mother of God,' she cried, 'I thought I was going to die.'

I took her hand in mine and squeezed it gently. 'You were very brave, mademoiselle, very brave. But please, calm yourself. You are quite safe now, and Monsieur Valdestin will look after you.' In order to deliver my reassurances I had knelt down beside her. She was wearing the same perfume as Thérèse Courbertin. My gaze lingered on the nurse's lips and the swell of her breasts. Annoyed by my own impropriety, I made some excuse and moved away.

Other doctors were arriving and peace was quickly restored. An orderly was mopping up Lambert's vomit and as I walked past he stopped me and said, 'What shall I do with this?' His fingers opened, revealing something in his palm.

'Where did you find it?'

'Just here.'

It was the object that Lambert had wanted me to take.

'Let me see.' The demoniac had obviously dropped it when the porters had manhandled him out of the ward. 'I'll look after it. Thank you.'

The orderly carried on mopping and I found that I was holding a bronze statuette. It was clearly supposed to represent the female form, and, although I am no expert on such matters, I estimated the thing to be very old. I had seen fertility charms that looked very similar in books about pagan civilizations. Where, I wondered, had Lambert obtained this little Venus? It was not uncommon for demoniacs to swallow objects and to regurgitate them later, but their provenance was usually obvious. This was quite different and emanated an aura of authentic antiquity. I looked around the ward and when I was sure that no one was watching, I slipped the figure into my pocket.

At the end of the day I returned to my apartment, where I discovered a letter from Soulignac. It was not the first. There had been two others, almost identical, containing the same parting request for us to meet again soon. I had previously claimed that Charcot's hysterics were taking up all of my time, but as I opened the third letter, already certain of its contents, I recognized that I could not defer Soulignac indefinitely. With some reluctance, I wrote a brief reply, suggesting that we might dine together at a restaurant on the Boulevard des Italiens.

We had hardly finished our oysters when Soulignac said, 'Well, what are we to do now? It seems to me that we have reached an important juncture. Although we did not accomplish our ultimate objective, we have nevertheless developed and tested a method for probing the greatest of all mysteries, and, we have collected together a series of case studies which appear to demonstrate the independence of personality from the brain. Perhaps it is time for us to publish?'

'But I experienced none of those things reported by our patients. There was no tunnel, no light . . . nothing.'

'Indeed, a disappointing result, but one which was not entirely unexpected. We were both fully aware that this might happen. Remarkable phenomena are not reported by all resuscitated patients. Be that as it may, our experiment could easily be replicated by others. That is how science proceeds. I assume that you have no desire to repeat the experiment yourself.'

'No.'

'Good. Frankly, I don't think I could be party to such a dangerous venture again.' The waiter arrived and set about removing our oyster shells. 'So, what do you say to a publication?'

I prevaricated. 'You are a distinguished surgeon and I have a position in the world's finest department of neurology. The scientific community will not be impressed by six cases, most of whom are dead and can say nothing more in support of their testimony. It would be foolish to risk our reputations.'

I urged circumspection, restraint and the more rigorous interrogation of patients. Premature publication might cost us our careers, our livelihoods. We argued through two fish courses, until, eventually, Soulignac conceded defeat. 'I suppose you're right. And in this matter your wishes must prevail. It was you and not I who very nearly made the ultimate sacrifice.'

Outside the restaurant we said goodbye to each other and I watched Soulignac as he marched off into a haze of rain. Why could I not tell Soulignac the truth? I attempted to reflect on my behaviour, but found it impossible to do so. My thoughts resisted connection and my motivation remained obscure.

6

Early Summer 1879

Thérèse Courbertin continued to raise objections to my suggestion that we find rooms in Saint-Germain. She seemed to have developed a superstitious attachment to our hotel in Montmartre, believing that as long as we continued to meet there we would never be found out. Yet, to me at least, it was self-evident that the existing arrangement was unsatisfactory. The hotel was too far away. Her opposition did not prevent me from investigating alternatives, and I soon discovered somewhere more suitable. The concierge, accustomed to handling delicate matters, made it known to me that a small gratuity would be enough to secure his confidence, and after only a few visits, Thérèse grudgingly conceded that I had been right all along. It was now much easier to conduct our affair. The apartment was perfectly situated, tucked away in a quiet cul-de-sac and in easy walking distance from our respective residences. Moreover, the interior, if a little dreary, was tolerably furnished.

Intimacy with Thérèse no longer felt like an optional indulgence but, rather, something necessary, vital: a form of sustenance that I could not do without. Inhaling her sweet, heady fragrance, I would lose myself in her beauty, become enraged by desire and batter her with my body until it seemed that her bones might shatter. Her eyes would show alarm, but then, quite suddenly, her expression would change as she abandoned herself to my fevered clutches. Something in her nature, something dark and aberrant, was gradually awakening in response to my need. Months passed and she became increasingly compliant. She was obviously excited by my violent passions and I interpreted her passivity as a form of consent. I knew that I was hurting her, but she did not protest, and the cast of her face, half-closed eyes, parted lips, cheeks flushed with pleasure, and the little moans that issued from her mouth encouraged me to further excesses. After these ravishments, these assaults on her flesh, I would make a token apology. 'I want you so much. You don't understand what it's like, not having you – as a wife – completely. It's unbearable.' But I was play-acting, feigning remorse and fully conscious that Thérèse was a willing accomplice.

As I lay on the bed, smoking a cigar, admiring Thérèse's exquisite body, its planes and intersections, its loose-limbed perfection, she turned to show me her outer thigh. The skin was marred by five oval bruises, corresponding with the fingers and thumb of my left hand. 'Look what you've done!'

'Forgive me,' I said, raising myself up and kissing each blemish. 'I got carried away.'

'What if Henri was to notice?'

If only, I thought to myself. If only he were more observant!

I still begged her to leave him. My constant appeals had not swayed her in the past, but I persisted nevertheless. She tried to mollify me with bland assurances: her marriage was sexless, they lived like brother and sister, she was always asleep by the time he came to bed, but none of it had any effect, because I was not jealous, as she seemed to think. I did not view Courbertin as a competitor. He was much less than that, a nuisance, a handicap, an obstacle, and why Thérèse should be so resistant to the dissolution of their disastrous marriage was beyond my comprehension. There was Philippe's welfare to consider, I understood that – of course I did – but Courbertin was not a vindictive or malicious man. He would not seek to remove the child. Everything could be resolved amicably. Thérèse had long since tired of hearing my opinions and increasingly her typical response was a heavy, impatient sigh. The ensuing silence was always tense and intractable. I suppose it was inevitable that my resentment would build and eventually find expression.

Circumstances had prevented us from meeting for two weeks and I was desperate to see her again. I went to the apartment early, hoping that she would make efforts to do the same, and passed the time drinking rum and pacing the well-worn carpets. When she finally entered, at the exact hour we had prearranged, I leaped out of my chair and threw my arms around her. I kissed her face, stroked her hair and started fumbling with the hooks of her dress. Her perfume was stronger than ever, almost overpowering. She put up some slight resistance, and when I did not stop, she twisted out of my embrace. 'Let's sit and talk,' she said. 'We don't talk as much as we used to.'

I did not want to talk. Even so, I attempted to comply and sat with her on the couch, holding hands, making conversation. It was difficult to concentrate, given the urgency of my desire. Before long, I was once again kissing her neck and reaching round to unfasten the back of her dress.

'No!' Thérèse cried, pushing me away. 'I don't want to. Not today.'

'Then why on earth did you bother coming?'

'To be with you!' Her eyes flashed angrily.

The tense exchanges that followed quickly escalated. Accusations were followed by counter-accusations, voices were raised and yet, even as we argued, my wanting of her did not diminish. I found her denial completely unreasonable, petty, callous and spiteful. Eventually, she burst into tears and laying a hand over her abdomen, informed me that she had a 'stomach ache' and was in considerable pain. I realized at once that she was speaking euphemistically.

The situation was beyond repair. We sat in uncomfortable silence, until Thérèse bid me a frosty adieu. I did not try to prevent her from leaving.

That evening, I found myself ordering absinthes in a dingy cafe near Saint-Sulpice. I poured water over the trowel, and with studied restraint, watched the sugar crystals dissolve and the green liquor turn opaque. I was aware that my thoughts were not as they should be, but I could not divert them from their course. I imagined Thérèse, in bed, with Courbertin beside her, his bloated face embedded in her hair, his arms around her waist. It was so unfair. Everything was on her terms.

Stumbling out of the cafe and onto the pavement, I hailed a cab and said to the driver, 'Take me to the Folies Bergère'. Until that instant, the idea of going to the theatre had not crossed my mind, and some part of me was still lucid enough to register mild surprise. The words had tripped off my tongue in the absence of any accompanying desire to be amused or entertained, yet I did not reflect on my impulsivity and simply climbed into the vehicle without thought.

The facade of the Folies Bergère was brightly illuminated and many carriages were parked outside. I went to the box office, bought myself a ticket, and made my way through the milling crowd. The auditorium was stifling, the air not merely warm, but hot. In front of me, the stage was only visible between columns of smoke that rose upwards, perpetually feeding a layer of cloud that hung like a stormy sky beneath the wide dome. I took my seat and gazed over bald heads and feathered hats at a man and woman performing a trapeze act. They were succeeded by a magician and then by a pretty chanteuse who practised her art in a state of semi-undress. The heat was overpowering and I decided to venture out into the garden: a covered space, planted with yew trees, resounding with the splash of fountains. It was a great relief to step through the doorway and breathe the cool night air. Couples sat at zinc-topped tables, heads tilted towards each other, almost touching, sharing drinks and stealing kisses; others sat alone, solitary gentlemen whose dark, hungry eyes feasted on the spectacle of so many whores gliding beneath the boughs and dispersing fragrances with their fans. I was captivated by their method of locomotion, which involved a languid swaying of the rump. Sitting down at an empty table, I called a waiter and ordered an absinthe. I don't know how many absinthes I had drunk earlier, but this additional glass, even though of modest size, was the one that finally interfered with my powers of perception. Everything became luminescent, fantastical.

Two of these whores were looking at me, one of whom had black hair, the other brunette. I tipped my hat at the latter and she came forward. Her face was caked with white powder, her eyes artfully elongated with a pencil and her lips were the brightest red. A smile opened cracks in her cosmetic mask: 'Buy me a drink, monsieur?'

'Of course, mademoiselle, my pleasure. What would you like? '

'A grenadine?'

'Certainly. Waiter?' I snapped my fingers. 'A grenadine.'

She sat down beside me and we made some small talk, which evolved into a pathetic, artificial flirtation; however, she quickly tired of this game and bluntly stated her terms. It was evident that she was anxious to clarify my intentions so as not to waste any time. Subsequently, we found ourselves in a grubby brothel a short distance from the theatre. I was still feeling angry with Thérèse, resentful, affronted, and some of this bad feeling was transferred onto my companion. 'If you want to be rough,' she scolded, 'there are specialists. Places you can go to.' Afterwards, she stood in front of a full length oval mirror, looking over her shoulder, inspecting her back. There was a small scratch. 'I'm sorry,' I said. 'This should make amends.' I tossed a pile of coins onto the eiderdown and when she saw the extent of my generosity, she rushed across the room and planted a kiss on my cheek. 'Just cut your fingernails next time, eh?' she laughed.

I emerged into the thin light of a grey dawn and managed to get a cab back to Saint-Germain. Throughout the night I had not felt at all tired, but as the sun began to rise I experienced a sudden, deep exhaustion. I longed for sleep.

Before retiring, I picked up the little figure that the demoniac had regurgitated and wondered where Lambert had got it from? As I handled the bronze, I noticed my fingernails. The whore had been right to admonish me. They were long and sharp, which was curious, because I had not neglected my toilet. I found a pair of scissors and gave them a trim, finding the activity more of an effort than usual. The substance of my nails had thickened. When I had finished, I drew the curtains and listened to the bells of Saint-Sulpice. I experienced a flicker of guilt, but the emotion was dull and muted. Standing by the window, I seemed diminished, an echo of my former self.

The whore's rebuke played on my mind. 'If you want to be rough, there are specialists. Places you can go to.' Even when I was living a dissolute life on Saint-Sébastien, visiting the brothels of Port Basieux with Tavernier, the pleasures I craved were never unorthodox: excessive, yes, but not exceptional. I was feeling increasingly frustrated, as if I was being denied an entitlement. The prospect of obtaining proper and full satisfaction proved a temptation impossible for me to resist, and, after making judicious enquiries I learned of an establishment situated in the Marais that had gained a reputation for accommodating patrons with very particular requirements. It was frequented by men of a certain type, effete, foppish individuals with slow mannerisms and drawling voices, many of whom claimed to be poets. I made their acquaintance in the waiting room, which was cavernous and lit by an iron chandelier. The wallpaper was made from red satin, embossed with Egyptian hieroglyphs, and the floor was littered with hookahs. Large Venetian mirrors reflected images of women sprawled on banquettes, their dressing gowns loosely tied, or falling open to reveal enticing glimpses of lace underwear or a silk stocking. Something about their disposition created an impression of exotic flowers with heavy heads, drooping in the humid heat of a conservatory. Occasionally, the madam would circulate, offering the sleepy clientele strawberries soaked in ether. On my first visit, she seated herself beside me, and after making some witty remarks, said, 'So, monsieur, what are you looking for?' We had a curious, elliptical discussion, and at its end, she said, 'If I'm not mistaken, monsieur, you'll be wanting to spend some time with our Lili.' She directed my gaze across the room to a diminutive figure, encased in a cocoon of smoke that issued in spirals from the bowl of an enormous pipe. The stem of the pipe was long and its ceramic bowl supported by a cage-like contraption containing an oil lamp. 'I can promise you, monsieur, Lili is very willing.'

The madam must have been a perceptive woman, because, although I did try some of the other girls, none of them was able to satisfy my desires as much as Lili. I would take her tiny hand and lead her to one of the upstairs rooms, where she would stand before me, swaying slightly, her ribs protruding through rice-paper skin, her nipples erect, her stomach a shadowy hollow.

'Do whatever you want with me, monsieur,' she would say in a voice made hoarse by her addiction, before advancing like a ghost, weightless and sacrificial. When we were coupled, I would abandon moderation, she would wrap her flimsy arms around my shoulders, pull me closer, and whisper enticements in my ear.

On one such occasion, my nostrils were filled with the sweet perfume that I had hitherto associated with Thérèse. It was unusually strong and, inhaling deeply, I became more and more intoxicated, losing all of my inhibitions and entering into a state of rapturous abandon. My hands travelled over her body, grasping, squeezing, until, wildly excited, my nails sank into her flesh. I raked them down her neck and chest, but was too transported, at first, to notice the injury I had inflicted. Then, I saw the three red trails, the blood welling up, the formation of glistening droplets that eventually trickled away. The air was suddenly as fragrant as honeysuckle and I found myself kissing and licking the broken skin. It was not iron that I tasted, but the sublime essence of the perfume that had tormented me for so long. Pressing my mouth against the wounds, I sucked and sucked until I was overwhelmed by an ecstatic swoon and lost consciousness completely.

When I awoke, Lili was sitting on the edge of the bed, inspecting the large white rose that she had previously worn in her chignon. The edges of each petal had darkened. Then, turning her smudged eyes towards me, she said, 'Are you all right? You collapsed on top of me. I had to struggle to get out from under you. You're very heavy – heavier than I thought.'

I reached out and touched the scratches on her neck.

'Forgive me,' I said. 'I don't know what . . .'

Looking down, she saw how I had scored her body; however, she merely blinked and assumed her habitually vacant expression.

What was happening to me? For the first time since my resuscitation, I experienced a reawakening of self-disgust, dismay at my own depravity. I could still taste the sweetness in my mouth, but it had turned sickly. Getting up from the bed, I picked up my jacket and went through the pockets until I found my cigarettes. The tobacco was soothing, but I still felt queasy and feared that I might throw up.

'I'm sorry,' I said to Lili, raising her chin with a crooked finger. But even as I said those words, the accompanying remorse had already begun to diminish.

I was still finding it difficult to sleep at nights. With the arrival of evening, I became restless and when I retired, the pillow quickly became hot and the mattress uncomfortable. I felt trapped, anxious and agitated, needful of open spaces. The apartment became airless and the walls seemed to close in on me. Not wishing to inconvenience the concierge, I would climb out of the window onto the pavement and walk the streets. These nocturnal excursions were mostly aimless, and I would wander from district to district without any notion of reaching a particular destination. More often than not, I found myself standing in front of Notre-Dame, looking up at the western facade, humbled by the upward thrust of the stone, the three sculpted portals, the Gallery of Kings, the circular perfection of the rose window and the delicate arches of the open colonnade. It had become strangely fascinating to me. I would circle the great edifice, studying its intricately carved exterior, impressed by the span of the flying buttresses which leaped audaciously from the ground to the roof and urged the eye to ascend even further: to the spire and the saintly statues that surrounded its eminence. And I was reminded of that night when I had looked down on those same statues from my impossible vantage point before plummeting through the cathedral, the earth and the pit.

Early one morning, I happened to see a priest unlocking the door to the north tower. He disappeared inside and a few minutes later reappeared, clutching some books. He then dashed off, his stride widening to hasten his progress. The sky was only just beginning to glow in the east. I crossed the road, opened the door and started to climb the spiral staircase. Although some candles had been lit, the interior was gloomy and it was necessary to navigate partly by sense of touch, feeling the walls for safety and guidance. I emerged abruptly onto the viewing platform above the colonnade. The panorama was breathtaking; roofs, domes and steeples receding in all directions, and the steel-grey river flowing beneath the arches of the Petit Pont and the Pont-Saint-Michel. In the distance I could see plumes of smoke rising out of factory chimneys and the purple masses of the surrounding hills. The parvis was empty, but the streets were coming to life. I could hear the sound of stallholders greeting each other, the rattle of carts and the whinnying of horses.

Clinging to the parapet were the famous gargoyles or 'chimera' of the cathedral: mysterious veiled birds, sleek predatory cats, goats, grotesque apes, dragons and semi-human things that were the stuff of nightmares, abominations that combined the characteristics of several species, freakish and unnatural. Open beaks and gaping jaws suggested a petrified dawn chorus of screeches, screams and mocking laughter. The balustrade was an infernal menagerie. Only one representation of humanity was included in this unholy assembly, a bearded sage, whose stone face expressed fear and speechless horror.

I found myself drawn to the most striking of all these creatures, a curiously melancholic personification of evil whose elbows rested on a cornerstone, and whose hands, distinguished by long fingers and sharp, tapering nails, supported a massive blockish head. His great, folded wings curled forward over his shoulders and two stump-like horns projected from his forehead. His eyes were deep cavities, his nose broad with flaring nostrils, and a swollen, lascivious tongue protruded from his open mouth. He seemed to exude indolence and lechery. Standing next to this Satanic likeness, I was reminded of the temptation of Christ.

It is recorded in the Holy Bible that the Devil showed Our Lord the kingdoms of the world, and said, 'All this will I give unto thee if thou wilt bow down and worship me.' Jesus did not question the Devil's right of possession. Evidently, the Devil's terms were valid, for when, as proud Lucifer, the Devil had been driven out of heaven by the archangel Michael, God decreed that the earth should be his domain. It has always been understood that the Devil is master here.

Looking out over the sprawling city, this proposition seemed incontestable. Here, surely, was the new Babylon: Paris, renowned for its vices, its tens of thousands of whores, its alcoholics and opium addicts, its voluptuaries, thieves, cut-throats and degenerates – a turbulent city of barricades and revolutions, blood and execution, of cruelty, lust, disease and madness. The melancholy demon was well placed to see it all, and I imagined him deriving much pleasure from observing the various permutations of human iniquity. Feeling uneasy, I returned to the stairs and, after descending to the street, made my way directly to the hospital.

After losing a night's sleep, I found it very difficult to function the following day. I felt drained of energy and had to put on my eye-preservers to prevent headaches. The problem of my abnormal sleeping habit was partially addressed by changing my working practices. Hysterical patients were monitored at regular intervals around the clock and I started volunteering for the unpopular night shift. This not only allowed me to catch up on lost sleep (when the rest of the world was going about its business), but it also pleased my colleagues and impressed Charcot. It was not possible for me to work every night. That would have been conspicuous. Even so, the compromise that I pursued was quite satisfactory.

I had not touched a battery for many months – not since before my period of infirmity. The day came, however, when I was referred an elderly gentleman who suffered from muscle weakness and I decided to treat him using electrical stimulation.

'Will it hurt, monsieur?' he asked.

'No. Not at all,' I replied.

The old man was not reassured. 'I was talking to Monsieur Fromentin, do you know him? He suffers from the same indisposition, and he said that he found the procedure quite painful.'

'Please,' I said, placing a friendly hand on the old man's knee, 'You have nothing to fear.' I switched on the battery and it began to buzz. Lifting up the rods, I passed them over the old man's exposed legs. 'See?'

'I can feel a prickling sensation,' said the old man, anxiously.

'Well, that's all right, isn't it?'

The old man nodded, but he did not look comfortable. He then said, 'It's getting hot.'

'Come now,' I responded tetchily. 'You are thinking too much about what Monsieur Fromentin told you.'

'No, it really is very unpleasant.'

The battery started crackling and there was a loud bang which made both of us jump.

'What on earth was that?' cried the old man. A ribbon of smoke was rising up from the machine and it had stopped buzzing.

'I am very sorry, monsieur, the device seems to be faulty. I'll have to get another one.' I went to the store room and on my return found the old man inspecting his legs.

'I've been burned,' he complained.

I inspected his skin and a few blisters had indeed risen.

'That is most unfortunate,' I said, 'but it won't happen again.'

I set the second battery down next to the first and switched it on. There was no buzzing sound. I tried the switch again and turned the dials but the machine was stubbornly inert.

'Is something wrong, monsieur?' asked the old man.

Again, I was obliged to apologize and went to get a third battery. Thankfully, this device was in working order and I was able to administer the treatment without further difficulty. The events of that morning set something of a precedent. Thereafter, I kept on having problems with electrical equipment. Batteries became temperamental in my hands. On one occasion, I was attempting to treat a hysterical contracture and the battery 'died' almost immediately. Yet, when Valdestin took the rods from me they promptly came to life again.

'You're jinxed,' he said, laughing.

'Yes,' I replied, pretending to enjoy the joke. 'It certainly looks that way.'

I was accustomed to receiving one letter a year, always around Christmas, from the mother superior of the Saint-Sébastien mission. Consequently, its unseasonal appearance among my mail immediately struck me as odd. On opening the letter, I learned that my old colleague Georges Tavernier was dead. He had fallen ill quite suddenly and his health had rapidly deteriorated. His assistant had been unable to treat the condition (which my correspondent neglected to identify). Tavernier must have been delirious at the end. Instead of calling for Father Baubigny to administer the last rites, he had requested the services of the Port Basieux bokor. That evening, sitting in a dingy restaurant with rotten floorboards, I raised a glass of rum to Tavernier's memory and took from my pocket an ugly thing of beads and hair. It was the amulet Tavernier had given me in the brothel we visited after the Piton-Noir ball. I worried the charm with my fingers and finally placed it on the table. The world is not always intelligible. When I left the restaurant, I did not pick it up. I left it there, an alien object, wedged between the pepper and the salt.

*

The examination room was painted entirely black and hung with etchings by Raphael and Rubens. Charcot had taken a personal interest in its refurbishment and had created a darkly atmospheric space in which he could initiate his disciples into the mysteries of differential diagnosis. When I arrived, a large number of my colleagues were already gathered there, among them, Henri Courbertin. We had not encountered each other for some time and he greeted me with characteristic warmth.

'Clément, my dear fellow, what a pleasant surprise!' He clasped my hand, smiled benevolently, and began talking about a monograph he had recently obtained on cerebral localization. Although I showed no interest and may have even stifled a yawn, he somehow managed to suppose that I was eager to read it.

'My dear fellow,' he continued, nudging me with his elbow. 'Why don't I lend it to you?' Before I could reject his offer he was saying, 'I'll leave it in my office for you to collect. I'm sure you will find it absolutely fascinating. Please,' he raised a finger, mistaking an emerging objection for gratitude. 'It's my pleasure.'

Charcot appeared in the doorway and marched through the assembly, distinguishing some of those present with curt acknowledgements, before taking his seat behind a bare table. The rest of us had to stand. He took off his top hat and angled his cane over his shoulder like a soldier's rifle. After he indicated his readiness to proceed, the drone of lowered voices heralded the appearance of a morose woman who was escorted out onto the empty floor.

Her hospital gown was removed and a flush of shame made her upper chest and face glow. Valdestin read aloud the woman's history and after a lengthy silence (broken only by the drumming of Charcot's fingers) our chief spoke directly to the patient: 'Madame, I would be most grateful if you would come forward.' He beckoned and she obeyed. He then raised his hand, 'Stop. Now, please turn around and walk back again.' Charcot touched his ear. 'Gentlemen, I want you to listen carefully. Now, madame, would you please walk backwards and forwards, just as you did before.' When she had done this, Charcot thanked her and continued in a more pedantic style of speech, 'If the ankle flexors and extensors are affected, as is sometimes the case, the foot will be absolutely flaccid. As the patient walks, she overflexes at the knee joint and the thigh lifts upward more than it should. As the foot hits the ground, the toes hit first and then the heel so that you can quite distinctly hear two successive sounds. The ataxic patient thrusts her leg forward in extension with almost no flexion of the knee joint; this time, the foot hits the ground all at once, making only a single sound. Here,' he gestured at the woman, 'we have a very typical example of the latter.' It was only then that he turned to see if we were impressed by his powers of observation. Some discussion followed, the woman was given a diagnosis, and the next patient was summoned. This procedure was repeated until noon, when Charcot rose from his chair, bade us all 'good day', and departed in the company of an associate professor and four junior doctors.

Those of us remaining filed out of the examination room and loitered in the corridor in order to enjoy a cigarette before resuming our clinical duties. It had become a point of etiquette to express disbelief at Charcot's brilliance before talking of other things, and for a brief duration the air was humming with superlatives. Once again, I found myself standing next to Courbertin, who, after honouring this servile obligation, spoke with jovial fluency about a number of inconsequential topics. It was only when I heard him say that he intended to take his wife and son to Venice in September that my attention was fully engaged.

'And how is your wife?' I asked.

A shadow seemed to pass across his face. His complexion was pasty and he was breathing heavily. 'She . . .'

'Yes?'

'She hasn't been very well lately.'

'Oh, I'm sorry to hear that. Nothing serious, I hope.'

His reply was hesitant, faltering. 'No, no. It's just . . .' He raised his arms and let them fall. 'Women!' Then, suddenly recognizing the impropriety of this exclamation, he pretended to make light of it. 'Enjoy your liberty while you can, Clément! With marriage comes great responsibility.' And with those ill-judged words, he set off down the corridor, pausing only to remind me of his prior commitment. 'I'll leave the monograph in my office. Tomorrow.' I watched him recede – a bumbling, perspiring fool.

That night, I could not stop myself from thinking about Thérèse Courbertin. I imagined how she might look in Venice, wearing a pale short-sleeved summer dress, carrying a parasol, crossing Saint Mark's Square or standing on the Rialto Bridge. And I imagined Courbertin, at her side, consulting his guidebook, his handkerchief permanently pressed against his damp brow. I imagined them returning to their hotel, a former merchant's palace with marble floors and gilded staircases – in bed together, listening to the sound of mandolins and lapping water. These flights of fancy made me aware of how much I still wanted Thérèse Courbertin. Indeed, I wanted her more than ever.

We had not spoken or written to each other for several months, not since our ridiculous argument. If Thérèse was as miserable as I suspected (a reasonable supposition, given Courbertin's remarks) then I was hopeful that the cause of this misery might be our separation.

The next day, I concealed myself in a doorway opposite the Courbertins' apartment block. At half past ten, Thérèse appeared and walked off in the direction of the Luxembourg Gardens. I followed her through the gates but kept my distance. She sat down on a bench overlooking the octagonal pool, the edges of which were surrounded by nurse maids and small boys launching toy boats. The sun came out from behind a cloud and its brilliance made my head ache. I put on my eye-preservers and drew closer to my quarry. It was obvious that Thérèse was in a reflective mood. She wasn't looking at the palace or the blooming flowers, but staring blankly out into space. I took one more step and slid on to the bench beside her. She was so self-absorbed that she didn't even notice my arrival and it wasn't until I had spoken her name that she turned around and gasped, 'Paul!'

'I'm sorry,' I said, 'I am so very sorry.'

'Not here,' she responded coldly. 'We can't speak here.' She got up to leave but I grabbed her arm and pulled her down again.

'No. Don't go,' I said. 'I won't let you. Not before you have heard what I must say. Please.' She stopped trying to escape and I released my grip. 'I behaved inexcusably – I know that – intolerably – but I beg you, please, please, take pity on me. I have been selfish and now recognize the magnitude of my stupidity. I adore you. I cannot go on without you. Please forgive me. I promise that I will never demand anything of you again. I love you – I do not deserve you – but I love you all the same and will always love you.'

Her eyes had begun to fill with tears, but she did not respond sympathetically. Instead, she stood up and took a few uncertain steps towards the balustrade. 'We can't talk here. Not like this.'

'Then let's go somewhere else.'

'No,' she sobbed. 'I can't do that.' She started to move away from me. I willed her to stop and, remarkably, she came to a sudden halt, jolting, as if she had reached the end of an invisible leash. Then, glancing back, she said,

'I'll write,' before descending the steps that led down to the pool. I watched her marching through the perambulators and squealing children until I lost sight of her.

Thérèse kept her word. She did write me a brief letter, full of hurt and anger. I wrote back: wretched, penitent. Soon, we were corresponding regularly, engaged in a subtle process of negotiation, the outcome of which seemed – with increasing likelihood – to be some form of reconciliation. For this to happen, however, it was necessary for me to make certain promises, one of which was never to ask Thérèse to leave her husband again. Needless to say, I accepted all of her conditions, and we were subsequently reunited in our secret apartment. There was some awkwardness at first, but in no time things were just as they were before.

7

Autumn 1879

Bazile opened the door, smiled broadly and shook my hand, 'Ah, Clément, what a pleasure it is to see you again. Forgive me for not responding to your note more swiftly, but I've been away. A family matter. In fact, Madame Bazile is still in Normandy.' I entered Bazile's parlour and had to pick my way through piles of books on the floor. 'I'm sorry,' Bazile continued, 'without Madame Bazile to keep things in order . . .' He drew my attention to the chaotic consequences of her absence. In addition to the scattered books, I saw a bicycle frame, some thick coiled rope, a lectern and a box of garden tools. There was also a small ginger kitten scampering around the room. Bazile scooped it up with one hand. 'I found him outside and thought I'd bring him in to keep me company.' The animal's ears drew back, its mouth opened wide and it hissed, apparently at me. 'Now, now, that's not how we welcome our guests,' laughed Bazile. He then put the kitten back on the floor, whereupon it darted under the sideboard and crouched, peering out from its shadowy retreat with glinting eyes. 'He's usually more sociable,' said Bazile, pulling a chair out from beneath the table. 'Please sit.' He then excused himself, and returned carrying a bottle of cider and two tankards. 'How have you been?' he enquired.

'Very well,' I replied. 'Apart from a little eye-strain.'

'You still look very pale.'

I shrugged. 'I haven't been out in the sun much, that's all.'

Bazile poured the cider and took his seat on the opposite side of the table. Our initial exchanges were, perhaps, a little more mannered than usual, but we were soon talking with the easy familiarity of old friends. 'So,' said Bazile, lighting his pipe and assuming a more serious expression. 'What next? The result of your courageous experiment was disappointing, but by now you must have given the matter much consideration and I have been wondering how you intend to proceed.' I explained to Bazile that he was mistaken, and that since recovering from my illness and returning to the Salpêtrière all of my time had been taken up by Charcot's hysterics. 'A shame,' said Bazile; however, he did not press me to reveal more and surprisingly allowed the subject to drop from our conversation.

The frequent replenishment of my tankard had brought me close to inebriation. Bazile, who was also guilty of over-indulgence, had digressed some distance from his initial topic, and was talking about the bells of

Notre-Dame. 'Emmanuel is the sole survivor. All the others were seized during the Revolution and melted down to make cannons. Guillaume, Pugnais, Chambellan, and Pasquier. John and his little brother Nicolas. Gabriel and Claude and the ladies, Marie, Jaqueline, Françoise and Barbara, who, like her saintly namesake, was reputed to have had the power to deflect lightning. Gone forever! Oh, what heavenly music they must have made.' He paused to imagine their lost voices.

'Why are there so many gargoyles on the cathedral?' I asked.

Bazile's reverie was so deep that he did not hear me properly. 'I'm sorry,' he said, blinking. 'What did you say?'

'The gargoyles,' I repeated. 'Why are there so many of them?'

'Strictly speaking, a gargoyle is a rain spout, albeit a rain spout that has been made to look like a monster. There are indeed many of these adorning the cathedral, but I suspect that you are, in actual fact, referring to the chimeras – the statues on the viewing platform.'

'Indeed.'

'They are not authentic, of course, but recreations in the medieval style, commissioned while the cathedral was being restored. Even so, there have always been hordes of hellish creatures on the balustrade. The originals were weathered away or removed when they became dangerous, but their claws and feet survived.'

'Dangerous?'

'By the end of the last century the cathedral was so eroded that it was not uncommon for the most dilapidated statues to fall off.' Bazile bit the stem of his pipe and spoke through his teeth. 'That must have been a sight, eh? Demons raining down from the sky and shattering on the parvis!'

'But why so many?' I persisted.

'There are certainly more devils on Notre-Dame than on any other building I can think of.' He took the pipe from his mouth and began to enumerate. 'There are the gargoyles and the chimeras. Then there are the carvings on the portal of the Last Judgement, which show sinners being led to hell in chains by demons. And on the north portal you can find Théophile kneeling before Satan.'

'Théophile?'

'Théophile, a seneschal who was supposed to have made a pact with Satan to secure advancement. He was saved from eternal torment by the intercession of the Virgin.' Bazile opened his mouth and released a cloud of smoke. 'The men who built the cathedral were keen to remind onlookers of the infernal domain.'

'Why so?'

Bazile looked at me as if I had failed to grasp something very fundamental. 'Because the cathedral is dedicated to Our Lady, and as her cult became more widespread, she was revered, not only as the queen of heaven and earth, but also, the queen of the underworld.'

'Our Lady is the queen of hell?'

'Yes,' said, Bazile insistently. He saw that I was doubtful and cited his source. 'When I first came to Paris I became the assistant of a scholarly priest of Notre-Dame. Do you remember, I mentioned it once before? His name was Father Ranvier and he was greatly interested in the carvings and statues of the cathedral. He was so knowledgeable that his opinion was frequently sought during the restorations. He had embarked on a fascinating history of the building that, after all these years, is still incomplete. I was his amanuensis.'

Placing a cigarette between my lips, I said, 'I was on the viewing platform recently. I hadn't been up there for years, and found myself quite intrigued by the chimeras.'

'In my humble opinion they are masterpieces.'

'Especially the winged demon.'

'Ah yes, the strix. I adore its melancholy expression, don't you?'

I lit the cigarette. 'The strix?'

'A name – of classical provenance – that has become associated with the winged demon because of the artist Charles Méryon. It was he who made the famous etching. You must know it: the winged demon, swooping crows, the tower of Saint Jacques in the background? Why it was that Méryon borrowed a name from Roman mythology is unclear, but in all probability his choice was somewhat arbitrary. He lost his mind and died in an asylum. Father Ranvier corresponded with him but Méryon's replies were unintelligible.'

Bazile tilted the bottle over his tankard but found it empty. Scuttling off to the kitchen he returned with yet more cider. We continued drinking and talking, but the subject of hell arose again in relation to a theological point, and I found myself speaking intemperately.

'Can any sin merit such a punishment? If Christian doctrine is correct, and such a place exists, then I must question our trust in absolutes, the reassuring polarities of good and evil, because a god who consigns his errant children to the pit cannot be meaningfully described as benign.' Looking across the table at Bazile, I saw in his eyes a combination of disapproval and compassion. 'I'm sorry,' I added. 'I have offended you.'

He sighed and said, 'Perhaps the disappointing result of your experiment has shaken your faith.'

I shook my head. 'I never had faith. Not really. That is why I sought to prove.' There was bitterness in my voice. 'People with faith have no need of evidence.'

Bazile made an ambiguous gesture. 'Perhaps we have had too much to drink.'

'Yes,' I agreed, pushing my tankard away.

As I was leaving, Bazile took something from his pocket and held it out for me to take. He tipped a silver cross into the palm of my hand. I was surprised by its weight and Bazile must have noticed. His brow furrowed momentarily before he declared, 'A small token of friendship. Let it be a reminder – you are always welcome here.'

I thanked him and motioned to leave, but hesitated in

order to ask a final question: 'What does it mean? Strix? You never said.'

'A strix is a nocturnal bird of ill omen,' Bazile replied, 'but one which feeds on human flesh and blood. A kind of vampire, I suppose.'

8

I had promised Thérèse Courbertin that I would never again ask her to leave her husband, and when I made that promise, it was one that I was confident I would keep. But as soon as our meetings were re-established, the urge to issue the same ultimatum returned, perhaps even stronger than before. Even so, I managed to exercise restraint and made an effort to talk to her in much the same way as I had at the very start of our relationship. We talked about events that had transpired during seances she had attended, spirit communication, inexplicable noises and the levitation of objects, the writings of Allan Kardec and many other subjects of esoteric interest. I wondered how she reconciled her spiritual aspirations with an illicit affair but, needless to say, I was not so stupid as to challenge her. What passed as her morality was clearly both idiosyncratic and pliable, a fragile system of values that would not bear the weight of too much scrutiny. It seemed to me, however, that at this particular juncture she was happier than she had been in a long time, insofar as an individual with Thérèse's constitution, so full of contradictions and prone to episodes of melancholy, could ever be described as happy.

I remember her so clearly, her supple body encased in a tight satin dress, her fur coat, the warm collar of which brushed my cheek as she offered me her neck, the sapphires that hung from her ears and the wisps of blonde hair that escaped from beneath her hat, her gloves, which, when raised to the lips, seemed to be saturated with her essence – the sudden ignition of her eyes and her glistening teeth.

Perhaps as a result of our temporary separation, Thérèse had come to appreciate the special nature of our union, our unique, if somewhat deviant, compatibility.

In order to increase our pleasure I introduced her to morphine, which had become fashionable among certain ladies, principally those who either hosted or frequented salons where stained glass, draped silk and the attendance of artists was obligatory. Medical suppliers were quick to profit from this craze, and small but beautifully finished enamel syringes were soon being manufactured to meet the demand. I was able to obtain a fine example, encrusted with pearls and lapis lazuli. Included in the purchase price was an attractive case made of ebony, with a lining of black velvet. Thérèse was naturally inclined towards experimentation and curious about altered states of consciousness. Moreover, one of her spiritualist acquaintances, a woman who I guessed was eager to associate herself with any new fad, had already acquired an enamel syringe and shown it off to her friends as if it were a new bauble. Under such favourable conditions, the task of persuasion was not very difficult.

Consigning Thérèse to oblivion was such a rare delight: slipping the needle beneath her skin, depressing the plunger and watching her face become serene, her eyelids heavy. After removing the needle, a bead of blood would well up from the puncture, unusually bright and red – like rose petals or rubies – and I would touch the droplet with a trembling finger and surreptitiously transfer it to my tongue. I could not stop myself, for the temptation was too great, and even though later I might reflect on my behaviour and be troubled by its implications, the pleasure of the moment far outweighed all subsequent considerations. There was something singularly appealing about Thérèse's bouquet, for it was at once both sweeter and more subtle than that of other women. It collected beneath her tresses, where I would bury my head and inhale deeply, and as I thrust myself into her, with savage insistence, her honey-like effusions incited brutality. I wanted to mark her flesh with my nails, but was forbidden to do so, and the frustration that I felt was insufferable.

When our love-making was over – for that, I suppose was what it was – she would curl into a ball and sleep, and I would feast my eyes on the gentle contours of her form, the arc of her back and the regularity of her buttocks. Through her translucent skin, I studied with some fascination the branching pattern of her vessels. I was strangely obsessed by the notion of her interior, and imagined Thérèse transformed into a medical wax-work, with her muscles and ligaments exposed. This exercise did not dampen my passion. Quite the opposite: contemplating her carnality (rump, flank and tenderloin) made her even more desirable. These meditations were increasingly associated with a creeping sense of unease, but I knew that it would pass. The feeling of not being wholly alive would return, and with it, a consoling anaesthesia.

One afternoon I was engaged in my habitual study of Thérèse in post-coital repose. She was sprawled out beside me, like a slumbering goddess, her arms angled either side of her head, one leg bent at the knee, the other extended. The sun was shining and a shaft of light disclosed flecks of gold among the chestnut curls of her pubic delta. I then noticed that the air was full of wink-ing motes, and lazily raised my arm, fingers outstretched, intending to catch a tiny blazing world. My open hand threw a shadow across Thérèse's chest. I made a move-ment and was puzzled by a curious phenomenon. The motion of my hand did not correspond precisely with the motion of its shadow. There was a slight delay. I wiggled my fingers to confirm my observation, and as before, the silhouette lagged behind. My professional instincts inclined me towards a neurological interpre-tation. Perhaps I was witnessing further evidence of damage to my nervous system? But such thinking was automatic and unconvincing. The shadow of my hand, now hovering over Thérèse's breasts, seemed to have an independent existence, being somewhat displaced from where I had expected it to fall. I abruptly closed my fingers, so hard that they produced a snapping sound, and, a fraction of a second later, their shadowy counterparts curled into the compact roundness of a clenched fist. Thérèse's eyes sprang wide open, the lids rolling back to such an extent that her irises were surrounded by gleaming whiteness. She gasped and clutched at her heart, struggling to draw breath.

'What's the matter?' I asked. She did not register my presence so I shook her and asked again, 'Thérèse, what's the matter?'

Her gaze gradually focused and she replied. 'It hurts, here.' She then began massaging her sternum. I took her pulse, which was racing, but there were no other symptoms.

'Did you have a bad dream?'

'No.'

'Then it's probably just cramp, a spasm of the intercostal muscles. You were asleep and the sudden pain woke you up with a fright.'

'No.' She rocked her head from side to side. 'I wasn't asleep. It felt like something was touching me,' she paused before adding, 'inside.'

I lay down beside her and drew her close. 'Cramp. That's all it was. There's nothing to worry about.'

'But the pain was so . . . bad.'

'Indeed. Cramps can be very unpleasant.' I stroked Thérèse's hair and whispered endearments into her ear, until once again she was asleep, or at least very close to it. The light faded as a cloud drifted in front of the sun, and my thoughts, although troubled, were also strangely excited.

As time wore on, my desire to take complete possession of Thérèse Courbertin – to have her as mine, and mine alone – grew so intense that my thoughts became fevered and my head filled with lurid fantasies. I imagined how it might have been, had we met in different circumstances, another life perhaps, in which Henri and Philippe had never existed, and in which I was free to do with her as I pleased.

There were rare moments when my conscience seemed to revive and protest, and then I would feel authentic emotions once again, self-loathing and disgust at my repellent daydreams. I thought of the nerves that connect the tongue and nose to the brain, and considered how oxygen deprivation might have affected their functioning. And how was it, I wondered, that for me, love and inflicting pain had become so hopelessly confused? I rationalized and rationalized, until, exhausted by an interminable and utterly sterile inner debate, I would fall into a state of torpid indifference.

Thérèse would sometimes say something that suggested the operation of a higher perceptual gift. She seemed to sense a presence in the room; however, her female intuition did not allow her to understand its nature or the extent of its influence and malignancy. On one of these occasions she became uneasy and restless.

Wrapping her arms around her body and shivering slightly, she said, 'I feel like we're being watched.'

'That's ridiculous,' I laughed.

'I never feel like we're truly alone.'

'What, do you think the concierge is spying on us? Do you think he peeps through the keyhole?' She shrugged and I continued, 'It's the morphine. It can create false impressions in the mind.'

She nodded, but her expression remained apprehensive.

We usually left the apartment separately, Thérèse first, and I a few minutes later. I did not always go home. More often than not, I went straight to the hospital or wandered the streets, brooding. I had managed to remain silent on the subject of Thérèse's marriage; I had made no more demands, but my resolve was weakening. Something in the core of my being felt tense and ready to burst.

Shortly before dusk, I found myself on the cobbled path that follows the river Bièvre. The air smelled rank and the surface of the bilgy water was mottled with green scum. Everywhere I looked there was refuse, broken pots, metal drums and heaps of decaying food infested with vermin. Men in flat caps were hanging pelts out to dry over wattle fences: they had just finished skinning animals and the workers' shirts were rancid. Other menials were unloading leather hides from a cart and throwing them into enormous vats.

I came to a shanty town of huts and beyond these were taller dwellings that seemed to have been constructed by simply piling one hovel on top of another. They leaned across the river towards each other, the upper storeys almost touching and compressing the sky into a fine, luminous strip.

An old woman, dressed in rags, was dangling her feet in the water. She was singing a sentimental ballad and took inebriate liberties with rhythm and pitch. When she heard me coming, she turned abruptly and whined, 'Charity, monsieur? A few coins, that's all I ask. I'll remember you in my prayers.' Her lips retreated to reveal a few blackened teeth. I walked on without acknowledging her plea and she immediately launched into an abusive tirade. A coughing fit cut short her string of insults.

After choosing a path that led away from the river, I entered a network of alleys that brought me to a dingy street enlivened only by the presence of a tiny cafe. It was getting cold, so I went inside and ordered a brandy from a moribund waiter with a drooping moustache.

The situation was intolerable. It couldn't go on. One way or another, I would have Thérèse Courbertin all to myself.

When I stepped out onto the street again, a full moon had risen above the rooftops. Looking up at the bright white disc, I felt a gentle heat on my face.

Two weeks later, I happened to be walking past the Courbertins' apartment, when I was overcome by a strong desire to see Thérèse. My feet began to drag and I found myself rooted to the spot. I knew, at some level, that it was madness to contemplate paying her a visit, but I was not deterred. Indeed, the longer I remained stationary, the more it was that I became determined to pursue what, ordinarily, I would have identified as a reckless course of action. A single thought came to dominate my mind: *You shall not be denied.* It was curiously resonant, like a spoken command.

I crossed the road and on entering the building asked the concierge for directions. There was something about his expression, his narrowed eyes and jutting jaw, which suggested suspicion; however, whatever doubts he may have harboured regarding my character, he answered, 'Madame Courbertin? Second floor, first on the left, monsieur.' I climbed the stairs and, as I neared the top, saw my double, rising and approaching from the opposite direction. A floor to ceiling mirror had been mounted on the landing and the person who confronted me was pale and haggard. I removed my eye-preservers and dropped them into one of my pockets. On the second-floor landing, there was yet another mirror, identical to the first, and once again I stopped, and after further consideration of my appearance removed my hat and combed my hair.

The Courbertins' apartment was easy to locate. I rang the bell and the door was opened by a fresh-faced maid.

'I have come to see Madame Courbertin.'

'Is she expecting you?' asked the maid.

'No.'

She raised her eyebrows and waited for some further explanation. Perplexed by my silence, she coughed nervously, and asked, 'Whom should I announce?'

'Monsieur Clément,' I replied.

The maid led me into what appeared to be a waiting room. Like most associate professors, Coubertin saw his private patients at home. I did not sit down, but instead examined a fine dry-point etching of a chateau beside a lake. The apartment was very quiet, although I could hear a muffled exchange taking place not very far away. A carriage clock chimed. The maid reappeared and requested that I follow her into the parlour, where Thérèse had situated herself by the fireplace. I bowed and said, 'Good afternoon, Madame Courbertin.'

She was wearing a grey dress with a pink blouse, and her hands clutched the edges of a tasselled shawl that she had thrown around her shoulders. I registered the potted plants, the photographs in silver frames, the leather sofas and the upright piano, the trappings and emblems of a comfortable, conventional existence.

'Monsieur Clément,' she replied, acknowledging my arrival with a tight smile. Then, addressing the maid, she said, 'That will be all, Isabelle.' The maid curtsied and left, but Thérèse waited for the girl's footsteps to fade before she asked, anxiously, 'What is it? What's happened?'

I turned my hat over in my hands. 'Nothing has happened.'

She appeared confused. 'Then why . . . what are you doing here?'

'I wanted to see you.'

'What?' Her features hardened and she glared at me.

'I wanted to see you,' I repeated.

'Dear God,' she paced up and down in front of the hearth. 'What are you saying?' She stopped abruptly and touched her brow. 'And what . . . what am I going to tell Henri? Have you taken leave of your senses?'

I sighed and said, 'I know that I shouldn't be here. But I hope that you will understand, when I say that I had no choice in the matter. I could not act freely. My heart. . .'

She made frantic movements with her hands, beating the air with downward movements while making hushing sounds. 'Must you speak so loudly?' Then, taking control of herself, she added with precise emphasis, 'Please leave.'

I shook my head. 'We can't go on like this. I am not prepared to—'

'Enough!' Thérèse interrupted. 'Henri will be returning shortly.'

I took a few steps forward but Thérèse retreated into a corner. Her expression, which had been stern and resolute, suddenly changed, becoming by degrees more uncertain. The colour drained from her face, she began to sway and I thought that she was about to faint. Moving forward, I took her in my arms and whispered to her in low, urgent tones, professing my love and begging her to put an end to our unhappiness. 'Have courage,' I said. 'It is in your power to release us from this wretched existence of secrecy and lies.' Her eyes glinted like those of a frightened animal and her bosom heaved with emotion. Emboldened by her fragrance I stroked her cheeks and kissed her neck. 'No, Paul,' she whimpered. 'No.' But I did not stop, even when she tried, weakly, to push me off. I felt invincible, excited by the fact that I was having my way with Courbertin's wife in Courbertin's parlour, and it seemed to me that, with every caress, I was demonstrating the insubstantiality of the psychological partition that Thérèse had erected to keep the different areas of her life separate. With every touch, I was forcing her to accept that the dissolution of her marriage was both inevitable and necessary. Courbertin was my inferior in every way. A feeble old man and a third-rate intellect.

'Please, Paul,' she ducked and escaped to the centre of the room, where she checked that her hairpins were still in place and repositioned her shawl. 'You must go now.'

I walked around the sofas, occasionally bending to inspect a framed portrait. When I reached the piano I noticed that there was some music on the stand. It was not a published piece, but an original composition copied out in black ink. Beneath the title, 'Serenade', was a dedication, 'For Thérèse'. The composer was Cécile Chaminade.

'Is this your piano?' I asked.

'Yes.'

'I didn't know you played. How strange, that we've

known each other all this time, and I didn't know that you played.' Thérèse's hand had risen to her mouth and her eyes were wide and staring. I turned the first page over and wondered how the music might sound.

'I would so love to hear you play. Would you do that for me? Would you play for me? It's only a short piece.'

Thérèse did not respond, but maintained her fixed position. The silence that followed was lengthy, eventually broken by the sound of a key turning in a lock. Someone had entered the hallway. 'Henri,' whispered Thérèse, folding the shawl around her body as if the temperature in the room had suddenly plummeted.

Courbertin called out, 'Thérèse, my dear?'

I could see that for a fleeting instant Thérèse had contemplated not replying, but on realizing that this would serve no purpose, she answered, 'Henri?'

We both listened to Courbertin's heavy approach. The door opened and on entering the room he caught sight of me and froze. I noticed that he was sweating and his breath was laboured. He glanced at his wife, who looked terrified, and then back at me. Dropping his medical bag to the floor, he cried out, 'Clément, what on earth brings you here?' He strode across the Persian rug with his arm extended.

'Your copy of Monsieur Varon's monograph,' I replied as we shook hands. 'I was passing and remembered that I should have returned it.' Reaching into my coat pocket I produced the volume and gave it to Courbertin. 'Charcot will be discussing cerebral localization at the research meeting tomorrow. I thought you might want to reacquaint yourself with some of Varon's theories.'

'Thank you,' said Courbertin. 'You're always so considerate, Clément. But really, there was no need.'

I gave Courbertin a conspiratorial look. 'The professor is not familiar with Varon.' It was generally accepted that an opportunity to impress Charcot should never be missed.

'Yes,' said Courbertin, slowly registering the implication. 'I see what you mean.' He tapped the monograph and smiled. 'Good man.' Then he turned to his wife, who was still standing somewhat dumbfounded in the centre of the room, and said, 'My dear, you haven't offered Monsieur Clément anything to drink?'

Before she could respond I said, 'You are mistaken, monsieur. Madame Courbertin has been most hospitable; however, I am running a little late and must now be on my way.'

'Very well,' said Courbertin.

Facing Thérèse, I said, 'Good day, madame.'

She lowered her head and responded, 'Good day, Monsieur Clément.'

Courbertin placed a kindly hand on my back and guided me into the hallway. 'A fascinating study,' he said, raising the monograph up as if it were sacred – Moses presenting the Ten Commandments to the Israelites. He then mentioned some obscure point of interest and sought my opinion on the matter. The answer I gave met with his approval. At the door, we shook hands once again and bid each other farewell.

I was due back at the hospital by eight o'clock and had several hours at my disposal. The thought of returning to my apartment was not very appealing so I walked to the river and smoked cigarettes on the quayside. I could see the cathedral, gilded by the setting sun, and, before long, I found myself crossing the Pont de l'Archevêché, responding to a silent but irresistible summons. I came to the rear end of the building and rounded the complex jumble of pinnacles and buttresses. Looking upwards, I saw that my progress was being monitored by a host of gargoyles. They protruded from the stonework at various levels of elevation: smooth muscular creatures, with extended necks and whose jaws, stretched wide open, evoked the din of hell. Their horizontal thrust was forceful, carrying with it a strong impression of exertion, as if they were straining to break free and at any moment might leap out into the void and take flight.

I arrived at the north portal and paused to study the stone reliefs and statuary. Three concentric arches, occupied by angels, maidens and learned men, enclosed a rough triangle in which many figures congregated on three levels. The lowest of these levels, the lintel, seemed to depict episodes from the infancy of Jesus Christ. The second level, however, was quite different. I had passed beneath the tympanum of the north portal on numerous occasions, without ever troubling to look up at these strange dramas, but now, having been made aware of their significance by Bazile, my curiosity was aroused.

The seneschal, Théophile, was shown five times, each appearance representing a stage in the telling of his story. Most of the figures had been splattered with white bird droppings, endowing the scenes with an eerie, wintry quality. In the first, Théophile was shown kneeling in front of the Devil. An earnest man stood by his side, holding the pact that the seneschal had evidently just signed, the terms of which promised worldly power in exchange for his soul. The second scene showed Théophile in prosperity. As he distributed pieces of gold with his right hand, a little demon was surreptitiously slipping more into his left. The next two scenes showed Théophile repenting and his subsequent salvation – a war-like Virgin Queen descending upon a vanquished Satan. Finally, in the upper register of the tympanum, Théophile was shown holding his head and marvelling at his good fortune.

I set off for the hospital but found walking more strenuous than I should have. An object in one of my trouser pockets was dragging me down. It turned out to be the silver cross that Bazile had given me. When I reached the Pont de l'Archevêché, I leaned over the railings and tossed it into the river. Thereafter, I made much better progress.

The night that followed was largely uneventful. I made hourly observations of Charcot's hysterics and was obliged to examine an epileptic patient who had had a seizure. Other than this minor incident, I was left to my own devices. Just before sunrise, I went for a stroll around the hospital grounds, and on my return felt unusually tired. I had some business to attend to in the plaster cast room which, being full of moulded body parts, resembled an art gallery or museum. The human form was not celebrated in this dusty depository, but maligned; all of the exhibits were twisted, deformed and diseased. I noticed that there was a chair in the corner. It looked welcoming, so I sat between its broad arms and was overcome by exhaustion. I closed my eyes and started to dream.

I was standing on the viewing platform of the cathedral, next to the statue of the strix. The sky over Paris was a flickering aurora of red light, broken by thick bands of black cloud. Fiery meteors dropped from the firmament, leaving incandescent trails and exploding with great violence when they reached the ground. On the horizon, I saw a conical mountain belching smoke and ash. It reminded me of La Cheminée. Most of the buildings in the vicinity had been reduced to burned-out, smouldering carcasses, and the river had become a channel of filth. I saw broken cupolas, crooked spires and mountains of rubble. In the middle distance was a strange edifice that I didn't recognize, a tangle of iron girders that might have risen to a great height before its destruction. Winged creatures wheeled around the burning remnants of the tower of Saint Jacques and I could hear their screeches, carried on a searing wind. It seemed that I was witnessing the last judgement, the final chaos.

It was then that I heard a voice.

'Behold: the divine plan.'

I turned slowly and discovered that the strix was looking at me.

'Do you want my soul?' I asked.

He licked his lips, leered and replied. 'No. It's mine already.'

I awoke with a start. The dream had been so vivid that it took me some time to recover. I could see the objects that surrounded my chair – a gnarled hand, a club foot and a bucket rimed with hardened plaster – but they all seemed less substantial than the apocalyptic images that refused to fade from memory. I raised my sleeve to my nose and thought that I could smell acrid smoke and flaming timbers. When I finally stood up, my legs were stiff and my temples throbbed with a painful beat. I had been asleep for more than an hour.

The research meeting was scheduled early and, after attending to my toilet, I went straight to the conference room. I was surprised to discover that most of my colleagues were already present, standing like sentinels around the large oval table. The associate professors had taken their seats and were gabbling convivially. There was some accommodating movement, a general repositioning of bodies, and I found myself looking down at Courbertin's bald head. He must have sensed my presence, because he interrupted his conversation to offer me a tacit greeting.

When Charcot entered, the associate professors stood to attention and they did not sit down again until he had invited them to follow his example. Consulting a sheet of paper that an assistant had helpfully placed in front of him, Charcot read out the agenda. Before discussing some new findings relating to cerebral localization, he wished to review the hysteria project.

'Gentleman,' said Charcot. 'I cannot emphasize enough the importance I ascribe to measurement. Some of you will no doubt remember the case of Justine Etchevery.' The associate professors produced a low, vaguely approving rumble of assent, but even the most junior doctors were conversant with this celebrated patient's history. 'Her retention of urine resulted in severe distension of the abdomen, and her survival, without developing any of the signs of uraemia, seemed to defy the laws of science. When the possibility of imposture was eliminated, some authorities suggested we were witnessing a miracle.' This provoked a ripple of sycophantic laughter. 'Gentlemen: measurement solved this mystery. Etchevery's vomit was found to contain urea, thus demonstrating an alternative pathway for excretion, and hysterical ischuria was distinguished from its rapidly fatal organic form.' Charcot proceeded to summarize some of the data that I had been partly responsible for collecting and then speculated on the potential significance of certain trends. A brief discussion followed, although none took issue with his largely unverified conclusions.

Our chief lit a cigar and whispered something to his assistants. The curtains were drawn, a screen erected, and the projector was switched on. A broad beam of light travelled over the heads of the seated professors and a photographic image of a naked woman appeared on the screen. Contractures had forced her hitherto supine body into the shape of an arch, supported only by the tips of her toes and the top of her head. Her buttocks were elevated some distance from the ground and she appeared to be thrusting her hips towards the ceiling. Charcot continued talking, and more images appeared. Gaping mouths, bulging eyes, bared teeth; a veritable gallery of human chimeras.

I was standing close to the projector, with my chin gripped in my right hand, and my right elbow cupped in my left hand. I noticed that I was casting a shadow on the back of Courbertin's jacket. Detaching my right hand from my chin, I opened my fingers, creating the illusion of a dark, spider-like form that, with a little encouragement, ascended Courbertin's spine and came to rest between his shoulder blades. The progress of the shadow had been slow and fractionally delayed. Charcot's voice sounded thin and remote: 'Gentlemen: it is important to recognize that hysteria has its own organizing principles, just like any other nervous ailment originating from a material lesion.' Tendrils of smoke rose from his cigar. 'The ultimate cause still eludes our means of investigation, but it expresses itself in ways unmistakable to the attentive observer.' As he elaborated, his words became less and less distinct until all that I could hear was a faint murmur.

My focus of attention was entirely on Courbertin. How absurd he looked. I considered the wispy strands of hair that had been raked across his head, the roll of flesh that hung over his collar, his short neck, his capacious trousers and flabby haunches: a man of modest abilities, who, by stubborn, bovine persistence and shameless ingratiation, had managed to secure a place at Charcot's table; a fraudulent man, anxious to please others and win their favour lest they should turn against him and expose his mediocrity; a man of nervous smiles and perspiration, clinging undergarments and wary confidences; and of course, a lucky man, who by an accident of chance, happened to come from a provincial town where a beautiful woman saw in him a means of escape. That such a pathetic specimen should represent an obstacle to the satisfaction of my desires was scarcely believable.

I lowered my hand and the shadow nestling between Courbertin's shoulder blades dropped a short distance. In my palm, I could feel something, a barely perceptible fluttering, like the wings of a trapped moth. I closed my eyes, and the trembling sensation became more intense, its definition increasing until it achieved a distinct periodicity. There could be no doubt as to what this curious phenomenon represented. I did not respond with shock, horror or surprise, but fascination. My tentative fingers closed around what I knew must be Courbertin's heart. I could feel its regular, vigorous beat – valves opening and closing, blood entering the atria, the ventricles contracting. The rhythm was hypnotic. Then, quite suddenly, the sensation vanished. Opening my eyes, I saw that Courbertin had shifted in his seat and positioned himself out of my shadow.

The photographic slide on the screen showed a cross-section of the brain. Charcot was gesticulating at certain structures with his cane, but I could not hear a word he was saying.

I altered my position and the shadow of my hand reappeared on the back of Courbertin's jacket. Once again, I felt his heart beating against my palm. The same thought that had provoked my rash actions the previous day sounded in my mind with identical declamatory resonance: *You shall not be denied.* I closed my fingers and began to squeeze. Immediately, Courbertin sat up straight. He began rubbing his chest and looking around the room. I squeezed harder, and harder still, until I felt the beat in my palm accelerate. Courbertin produced a handkerchief and mopped his brow. He was shaking, and it took him several attempts to stuff the handkerchief back in his pocket. His sweat tainted the air and I could smell his panic. He muttered something to the man sitting next to him and then stood up. Our eyes met briefly as he hurried into the darkness between the projector and the door. He had looked nauseous, sickly, and his forehead was covered in glistening droplets. Charcot registered the disturbance and threw a glance in our direction, but his delivery did not falter. 'With respect to the management of hysterical young women, I recommend extra, that is to say, punitive cold showers, beyond five or more per day if they are to be mastered.' My hearing was now totally restored. I could hear Charcot's voice and, behind me, the door being opened and softly closed.

When the research meeting ended, I went straight to my apartment and slept soundly for the rest of the day. In the evening, I returned to the hospital, and met Valdestin, who was just leaving.

'Did you hear about Monsieur Courbertin?' he asked.

'No,' I replied.

My colleague shook his head and produced a heavy sigh. 'Died this morning – a heart attack – on his way home in a cab.' Valdestin made a helpless gesture. 'The driver thought he was asleep.'

The feeling of not being wholly alive seemed to rush into my body and its coldness made me numb and unresponsive. Valdestin mistook my impassivity for grief. 'I'm sorry, Clément. You were better acquainted with him than I.' Then, attempting to console, Valdestin added, 'He always spoke very highly of you.'

A thought formed out of the nothingness in my skull: *She is mine now.*

9

The Salpêtrière was well represented at Courbertin's funeral. Charcot and Madame Charcot were present, as were most of the associate professors and a respectable number of junior doctors. Thérèse looked beautiful in black, tall, slender and alluring, her widow's veil endowing her with an aura of mysterious glamour. One of her hands rested on Philippe's shoulder. Standing next to Thérèse was a man who reminded me of Courbertin. He was clearly a relative and I supposed that he must be a brother or a close cousin. At his side was a dowdy wife with dull, lifeless eyes.

The priest swung his censer over the coffin and mumbled prayers. Birds sang. The sun was bright and my skin started to prickle, so I edged into the shade of a mausoleum.

Some distance from the principal mourners stood a tight knot of people who I suspected might be members of Thérèse's spiritualist circle. The women sported enormous hats festooned with black ribbons, and one of the men was wearing a cape so long that it touched the ground. A frail old lady, who sat on a portable chair in the centre of the group, kept on staring at me. Whenever our gazes coincided, she quickly looked away.

After Courbertin had been buried, the crowd began slowly to disperse. I watched Charcot go over to Thérèse and offer his condolences. Valdestin, who was standing in front of me, turned round and said, 'Do you think we should say something too?'

'No,' I replied. 'I think we should leave now.'

I had already written to Thérèse – twice, in fact – and on both occasions I had endeavoured to be sympathetic without also being hypocritical. Thérèse did not love Henri Courbertin, perhaps she had never loved him, and, although I expected her to show some outward signs of grief, I did not expect his death to affect her very deeply. The replies that I received were measured and gave me no cause to suspect that I might be wrong; however, when we finally met, three days after the funeral, Thérèse was clearly troubled.

'What is it?' I asked.

'Henri must know now,' she replied.

'Know what?'

'How I deceived him. I keep on imagining Henri, on the other side, heartbroken, appalled.'

Taking her hand in mine, I tried to console her, 'You placed your domestic responsibilities before your own happiness. That was a selfless thing to do.'

'There was nothing selfless about my behaviour,' she responded. 'I was frightened of losing Philippe, that's all.'

'You cannot blame yourself for what happened, and if, as is commonly supposed, the newly departed are obliged to examine their consciences, then Henri will appreciate that he too was at fault. He neglected you, patronized you and made no real effort to understand you.' A long silence ensued and I added, 'What's done is done. He is no longer with us and we are now free to do as we please.'

On hearing these words, Thérèse's expression became anxious and some lines appeared on her brow. 'We cannot be together. Not yet. It's too early and people are sure to talk.'

'If they wish to gossip,' I said, sweeping my hand through the air with scornful disregard, 'let them, I really don't care.'

'Perhaps not,' said Thérèse, 'but I do. A woman has good reason to concern herself with the opinion of others.'

'Then perhaps we should leave Paris altogether, start a new life in a spa town. Lamalou-les-Bains, perhaps? I could get a position in the sanatorium where Charcot sends his patients for the thermal cure.'

'What about Philippe?'

'What about him?'

'Are you prepared to—'

'I'll treat him like a son,' I interrupted. Something in my voice, a strained note of impatience, must have betrayed my insincerity.

Thérèse looked down at the floor and said, 'I think we need to consider our situation very carefully.'

We did not make love that day; however, when we met again (for the second time after Courbertin's death) Thérèse responded readily to my tentative caresses, throwing her head back to expose her long neck, welcoming each advance with a tremulous, breathy sigh. As my passion mounted, I found myself treating her roughly, my nails digging into her skin, the urge to tear and rip so powerful that I only stopped when she emitted a cry. I removed my hand, but she drew my fingers back to her flesh. 'More,' she whispered. 'More.' Her invitation was so exciting that my passion found its ultimate expression prematurely. Such was the violence of my paroxysm, and so depleted did I feel after, that I was completely unable to recover my potency. I was still lying on top of her when Thérèse said, 'I attended a seance last night.'

'Oh?' I responded.

'I received a communication from the realm of the spirits.' She hesitated before adding, 'From Henri.'

'Did you?' I rolled off her body and reached for my cigarettes. After lighting one, I said, 'What did he say?'

'He said that Philippe and I were in great danger.'

'How, exactly?'

'The medium, Madame Gravois, was unable to be more specific. She said that the communication was very faint.'

'I don't think you should go to these seances any more. I'm not sure you are in the right frame of mind.'

'Do you think it was him? Coming through?'

'I don't know.' I stroked a damp strand of hair from her forehead and wanted to say something more comforting, but all I achieved was a flat repetition of the same sentence.

The question of when we should make our relationship known to the wider world was raised intermittently, although with decreasing frequency. Since Courbertin's demise, it no longer seemed quite so necessary that we should live under the same roof. The proximity of a child would, I realized, very likely dampen our ardour and we had had insufficient opportunity to enjoy our newfound liberty. One rainy afternoon, Thérèse asked the inevitable question: 'Do you still want to marry me?'

'Yes,' I replied, without making eye contact.

Her instincts must have served her well, because she had the good sense not to press for a date.

Weeks became months and we continued to meet in secret. The Saint-Germain apartment, which had always had a dusty, mouldering atmosphere, was now looking distinctly shabby and ill-used, and something of its character seemed to have found a corresponding weariness in Thérèse's soul. Her movements had become slow and languid, her gaze unfocused. This may have been because of the morphine, which she now injected on her own as well as in my company. Even so, there was something about her lassitude that seemed to require more than just a chemical explanation. When I contemplated her malaise, my brain supplied an apposite image: a wilting flower. Yes, that was what she had become, a wilting flower, with petals turning brown at the edges.

Thérèse continued to encourage my excesses. She permitted me to tug at her hair and bite her so hard that impressions were left in her flesh, to rut on her back like an animal. She would get down on her knees at my command and, taking me into her mouth, prolong her humiliation until I found release. She was incapable of disobeying me and exquisitely responsive to my needs. Indeed, there were moments when it seemed that I had only to think of a novel transgression and she was at once positioning herself for my convenience.

This willingness to comply with my wishes seemed to extend into other areas of her life. It occurred to me that she had not mentioned her spiritualist circle for some time and I pointed this out.

'I stopped going,' she replied.

'Why?' I asked.

She coiled a lock of hair around her finger and pouted. 'You were right. It just made me upset.'

Beyond the walls of our retreat, the city went about its business, and when we emerged, we would join the flow of pedestrians and blend into the anonymous traffic. I would usually go to the hospital, and she would usually go home, and so it went on. Although I often crossed the large open square in front of Saint-Sulpice, I no longer ventured inside the church, and rarely spared a thought for my old friend the bell-ringer, but a chance encounter quite literally brought us together again. We were both rounding the Fountain of the Four Bishops, and neither

of us was paying very much attention to his surroundings, when we stepped into each other's paths and
collided.

'Paul!' Bazile took my hand and shook it vigorously.
'How good it is to see you again. Where have you been?'

'I'm sorry,' I replied. 'The hospital, you know how it
is – Charcot works us like mules.'

'Why don't you come inside for a cider?' He gestured
towards the north tower. 'Surely you can spare a few
minutes?'

'That is very kind of you, but I must decline. My day
has been very demanding.'

'Then next week, perhaps?'

He was insistent and did not let me go until I had
committed myself to a dinner engagement. At the time, I
felt quite irritated by Bazile's tenacity, but in due course
I would be grateful.

Memory is not reliable, and a distinctive event can easily
erase the impressions that preceded it. Consequently I
have only the poorest recollections of Thérèse's arrival
at the apartment and what happened immediately after:
skirts and stockings on the floor, my thumb on the
plunger of the syringe, writhing limbs, parted lips, tears
rolling down her cheeks, leaving gritty black trails of
mascara. But what followed, I remember all too clearly.

She was lying on the bed, her body curled around a
pillow that she clutched against her breasts. On her back,

I could see the imprints of my barbarity, scratches, bruises, bleeding traces, and I experienced a certain creative pride in my accomplishment. She was exuding her inimitable fragrance in copious quantities. It seemed to fill the room like a thick, scented fog. I imagined its restless movement, pouring out of her wounds, flowing over the bedclothes, cascading to the floor and creeping into corners and crevices: the oil of the damask rose, figs in honey, sweetmeats, glazed fruit, lavender, civet and bergamot: all of these things combined, and yet so much more – luscious, heady, delight – beyond description. I brushed my mouth against her lacerations and licked the blood off my lips. With eager fingers I tore a scab from her shoulder and examined it closely: a red-black crystal that when held up to the gaslight seemed to glow like a garnet with a dancing spark imprisoned at its core. I placed the scab on my tongue, and, as it dissolved, my palate was suffused with new registers of sensation. My body was electrified and I was filled with a profound sense of well-being. The skin where the scab had once been darkened and a bead of blood appeared, ripening until it reached its natural limit of expansion, before trickling from one shoulder blade down to the other. I licked at the rivulet of blood, and licked again, until my mouth was pressed against the source and I was sucking with the concentrated energy of a newborn baby. Thérèse stirred and made a mewling sound, but her personality was submerged in a bottomless opiate sea. The blood was intoxicating, and when I had sucked the capillaries dry, I raised myself up, my knees sinking into the mattress as I became upright.

Thérèse's neck was exposed and beneath its gleaming surface I could see the pulsing of her carotid artery. I was seized by a desire to slice it open and quench my thirst: a thirst that was suddenly urgent and demanding.

She is yours, now – all yours. The thought was sonorous and persuasive. *Yours to enjoy.*

Thérèse was very still, so still that even her breathing was impossible to detect. Only the pulse on her neck indicated that she was alive. My thoughts progressed logically: *Her surrender excites you. The ultimate surrender is death. Therefore, in order to experience the ultimate pleasure. . .* I raised my hand and a faint shadow crept across the spoiled surface of Thérèse's back. At once, I could feel the moist heat of her interior, the throbbing of her heart. My fingers closed and I began to exert pressure. A rasping sound emanated from Thérèse's throat as she struggled to take in air.

The bells of Saint-Sulpice rang out, their peal oddly transformed into a harsh, plangent clangour.

I looked towards the window and what I saw made me freeze. A paralysing horror robbed me of the power to move. In the glass, I did not see a copy of myself, but a demon, a hideous creature, leering, salivating, grinning maniacally, its arm lifted high, displaying a set of lethal talons. Its eyes were yellow, eyes that I recognized – eyes that, once seen, could never be forgotten – poisonous eyes radiating malice and wickedness. I felt as if I were standing on the edge of an abyss. The sweetness in my mouth turned sour and I screamed. Leaping off the bed, I ran to the washstand, where I coughed a thin stringy liquid into the bowl. Thérèse said something, a soft murmur, but she was still asleep. I saw clearly what, until that moment, I had been blind to. The cuts and bruises that covered her body were no longer pleasing to look at, but repellent. She looked pitifully thin – wasted, broken. I stepped towards the window, my whole body quivering, but all that I saw was my own ghostly reflection suspended in darkness.

10

That night, I had bad dreams: awful, vivid dreams of hell and damnation. In the last of these, I found myself returned to that bleak arena of boulders and belching magma pools, and once again witnessed the arrival of a troupe of demons. As before, the leader was carrying a naked woman and, when he threw her onto a rock and began hammering nails through her hands, I realized that it was Thérèse Courbertin. She was writhing, shrieking, straining to break free, begging for mercy, while all around her the demons flapped their wings and created an infernal din. I was not frightened, but excited by what I saw, and utterly indifferent to Thérèse's ordeal. She squirmed, twisted and cycled her legs furiously in the air, all the time, wailing and screeching. I drew closer, close enough to catch her ankles, pull them apart, and hunker down between her thighs. She was yelling, 'No – please – no,' but I was deaf to her cries. I leaned forwards, punched a hole through her ribcage and ripped her heart out. Then, I held the organ up, a grisly trophy, the aorta dangling, before crushing the ventricles over my open mouth and squeezing the blood out like water from a sponge. The fragrant liquid scattered over my face and trickled down my gullet. I stretched my wings, howled at the roiling sky and awoke with a bestial moan still issuing from my mouth. The bed sheets were clammy, and during the course of my troubled sleep I had torn them to shreds.

I was haunted by images of Thérèse, fleeting impressions of her flesh, her curves and crevices, the neatly folded pleat of her womanhood, all of which made me eager to see her. I knew, of course, that I must resist the urge, that if we met again she would be in mortal danger. But exercising self-control only seemed to increase the urgency of my desire, and a prolonged inner struggle ensued. It was as if my mind had been divided and I was no longer a single person, but two antagonistic personalities: one permissive, encouraging me to satisfy my needs, the other prohibitive, demanding abstinence. My head swam, I felt sick and dizzy; I vacillated between states of acceptance and denial, insight and confusion.

What was I to do? Find a church and pray? Ask the all-knowing God to intercede? He, who created everything and watched, impassively, as the ripples of cause and effect spread from His person, bringing evil and suffering into being – our Holy Father and architect of hell. I sank into a quagmire of theological debate, becoming desperate for the reassuring certainties of science. Once again, I tried to make sense of my experience with reference to peripheral nerve damage, and, once again, the demon had cause to celebrate another victory.

A week later I kept my dinner engagement with Bazile. He and his wife welcomed me with their customary warmth and, after aperitifs and some cheery exchanges, we all took our places at the table. Madame Bazile had prepared a succulent belly of pork served with vegetables and a creamy sauce. The cider, however, was rather sour and I was unable to drink very much of it. 'No more,' I said, placing my hand over the tankard, 'I really should stop.'

'But you've hardly had any,' pleaded Bazile.

I feigned embarrassment. 'Last night . . .' My expression communicated remorse.

'Oh, I see,' said Bazile. 'You over-indulged? That is most unfortunate, because my dear wife returned from Normandy with several bottles of my favourite cider, a speciality of the region where she was born. You really must try some! I asked her to pack an extra bottle, a very heavy one, might I add, just for you!'

'Don't listen to him, Monsieur Clément,' said Madame Bazile, 'It was no trouble at all.'

Bazile excused himself and returned to the table with another jug, but the new cider tasted no different from the old – again, the same sourness, an acrid undertow. I doubt that I was able to disguise my dislike of the beverage, because Bazile said, 'Being uncommonly sweet, it is something of an acquired taste, but persevere and I'm sure you will learn to appreciate its virtues.' Not wishing to upset my hosts, I was obliged to drink the whole lot while making dishonest remarks about its vitality. It made me feel quite ill.

When we had finished eating, Madame Bazile retired for the evening. Bazile lit his pipe and our conversation soon became more serious. Before long, we were engaged in one of our deep philosophical discussions, but as the evening drew on, I was gradually overcome by a creeping sense of despair. Great rifts of nothingness seemed to be opening up inside me.

'What is the point of prayer?' I asked. 'God is supposed to be unchanging. Even before a prayer is recited, He must have already decided whether or not He will answer it.'

'There is no contradiction,' said Bazile. 'Prayer is not separate from the causal order of the world, but an essential part of it. We bring about by prayer those things that God has already determined should result from prayer.'

I found the circularity of his argument irritating: 'If human beings are not free to make choices, then there can be no such thing as morality. We are only good or bad insofar as God wills it so. Either God is all-knowing, in which case we are not free, or we are free, in which case God is not all-knowing.'

'The God in whom I believe is perfect,' said Bazile gravely, 'and all-knowingness is a fundamental condition of His perfection.' The bell-ringer pressed more tobacco into the bowl of his pipe. 'All-knowingness and freedom need not be considered irreconcilable. Just because God knows that you will do something does not mean that he is responsible for your actions. Rather, God has fore-knowledge of what it is that you freely decide to do.'

'Sophistry,' I said, shaking my head.

Bazile sucked on the stem of his pipe. 'Yes, to an extent. I accept that charge. Complex ideas do not lend themselves to easy expression. Perhaps we have reached that point at which language itself is no longer service-able and, as a consequence, arguments appear more suspect. Indeed, one must suppose that, ultimately, God is unknowable because the human intellect is of limited capacity. You would not try to scoop up the ocean with a thimble, so why do you expect your mind to encompass the infinite?'

'If God is unknowable, why conclude that He is per-fect or benign? Why make any assumptions about His goodness? The Bible exhorts us to be kind, but the world, with all of its manifest imperfections – injustice, cruelty and disease – does not look like the handiwork of a loving Father.'

Bazile frowned. 'As a doctor, you must have seen many children being subject to painful medical procedures?'

'Yes.'

'A very young child cannot understand why it must suffer. It is incapable. But such suffering is necessary. Evils may be the price we pay for the greater good that outweighs them.'

'You truly believe that this is the best of all possible worlds?'

'Yes. How could imperfection arise from perfection? The existence of injustice, cruelty and disease do not demonstrate that the world was not perfectly created. These things are requisite, unavoidable, in ways that perhaps we will never fully appreciate.'

I was not impressed by any of Bazile's arguments. They seemed facile, slippery, specious, an uneasy attempt to gloss over the glaring inconsistencies and stark contradictions that lay at the very heart of his religious convictions.

What had I been hoping for? The prospect of redemption? To be persuaded that I could still alter my destiny? As our dialogue continued, the rifts inside me widened, and despair was replaced by a feeling of desolation.

'I do not understand how you are able to sustain your faith,' I said to Bazile. 'It is beyond me.' The tone of my voice was contemptuous. I might as well have called him an imbecile.

The atmosphere in the room became tense and uncomfortable. Bazile affected indifference, but it was obvious that I had offended him, and our subsequent efforts to revive the conversation stalled.

'It is a curious thing,' said Bazile, yawning, 'but for some time now, whenever we have been together, I have become very tired: unnaturally so.' He turned his eyes on me. There was something disturbing about the probing intensity of his gaze. 'Intellectual rigour!' he added with a wry smile. 'Perhaps I'm not used to it any more.

Madame Bazile is a devoted wife and an excellent cook, but relatively untroubled by the great mysteries.'

'I think I had better go,' I said, rising abruptly.

'If you wish,' Bazile replied.

'Please thank Madame Bazile for an excellent meal. The pork was exceptional.'

Bazile took his own coat as well as mine from a peg on the wall and we descended the bell tower together. Outside, the pavements were glassy with rain. Before I made my departure, we shook hands, albeit rather stiffly.

'Goodbye,' said Bazile.

I nodded, put on my hat and marched across the square. When I reached the other side, I turned to look back and fancied that I could still see the bell-ringer standing beneath the mighty colonnade, a barely discernable figure in the shadows. I quickened my step and headed off into the night, giving scant consideration to my route or destination.

My black mood worsened and I began to feel totally divorced from my surroundings. I did not see the shopfronts, cafes and advertisements. The city made no impression on my senses. I was in the world, but set apart from it, estranged, alienated and alone. Grief and bitterness curdled in my stomach. Everything seemed futile, a divine joke, a preordained pantomime without meaning or tangible purpose.

I had died, travelled to hell and returned, possessed by a demon: a predatory evil that had discovered pathways of easy influence along the soft grain of my many flaws and weaknesses, my arrogance, lechery and self-pity. I had been a willing accomplice to murder, lending the demon my shortcomings and deficiencies so that it might perform its heinous deed. And, inevitably, I would be its accomplice again, my debased love providing it with the means and opportunity to destroy Thérèse. I recalled her scarred flesh, her languid movements, the emptiness in her eyes, and realized that her descent into depravity must also be counted as one of the demon's accomplishments. It had reached into her mind and cultivated latent proclivities to ensure our mutual ruin.

A demon has many goals – to corrupt, to defile, to propagate suffering – but all of these are secondary to its principal goal, which is to take souls to hell. Well, my demon had already achieved this end. I was not, at that moment, in the hell of fire and brimstone but in another hell, a far worse hell, the hell of my own guilt and desperation.

An angry voice: 'Get out of the way!' A carriage was coming towards me, lamps glaring. 'Monsieur!' I dodged the vehicle but was drenched with spray when its wheels rolled through a puddle. The driver swore and shook his fist.

I was standing on the Pont Neuf.

How could I justify my continued existence? If I lived, the demon would surely prevail and Thérèse would die. I climbed onto the low wall and looked down into the black water. My death had brought the demon into the world, and my death might also be the means to expel it. I was already damned, so what did it matter if I took my own life? At least Thérèse would survive, and in the end all choices are sanctioned by God!

I launched myself into the void and was surprised when, instead of falling forwards, I fell backwards. Someone had grabbed my coat, and I found myself lying on the pavement, gazing up at low, faintly glowing cloud. Bazile's face appeared. 'If you kill yourself,' he growled, 'it will become more powerful than you can possibly imagine.'

11

I can remember little of what transpired immediately after, a general impression of passing through familiar streets, rain, Bazile at my side, occasionally grasping my elbow to make me turn left or right, fragments of speech – 'poor fellow', 'be strong', 'you are no longer alone' – and finally, Saint-Sulpice coming into view, flat and unreal as if painted on a curtain at the opera. It seemed that one minute I was on the bridge and the next seated in Bazile's parlour nursing a bowl of steaming tea.

'How did you know?' I asked.

'There were indications,' replied the bell-ringer. 'Certain signs.' He struck a match and lit his pipe. 'However, your evident discomfort drinking the cider this evening confirmed my suspicions. I had added holy water.' Bazile gestured in such a way as to suggest that he was unhappy about having deceived me. 'The small quantity you drank revived your conscience, gave you the strength to put up a fight; however, a demon is a subtle adversary, and even the best intentions can be subverted to serve its aims.'

'I was trying to . . . thwart it.'

'Indeed,' said Bazile, 'but self-slaughter is a sin, a sin born of despair. A demon feeds on misery, nourishes itself on negative emotions. Tonight, had you succeeded in ending your life, not only would you have insulted your Maker, but you would have also empowered the very evil you sought to frustrate! No longer obliged to cause suffering by exploiting the frailties of its host, the demon would have been liberated, free to do its mischief without constraint.' Bazile produced a small cross attached to a thread-like chain. 'Put this on. Now, my friend, you must tell me everything.'

I made my confession. I told him of my time on Saint-Sébastien, how I had witnessed the murder of Aristide, and how I had carelessly sworn to tell no one, and how I had broken my oath. I told him what had really happened on the night of the experiment, and how I had journeyed to hell and witnessed unspeakable horrors. I told him how I had been resuscitated and how I had awakened a changed man: sensitive to sunlight and the smell of blood, alert at nights and tired during the day, my fingernails grown thick and sharp. I told him about the demoniac and the little Venus, my affair with Thérèse, the brothel in the Marais, the death of Courbertin and the image of the demon in the window. And when I was done, I broke down and wept.

'These tears are precious,' said Bazile. 'For many months, your soul has struggled to resist spiteful tyranny, your natural emotions smothered by a suffocating malevolence and now, at last, your humanity is restored.'

'What am I to do?' I asked, pathetically.

'We will consult with Father Ranvier.'

'Who?' The name sounded vaguely familiar.

'My old mentor,' replied Bazile.

'But I am expected at the hospital.'

'I will send word of your indisposition.'

'Will he be able to help, this priest?'

'I am sure he will.' Bazile rose from his seat. 'Would you like some more tea?'

'Yes,' I said placing my head in my hands. 'Thank you.'

I heard Bazile leave the room and sounds coming from the kitchen. As I waited, the cross hanging from my neck seemed to grow heavier and heavier until I was experiencing considerable discomfort. I slipped my fingers beneath the chain and lifted the tiny links off my skin, but as I did so, my nails caught the clasp and released the fastening. The cross and chain dropped onto the table top. I immediately felt relieved and straightened my spine, but only temporarily, because relief was quickly superseded by panic. The walls seemed too near, the temperature too hot; I felt trapped, entombed, and it became difficult to breathe. All that I could think of was getting outside, where I could fill my lungs with the cool night air. I crept over to the door, opened it and immediately set off down the stairs. Darkness prevented me from making a quick escape and I had not got very far when I heard Bazile calling my name and chasing after me. His hand landed on my shoulder and he spun me around, 'Paul!' I detected some shadowy movements and once again I felt the weight of the cross and the bite of the chain. 'Where are you going?'

I felt dazed, bemused. 'I don't know . . . It's stifling up there.'

'Why did you remove the cross?'

'I didn't.'

'You must have.'

'It was an accident.'

Bazile took my arm and said, 'Come now. The tea is made.' We ascended the stairs in silence and as soon as we were back in the parlour, Bazile locked the door and removed the key. 'I'm sorry, Paul. But I would not forgive myself if anything happened to you. Dawn is nearly upon us. Please, sit down and drink your tea.' He excused himself and I heard him speaking to his wife. When he reappeared, he pointed at the window, which was grey with the first light of the new day. 'The sun is up,' he said with a kindly smile. 'We must go.'

After leaving Saint-Sulpice, we went directly to my apartment in order to collect the little Venus. 'Father Ranvier will be most interested in this figure, I am sure,' said Bazile. I wasn't very hungry, but my companion insisted that we stop at a cafe and I managed to eat a few rolls. The bells of Saint-Sulpice rang out and I threw a questioning glance at Bazile. 'Madame Bazile,' he said, smiling. 'And very skilled she is too!' Rising from his chair, he dropped some coins into an ashtray and indicated that it was time for us to depart.

'The cathedral is this way,' I said.

'We are not going to the cathedral.'

I was surprised, given that Bazile had described his mentor as a scholarly priest of Notre Dame. 'Where does Father Ranvier live?'

'Lately, in the Hôtel Saint-Jean-de-Latran.' Bazile paused, and I could see that he was considering whether or not to elaborate. 'I regret to say that Father Ranvier has never been properly appreciated by the Church. The Bishop considers some of Father Ranvier's views,' again Bazile paused before adding, 'unorthodox. Perhaps I should be more respectful, especially where a bishop is concerned, but in my opinion, Father Ranvier has been denied the privileges he deserves.'

When we arrived at the Hôtel, the vestibule was empty and we went straight up to the second floor.

'Shouldn't you have sent a note?' I asked. 'It is still very early.'

'Given what has transpired,' said Bazile, 'I am sure that Father Ranvier will forgive us for neglecting formalities. Besides, I know the hours he keeps. He rises at four thirty every morning and has done so for years.'

We came to a scuffed door and Bazile knocked three times. After a short interval a frail voice called out, 'Who is it?'

'Édouard.'

The door opened and standing before us was a

venerable gentleman whose seamed face was surrounded by a tangled mass of wisps and curls, made all the more striking on account of their whiteness. He squinted at us through oval spectacles with watery grey eyes so pale that they were almost colourless. It was difficult to estimate his precise age, but I fancied he must be at least eighty. Embracing my companion, he cried, 'Édouard, Édouard.' Then, taking a step backwards, he acknowledged my presence with a shy inclination of his head.

'My friend, Monsieur Clément,' said Bazile.

'The nerve doctor?'

'Yes.'

'Please come in.' The room we entered was spacious and resembled a library. Tall bookcases lined the walls and the air smelled of wax, dust and leather. 'Fetch more chairs,' said the priest. Bazile did as he was instructed and we all sat around a table, the surface of which was covered in statuettes of the Virgin, star charts and astronomical calculating devices. 'So,' said the priest to Bazile, 'what brings you here at this early hour?'

'Monsieur Clément,' said Bazile, 'is greatly in need of your assistance.'

'Really?' said the priest, exchanging the spectacles he was wearing for another pair.

Once again, I was obliged to tell my story. It was, perhaps, a little easier on this second occasion and, as I spoke, the priest listened intently. His expression was sympathetic and the creases around his eyes deepened when distress or embarrassment made me falter. When I reached my conclusion, the priest exhaled and whispered, 'Astonishing!'

'The figure,' said Bazile. 'Show Father Ranvier the figure.'

I took the little Venus from my pocket and handed it to the priest. He produced a magnifying glass and, closing one eye, peered through the lens.

'Do you know what it is?' asked Bazile.

'Yes,' said the priest.

'It looks very old.' I interjected.

'It is very old. Third century BC, or thereabouts, and almost certainly the work of the Parisii, the Celtic tribe who occupied the Île de la Cité before the Romans came.'

'You don't think it could be a copy, a replica?'

'No.' The priest turned the figure over. 'What we have here is a sacramental object, probably used to propitiate Cernunos, the horned god – their god of the underworld.' He put the magnifying glass down and continued, addressing his remarks to me rather than Bazile. 'Unlike other Celtic tribes, the Parisii rarely produced representations of animals and warriors. They were much more likely to make effigies of women and . . .' his lips twisted before he completed the sentence, 'demons.' The priest picked up the figure and handed it back to me. 'Nearly two hundred years ago, workmen digging beneath the choir of the cathedral unearthed four stone altars, now presumed to have been part of an ancient temple. The face of Cernunos is carved on one of these altars, and an individual unfamiliar with the old gods would probably say that it is the face of the devil.'

I felt confused and unsure of what the old priest was implying. He must have detected my confusion, because he leaned forward and his expression softened. 'It will all become clear, monsieur, I promise.' Then, touching his fingertips together, he continued: 'Our city has an exceptionally bloody history. No other capital in Europe has witnessed so much violence and cruelty. It is as though there is something bad here, a pernicious influence that makes men turn against each other. And, invariably, when they turn against each other they also turn against the cathedral. For hundreds of years, the mob has congregated in front of Notre-Dame, brandishing weapons and flaming torches. United by a common savage instinct, they have repeatedly attempted to raze the cathedral to the ground. In 1793 they put nooses around the twenty-eight kings and pulled them off the facade, roaring with delight as each one fell. The statues were then decapitated, smashed and thrown into the Seine. Between 1830 and 1848, Paris was barricaded almost thirty times by its rebellious workers and, every time, the cathedral was attacked. And you will recall, no doubt, the most recent uprising, when the cathedral was set on fire and the archbishop executed. Why should this be?' The old priest sighed. 'Why is Paris such a violent city, and why is it that the mob nearly always directs its ire at the cathedral?'

I recognized that these questions were rhetorical and remained silent.

'Many of our churches are built on sites already associated with worship, such as holy wells, shrines and sacred caves. Those who have studied Hermetic philosophy suggest that these sites are, in fact, spirit portals, locations where the partition between this world and other worlds is weak or ruptured. At Notre-Dame, the partition is at its weakest between our world and the underworld, and by the underworld, I mean Sheol – Tartarus – hell. That is why the Parisii worshipped a horned god. They had knowledge of demons and sought to propitiate them through human sacrifice, usually a young female. In subsequent generations, men whom we would now describe as magicians succeeded in repairing the breach, thus preventing demons from gaining entry into our world. However, the partition is imperfect, and the malevolent powers that inhabit the underworld can still extend tendrils of influence, inciting violence and inducing the rabble to attack the blessed stones that now protect the portal. For reasons that I cannot explain, when you conducted your extraordinary experiment, your soul was able to pass through the partition and, of course, when your soul returned, it was no longer alone – but accompanied.'

It was evident from Bazile's neutral expression that he was familiar with Father Ranvier's startling cosmology. I, on the other hand, had enormous difficulty assimilating what I was being told. Although I was prepared to accept the reality of my own demonic possession, what I was now being asked to believe was strange beyond imagining. Yet there was something very persuasive about this priest, who spoke with calm confidence and whose scholarship did not rely on ponderous citations or frequent lapses into Latin and Greek.

'Please,' said Father Ranvier, 'may I see your hands?'

I held them out and he lowered his head to inspect my fingernails. They had not been trimmed since the previous day and had already grown long and sharp.

'You will recall,' said Father Ranvier, 'that the most celebrated chimera of Notre-Dame, the winged demon, also possesses very long fingernails.' Ranvier glanced at Bazile. 'You see? Poor Méryon understood the significance of this. Demons have a predilection for blood. They modify the physiology of their hosts to make them better instruments for the satisfaction of their need. That is why Méryon titled his etching of the winged demon "The Strix". Poor, poor man. Baudelaire thought he was possessed. I fear the poet may have been right.'

The fatigue that typically came over me during daylight hours was hindering my ability to concentrate. Father Ranvier and Bazile continued talking, but I was not always able to follow their exchanges. They spoke about a thirteenth-century treatise on diabolical manifestations, and then Marcel, a bishop of Paris reputed to have battled with vampires in the fifth century. When their conversation returned to my situation, Bazile said, 'Well, Father? Do you think you can help Monsieur Clément?'

'Yes,' replied the priest. 'Yes, with your cooperation,

Édouard, I can help Monsieur Clément. But I must make one thing perfectly clear,' he glanced from Bazile to me and back again. 'The undertaking that lies ahead of us is highly dangerous. The demoniac who ran amok at the Salpêtrière – or at least the thing that had seized control of his faculties – recognized the presence of a superior power. Our adversary occupies an elevated rank in the infernal hierarchy. One does not confront such an entity with anything less than extreme trepidation. To do otherwise would be folly.' Father Ranvier tapped the ends of his fingers together. 'I can perform an exorcism and, by the grace of God, the demon will be cast out; however, that will not be the end of it. The demon will continue to exist in our world and retain its capacity to do harm.'

'Why can't it be sent back to hell?' asked Bazile.

'Once,' replied Father Ranvier, 'there were books containing rituals for that purpose. But now they are all lost.'

'Then what are we to do?' I asked, desperation making my voice ragged.

'We must attempt to confine it.'

'You mean to imprison the demon?'

'Yes,' said the priest. 'The Holy Roman Emperor Rudolf II is reputed to have acquired a demon in glass which he subsequently exhibited in his museum of oddities. At that time, the practice of trapping spirits in glass and gemstones was quite common among the magical elite.' Father Ranvier got up and shuffled over to one of the bookcases. He ran his finger across a row of spines and when he had found the tome he was looking for he returned to the table. The text, faded to ochre-brown, was dense and annotated throughout by different hands – some cramped, others more broad and flowing. Father Ranvier began to read: 'Procure of a lapidary good clear pellucid crystal. Let it be globular or round each way alike and without flaws. Let it then be placed on an ivory or ebony pedestal . . .' The priest raised his head. 'Édouard, can you obtain the keys to the crypt of Saint-Sulpice?'

'Yes. Of course.'

'Then let us meet there tomorrow, at dawn. I must make preparations. Do not eat or drink anything, except water, and keep a close eye on Monsieur Clément. He must not be left alone for a second.'

12

Bazile and I spent the rest of the day in the north tower of Saint-Sulpice. He had taken the precaution of locking the door, but this really wasn't necessary. As the day advanced, I became tired and subsequently fell into a prolonged, dreamless sleep. When I awoke, it was past ten o'clock and the sky beyond the semi-circular windows had turned from grey to black. After attending to my ablutions, I sat down at the table.

'Can we go for a walk?' I asked Bazile.

'No,' he replied. 'I think that would be most unwise.'

He handed me a book of religious meditations and suggested that I read them.

'Where is Madame Bazile?'

'I've sent her away.'

'Normandy?'

'No: just round the corner. She's staying with a friend – a widow.'

'I'm sorry.'

Bazile raised his eyebrows, 'What for?'

'This imposition. Your inconvenience.'

He shrugged, dismissed my apology with a gesture

and lowered his head over the open pages of a Bible that he had evidently been studying while I was still asleep. The room was poorly ventilated and I was soon feeling extremely uncomfortable. 'Édouard,' I said, 'I need some air. Please, let us go outside, just for a few minutes. I am . . .' I paused to find the right words, 'quite sane. I can assure you, I won't try to run away.'

Bazile sighed. 'Can't you see what it's doing, Paul? Please, rest and ready yourself.'

I tried to read through the meditations but found the piety of the authors overblown and their blandishments vaguely irritating. My discomfort increased and I loosened my collar. As my fingers brushed the chain around my neck, I was reminded of the cross that hung beneath my shirt, and I noticed that it was not merely warm, but hot, as if the heat from my body was accumulating in the metal. I glanced across the table at the top of Bazile's head, his thick black hair divided by a makeshift parting. He was so engrossed in the Gospel of Saint John that his nose was almost touching the page. I looked from his crown to a large silver candlestick, and the idea of connecting one forcefully with the other entered my mind with a kind of casual indifference. The cross was now burning with a fierce heat, yet the pain was curiously cleansing. I pressed my palms together and offered Bazile my hands. 'You should tie me up. I am having thoughts. Unwanted thoughts.'

Bazile's eyes widened as he registered the implication of my appeal. 'It seems then, that the battle has already begun, but the very fact that you are able to make such a request clearly demonstrates that the first victory has been yours. No, I will not bind you. Let my belief in your innate goodness serve to strengthen your resolve.' He then recited the Pater Noster, raising his voice on reaching the words, 'deliver us from evil'.

The night wore on. I experienced more unwanted thoughts, some accompanied by obscene images of degradation, others by violent urges of increasing intensity. Bazile suggested that we kneel and pray together, but prayer had little effect. Disturbing thoughts and images continued to assail my mind and it was only after the middle hour of darkness had come and gone that finally I detected a subtle change, a shift in the balance of power, the gradual reduction of the demon's influence.

Bazile filled two oil lamps and lit the wicks with a match. 'Are you ready?' he asked.

'It isn't dawn yet,' I replied.

'The sun will be up within the hour,' said Bazile. 'Come.'

We descended the stairs of the tower and made our way directly to the crypt. As the door opened, a breath of air carried with it the smell of damp stone. I could not see very far ahead; indeed, it seemed as if we were walking through a void. The rich acoustic, however, betrayed the crypt's unusual size, its unseen vastness. Eventually, we came to a rectangular area defined by columns and arches.

'The remains of the original Saint-Sulpice,' said

Bazile, 'The present church was built on the site of this earlier building, a modest house of prayer where parishioners worshipped for more than five centuries.'

I judged that these crumbling remnants must be of medieval origin, although they might just as easily have survived from a more distant past: Roman times, or perhaps even earlier. Bazile and I smoked, paced up and down and engaged in some desultory conversation, and in due course my companion consulted his pocket watch and said, 'I'll see if Father Ranvier has arrived.' He picked up one of the oil lamps and marched off, soon disappearing from view. I peered into the murky distance and listened: a key turning in a lock, a door closing, the lock again, and then silence.

Almost immediately, I experienced an irrational terror of abandonment and my breathing became irregular. This 'attack' was far worse than any I had experienced before and came with a chilling suggestion of premature burial. I thought of Saint-Sulpice, directly above my head – its baroque bluffs and cliff faces, the immense dome above the transept crossing, all of that colossal weight, bearing down on the columns of the old church – and had to wrestle with a strong impulse to chase after Bazile. I imagined the vault collapsing, entrapment and a slow, agonizing death. Shadows leaped across the walls and I was overcome by a profound sense of being alone. It came as a great relief, therefore, when a few minutes later, I heard Bazile returning with Father Ranvier: footsteps, and the reassuring strain of human voices. The two men emerged from the gloom, Father Ranvier holding the oil lamp aloft, and Bazile struggling to manage what looked like a portable table under one arm and a canvas bag under the other.

'Monsieur Clément,' said Father Ranvier. He stood in front of me, gripping my arms above the elbow. 'A difficult night, I hear. Still, by God's grace you have survived the ordeal and by His grace we will be triumphant.' Placing his hands on his hips, the priest looked around at the columns and arches before adding, 'Hallowed ground! We have this to our advantage. Édouard, set up the table here, and then clear away anything that can be moved.'

In spite of his age, Father Ranvier went about his preliminaries with surprising vigour. He took a white cloth from the canvas bag and spread it over the table, pressing out any creases with his palm. Several items were laid out: a crucifix, two candles and a lead-capped wand – unwrapped from a handkerchief of blue silk. It did not seem right that a crucifix, the principal emblem of the Church, should be placed next to an object commonly associated with stage magic, and Bazile's remark about the Bishop not valuing Father Ranvier's scholarship came back to me. Suspicion was swiftly displaced by curiosity when the priest produced a sphere of glass so heavy that lifting it out of the bag made him grimace. I came forward and offered to help him, but he turned on me and said with unexpected ferocity, 'No, monsieur. You must not touch this.' He positioned the sphere on an ivory base some distance away. On his return, Father Ranvier ran a length of cord around the table, making minute adjustments as he did so to ensure its circularity. He chalked various words and symbols around the circumference and drew a complex triangular figure inside; then he lit seven candles, which he placed at regular intervals equidistant from the table so as to create a 'greater circle' of light. Next, Father Ranvier produced a straitjacket and a leather strap. Naturally, I associated such restraints with lunacy and incarceration. Perhaps all doctors who specialize in the treatment of brain disorders have a fundamental fear of suffering the same fate as their patients.

'I can't.' I said. 'Absolutely not!'

'But, monsieur,' said Father Ranvier, 'you have already experienced the demon interfering with your mind, is that not so? And there will be worse, I am sorry to say, much worse, before our work is done. Our enemy will not relinquish its claim on your soul without contention, and when it is forced to accept the sovereignty of Christ, it will be enraged, disposed to perform acts of violence. If you do not wear these restraints, you will be placing all of us in terrible danger.'

I could not argue. There was no logical objection and I duly submitted. After the jacket had been fastened, I sat on the ground, and Bazile bound my ankles together. 'Have courage, my friend,' said the bell-ringer. 'Have courage.' But I could see that he was troubled.

Father Ranvier and Bazile stepped into the circle, after which the priest instructed Bazile to touch the ends of the cord together and to seal the break with candle wax. 'Édouard,' said Father Ranvier, 'you must not step outside this circle. Whatever happens, do you understand?' Bazile nodded and Father Ranvier handed him a black leather volume. 'Let us begin.'

The two men knelt on the ground and began a series of invocations, beginning with the Litany of the Saints. A psalm preceded an antiphonal appeal on my behalf.

'Save this man your servant.'

'Because he hopes in you, my God.'

'Be a tower of strength for him, O Lord.'

'In the face of the enemy.'

'Let the enemy have no victory over him.'

'And let the Son of Iniquity not succeed in injuring him.'

When the invocations were concluded, Father Ranvier and Bazile stood up for the summoning.

'Unclean Spirit! Power of Satan! Enemy from hell!' The priest's voice was resolute. 'By the mysteries of the incarnation, the sufferings and death, the resurrection and the ascension of Our Lord Jesus Christ; by the sending of the Holy Spirit; and by the coming of Our Lord into last judgement, make yourself known to us!'

I had imagined that the ritual would proceed without effect for some time, that there would be a certain amount of waiting before the demon was compelled to respond; however, when the summoning was ended, I felt a 'change', subtle at first, almost imperceptible, but gradually intensifying until the reality of the phenomenon was beyond question. Glances were exchanged and it was obvious that Bazile and Father Ranvier could also sense it: a presence, seeping into the atmosphere, nowhere and everywhere, a hiss beneath the silence, bringing to each of us an acute and almost painful awareness of our human frailties – the softness of flesh, the frangibility of bone, the precarious equilibrium of the mind. Its essence was threat, a wordless but unmistakable threat to the self. I tensed my muscles as if in readiness to receive a blow, and it seemed that this reflexive, physical reaction was complemented by some inner psychological equivalent: a contraction or shying away at the very core of my being.

Father Ranvier made the sign of the cross and cried out, 'God, Father of Our Lord Jesus Christ, I invoke your holy name and humbly request that you deign to give me the strength to expel this unclean spirit that torments this creature of yours.'

There was a strange abrasive noise, like two rocks being scraped together, and a dusty shower of granulated mortar fell from above. I stared up at the vault and saw nothing remarkable, apart from a billowing sail of spider's silk. My fear of being buried alive returned and I called out, 'The vault is unstable. Quick, release me. We must get out!' Bazile and Father Ranvier looked at me with blank expressions. 'Didn't you hear it?' I implored, my voice becoming shrill with exasperation.

'Hear what?' asked Bazile.

I rolled my eyes upwards. 'The stones shifting!'

'I heard nothing,' said Bazile.

'Nor I,' said Father Ranvier.

'Please. We must get out at once.' I struggled hopelessly to break free.

'Monsieur Clément,' said Father Ranvier. 'It is the enemy, interfering with your mind again.'

I could not accept this. The mortar was real. 'Édouard, help me. Please.' Bazile winced and repeated his earlier exhortation: 'Have courage, my friend, have courage.' As he spoke these words, I noticed that his breath was clouding the air. It was getting colder and a shiver passed through my body.

Father Ranvier began to recite the twenty-third psalm. 'The Lord is my shepherd, I shall not want; He makes me lie down in green pastures. He leads me beside still waters; He restores my soul.'

I felt a curious loosening of the constituent parts of my character, a loss of integrity, a shift towards disintegration. Bazile was looking nervous.

'Even though I walk through the valley of the shadow of death, I fear no evil . . .' Father Ranvier faltered as the temperature plummeted. 'For Thou art with me; Thy rod and staff, they comfort me.'

The impression we all shared, I am sure, was of approaching menace, inestimable power, and I was overcome by a visceral, bowel-gripping fear. My teeth chattered and the world around me seemed to pitch and roll. When Father Ranvier had finished the psalm, he threw his arm out, fingers outstretched, as if he were a god releasing a thunderbolt. Stamping his foot, he roared, 'I exorcize you, Most unclean spirit! Invading enemy! Filth! Be uprooted and expelled from this creature of God.'

My head felt as if it had been struck by an axe. I experienced blinding, white hot pain, and then there was darkness, oblivion.

13

On opening my eyes, I was aware that a period of time had elapsed, but could not judge how long. It could have been minutes or hours. I was lying on my side some distance from my previous location. Two of the candles in the outer circle had been knocked over; my body ached and my thoughts were sluggish. Father Ranvier was chanting and Bazile was crouched at the edge of the circle – although still within it – studying me closely.

'Clément, are you back?'

'What happened?' I asked. 'Is it over?'

'No, my son,' said Father Ranvier. 'It is not over.'

'I am still . . . possessed?'

'You are,' said the priest.

'What happened?' I repeated.

'You lost consciousness,' answered Bazile.

'Indeed,' I replied, annoyed that he was merely stating the obvious. 'But what happened while I was gone?'

Bazile glanced at Father Ranvier and something passed between them: an unspoken request to proceed received reluctant approval.

'You were raving – speaking gibberish – and . . . It spoke to us. A voice, coming through you.'

'And what did it say?' Bazile shook his head. 'Tell me!' I demanded.

'Horrible things, obscenities.'

'You must tell me what was said!'

'It spoke of your friend, Madame Courbertin.' Again, Bazile consulted the priest, who sighed and indicated that he should continue. 'It said that she will not live long, and, very soon, it will have the pleasure of tasting . . .' Bazile shuddered, '. . . tasting her blood in hell'.

'The enemy is a liar – the great deceiver!' cried Father Ranvier. 'We must take no heed of what it says.'

I tried to sit up. 'Help me? Please. I can hardly move.'

Bazile started towards the circle's edge but Father Ranvier grabbed his arm and pulled him back. 'No! You must not!'

'But Monsieur Clément is in pain. Surely I can. . .'

'No!' The priest cried. 'You will stay in the circle!'

Bazile looked down on me, his expression full of pity. 'I am sorry, Clément.'

The priest returned to his table and began to recite a formal chastisement of the demon. He began in hushed tones, but was soon invoking the 'word made flesh' and delivering urgent reprimands. My head throbbed and I felt nauseous.

'You are enjoined in His name! Depart from this person whom He created! It is impossible for you to resist!'

As the priest's haranguing of the demon went on, the pain in my head became intolerable. I passed out several times, and on regaining consciousness found myself first on one side of the circle, then the other, feeling worse and worse on each successive reawakening, until everything became confused and blurred. I can recall, however, a brief interlude during which I seemed to recover my mental faculties and reasoned thus: you damaged your nervous system during the experiment and have since been suffering from delusions and hallucinations. You did not go to hell and did not return possessed. Courbertin died naturally and, because of your guilty conscience, you imagined it was you who had killed him! You cannot trust your memories: they are adulterated by fantasies and dreams. Charcot is right. Demoniacs are hysterics and hysteria is a condition of the nervous system.

I called out to Bazile, 'Stop! No more! I have misled you! I see it all clearly now. I am insane. I need sedation, electrical therapy, the water cure. Please, I am sick. Take me to the Salpêtrière! Take me to Charcot, I beg you.'

'Ah, Monsieur Clément,' said Father Ranvier, 'the enemy is now at his most dangerous. Do not be seduced by superficially attractive arguments. Even if you doubt the existence of God, our foe can yet be beaten, but if you doubt the existence of the Devil, all is lost.' His words resounded in the recesses of the old church, returning 'all is lost' as a portentous echo. The columns began to waver like fronds in a stream and I sank into a prolonged delirium.

I saw lurid visions: Thérèse, writhing luxuriously beneath a grotesque incubus, the winged demon of the cathedral taking flight and Courbertin climbing out of his grave and walking the streets of Montparnasse with the stilted gait of the living dead. I saw medieval towns-folk dancing with skeletons, oceans of fire and the discoloured eyes of the Port Basieux bokor.

It seemed that I was in this fevered lunatic frenzy for an eternity, time enough for the great pyramids of Egypt to become dust. And when finally I awoke, rising up through the cloudy medium of my disordered imaginings, my body welcomed me with blinding pain: no longer restricted to my head, but spread through every burning nerve. My face was pressed against the ground, but I could see the cloth of the straitjacket, scuffed and torn. In my mouth, I could taste blood, not sweet and fragrant, but sharp and metallic.

Bazile and Father Ranvier were looking at me with horrified expressions. They were both sitting cross-legged and breathing heavily, as if they had recently completed a task that had required sustained physical exertion. Father Ranvier looked tired and dishevelled – his spectacles were tilted at a steep angle across his nose and his purple stole was unceremoniously wrapped around his neck like a scarf. The cold was unbearable. I rolled onto my back. On my forehead beads of perspiration had turned to ice, and the air smelled faintly of sulphur.

'What happened?' I croaked.

Bazile stood up at once. 'Thank God! You're alive. I

thought it had killed you.' He looked up at the vault, then down to me, and I guessed that he was estimating the distance I had been raised and dropped. Turning towards Father Ranvier, Bazile said, 'We must stop now. Monsieur Clément may be injured. We can't go on.'

'No. That is not possible.'

'But he might be in urgent need of medical attention. And this abomination, this hideous thing . . .' Lost for words, Bazile waved his arms in the air. He swallowed and continued hoarsely, 'This is not what we expected.'

'We have no choice,' said the priest. 'We are bound to finish what we have started.'

'Bazile,' I cried. 'You really must help me.' I coughed up a clot of blood and spat it out.

The bell-ringer was about to step out of the circle, when the priest lunged and took hold of his leg.

'Édouard!' cried the priest. 'It is not safe.'

'Monsieur Clément may be dying.'

'Indeed, and we must save his soul. That is our principal obligation.'

The priest stood, raising himself up by pulling on Bazile's coat.

'I cannot stand by and watch him suffer!' said the bell-ringer.

The priest's eyes were ablaze with fanatical zeal. 'Have faith, Édouard!'

I remembered Bazile once talking of some spiritual crisis he had experienced in his past, and I sensed that a much greater struggle was taking place than was readily apparent. 'Have faith!' demanded the priest again. Bazile made an abrupt movement and shook off the priest's determined grip.

'It cannot be right,' said Bazile, 'To abandon him. Not like this.'

'And what about your wife?' the priest responded. 'Is it right to abandon her? If you step out of this circle, then the husband whom she next meets may be a very different man to the one she married.'

The riposte was well chosen. Bazile was torn, uncertain, and Father Ranvier, observing his indecision, seized the opportunity to carry on with the exorcism. 'Get out, impious one! Get out! Out with your falsehood! He who commands you is He who dominated the sea and the storms. Hear, therefore, and fear, Satan! Enemy of the faith! Enemy of humankind! Source of death! Thief! Deceiver!' Each accusation felt like a cudgel landing heavily on my skull. 'Depart this person!' bellowed Father Ranvier. 'Root of evil! Warp of vices!' He shook his fist and bared his teeth. 'Out, out! In the name of Michael, most glorious prince of the heavenly army! In the name of the blessed apostles, Peter and Paul, and all the saints! In the name of Jesus Christ, God and Lord! And in the name of Mary, mother of God, immaculate virgin, queen of heaven and hell: I cast you out! Be gone, demon, be gone!'

Father Ranvier's frame sagged. It was as though this final invocation had sapped all of his remaining strength. He looked impossibly old, like an ancient tree, desiccated and encased in cracked bark. A clump of hair had dropped over his forehead and his slack mouth resembled a hastily sewn suture. His gravitas had withered away, leaving nothing in its place but a suggestion of weary dotage, or even worse, senility. The silence that followed was exceptionally dense. Like the silence after snow at night – layered, unearthly – and I watched with horrible fascination as each candle began to dim, each flame dwindle to a faintly glowing point of light. From somewhere in the darkness came the sound of respiration: moist, low-pitched and reminiscent of a large animal. The in-breath was short and harsh, like a gasp, the out-breath long and accompanied by a liquid rattle.

'What is that?' whispered Bazile. But the priest did not reply.

The presence, formerly experienced as an abstract threat to the self, was now more substantive and possessed recognizable attributes: predatory intelligence, a savage disposition and malign purpose. It seemed, though – and I am not sure how, exactly – that it impinged upon the senses primarily as a noxious stench, vile and fetid. My empty stomach contracted and I began to retch. The will to destroy and obliterate was so fundamental to its nature, that proximity alone was sufficient to stress the fault lines of the mind and encourage fragmentation. A descent into madness seemed imminent. This effect was not confined to the inner world of the bystander. Once again, I heard stones shifting and felt a sprinkle of mortar on my face. It was as if materialization had placed an unbearable strain on the physical universe. Everything, from the bones within my aching body to the vault above my head, seemed in danger of being torn apart by indiscriminate and wayward forces. And at the centre of this 'system' was a molten core of hateful intent, a desire – no, more than that: an insatiable craving, lust – for human torment. I could sense its excitement, the registration in its consciousness of our vulnerability, its salacious hunger for flesh and its thirst for blood.

There was a ruffling of leathery wings and a loud snap, like the sound of a loose awning in the wind. The candles went out and we were plunged into darkness.

'Father?' said Bazile. Instead of the old man's voice, I heard a clop – as if a horse were tentatively testing the ground with its hoof. 'Father Ranvier?' Bazile persisted, but the priest seemed to have fallen into a kind of trance.

The bell-ringer struck a match and I saw his disembodied face floating above the ground as he searched desperately for the oil lamps. He found one, lit the wick, and adjusted the regulator to produce more light. When he looked up again, he screamed, the same scream that had issued more than once from my own mouth when confronted with the incomprehensible. The demon had emerged from the shadows. It moved quickly: stance forward-leaning, like a bull preparing to charge, septic eyes, eager and luminescent, horns tapering to points of precise and deadly sharpness. A snarl revealed fangs and the slithering fork of its tongue. It lashed its tail, whipping up a spray of stone chippings that stung my face. Terror, indescribable terror, made me jabber and weep. To see it again, at close quarters and unquestionably real, reduced me to mewling idiocy.

Father Ranvier, who had until that moment been immobile, seemed to recover his senses. He snatched the wand from the table and aimed it at the demon, muttering something in a language I did not recognize. Then, at the very top of his voice, he yelled, 'Adon, Schadai, Eligon, Amanai, Elion.' Bazile had fallen to his knees, both hands clamped tightly over his mouth. 'Pneumaton, Elii, Alnoal, Messias, Ja, Heynaan . . .'

The demon halted at the edge of the protective boundary and glared at the priest. I saw its arms rising, talons opening out in the lambency of the oil lamp, and slowly Father Ranvier began to ascend. He gained height, until his head almost touched the ceiling and then drifted out of the circle. At first, his limbs flailed around, but he was soon overcome by superior forces and his attitude became stiff and erect, like a soldier standing to attention. There was a ripping sound, and the priest's cassock and underclothes dropped to the ground in shreds, revealing a scrawny physique. Bereft of dignity, his shrivelled genitalia retracted into a wiry nest of grizzled hair. He began to rotate and his wrinkled buttocks came into view. When the turn was complete, his bladder failed, and a stream of urine trickled down his thighs and dripped from his calloused feet. The demon raised its arms for a second time and brought them down forcefully, emitting an effortful aspiration. What I saw next was so horrible, so utterly repulsive, that I very nearly swooned. Father Ranvier's skin was stripped from his body. It came away in one piece, like the slough of a snake, and for a brief moment stood on its own – a papery, hollow man – before collapsing. The priest shrieked and I flinched at the thought of so much pain: shrill, howling, bright-hued pain, incandescent scalding agony. His exposed muscles looked raw, lobster red, and glistened as if coated with a reflective laminate. Father Ranvier's face, although hideously transformed, was still recognizably his own. A few tufts of white hair still adhered to his bleeding scalp and his pale eyes were as distinctive as ever. His jaw trembled and the muscles attached to it began to bunch. He was evidently making a supreme effort to speak. After a few unsuccessful attempts, I heard him croak the word, 'Tetragrammaton.' And, a second or two later, his body burst into flames. Instinctively, I curled into a ball to protect myself from the scorching heat.

My terror had reached a limit beyond which there was nothing except mute vacancy. When the conflagration had exhausted itself, I straightened my back and peered through a veil of thick smoke. Father Ranvier's incineration had been total, and nothing remained of him except the smell of cooked meat and charred flakes in the air. The triumphant demon had not budged. It swung its head round and looked at Bazile, who was cringing and repeating, 'Merciful heaven, preserve us!' Then, reversing the movement, it fixed its eyes on me.

A faint white light had appeared, softly glowing in the middle distance. Its gentle insinuation dispersed like milk in water. I was too much in the thrall of those venomous eyes to be distracted. However, the light grew brighter and I realized that its origin must be the sphere of glass. The demon's expression altered and – insofar as one can interpret the rearrangement of such crude features – the alteration suggested wariness or caution. Shafts of brilliance were soon shining through the hazy atmosphere and the light became so bright that I could no longer look at it directly. I heard the demon snort, a deep growl, and then a stuttering, scraping sound, as if it were digging its talons into the ground to resist traction. There was more shattering of stone and I realized that a struggle was taking place. I was buffeted by a blast of air as the demon beat its wings, and then it roared: an appalling expression of towering rage. There was more lurching, and crashing, and I thought the vault was finally going to come down on our heads. But instead, there was a strange rushing, experienced more in spirit than through the senses, followed by an abrupt and total silence. The bright light was suddenly extinguished and for some time the ground shook – a soft, prolonged tremor. When I looked up, the demon was gone.

Bazile stepped out of the circle and walked towards the glass sphere. On reaching his destination, he craned forward, examined the object and drew back suddenly.

He made a hurried sign of the cross, removed his coat, and threw it over the sphere in a single movement. On returning, he knelt and helped me to get out of my restraints.

'Are you all right?' he asked.

'I don't think anything is broken.'

He nodded and whispered, 'God in heaven!'

Both of us were in a state of shock.

As I sat, with my back against one of the columns and rubbing my sore legs, Bazile lit more candles and started to clear up Father Ranvier's materials. He collected all of the items together, including the sphere (which he kept wrapped in his coat), and put them in the large canvas bag. He then turned his attention to Father Ranvier's remains. Although he was able to handle the shredded clothes, when it came to picking up the priest's skin he baulked, and I saw him turn away. After composing himself, he made another attempt, but the 'bundle' he had lifted unravelled, revealing its human outline. Bazile's face crumpled in disgust and only after several more endeavours did he manage to fold the skin into a shape that would fit into the bag. Finally, he erased the chalk marks with the heel of his shoe and I was reminded, curiously, of my old associate Tavernier, destroying the vèvè on our journey to Piton-Noir.

When I looked at my pocket watch, I thought it had stopped. 'What is the time?' I asked. Bazile consulted his own timepiece, and we discovered that only an hour had passed since our arrival. Clearly, the materialization had violated so many natural laws that even the flow of time had been affected. We climbed the stairs of the north tower and stumbled into Bazile's parlour. Taking our usual places at the table, we sat, dazed, saying nothing, until the morning was well advanced, and even then, all that we could utter were short declarations of horror and incredulity.

'When you depart, you must take the crystal with you,' said Bazile.

'I don't want it!'

Bazile sighed. 'I am sorry, Clément, but it is your . . . responsibility.'

'I can't.'

'I am afraid you must.'

'We could destroy it. Yes, let us do that.'

'And risk the release of what is now trapped inside?'

'Then I shall bury it!'

'And what if someone digs it up?'

'I'll take it somewhere remote. A distant country.'

'Wherever you go, it won't be safe. The glass might break.'

'What are you suggesting, Édouard? That I carry this abhorrent thing around with me for the rest of my life?'

'Yes. And perhaps at some point in the future you will find a solution to your predicament. But until then . . .'

'And what if I die before that is possible?'

'You will have to make some form of provision. I am sorry.' Bazile glanced over at the canvas bag.

'What are you going to do with Father Ranvier's remains?'

Bazile stood up and went to his sideboard. He removed a large scissors and set them down by the stove.

'One cannot expect the authorities to believe us. If we implicate ourselves in Father Ranvier's disappearance, then we will both become suspects in a murder investigation.'

Again I was reminded of my time on Saint-Sébastien, and how Tavernier had urged me not to go to the police. I was visited by a sense of déjà vu.

Bazile removed Father Ranvier's skin from the canvas bag and unfolded it on the floor. It looked like a slumbering ghost, transparent and slightly greenish. The priest's beard and most of his wild white hair were still attached and served as a vivid reminder to us that only minutes earlier this ghoulish sheath had been occupied. The bell-ringer squatted, opened the stove door and began cutting. I saw him detach Father Ranvier's right hand, now a drooping glove, and toss it onto the flames. The skin began to crackle and the room filled with a smell not unlike roasted pork. Bazile closed the stove door and said, 'I think I am going to be sick'.

14

I spent most of the following two weeks lying on my bed, looking up at the ceiling, smoking, thinking. Although I had not broken any bones, I had sustained some superficial injuries and I was suffering from exhaustion. Be that as it may, I felt quite changed – restored – much more my former self. Like the rest of humanity, when the sun had dropped below the horizon I began to feel tired, and when the sun rose I felt refreshed and alert. My fingernails grew at a normal rate and I was able to discard my eye-preservers. Even my nightmares were different: no longer vivid, fiery visions, but dark reflections, like moonbeams on water. I was still haunted by impressions of recent events, particularly the exorcism, but I also experienced episodes of giddy excitement when I remembered that I was now free of the demon's influence.

During this period of convalescence, I wrote several letters to Thérèse, declaring my affection and expressing my desire to see her again soon. I received only one reply which was short and apologetic: our next meeting would have to be postponed, because Courbertin's cousin was in Paris and she was occupied with the settlement of some family business. I thought nothing of this. Later that afternoon Bazile arrived with a selection of cold dishes prepared by his wife. We ate together at my dining-room table, but our conversation was subdued. It is said that shared adversity brings people closer together, but in our case something indefinable seemed to have come between us.

'Where have you put the crystal?' he asked.

I pointed at a chest of drawers. He nodded and his expression became pained.

I said, 'Father Ranvier's end was so unexpected. I am concerned that he meant to do something more. I worry that the ritual was not finished.'

Bazile chewed his lower lip. 'I cannot say for certain, but as far as I know, there was nothing else to be done.'

'Was there anything in Father Ranvier's bag to suggest otherwise? Items that he had not made use of?'

'Additional candles, a book of prayers,' Bazile replied. 'Nothing significant.'

I was mildly reassured. Even so, a general state of anxiety persisted. I wanted to know more about what had happened during the exorcism, particularly when I had been unconscious, but Bazile would not be drawn. He simply paraphrased Father Ranvier. 'Lies. All lies and wicked deception. You do not need to know such things.' He was clearly relieved when I allowed him to change the subject.

That evening, I devoted my thoughts entirely to Thérèse. I was undecided as to whether I should give her a full account of my remarkable history. She was open-minded, inquisitive and fascinated by the supernatural, yet I imagined that even she, on hearing such a fantastic narrative, might doubt the storyteller's sanity. Moreover, such an account would necessarily be incomplete. How could I explain what had happened to Courbertin? Although I was not, strictly speaking, responsible for his death, I had wanted to be rid of him and suspected that my ill-will had played a significant part in his demise. Remembering Courbertin filled me with grief, for he had been a kind, generous man.

I yearned to see Thérèse again, ached to see her face, touch her cheeks and kiss her lips. I conjured consoling images: Thérèse rising in the morning, laying out her towel and stooping to pick up a sponge, droplets glistening on her wet thighs and sunlight in the tangled mass of her hair. I wanted to cradle her in my arms, stroke her brow and hear her contented sighs. Another life suggested itself: a country practice, my new wife tending roses in the garden and little Philippe paddling on the shore of a wide blue sea.

When Thérèse's second letter arrived I could hardly believe what she had written. She was very sorry, but after much soul-searching, she had come to the conclusion that our relationship must end. We had not made each other happy. Now that Courbertin was dead, Philippe must be her priority.

I remembered the last time we were together, her body covered in cuts and bruises, and supposed that her decision must be connected with my acts of violence. Immediately, I went to my bureau and scrawled a frantic reply. I pleaded, grovelled, begged her to reconsider, confessed my faults and promised to change. But her position became entrenched and it soon became apparent that she was very angry with me. She blamed me for her 'moral decline' and declared, using forceful language, that she now meant to recover her 'dignity' – something that, for obvious reasons, could not be achieved if our 'association' continued. I resolved to see her that instant, to tell her the truth, to tell her everything; however, as I was running down the street, coat-tails flapping in the rain, common sense prevailed. How would presenting myself on her landing, drenched and raving like a maniac about demons help my situation? I stopped running, turned round and walked back to my apartment, where I composed another hopeless letter.

The following Monday I resumed my duties at the Salpêtrière. Charcot was delighted to see me back on the wards again and made some polite enquiries about my health. I told him that I had caught a chill and that my old respiratory problem had returned. He made some sympathetic remarks, patted me on the back and departed, dispersing papal benedictions with one hand while twirling his cane in the other.

I could not stop thinking about Thérèse. I missed her terribly. Indeed, I missed her so much that my mind began to play tricks on me. One morning I awoke and saw her standing at the end of my bed. She was wearing a dress of black silk and crimson lace and her eyes were abnormally large and bright, like emeralds set in white marble. Even though I realized she wasn't really there, her name escaped from my lips and I reached out my hand. The hallucination faded and joy was replaced by misery. I took to loitering outside her apartment, and after several weeks of agonizing indecision, I finally entered the building. I climbed the stairs and knocked on her door, which was opened, not by a maid, but by a man who looked vaguely familiar. It was the gentleman who I had seen at Courbertin's funeral, the one who had been wearing a long cape. I introduced myself and asked to see Madame Courbertin. The man shook his head. 'I am afraid she is not receiving visitors today.' He then shut the door in my face. Thereafter, all my subsequent letters were returned unopened.

A few months later, gripped by the same impulse, I walked to Thérèse's apartment again. I informed the concierge that I had come to see Madame Courbertin.

'She doesn't live here any more,' he replied, stubbing out a cigarette. 'She's moved away.'

'Where?'

'She said something about going back home to live with her parents. Her husband died, you know. Dreadful shame.'

'And where do her parents live?'

The concierge shrugged. 'How should I know?'

Everything around me seemed to go dark.

'Are you all right, monsieur?'

'Yes,' I replied, touching the wall to steady myself. 'Thank you.' I left the building, muttering, 'I have lost her.' But then I remembered that Courbertin and Thérèse had come from the same town. Over the next few days I made some discreet enquiries at the hospital and established without much difficulty that Courbertin was a native of Chinon. I nurtured a fragile hope that, with the passing of time, Thérèse might forgive me. This prospect, however unlikely, became the single most important reason for my continued existence.

The season changed. I busied myself at the hospital and worked hard. Charcot took me aside and informed me that my valuable contribution to the hysteria project had been 'officially' noted. Occasionally, I met with Bazile, but we were no longer at ease in each other's company. Life seemed dull and empty. Most evenings were spent alone, reading works of hermetic philosophy and ritual magic, but none of them contained what I was looking for.

On the Boulevard Saint-Michel is a shop that stocks plain, hard-wearing furniture. I had been meaning to go there for some time. When the opportunity finally presented itself, I stepped into a warm interior that smelled strongly of beeswax and sawdust. Down in the basement, I discovered several chests, one of which was made from solid oak. I asked the proprietor if it could be reinforced.

'There is no need, monsieur,' he replied, rapping the wood with his knuckle. 'It is virtually indestructible.' Ignoring his objection, I told him of my requirements. He listened heedfully and then said, 'Lead? Iron plates? But you won't be able to move it, monsieur. It'll be too heavy.' I dismissed his remark and negotiated a price. He was still shaking his head when our business was concluded. As I was preparing to leave the proprietor asked, 'What do you intend to keep in it?'

'Family heirlooms,' I replied.

'They must be of great value.'

'Indeed.'

'Well, rest assured, monsieur: they will never be stolen. It would be easier to rob a bank!'

One day, I was speaking to Valdestin and he asked me if I knew of anyone who might be interested in an unusual appointment. A friend of his, a neurologist named Trudelle, had agreed to become 'house physician' to a wealthy Touraine family. Unfortunately, only weeks before he was due to leave Paris, he had met a factory owner's daughter, fallen in love and decided that his interests were best served by remaining in the capital. The family were very disappointed and Trudelle, overcome with guilt, felt obliged to help them find a replacement.

'Well?' said Valdestin. 'Do you know anybody who would be interested in such a position?'

'Yes.' I said. 'Me.'

'Have you gone mad? Charcot always rewards industry, and, given the way you have been working lately, he will almost certainly recommend your advancement next year.'

'I could do with a change.'

'Clément! Don't be absurd!'

'Tell me: where can I find Trudelle?'

Valdestin said that I was being foolish, but I was insistent, and in the end he handed me one of Trudelle's cards. I think I had already made up my mind to get away from Paris. The same restlessness that had preceded my sudden departure for Saint-Sébastien had taken hold of me and I had been simply waiting for the right opportunity to present itself.

I visited the Du Bris family at their hotel, a fine establishment situated near the opera house. Gaston Du Bris was a big man, ruggedly handsome with longish hair and a pock-marked face. His wife, Hélène, was pretty and courteous. They had with them the eldest of their three children, Annette, whose delicate features and winning naivety made her appear somewhat younger than her twelve years, and Hélène's brother, Tristan Raboulet – a man in his mid-twenties whose dress and casual manners were perhaps a little too informal given the occasion. Both Annette and her uncle suffered from epilepsy and their seizures were becoming more frequent. I examined the two patients, discussed their symptoms, and enquired as to what treatments they had so far received. Their local doctor and a so-called 'specialist' at the hospital in Tours had prescribed largely inert substances. I was broadly in agreement with Trudelle, whose prescribing habits were at least more current. Nevertheless, he had neglected to consider the full range of options and I advised accordingly.

'With respect,' I said to Du Bris. 'I am not sure that you need to employ a house physician. Perhaps you should see first how your daughter and Monsieur Raboulet respond to the new medications?'

Before Du Bris could answer, his wife said, 'No.' She wrapped her arms protectively around Annette. 'The seizures are so terrible. Only last week I thought . . .' She shook her head and her eyes moistened.

'It is always very upsetting,' I said with sympathy, 'to see those whom we love in distress. But the seizures are likely to be less frequent and certainly less severe.'

'Even so', said Hélène. She glanced at her husband – a silent appeal for support.

Du Bris nodded and said, 'Monsieur, you seem to be suggesting that we can expect to see an improvement, but the new medications are not a cure. Have I under-stood you correctly?'

'Indeed.'

'Then I agree with my wife. Having a doctor – a col-league of Charcot, no less – accommodated at Chambault would be very desirable.'

Hélène breathed a sigh of relief.

We discussed certain practical matters and an arrangement was made for me to visit their estate in due course. As I was leaving, Raboulet sidled up to me and said, 'Monsieur Clément, would you be so kind as to recommend a good play?' He looked excessively disappointed when I was unable to. So much so, that I felt obliged to tell him about a concert I planned to attend that very evening: piano pieces performed by a Russian virtuoso. He promptly scribbled the details on the cuff of his shirt, seemingly indifferent to his brother-in-law's disapproval.

I had not expected to see Raboulet at the concert, he seemed too feckless and disorganized; however, during the interval, we met in the foyer and he enthused about the music. 'Thank you, monsieur. A thrilling programme. I am so glad I came.' He was a talkative fellow and I learned that he had a wife called Sophie, and a baby daughter called Elektra after the protagonist of his favourite Greek tragedy. 'I can't think why you would want to leave Paris for the country, monsieur,' he said, making flamboyant gestures. 'There really is nothing to do. You don't get heavenly concerts like this in the village! Still, if you're mad enough to forgo such pleasures then I will be overjoyed. You have no idea how much I crave educated conversation.'

The following week I travelled to Chambault. It was an extraordinarily beautiful chateau, surrounded by exquisite gardens. On my arrival, Annette handed me a little watercolour of a gentleman in a frock coat carrying a black bag.

'For you,' she said.

It was surprisingly accomplished and I recognized myself immediately.

'Thank you, Annette. The likeness is astonishing.'

'Please come and live with us,' she said, her brow tensing. 'Please come and make me and Uncle Tristan better.' Her appeal was so direct, so earnest, that I was quite moved.

I was introduced to Annette's brothers, Victor and Octave, and Du Bris's mother, Odile – a formidable old woman whose presence was quite oppressive. Hélène hovered in the background, quietly observant and slightly agitated. She was clearly anxious that I should find everything to my satisfaction. Du Bris showed me the suite of rooms that would be mine if I chose to accept the appointment. They were spacious and adjoined a massive library. As we were walking through, I stopped to read the titles and discovered that many of the books were about esoteric subjects.

'Are you a student of the occult?' I asked.

Du Bris laughed out loud. 'Me, good heavens, no! I'm afraid I'm not much of a reading man. Riding, shooting – yes; but not reading!'

'Then whose—'

'Almost all of the books you see here once belonged to Roland Du Bris – my great-great-great . . .' he stopped to calculate the precise relationship, but gave up and said instead, 'An ancestor who lived here hundreds of years ago.' He seemed impatient to proceed. 'Come, monsieur. You must see the dining room. We have a tapestry on the wall that once belonged to the first King Louis.'

That night I stayed in Tours, meaning to get the early

train back to Paris the following day. In the hotel parlour, I discovered a map of the area. I traced the course of the river Loire, from Tours to Candes-Saint-Martin, and then moved my finger from left to right until it came to rest on Chinon. 'Not far,' I thought to myself, 'not far at all.' Before retiring, I asked the porter for some paper and wrote a letter to Du Bris accepting his terms.

I was ready to leave Paris before the onset of winter. I said goodbye to Bazile and later that same afternoon walked to the cathedral. The sun was setting and the stone of the western facade was ablaze with red-gold light. Looking up at the central portal I saw devils and demons, endless permutations of human suffering: an eviscerated sinner trailing his insides, another tumbling headfirst into a boiling cauldron and an erring bishop with the clawed feet of a succubus digging into his shoulders. I saw cascades of intertwined bodies, naked and vulnerable, descending into torment, leering grotesques, prodigies, instruments of torture. Among all of this obscene cruelty one scene in particular stood out: a woman, upside down, with toads and serpents biting her breasts, a hook in her belly, about to have her loins devoured by lascivious demons. I remembered the exorcism, Bazile's stunned voice, 'It spoke of your friend Madame Courbertin . . .' I wanted to pray for her, but the words stuck in my throat. How could a perfect, all-knowing and all-powerful God permit the existence of hell? I had not found an answer to this question and doubted that I ever would.

My first winter at Chambault was mild. Both of my patients responded well to the medication that I had prescribed and further improvements were achieved with regular herbal infusions. Raboulet had only two seizures between Christmas and Easter, while Annette had only one. The family were extremely appreciative and I was treated more like a guest than an employee. I had plenty of free time, most of which I spent in the library, and when I wasn't reading, I went out riding by the river. Once or twice, I was tempted to take the road to Chinon, but I managed to resist. Life at Chambault was delightful. The estate was a little Eden and I had slithered in like a serpent.

PART THREE

Redemption

15

Chambault

The sun had climbed to its highest point and the white
facade of the chateau shone with a radiance of exceptional purity. We had gathered at the edge of the lawn
beneath the boughs of a wild cherry tree. Hélène Du Bris
was seated at my side, paintbrush in hand, carefully
introducing stipples of vermillion onto the green wash
of her watercolour. Raboulet was lying on his back,
vacantly gazing up through the overhanging branches,
and behind him, sitting on the grass with her back
against the trunk, was his wife, Sophie, their sleeping
infant cradled in her arms. Odile Du Bris had covered
her legs with a woollen blanket and was also asleep;
I could hear her stertorous breathing. Mademoiselle
Drouart, the governess, had organized a game for the
children, and Victor, Annette and Octave were chasing
up and down the steps which led to the ice house, their

voices shrill with excitement. As usual, Du Bris was absent.

Earlier, the cook – Madame Boustagnier – had brought us a basket of freshly baked bread, goat's cheese and apricots. Only a few hollow crusts remained. She had also packed two bottles of wine from the cellar. The red from the estate – distinctive and spicy – had acted on my brain like a potent soporific and my limbs felt swollen and heavy. A butterfly settled on Hélène's easel. Its transparent wings trembled and opened to reveal markings of exquisite delicacy, a network of dark lines against a background of vivid orange. Hélène turned to see if I was looking, and when our eyes met, she smiled and said, 'Do you know what it is, monsieur?'

'No,' I replied, 'I'm afraid I don't.'

'So very beautiful . . .'

'Indeed, madame, and probably quite rare.'

Hélène continued painting, and perhaps because of the wine, I found myself incautiously staring at her. She was wearing a close-fitting gown of blue silk, cut to show the suppleness of her figure. Her arms emerged from short sleeves trimmed with white lace, and I noticed that her skin had darkened during the course of the summer to a sensuous olive. Her hair was piled up loosely on top of her head and held in place by a set of ivory combs. The nape of her neck was visible through a faintly glowing haze of blonde down.

'Monsieur Clément?'

It was the old woman. She had woken up. I rose, a flush of embarrassment warming my cheeks.

'Yes, madame?'

'Would you get me my blanket? It has dropped to the ground.'

'Of course.'

I picked up the fallen mantle and laid it across her legs. When she said, 'Thank you', I thought I detected a certain coldness in her voice. If she had observed me gaping at her daughter-in-law, there was nothing I could do. I made some solicitous remarks and returned to my chair.

Raboulet stood and brushed some grass from his trousers. He lit a cigarette and, addressing no one in particular, said, 'You know, I heard something quite extraordinary the other day. A fellow from Bonviller is supposed to have sold his wife. Apparently, he sold her along with all the furniture in his house for a hundred francs.'

'Who told you that?' asked Hélène.

'Fleuriot,' Raboulet replied. 'He told me that the notary refused to register the sale but the people involved decided to carry on regardless. They signed a document before three witnesses in the marketplace.' The old woman grumbled disapprovingly. 'Now, that can't be right, can it?' Raboulet went on, 'I mean to say, a man can't just sell his wife, surely? What do you think, Monsieur Clément?'

'Parties can agree to conditions without recourse to

law, and often do. I recall there was a similar case reported in Rive-de-Gier, not so long ago.'

'Who would have thought it?' said Raboulet.

'These peasants are brutes,' said the old woman.

'Let us hope,' I said, 'that in the fullness of time, compulsory schooling will have an improving effect.'

'Education is all well and good, monsieur,' snapped the old woman, 'but it will not be enough. The peasantry suffer from a moral weakness. I have lived here all my life and know what they are like. Believe me. They are godless and intemperate.'

'Oh, madame,' said Raboulet, extending his arms and tacitly begging the old woman to reconsider her judgement. Her unforgiving expression did not soften and she turned her head away sharply.

Undaunted, Raboulet continued to inform us of the latest gossip: an argument involving the blacksmith, the appearance of gypsy caravans by the river. His chatter was mildly diverting and occasionally prompted some frivolous banter. Thankfully, the old woman fell asleep again, so we were spared more of her scolding piety. When Raboulet had exhausted his stock of stories, he strolled around the cherry tree a few times before positioning himself between two moss-covered statues of cherubs. He gazed out over the lawn and waved at the children, who stopped their game to return his signal.

'I think I'll join them,' he said. 'They look like they're having fun.'

He picked up a straw hat and stepped out of the

shade and into the fierce midday heat. He was dressed in a pale summer jacket and baggy trousers. His gait was shambolic, as if his limbs were connected to his body only by threads of cotton, and his rangy, uncoordinated step reminded me of a marionette. The children became boisterous at his approach, and I could hear Mademoiselle Drouart attempting to calm them down.

Hélène leaned back in her chair and considered her watercolour. She had only included the southern tower of the chateau, with its conical roof and ornate chimney stack; however, the building supplied a vertical line which divided the picture into pleasing and complementary parts. I said, 'The fallen leaves are particularly well executed.' Hélène was so modest that my praise baffled her. 'No. Really, madame,' I persevered, 'I think it's rather good.'

'You are very kind, monsieur, but I am perfectly aware of my limitations.' She paused and a line appeared on her brow. 'Did you meet many artists when you lived in Paris, Monsieur Clément?'

'Yes, a few, but none of renown: the closest I came to artistic genius was to stand in the same room as Gustave Doré. We were never introduced. He was pointed out to me – a distant figure standing next to the punch bowl – by one of my medical colleagues.'

'You must find life at Chambault very slow, monsieur.'

'Not at all.'

'I worry that we will lose you one day: that you will

225

get bored with us and our provincial ways and return to the city.'

'I wouldn't dream of it.'

She looked at me in disbelief.

'I am very happy here,' I continued, eager to reassure her. 'I adore the peace, the tranquillity.' Directing my gaze to the noisy group on the other side of the lawn, she raised her eyebrows. I laughed. 'They don't disturb me when I'm in the library.'

'How are your studies proceeding, monsieur?'

'It is a privilege to have access to such a collection.' My response was a subtle evasion and I was relieved that it passed without notice.

Suddenly, the children were racing towards us, pursued by their uncle. Mademoiselle Drouart was following behind, unhurried, striking a graceful pose with her parasol. 'I won, I won,' shouted Victor, as he passed between the two mossy cherubs and collapsed on the ground. I was aware that Annette had purposely decreased her speed so as to allow both of her brothers to beat her. This little act of charity was strangely touching. She had inherited her mother's hair and eyes, and her face, although still that of an innocent, could communicate emotions of surprising depth and maturity. Raboulet arrived next, grinning and coughing after his exertions. He slumped down next to his wife, who looked at him with mock exasperation. Mademoiselle Drouart collected the children together and led them to an adjacent tree, where she began reading to them from a volume of fairy stories.

I closed my eyes and listened to the soft murmur of her voice, the humming of an inquisitive honeybee, and the gentle rustle of Hélène's skirts. I must have dropped off, because when I opened my eyes again, Annette was standing in front of me, a bracelet of tiny flowers in her outstretched palm.

'That is very pretty,' I said.

'I made it for you,' she whispered.

'Thank you.' I replied. 'It is too small for me to wear, so I shall keep it on my desk.' The child gave me the bracelet and I placed it in my breast pocket, making sure not to break any of her carefully constructed links.

'The demoiselles wear flowers.'

'Who?'

'The demoiselles. The fairies of the forest. Madame Boustagnier told me about them.'

'Is that so?'

Raboulet stirred: 'Ha! The doctor doesn't believe in fairies, my dear. He is a man of science, which means that he doesn't believe in anything that he cannot touch or see.'

'But you can never see the demoiselles,' said the child. 'It is impossible. They disappear if anyone gets close.'

'There you are, monsieur,' said Raboulet. 'Science's problem in a nutshell. Although there is no evidence to suggest the existence of certain phenomena, belief in them will persist forever because they cannot be refuted.' Raboulet liked to remind me that he had read one or two volumes of philosophy. 'This is why,' he continued, 'science will never replace the idiocy of religion.'

Hélène swivelled round to make sure that Odile was still unconscious. Anxiety became relief and she waved a cautionary finger at her brother.

'I could see she was asleep from here,' said Raboulet.

'Is that true, monsieur?' asked Annette. 'You do not believe in anything that cannot be seen or touched?'

'No,' I said, stroking a wisp of hair out of her eyes. 'That is not true. Thank you for the bracelet.'

A light breeze, carrying with it the perfume of roses, made the boughs above our heads creak. Some leaves fell and their descent was accompanied by birdsong.

Earlier that summer, I had written a letter to Thérèse. I did not know her address, but had assumed, correctly, that Chinon was so small a town that an envelope carrying her name would not present the postal service with too great a challenge. I had been half expecting her to return the letter unopened, so I was mentally unprepared for her reply, which arrived only two days later. The script was jagged, forward leaning, and in some parts made almost illegible by trails of splattered ink. It was not necessary to read the words to gauge the strength of Thérèse's emotion. She had apparently committed her thoughts to paper, without pause, and in a blind rage: 'I never want to see you again. What you did to me was unforgivable and every day I suffer as a consequence. Perhaps it is only right that a woman who neglected her son and deceived her husband should be punished. Why do you persecute me so? Please, leave me alone. Please, go back to Paris.' I would sit in the library, reading and rereading this letter. It was not her anger that I found so upsetting, but rather her pleading. News of my arrival in the Loire had reduced her to scrawling desperate entreaties: 'I beg you to respect my wishes. Please, please be merciful.' To think of her so frightened and wretched filled me with sadness.

Old buildings are said to make noises, but Chambault was remarkably quiet at night. I folded Thérèse's letter and slipped it into a volume of alchemical writings. When the dogs started barking, I assumed that they had been disturbed by a mouse or a wild cat, but they did not stop, and after several minutes I too detected the sound of an approaching trap: whip cracks, the jangling of the bridle, the rattle of wheels on the village road. The courtyard gate was closed and the vehicle was obliged to stop outside. There were raised voices and someone rang the bell. Louis, one of the servants, called down from a window, a door slammed and there were hurried footsteps. I tidied my things and slotted the alchemy book back into its space on the shelf. The commotion grew louder and I decided to investigate. When I stepped into the antechamber, I was confronted with Du Bris, entering from the other side. He was in his dressing gown and clutched a rifle in his hands. Keeping pace with Du Bris was Louis, still in his nightshirt, and holding up an oil lamp. They were followed by Father Lestoumel, the curé, and a burly man from the village carrying a girl in his arms. Even from a distance I could see that her limbs were shaking.

'Quick,' I said. 'This way, please.'

At the opposite end of the library was the door to my rooms. On entering the study, I lit some candles, ordered the man to lay the girl out on the divan and commenced my examination. Her head was rolling from side to side, she was uttering incoherent phrases and her face was lacquered with perspiration. Lank black hair was plastered across her forehead. I asked Louis to hold the lamp higher, and as he did so I saw that the girl's skin had a bluish hue. There were blood stains down the front of her smock and her breathing and heart rate were rapid.

'How long has she been like this?' I asked.

'Allow me to introduce Monsieur Doriac,' said the curé, 'the girl's father.' He invited the man to step forward. 'Speak, Thomas. Answer the doctor's question.'

'She's been poorly for weeks,' said Doriac. He was a big, awkward fellow with lumpy features.

'Indeed,' I said, 'but how long has she had this fever?'

'Two days.'

'When was the last time she had anything to drink?'

'I don't know. My wife's been looking after her.'

'Why didn't you call Monsieur Jourdain?'

'We did. He came on Tuesday and prescribed some pastilles. They didn't help, so my wife . . .' Doriac became uncomfortable and he did not finish his sentence.

The curé bowed and spoke confidentially into my ear, 'I went to fetch Monsieur Jourdain earlier this evening, but unfortunately I found him indisposed.' What he meant was that the reprobate had, yet again, drunk himself into a state of insensibility. 'I'm sorry, monsieur, but there was nothing else I could do. I didn't want to risk driving her all the way to Bleury-en-Plaine.'

I listened to the girl's lungs and heard exactly what I dreaded: a horrible crackling as she drew breath. Du Bris must have observed my reaction. He clapped a hand on Doriac's back and said, almost jovially, 'Come, monsieur, let's leave the doctor alone, we mustn't distract him. How about a cognac? You look like you could do with one, and you, Father Lestoumel? Would you like to join us? No? Very well. Come, monsieur.' Du Bris steered Doriac towards the library and beckoned Louis. It was obvious that he fully understood the gravity of the situation. I emptied some water into a bowl and tried to cool the child's forehead with a damp flannel. I then prepared a solution of salicin. While I was dissolving the powder, I asked Father Lestoumel the child's name, and he said that it was Agnès. Positioning myself so that I could raise her up a little, I held the glass to her lips. Her breath was fetid. 'Agnès,' I said, 'listen to me. Keep your head still. You must drink. It is important that you drink.' The poor creature was delirious. I tilted the glass but she didn't swallow anything. The liquid came straight out of her mouth and cascaded down her front.

The curé caught my eye and said, 'When Jourdain's pastilles didn't work, Doriac's wife rode out to Saint-Jean to see Madame Touppin.'

'Who?'

'Madame Touppin. She is reputed to be a healer. In reality, she is nothing but an ignorant hag who sells charms and potions to the gullible and superstitious. She told Madame Doriac to slice a living white dove in two and to place the palpitating halves on the child's chest.' When the curé saw my expression, he added, 'Yes, I know: you wouldn't think it possible in this day and age, but I promise you, monsieur, it is true. Unfortunately, I didn't hear of this obscenity until today, otherwise I would have acted earlier.'

'Are you suggesting that the Doriacs actually . . .'

'Followed Madame Touppin's advice? Yes, and Madame Doriac was willing to wait indefinitely for the treatment to take effect. Naturally, as soon as I saw Agnès, I realized she was in need of urgent medical help, and set about persuading Monsieur Doriac to think again about Jourdain.'

'Really, Father, it is not acceptable that a doctor should be so regularly – as you say – indisposed.'

'Yes,' said the curé, bowing his head. 'You are quite right.' But I could tell by the defeated croak of his voice that he had no appetite for further arguments with the village council.

Taking pity on him I said, 'There is only so much that a priest can do.' He sighed and showed his appreciation with a grateful smile.

'Agnès,' I persisted. 'Drink. You are unwell and must

take some medicine to get better. Please, Agnès, you must try.'

It was futile. When I removed the glass from her lips, it was half empty, and she had imbibed nothing. The stream of nonsense issuing from her mouth continued unabated. Her forehead was burning and I could feel the heat coming off her body in waves. The effect was like standing close to a stove. I set the glass aside and removed the girl's smock, manipulating her arms and pulling the garment off over her head. The revelation of her naked flesh made the holy man cover his eyes. I soaked the flannel and began wiping away a layer of filth, and as I did so, her shivering became more violent. It seemed to me that her skin was a deeper blue than it had first appeared. The curé overcame his scruples and, after a minute or so, lowered his hand.

'Are we too late?' he asked.

The child looked pitiful. She was wasted and her ribs were clearly visible. Foamy sputum, flecked with clotted blood, oozed from her mouth. Wiping it away, I found it difficult to be anything other than frank: 'I am not very hopeful.'

Father Lestoumel nodded. 'Yes, I feared as much. Doriac will be devastated.' He searched in the folds of his cassock and produced a small bottle of holy oil. 'May I?'

I gave my consent and he began to administer the last rites. Rising, I crossed the floor and removed a hypodermic syringe from my bureau. It was my intention to deliver an anti-pyretic intravenously. If the child's fever could be reduced, then there was a slim possibility she might pull through. I could hear Father Lestoumel praying as I busied myself with my bottles, but then something changed. It took me a few moments to identify what was different. Agnès had stopped mumbling.

'Monsieur Clément?' The curé's voice was timid, uncertain. I rushed back to the divan and grabbed the child's wrist. There was no pulse. 'Has she gone?'

'Yes.'

The curé made a cross in the air and continued with his prayers.

Had I hesitated for the briefest interval, I would probably have done nothing, but instead I impulsively ran to the cupboard where the batteries were stored and removed one at random. Placing the mahogany box on the floor next to the divan, I raised the lid. The cells elevated and the elements were instantly plunged into a reservoir of dilute sulphuric acid. I made some adjustments to the coil and the device began to emit a soft buzz. Picking up the electrodes I held them over the child's heart.

'Monsieur,' the curé stirred from his ritual. 'What are you doing?'

Two glowing lines of liquid energy, like miniature bolts of lightning, bridged the gap between the electrodes and Agnès's body. The curé gasped as the girl's eyes opened and her chest heaved. A muscular spasm caused the child's back to arch, and she maintained this position for a second or two, her stomach thrust upwards, before she became limp and fell back. The impact of her land-ing seemed to knock the air from her lungs, which escaped in the form of protracted, rattling sigh. A further charge had no effect, and when I raised the electrodes, I saw that they had left behind two burn marks. Although Agnès's eyes had opened, and remained open, I was only too well acquainted with the glassy vacant stare of the dead – that chilling emptiness. She was beyond help now. With precise movements, I altered the position of the metal rod within the coil, pushed the electrodes into their cavities, and closed the lid. The buzzing ceased, creating a paradoxical, roaring silence.

'She seemed to come back,' said the curé, 'I have never seen such a thing. I didn't know that . . .' his perplexity rendered him speechless. Nervously worrying the beads of his rosary, his gaze travelled slowly from the dead girl to the battery. 'What is this machine?'

'An electrical device.'

My voice sounded alien, strained and distant. Perhaps it was the peculiarity of my delivery that made Father Lestoumel transfer his attention from the machine to me, and his strong pastoral instincts made him reach out to rest a solicitous hand on my shoulder. I should have acknowledged the gesture, but instead, I stood up and returned to the cupboard from where, among my phar-macological preparations, I took a bottle of rum. I didn't trouble to offer the curé a glass. Sitting down at the table, I rubbed the bristle on my chin and stared across the room at the corpse.

'You are a good man,' said the curé, 'and good men are always welcome in my church.' Emboldened by some inner sense of conviction, he added, 'There is nothing that God cannot or will not forgive.' He could be remarkably perceptive for a country priest.

I finished the rum and said: 'Shall I tell Doriac, or will you do it?'

16

I was preparing an infusion of passionflower and skull-cap when a rap on the door was followed by a tentative enquiry.

'Monsieur?'

I called out, 'Come in,' and Raboulet entered. His hair was mussed and a crumpled linen jacket hung loosely off his shoulders. He hadn't attached a collar to his shirt and he had neglected to shave. I indicated that he should sit, and he slumped down on a chair, extending his legs and placing his hands behind his head.

'Shame about the girl,' he said. 'I just heard; Hélène told me. Was it pneumonia?'

'Yes.'

'Poor child, why on earth did they drag her all the way out here?'

'Monsieur Jourdain was indisposed.'

Raboulet nodded. 'I slept through the whole thing.'

'There wasn't anything you could have done.'

'Like a baby. I thought you'd reduced my bromide.'

'I have. But even small doses have a sedative effect.'

I stirred some honey into the infusion and passed him the glass. 'How have you been feeling?'

'Not too bad.'

'No unusual experiences . . . sensations?' The young man shook his head. 'Good.'

'I was thinking of taking a boat out, later today. No one wants to come with me. I was wondering . . .'

'You can't row on your own.'

'But I've been doing so well.' He took a sip. 'How about you, monsieur? Can I tempt you out onto the river?'

'Not today, thank you.'

'Ah, yes. Forgive me. You must be tired.'

Raboulet stood up and crossed over to the window. Beyond the formal gardens, a carpet of wildflowers stretched off into the distance; aspen quivered on the horizon.

'I get so bored,' said Raboulet. 'There's so little to do.'

I felt sorry for him. 'Perhaps you'll be able to get away from here one day.'

'Do you really think so?' His voice was eager.

'I can't make any promises, but if things continue to improve . . . who knows?'

He finished his infusion and we sat and talked for a while. We smoked some cigarettes and played a game of bezique. When I declared two hundred and fifty I still had two aces. For several weeks, I had been letting Raboulet win, and judged that it was probably about time for him to lose again. Raboulet grinned and vowed to take his revenge. I was to expect, so he declared with counterfeit theatrical anger, 'a humiliating defeat'. As I put the cards away, he asked, 'What do you keep in there, Clément?' I looked up and saw that he was gesturing towards my wooden chest.

'Delicate scientific instruments,' I replied, 'and new preparations that I have yet to test.'

He responded reflectively. 'Yes, of course.' The tone of his voice carried an underlying implication of self-reproach, as if he was thinking: how stupid of me to ask such a question, a doctor can't leave expensive equipment and dangerous substances lying around the place. 'Oh well,' he added, rising from the chair and glancing at my table clock, 'I suppose I'd better leave you to your books and potions. Will you be dining with us this evening?'

'I'm not sure.'

'If you do decide to join us, don't forget the cards, eh?'

My mind was still clouded with memories of Agnès Doriac. After the curé's departure, I had stayed up for most of the night, drinking the remainder of my rum. Had I been less distracted, I might have responded more warily, but I let Raboulet leave, without asking any questions, as if nothing out of the ordinary had happened.

I spent the rest of the morning in the library. Madame Boustagnier, ever solicitous, brought me some soup and bread at midday. Just after two o'clock, the bell rang, and Louis came to inform me that Monsieur Doriac had returned. He wanted to speak with me.

'Shall I tell him that you are otherwise engaged, monsieur?'

'No!' I snapped. 'I'm perfectly happy to see him.'

'Very good, monsieur. He is waiting in the courtyard.'

'Why?'

'He wouldn't come in, monsieur.'

'Did you ask him?'

'It was his preference to remain outside.'

I put on my jacket and made my way downstairs. The dogs were barking and I was annoyed that nobody had taken the trouble to calm them down. Doriac was standing by the well, holding a wide-brimmed hat in one hand and a basket in the other. He started towards me, his upper body swaying as he lumbered across the cobbles. Damp patches were visible beneath his arms.

'Monsieur Doriac. Please, why don't you come in?' He looked down at his clogs. They were coated with white dust and he was clearly concerned that he would bring dirt into the chateau. 'You can clean your clogs in the kitchen.'

He shook his head. 'No. I can't stay.' He extended his hand and offered me the basket. I took it from him and peering inside, saw that it was full of straw and eggs. 'Thank you for trying to save my daughter. Father Lestoumel told me you tried very hard. I know it isn't much, but it's all that I have.'

I didn't want to deny him or his family their supper, but I had to accept his gift; to do otherwise would have been churlish, or even worse, insulting.

'Thank you, monsieur,' I said, inclining my head. 'You are most kind. Agnès was very sick. I am so sorry.' Doriac took a step backwards. Now that he had accomplished his task, he seemed anxious to leave. I looked about the courtyard and, noticing that it was empty, asked, 'Where is your trap, monsieur?'

'I don't have a trap.'

'You had one last night.'

'The curé . . .' Doriac's explanation did not proceed beyond naming the person who had obviously obtained the vehicle.

'You walked?'

'Yes.'

'All the way?'

'Yes.'

'You must be exhausted. Please, allow me to drive you back to the village.'

'No,' Doriac replied assertively. 'I can walk.'

I thanked him again for the eggs and he put his hat on. He looked up into the blueness of the sky, turned, and began his long walk home. The large wooden gates had been left open and he was able to leave through the archway that usually admitted carriages. I watched him pass the little fountain and take a pathway that veered off to the left. He didn't look back and proceeded slowly, head bowed, his ponderous tread suggesting the grim determination of an ox. When Doriac had disappeared from view, I went to the kitchen, where I found Madame Boustagnier chopping vegetables. I gave her the eggs, informed her that it was my intention to dine alone, and requested an omelette.

'Where did you get these, monsieur?'

'They were given to me by Doriac.' She looked at me quizzically. 'The man who came here last night with the curé.'

'Ah, yes,' she replied. 'The girl's father.' Her face became anguished and she made the sign of the cross with fluid dexterity. 'God rest her soul.'

'The omelette must be made with these eggs,' I said, 'And these eggs only.'

'What? All of them, monsieur?'

'Yes,' I said. 'All of them.'

She reached into the basket, lifted one out, and inspected its speckled surface with interest.

'It's cracked.'

'That doesn't surprise me, Madame Boustagnier. Monsieur Doriac came on foot, carrying that basket all the way from the village.'

'I'll remember him in my prayers.'

I shrugged. 'If you think it will help.'

Cradling the cracked egg in her rough pink hands, she placed it back in the basket with affecting tenderness.

I had just finished giving Annette her infusions when her mother appeared in the doorway. Hélène was wearing a black dress and a silver necklace, her hair was tied back and two garnet teardrops hung from her earlobes.

'Are you finished with Annette, monsieur?'

'Yes, madame.'

'And is she well?'

'Very well.'

The child addressed her mother: 'Monsieur Clément put only one spoonful of honey in my medicine.'

'Oh, why was that?' asked Hélène.

'He said that I am sweet enough already.'

'Monsieur,' Hélène said in mild reprimand, 'you will give Annette an inflated opinion of herself!' I was somewhat embarrassed by the child's disclosure, and made some light-hearted remark before pretending to rearrange my bottles. I could hear Hélène's skirts sweeping the floor as she crossed to the window. 'Monsieur,' she continued, her voice a little strained, 'My mother-in-law has asked Father Lestoumel to say a Mass for the repose of Agnès Doriac's soul, and she was anxious that you should be informed. The service will be held tomorrow afternoon, in the chapel.'

'Please thank Madame Du Bris for her kind invitation; however, I must decline.'

Hélène nodded.

'Monsieur Clément?' I turned and saw that Annette was standing beside my wooden chest.

'Yes?'

'What do you keep in here?' She dragged her hand over the lid, creating a channel through the dust.

'Why do you ask?'

'It is so very large.' She caressed the padlock and insinuated her finger into the keyhole.

'Dangerous substances,' I said. 'Chemicals.'

The child seemed satisfied with my answer.

'Come, Annette,' said her mother, 'you have an English lesson with Mademoiselle Drouart and we mustn't keep her waiting.' Annette moved, but her hand seemed to linger on the lid, delaying her departure, for a brief moment before she succeeded in pulling away.

Hélène regained my attention. 'Will you be dining with us tonight, monsieur?'

'No. I intend to retire early.'

'As you wish, monsieur.'

I stood at the doorway, watching Hélène and Annette as they walked through the library. Even then, as my thoughts raced, I could not stop myself from admiring Hélène's figure and her graceful carriage. When they had reached the astronomical globes, I called out, 'Annette.' Mother and daughter stopped and turned to face me. 'Annette, would you come here, please.' I beckoned, and the girl returned. Lowering my voice, I asked, 'Annette, have you been talking to your uncle Tristan about what's in my chest?' She shook her head. 'Perhaps you were playing some sort of guessing game?' Again she shook her head. I smiled and added, 'Oh, I forgot to give you this.' I produced a boiled sweet from my waistcoat. 'Thank you, monsieur,' she said, before running back to her mother.

When Hélène saw what I had given Annette, she cried, 'You spoil her!'

I made a gesture, communicating my helpless affection for the child. Mother and daughter performed a pleasing synchronous revolution and marched into the shadowy antechamber. I needed to think and decided to go outside for a stroll.

Chambault did not possess a single large garden, but a number of relatively small gardens, all exquisite examples of the horticulturalist's art: intimate, scented spaces in which to sit and meditate or find solace in beauty. I crossed the courtyard and walked out into the Garden of the Senses, a system of concentric perennial beds rippling out from a central fountain, and from there entered directly into the Garden of Healing – a favourite haven of mine, planted with medicinal herbs. Sitting on a bench beneath a willow tree, I inhaled the calming fragrances. The sun was setting and the pale turrets of the chateau turned pink in the pastel light. I did not move until the sky had darkened and some precocious stars had appeared above one of the conical roofs.

On my return, I informed Madame Boustagnier that I was ready to dine, and a tray was brought to my rooms: an omelette, some bread, a dish of strawberries and a bottle of fruit brandy. As I ate, I was troubled by a peculiar sense of having stumbled across some important fact, but I was unable to say what it was, exactly. This feeling seemed to be connected, in an obscure way, with Doriac's eggs. When I had finished eating, I took off my collar and waistcoat and lay on the divan. For over an hour, I smoked and stared at the chest, trying to persuade myself that the curiosity expressed by both Raboulet and Annette concerning the contents was nothing more than a bizarre coincidence.

Raising myself up, I went over to the table and lit another candle. It was then that I noticed something different. I went down on my knees, and saw a line on the floor, just to the left of the chest. On closer inspection, I realized that the line was created by an edge of dust. The cause was obvious: dust had collected around the chest, and the chest had been moved approximately four centimetres to the right. There were no scratches on the floorboards. The chest was a very heavy object, made from solid oak, trimmed with brass, and lined with lead: the underside was reinforced with iron plates. When I arrived at Chambault, six powerful men were needed to carry it up the stairs. Although the chest had been displaced by a relatively small distance, this could not have been the result of an accidental knock, and nobody in the chateau was strong enough to push it. I was overcome by a feeling of dark foreboding – cold, obstinate dread.

For several hours I paced around the room, before going down on my knees yet again to examine the line of dust. No matter how many times I looked at it, I was obliged to reach the same conclusion. The chest had moved. I retired to my bed, but did not fall asleep for several hours. When finally I drifted off, I dreamed of Madame Boustagnier in the kitchen: a residue of memory from the previous day. She was inspecting one of Doriac's eggs, just as she had in real life. Once again, I heard her say, 'It's cracked.' Her voice sounded so loudly that I awoke. The meaning of the dream was all too apparent. Now I understood the cause of that insistent nagging feeling, of having encountered some important but unidentifiable piece of information. I imagined the pitch-black interior of the chest – a flaw in the glass, a hairline crack, spreading. My heart was beating wildly in my ears. I would have to open the chest to assess the damage, for that was the only explanation. It hadn't been opened in over a year, and the prospect of doing so filled me with horror.

17

I came upon Odile Du Bris just as she was leaving the chapel. A veil covered her face and a wrinkled hand clutched Louis' forearm for support. On hearing my approach, she looked up and said, 'Ah, Monsieur Clément. Do you have a moment?' She dismissed Louis with an imperious gesture and permitted me to escort her back inside. The space we entered was roughly circular and dominated by an ancient plaster altarpiece. The relief figures and ornamentation were crudely executed and painted in faded reds and gold. In front of the altar was a small table, entirely covered in blue brocade, on which rested an open prayer book. The deep, rounded depressions in the well-worn hassock showed where two protruding kneecaps were frequently accommodated.

Odile Du Bris lowered herself onto a chair and indicated that I should close the door. I performed the task and stood before her, my hands clasped behind my back. She looked me up and down and then said, 'Did Hélène invite you to the service, monsieur?'

'Yes,' I replied.

'You did not come.'

'No.'

She took a deep breath and expressed her disapproval with a lengthy sigh. Then, lifting her veil, she fixed me with a cold stare.

'How is my granddaughter?'

'Very well, madame.'

Odile's expression softened slightly and she fussed with her lace shawl. 'I worry about her.'

'There is no need to be unduly concerned.'

'She doesn't act her age,' Odile sneered. 'She doesn't comport herself as a young woman should.'

'Madame, she is only—'

'She talks nonsense about fairies and goes about as if she is in a dream. It is not right, monsieur.'

'Annette is very imaginative – a thoughtful child. It is her nature.'

'Thoughtful, monsieur? There is a difference between thinking and wool-gathering.' I did not want to argue with the old woman. When she spoke again, her voice was less confident and trembled slightly with emotion. 'You must make Annette better, monsieur. You must.' Her eyes moistened and she pretended to adjust her veil. When she had completed the manoeuvre she allowed the gauze to drop in front of her face. She was a proud woman and it was all too easy to forget her age and infirmity. I took a step forward and rested my hand on hers for a fleeting moment, just enough to communicate that I was aware of her distress, and then withdrew. Odile nodded and assumed her stiff attitude. When she spoke again, there was metal in her voice. 'I never approved of the marriage. But my son is headstrong. Had his father been alive . . .' She straightened her back, and drew obvious satisfaction from some imaginary scenario. A half-smile appeared and then faded as reality reasserted itself on her senses. 'There's something in their blood,' she added with contempt.

'I'm sorry?'

'The Raboulets. Look at Annette's uncle.' She shook her head. 'And there were others. Old Raboulet was just the same.'

'It is quite true, madame, that there are certain constitutional vulnerabilities that can be passed down from generation to generation. But if a condition can be managed, then individuals so afflicted can expect to live a full and happy life.'

Odile snorted. 'Annette will not be a child forever. What hope is there for the girl when she reaches maturity? She's not far off it! How many suitors can we expect?' Odile pushed out her chin defiantly. 'A good match with a local family is out of the question. Even if we send her to Paris, enquiries will be made and, I can assure you, people talk. If she could only be more sensible, more womanly, at least then there might be a chance.'

'Your granddaughter is kind and has many endearing qualities. There is nothing deficient in her make-up. Indeed, in many respects, I think she exhibits sensitivity and intelligence in advance of her years.'

Odile tutted and looked away. 'Monsieur. Would you be kind enough to call Louis?'

A filigree candelabrum had been placed on the altar next to some pots of dried lavender. The air was laden with scent and the light that passed through the stained-glass windows created pools of amber on the flag stones. I had been dismissed.

I passed from the Garden of Healing into the Garden of Intelligence, a delightful assortment of yellow and blue blossoms surrounded by pergolas of rose and humming-bird vine. The path led me to an uneven staircase which I climbed until the Garden of Silence came into view: a rectangular lawn, contained by low box hedges, with a Roman urn standing on a pedestal at its centre. Beyond the terraces which dropped away at my feet, the cor-belled turrets of the chateau emitted a warm glow in the early light, as if the sun's rays were being refracted through honey. I inhaled the morning air, which was cool and fragrant with lilac and the white chocolate undertow of clematis. A pallid wafer moon floated above the chim-ney stacks, more like a recollection, a thing imagined, than another world.

As I walked around the Garden of Silence, I felt strangely cleansed and began to feel more hopeful. There was no need to act rashly. Perhaps it was a temporary phenomenon. I should be patient and review the situa-tion pending further developments; if there were none, it would be wise to leave the chest alone. The death of the Doriac girl had probably upset me more than I had realized. Attempting an electrical resuscitation had been ill-judged. Undertaking the procedure was bound to bring back bad memories. I should have left the battery in the cupboard and allowed the girl to die naturally. The whole episode had unsettled me.

On returning to my rooms, I enjoyed a breakfast of freshly baked rolls, fruit conserve and a brackish, aromatic coffee of exceptional strength. The walk had sharpened my appetite and I ate with relish. I spent the remainder of the morning in the library reading Montaigne, most notably, his essay titled 'How our Mind Tangles itself Up'.

It occurred to me that I had spent most of the year either cooped up in the library or riding around the estate. Perhaps it would be appropriate for me to spend some time away from Chambault? Raboulet and Annette had not had any seizures in over six months and I broached the subject with Du Bris.

'How long will you be absent?' he asked.

'A week or so,' I replied.

He turned his palms outwards and smiled. 'That seems perfectly reasonable. Where are you going?'

I heard myself reply: 'Chinon.'

18

Louis drove me to the village and it was there that I caught the diligence. The journey was not arduous and I glimpsed Chinon for the first time in the late afternoon. It was an impressive sight, ramparts and towers on a low ridge, the pale stone blushing as clouds passed in front of the sun. The approach road was well maintained and the vehicle made very good progress. Within minutes of crossing the river Vienne I was standing in the market square.

It was relatively easy to find an inn. I was shown a room which, although not spacious, was comfortably appointed and, after a short rest, I ordered some bread and cheese. This I ate outside, beneath a canopy of bright red flowers. I then went for a stroll.

The crooked medieval streets were mostly deserted. Apart from an old woman sitting in a doorway and a mangy stray dog, I saw no other living creature. I turned off the main thoroughfare and ascended a steep cobbled path that rose higher and higher until it reached the town's lofty fortress. From this vantage point the view was quite spectacular. I gazed south, over a patchwork of rooftops and timbered gables, beyond the river, where fields and vineyards rolled away to the shimmering horizon.

'She is down there', I thought to myself. 'Somewhere.'

The impulse that had made me travel to Chinon was obscure. I wasn't wholly sure what I was doing there. Of course, there were superficial justifications – reconnaissance, information-gathering, testing my nerve – all of them quite ridiculous. In reality, I wanted to find Thérèse and tell her how much I loved her. I wanted to take her in my arms, feel her warmth and touch my lips against her hair. I hoped that when she looked into my eyes she would see the torment, anguish and remorse, recognize my plight and take pity on me. Even though I could no longer believe in an all-knowing, all-powerful God of love, I was still prepared to believe in love itself. In a universe without certainties, love had become my rock, my pole star, my still centre. Love was all that I had left.

Over the next few days – I cannot remember how many – I wandered the streets, anxious, expectant, my heart racing whenever I saw a woman in the distance. One evening, and one evening only, I drank myself into a stupor. When I awoke the following morning I went to the post office, but a headache prevented me from making the relevant enquiries. Instead, I sat in a cafe, where I overheard two men talking about market day. Later, I asked the waiter on which day of the week market day fell, and he replied, 'Thursday.'

In a town the size of Chinon, all of the inhabitants

would be out on market day, buying provisions, gossiping, meeting friends. She would be there: a tall, well-dressed woman, conspicuous among the hoi polloi, moving from stall to stall, graceful, poised. The image persisted in my mind like a premonition.

I slept badly on Wednesday night and when I awoke on Thursday morning I felt agitated and fearful. Breakfast was served in my room but I hardly touched it. I went to the market square early and watched the stallholders laying out their produce and wares. People began to arrive, money changed hands and acquaintances gathered together in small noisy groups. I circulated around the square, studying the merchandise: wicker baskets, glazed pottery, brightly painted plates, goat's cheese, cured meats, quince jelly, pickled samphire, almonds and prunes stuffed with marzipan. A gypsy was trying to sell a piebald horse. One of the stalls was covered with a chaotic jumble of household items and I caught sight of myself in an oval shaving mirror. I looked unkempt, even disreputable. How would Thérèse react if she saw me like this? I straightened my hat and tried to look calm and dignified.

A mass of dark cloud was building overhead and the temperature began to drop. I had been patrolling the market for over an hour and was about to give up, when the crowd parted and I saw a gentleman dressed in a brown jacket and trousers. His skin was tanned and he sported a large bushy moustache. He was holding the hand of a child. Although the boy had grown, I recognized Philippe immediately. For a moment, I froze, but then I stepped forward and, making a show of glad surprise exclaimed, 'Philippe. Good heavens! Philippe, my dear little friend! Do you remember me?' The boy's expression remained blank, so I continued, 'Surely you remember me!' I then offered the old gentleman my hand, which he shook with unexpected firmness.

'Monsieur Arnoult. And you are?'

'Monsieur Clément.' I paused to see if the name meant anything to him, then added, 'I was a colleague of Philippe's father.'

'A doctor?'

'I worked with Henri at the Salpêtrière. Dear Henri; he is sorely missed.' I narrowed my eyes and looked from Arnoult to the boy, and back again. 'You must be Philippe's grandfather – on his mother's side?'

'Yes,' Arnoult replied. 'That is correct.'

'And how is Madame Courbertin?' I asked, attempting to sound natural, but my voice came out strained and hoarse.

Arnoult winced and stroked Philippe's hair. 'Not very well, I'm afraid.'

'Nothing serious, I hope.'

'Unfortunately, she is very ill.'

'Very ill?' I repeated. 'What is she suffering from? I do not wish to pry, monsieur. I only ask in order to establish if I might be of service.'

Arnoult turned Philippe towards a knot of gabbling women. 'Go and help your grandmother.' The boy ran off and the old man readied himself to answer my question. 'She had a condition, a stomach complaint, and took morphine to control the pain. Unfortunately, she was not very good at regulating her medicine and often took more than was good for her. Our doctor, Monsieur Perrot, tried to get her to reduce the amount she was taking, but this proved very difficult. She had temper tantrums, bad dreams and screamed like a mad woman in the night. The boy was terrified.' Arnoult shook his head. 'We couldn't go on like that. It was impossible. My daughter resumed her habit and became weaker and weaker. Her heart is not strong.'

There was a rumble of thunder and it started to rain. The people around us began to scatter.

'I am sorry,' I whispered.

'You knew her well?'

'Yes,' I replied. 'Henri was very good to me.'

'What was your name again?'

'Clément. Paul Clément.' It still meant nothing to him.

Philippe was standing next to his grandmother. She indicated her intention to find somewhere to shelter by placing a hand over her head.

'Excuse me, monsieur,' said Arnoult, 'I must go.' He advanced a few steps and then stopped. Looking back, he said, 'We live by the river.' He recited an address. 'If your business detains you in Chinon . . .'

'Thank you. I would very much like to see her again.'

'Then come this afternoon,' said Arnoult. 'I would appreciate a second opinion.'

Arnoult pressed his hat down to ensure that it would stay on and hurried off in pursuit of his wife and grandson.

At one o'clock I walked to the embankment and followed the river until I came to a house that was set back from the road. It was a substantial property with peeling paintwork and faded green shutters. I rang the bell and the door was opened by Arnoult, who invited me in and introduced me to his wife. Madame Arnoult was a handsome woman with strong, regular features. Her smile was an exact copy of Thérèse's.

'How is she?' I asked.

'Not good,' Arnoult replied. 'Her condition has deteriorated. We called Monsieur Perrot when we got back from the market. He is with her now.'

I ascended a staircase and was shown into a musty bedroom. When I saw Thérèse, my legs gave way and I would have fallen to the floor had not the old man grabbed my arm. 'Monsieur?'

'I'm all right,' I said, 'I'm sorry.'

He released his grip. The woman lying beneath the eiderdown was hardly recognizable as my beloved Thérèse. Shadows gathered where I expected to see her eyes, and her angular jaw bone defined the precise limit of her chin. Her skull was too present, too eager for exposure. She was wasting away.

Arnoult drew my attention to a middle-aged gentleman standing by the window. 'Monsieur Perrot,' he said. I nodded, moved to the bedside and sat on a wooden chair. Lifting Thérèse's limp hand, I noticed that her fingers were blue. I was vaguely aware of Arnoult continuing: 'Monsieur Clément was a colleague of Henri, they worked together at the Salpêtrière.'

'Thérèse,' I whispered. 'Thérèse. It's Paul. Can you hear me?'

Perrot came forward. 'She lost consciousness an hour ago.'

Arnoult spoke again. 'Monsieur Perrot? Monsieur Clément? Something to drink?'

'An anisette,' said Perrot, 'mixed with water.'

'And you, Monsieur Clément?'

I looked up. 'Nothing for me, thank you.'

Arnoult left the room and Perrot asked me if I had been informed of Thérèse's medical history.

'Her father mentioned morphine,' I replied.

Perrot lowered his voice. 'She had a long-standing addiction. The old man thinks that it all started with a stomach complaint.' He shook his head. 'I did everything I could to get her off it, but without success. She has been very ill for several months now. Very ill.' He tapped a stuttering rhythm over his heart and looked at me knowingly. 'She saw a cardiologist in Tours. He wasn't very optimistic.'

Thérèse coughed and emitted a low groan. Her lips were cracked and a white residue had collected in the corners of her mouth.

'Do the family know?' I asked.

'I think Arnoult understands. I'm not sure whether his wife does.' Perrot removed his stethoscope. 'Were you close?'

'Yes,' I replied, turning away to conceal my grief. 'We mixed in the same circles – in Paris.'

'Poor Philippe,' Perrot continued. 'First his father, then his mother. Dreadful.'

Arnoult returned and handed Perrot his anisette. The doctor drank it while making some bland remarks, before picking up his leather bag. 'Well, I must be on my way. Madame Musard has a fever and I promised to see her again.' Looking over at Thérèse, he added, 'I'll be back as soon as I can. Stay where you are, Arnoult, I'll see myself out.' We listened to Perrot descending the stairs and the front door opening and closing.

'What do you think?' asked Arnoult. 'Is there any hope?' I couldn't answer him. My throat was too tight. Arnoult sighed and said, 'I thought as much.' He sat on the opposite side of the bed and bowed his head. After a few minutes, he stirred and said, 'Why Chinon, monsieur? What brings you to our town?'

I told him a little of my circumstances and said that I was taking a short holiday. He then asked me some questions about my life in Paris and I exaggerated how well I had known Henri. Arnoult's questions were innocent enough, but he clearly found it curious that his daughter had never mentioned me. I found the pretence tiring and wanted Arnoult to leave. I wanted to be alone with Thérèse.

It was an overcast day, and by mid-afternoon the room was quite dark. Arnoult lit some candles and then dozed off. He was relieved by his wife, who took his place. She asked me the very same questions and I repeated identical falsehoods. Perrot returned at eight o'clock and undertook another examination. He offered me his stethoscope and I was obliged to listen to the irregular beat of Thérèse's heart.

I remembered our apartment in Saint-Germain: the shadow of my hand on her back, her rasping as my fingers closed. Was this my fault too?

When Perrot left the room I could not restrain myself any longer. I wrapped my arms around Thérèse's neck and sobbed into her lank hair, 'I'm so sorry – so very, very sorry.' She felt flimsy, insubstantial, and I feared that if I handled her too roughly her ribs might snap. Withdrawing a little, I kissed her forehead and then her lips. 'Please forgive me,' I pleaded.

There were footsteps on the landing. I quickly found my handkerchief and wiped away my tears, but this clumsy attempt to hide my emotion proved futile. My voice was thick and my eyes were still prickling. Arnoult's expression was sympathetic, but I also detected a hint of suspicion.

'Would you like something to eat?' he asked.

'It is kind of you to offer,' I replied. 'But no, thank you. Perhaps I should go now. I do not wish to intrude.'

Madame Arnoult arrived with Philippe. She guided the sad-looking boy around the bed and said, 'Say goodnight to your mother, child.' Philippe planted a kiss on Thérèse's cheek and recited a touching prayer – an entreaty to the Blessed Virgin.

As he was leaving I stopped him and made him stand squarely in front of me. 'Philippe, your mother is very ill, and she has not been well for a long time. Illness changes people. But we will remember her how she was, when she was healthy and happy. She loves you, Philippe. She told me so on many occasions. She loves you more than any-thing – anything in this world.' I let him go and his grandmother took his hand. At the door, he paused, and said, 'Goodnight, monsieur.' But there was no warmth in his voice.

When Philippe and his grandmother had departed I sat in silence with Arnoult until the sky turned black. The old man drew the curtains and I said, 'May I come tomorrow?'

'If you wish,' he replied.

The following morning Thérèse was no longer at peace. She was in an agitated state, plucking the eider-down and mumbling. Occasionally, her eyes would open, but she registered nothing. Her fingers were freezing and I rubbed them incessantly to keep them warm.

Perrot appeared just before noon.

'She's uncomfortable,' he said. 'I think she needs sedation.' He gave me the opportunity to object, but he was her physician and I did not want to interfere.

Hours passed. I went for a walk and returned when it started to rain. Madame Arnoult had prepared a meal for her husband and Philippe. I did not join them, knowing that while they ate together I could be alone once more with Thérèse.

She was lying very still and her breathing was shallow. Quite suddenly, her eyes opened and she seemed to focus on me. I clasped her hand. 'Thérèse,' I cried. 'It's me, Paul. Do you see me? Oh, Thérèse, my darling, how I love you: how I love you! ' I saw the light of recognition flare in her eyes. Then surprise turned to fear. She was terrified. Beneath my thumb, I felt the last movement of blood in her veins. Her eyes remained open, but she was dead.

I sat on the embankment indifferent to the downpour. The surface of the water became choppy as an unseasonably cold wind gained strength. I remembered the demon's prediction: Thérèse would die and it would have the pleasure of tasting her blood in hell.

Father Ranvier and Bazile had insisted that this vile taunt signified nothing, but they had clearly underestimated the demon's power.

I stayed out until nightfall and, after returning to the inn, I slept in my wet clothes. The next morning I caught the diligence back to the village. My muscles ached and I shivered all the way. I paid a farmer to take me to the chateau in a trap, and on my arrival went straight to bed. Although the weather was now perfectly pleasant, the sheets felt like ice and my teeth chattered. Louis came to see if I wished to dine with the family, but I was feverish and by that time quite unwell. Raboulet came up after dinner to see if I needed anything, but I sent him away.

'I have an infection,' I said. 'I should be left alone.'

'But you must eat,' Raboulet protested.

'Get Madame Boustagnier to leave some bread and water outside my door. That will suffice for now. If I need more I will call Louis.'

I was burning and my mouth felt as if it had been packed with hot ashes. Even after taking salicin my temperature remained perilously high and my mind was invaded by vivid memories and epic nightmares. I saw myself handing Thérèse an enamel syringe and saying, 'For you: a special gift.' I saw a funeral cortège marching solemnly behind a white coffin carried by leering demons and I saw Thérèse trailing torn cerements, wandering vulnerably across the fiery expanses of hell. It is impossible for me to describe my misery. I wept and wept until I seemed to have no substance.

The illness lasted for two weeks, after which I began to feel a little stronger. One day, towards the end, I awoke to find Annette sitting next to my bed.

'What are you doing here, child?' I asked.

'I came to see you,' she replied.

'Please. You must leave now or you will become unwell too. Does your mother know you are here?'

'No. She told me that I shouldn't come.'

'Then you had better go before she notices that you are missing.'

'It isn't right.'

'What isn't right?'

'You being here, all on your own.'

'I am perfectly happy.'

'No. I don't think so. I think you are sad.' She pointed to a glass on my bedside cabinet. 'I have made you a hot sugar and lemon drink. Madame Boustagnier said that it is good for chills.' She stood and pressed her cool palm against my forehead. Imitating my attitude and manner she said, 'Yes, a definite improvement.'

'Clean your hands before you leave,' I said with stern emphasis.

Annette walked over to my washstand and poured some water. Dipping her fingers in the bowl, she said, 'Are you very ill, monsieur?'

'No. Not very ill.'

'Good. I prayed for you in the chapel. I prayed that you would not die.'

'Thank you. That was most considerate.'

'Why does God listen to some prayers and not to others?'

'I don't know. Perhaps you should ask the curé.'

She considered this advice and then said, 'Yes. Perhaps I should.' After drying her hands she walked to the door. Her movement was so smooth it seemed to arise in the absence of any friction. 'Don't forget your drink, monsieur.'

'No,' I replied. 'I won't.'

She raised her hand, her expression coy.

'Goodbye, Annette. And thank you.'

I listened to her steps receding and when she was gone, for the first time since my return from Chinon I was aware of the birds singing outside my window.

My recovery was slow. A month later I was still quite weak; however, my old routine was eventually re-established. I monitored Annette and Raboulet's health, administered medicines, went riding by the river and read late into the night. But I was not the same man. I was altered. Something of my former self had died that day in Chinon: something essential, something that would never again be revived. A particular image suggested itself when I reflected on my inner desolation: my heart, shrivelled up like the head of a dead rose.

On the days when I was feeling more robust, I would go on lengthy excursions up into the hills where the cave-dwellers lived. They were poor farming folk who had created homes for themselves by digging into the soft tufa cliffs. Their infants were often sick and many would have died without my care. Why was I doing this? It is difficult to say. But if I had any reason at all, it was simply to spite God.

19

SEPTEMBER 1881

Mademoiselle Drouart had entered the antechamber and I saw her hesitating on the threshold of the library. She was about to knock on the door jamb when I called out, 'Please, mademoiselle. Do come in.'

Her heavy heels sounded loudly on the floor as she marched towards me.

'Good morning, monsieur.'

'Good morning, Mademoiselle Drouart.' I drew a chair out from under the table and the governess sat down. She was young and in possession of a flawless complexion, yet she was habitually serious and had a tendency to frown. Her chestnut hair was tied back and she wore a pair of spectacles that made her look like a spinster. She was carrying a portfolio. I took the seat opposite and noticed her stealing a quick glance at the book I had been reading.

'I am sorry to disturb you, monsieur, but I need to tell you something. It concerns Annette.' She placed the portfolio on the table, untied the ribbon and opened it out. 'Yesterday, we drove down to the village in order to make some drawings of the church.' Sorting through the loose papers, she selected a few for my consideration: pencil and charcoal sketches of Saint-Catherine's steeple, executed in a free hand and rich in detail. Mademoiselle Drouart registered my tacit appreciation and added, 'I think Annette must have inherited some of her mother's talent.'

'It would certainly seem that way, mademoiselle.'

'She is quite accomplished,' said the governess, 'which is why I felt it necessary to speak with you.' She offered no further clarification so I gestured for her to continue. 'In our lessons, I have always stressed the importance of being true to the eye. Paint what you see. That is what I say, and that is exactly what Annette does. However, yesterday, she introduced something into her sketches that wasn't really there. Now, if her brothers did this I would think nothing of it, but where Annette is concerned, I am mindful of her condition.' Mademoiselle Drouart selected two more sketches from the portfolio and pushed them across the table. I saw what she meant immediately. The spire of Saint-Catherine rises out of a square tower, and leaning over the indented parapet was a figure in silhouette – a winged creature with horns projecting from its head. I did not respond and Mademoiselle Drouart, assuming I had not identified the aberration, added helpfully, 'The gargoyle, monsieur. There is no such thing. Yet, it appears in all of the sketches Annette made while looking up at the steeple from the south side of the church.' More pictures appeared in front of me, all showing the same winged figure. 'There are two gargoyles at the rear of the church, but these are quite different from the one shown here. They are simple and stylized. Unembellished. Clearly, Annette has not confused them. When Annette used to have seizures, a few days before, she would sometimes refer to people and objects that I could not see. I wondered whether the gargoyle in these sketches represents something similar, something medically significant.'

I rubbed my chin and attempted to remain calm.

'Did you talk to her about it?'

'No. I wanted to seek your opinion first. I didn't want to berate her for something over which she has no control.'

'Very wise, mademoiselle.'

'Nor have I said anything to Madame Du Bris. I did not wish to worry her unnecessarily.'

'You are most considerate, mademoiselle.' I searched one of the drawers and found a cigar. In order to conceal my trembling hand, I turned away as I lit it. 'Annette is an imaginative child, mademoiselle, and even though she has not, to date, been inclined to introduce imaginary elements into her drawings, it is, I daresay, the most likely explanation. Her condition has been controlled for many months and I have not noticed anything that would lead me to conclude that she is about to have another seizure. Even so, one can never be too careful, and I am most grateful that you have brought these sketches to my attention.' I drew on the cigar and continued, 'I might give her an additional infusion tomorrow. Just to be on the safe side. It is in my nature to err on the side of caution.'

'What should I do with these?' The governess traced an arc in the air over Annette's drawings.

'Could I keep them?'

'Certainly.' Mademoiselle Drouart stood and, glancing at my book again, said, 'Ah, Montaigne, he is such good company. I am very fond of his essay on the education of children.' She took off her spectacles and, wiping the lenses clean with a starched handkerchief, quoted the great essayist: 'Only fools have made up their minds and are certain.'

'Indeed,' I replied. 'In life, the correct course of action is rarely obvious.'

She placed her spectacles back on her nose, smiled and said, 'Good day, monsieur.'

I bowed my head and remained in that position, looking down at my shoes. Outside, two birds started a fitful chirruping that became increasingly fluid until the library was filled with their song – a melodious duet of startling complexity.

After lunch, I saddled up one of the horses and rode to the village. Saint-Catherine's spire came into view long before I reached the market square and I immediately began to feel anxious. I knew already that I would find nothing there to alleviate my fears, but I kept going, nevertheless. Having travelled so far, I was reluctant to abandon hope entirely. The main road, which passed through the centre of the village, was empty, and most of the houses had their shutters closed. I dismounted, and a cloud of white dust rose up as my feet hit the ground. I proceeded directly to the church, where I took one of Annette's drawings from my pocket. Shading my eyes, I looked upwards, and compared her artwork with the original. There were no gargoyles leaning over the parapet, nor was there anything that might be mistaken for a gargoyle. I walked around the tower in order to view it from several different perspectives, but the architectural lines remained stubbornly simple. There wasn't even the consolation of a mysterious shadow.

My legs felt weak and I made my way unsteadily across the square to the inn. The door had been left open and, when I stepped inside, it took a few seconds for my eyes to adapt. Fleuriot was washing glasses and his only customers were Pailloux and a young man with sharp features whom I did not recognize.

'Good day, monsieur,' said Fleuriot.

Pailloux turned around, revealing his red swollen nose and saluted me. His companion grinned.

I ordered an anisette and sat at the counter. As Fleuriot prepared my drink he said, 'Have you seen the gypsies, monsieur?'

'No.'

'They're back again: camped out by the river. If you go up the hill,' he jabbed his thumb backwards, 'you can

271

see their caravans. One of them came here this morning – big fellow, as brown as a berry – carrying an enormous pair of scissors. He went around all the houses asking the women if they'd sell him their hair.'

I must have looked puzzled because Pailloux called out, 'Wigs, monsieur. The gypsies collect sackloads of hair and take it north. The wigmakers offer a good price.'

There then followed a conversation about irregular transactions, during which Pailloux claimed to have known a man who was once offered a diamond in exchange for his teeth by a dentist. The young man was suddenly distracted by something outside and, reaching over the table, he pinched Pailloux's sleeve. With a discreet nod he directed the drunk to look through the window. My curiosity was aroused and I shifted position to get a better view. Du Bris was standing in front of the church, talking to a woman.

'Oh, he's a bold one,' muttered Pailloux. 'Look at him – in broad daylight too.'

'That's enough,' said Fleuriot.

Pailloux shrugged, 'What difference does it make?' The young man continued to grin inanely. 'It's hardly a secret any more.'

I looked at Fleuriot inquisitively and he waved his hand in a manner to indicate that I should take no notice. The drunk went on. 'Some men are never satisfied. It's not as if his wife isn't a beauty.'

'Pailloux!' Fleuriot's voice had hardened.

'What?' asked the drunk.

'Enough!' Turning to address me, Fleuriot added, 'I'm sorry, monsieur,' and then quickly changed the subject. The atmosphere thereafter was somewhat strained.

I finished my anisette and when I walked out into the sunlight there was no sign of Du Bris. Both he and the woman he had been talking to were gone. Before leaving the village, I took one last look at the church, then mounted my horse and rode back to the chateau.

As I entered the courtyard Hélène Du Bris was coming out of the kitchen, carrying a basket full of fruit.

'Ah Monsieur Clément!' she exclaimed, 'You have returned. Why don't you come and join us? We're sitting by the cherry tree.'

'Thank you,' I replied, 'that is most kind.'

I left the horse with the stable boy, brushed my jacket and walked through the Garden of the Senses. Massive purple flowers shaped like the bells of trumpets blocked my path, and a swarm of pale blue butterflies flew in all directions as I pushed the blooms aside. The air smelled of citronella. I made my way through the fragrant jungle and stepped out onto the lawn. Raboulet was lying on the grass, reading a book, and his wife Sophie was marching up and down, trying to get their infant to sleep. Hélène was sitting at her easel, painting, and Annette was standing next to Odile, passing her slices of fruit. When I reached the cherry tree, greetings were exchanged, and Hélène offered me the vacant chair at her side.

'Where are the boys?' I asked.

'With Mademoiselle Drouart. She has taken them up into the forest.'

I leaned forward to examine Hélène's watercolour. The subject was one of the moss-covered cherubs spaced at regular intervals around the edge of the lawn. I glanced from her reproduction to the original and was impressed by how she had managed to duplicate the various shades of green.

'You are a fine colourist,' I said.

With typical modesty, she responded, 'The light is very favourable today. Would you like some fruit?'

'Thank you.'

Hélène addressed her daughter, 'Annette: Monsieur Clément would like some fruit.' Annette picked up a basket – the one I had seen Hélène carrying on my return from the village – and brought it to me. She tilted the rim, revealing an assortment of apples, grapes and pears. I took an apple and Annette returned to her grandmother.

The sun was low and bright. On the other side of the lawn a wild cat was stalking lizards.

'One of the fountains has stopped working,' said Hélène.

'Has it?' I responded.

'Yes. Monsieur Boustagnier says that there must be an obstruction.'

'Will he be able to undertake repairs?'

'Not without digging up the Garden of Intelligence.'

Our conversation about the fountains became more general, and before long Hélène was enthusing about a new project. There was a field behind the Garden of Silence that was rather wasted – a large area of weeds and wild flowers. She was thinking of building a maze on it. 'I have always been peculiarly fascinated by mazes,' she said, emphasizing the cherub's capricious disposition with a skilful touch of her brush. 'Perhaps my father is to blame. He had a great love of Greek myths and when I was a child he often repeated the story of Theseus, the hero who ventured into the great labyrinth and killed the minotaur.'

'Yes, mazes are indeed fascinating,' I mused. 'They have about them a delightful air of mystery; however, I am inclined to believe that their universal appeal owes much to their symbolic significance.' Hélène gestured for me to continue. 'Consider how we negotiate a maze: we set off on a journey, not quite sure where we are going. We choose to go this way or that way, up here or down there. Some of our choices are good, others bad. Sometimes we progress towards our goal, but we are frequently frustrated or get lost. It seems to me that mazes are very much like life itself.'

Hélène turned to face me and I saw that my comments had unsettled her. She looked sad, distraught. 'That is so very true, monsieur. We make decisions without knowing what lies before us and we are obliged to accept the consequences. There is no way out.' Her eyes moistened. 'Is it any wonder that . . .' She stopped herself and seemed embarrassed.

To save her from further embarrassment, I gallantly pretended that I had just remembered something important: in fact, a trivial costing error on a pharmacist's invoice. The ruse worked and Hélène's customary good humour was restored; however, I could not help but connect her sudden emotion with Pailloux's indiscreet remarks. The thought of her being wronged made me feel quite angry, but there was nothing to be done. It was not my place to intervene with respect to such a private matter.

Our conversation petered out and my thoughts returned to Annette. She seemed no different: still the same girl, the same innocent creature whose smile was perhaps the last thing in the world that could raise the ghost of my lost humanity. I watched her closely, saw her straighten Odile's blanket without fuss, such that her little ministration went completely without notice – which of course was her intention. Once again, I succumbed to the seductive comforts of self-deception. 'Yes', I said to myself. 'One must not jump to conclusions. The drawing of the gargoyle might well be a pathological phenomenon, the result of a freak electrical discharge in the brain.' But I was soon to be shaken out of my idiotic complacency.

Odile had been telling Annette stories from the Bible, most of which included examples of divine retribution on a grand scale: plagues, floods, the destruction of cities. Presumably, the old woman's purpose was to instil in her granddaughter some of her own God-fearing piety.

Odile's noisome monologue was interrupted when she paused to take some refreshment. Annette lifted the fruit basket and Odile detached some lustrous grapes from an already half-eaten bunch. It was then that Annette said, 'Could God create a stone so large and heavy that he could not lift it?'

The old woman answered with irritation, 'What sort of question is that, child?'

Annette was puzzled by her grandmother's response. 'You said that God is all-powerful.'

'Well, so he is! He can do anything!'

'But if he made a stone that he could not lift, he would no longer be all-powerful. It would be something that he could not do.'

'Don't be foolish, child!'

'Actually,' Raboulet set his book aside and sat up, 'that is an extremely interesting question.'

'Tristan!' Hélène threw a cautionary glance in her brother's direction, but he was not discouraged.

'No, really. It's rather clever. What do you think, Monsieur Clément?' He winked mischievously. 'Could God create a stone that he could not lift?'

'It is a question that has troubled theologians for many centuries', I replied. 'What made you think of such a thing, Annette?'

'I don't know,' she replied. 'It just came into my head.'

'In which case,' the old woman scolded, 'you should think more carefully before opening your mouth.'

Raboulet ignored Odile and said, 'Are you serious, Clément? Have theologians really considered this question.'

'Yes. It is sometimes referred to as the omnipotence paradox.'

'And what did these wise men conclude?'

'They concluded that the question is invalid.'

'Well,' he said, smirking, 'I can see why. The question seems to admit only two possible answers, both of which are rather disconcerting,' he paused and added under his breath, 'for believers.'

'Enough of this talk,' said Odile, glaring at Raboulet. 'The child is already confused enough. She should not be encouraged to ask absurd questions.'

Raboulet inclined his head, 'My apologies, madame. You are quite right. Thinking too much never did anyone any good – particularly young women.' His sarcasm was lost on Odile, who raised her chin, inflated her chest and engaged in some self-satisfied preening.

That night I could not sleep. I got up and walked through the gardens. Monsieur Boustagnier had suspended rocks from the almond trees and they knocked together as I passed. These weights bent the branches and made them produce more fruits.

Annette had wanted to know what I kept in my wooden chest. Then she had seen a gargoyle on the church. And now, one of the most problematic questions known to the medieval church had simply popped into her mind. I could no longer deny that something very strange was happening.

The world turns and we move from light into darkness, from darkness into light. With light comes warmth, with darkness, cold. Everything that lives and breathes depends on the light for its continued existence. All growth is stunted by darkness. When light is plentiful, the earth is fertile, but when light is scarce, the winter months bring death and corruption. From the earliest times, light has been associated with good, darkness with evil.

I had made my decision. The chest in my study could only be opened during the day, and preferably when the light was at its strongest. To attempt to open it at night would be folly. I went to the kitchen and informed Madame Boustagnier that I did not require lunch, and on my return bolted the first antechamber door, the second antechamber door and the door between my study and the library. I then found a jar full of keys that I kept hidden at the back of the cupboard. Tipping the keys onto the floor, I selected two from the jumble. I unlocked one of my desk drawers and removed a metal cash box. This too, needed to be unlocked. Inside was a third, more substantial key, its blade a complicated knot of serrated projections.

The time had come.

Light streamed through the windows, illuminating a

swirl of glittering motes, and I tried to steady my agitated nerves by observing their slow, circular motion. The attempt was futile. My heart felt swollen and heavy – my breath came in gasps.

Like a condemned man, I walked over to the chest, knelt down and inserted the key into the padlock. The key did not turn at first, and I had to use considerable force before a loud snap signalled that the shackle was free. I removed the padlock and, gripping two leather straps, heaved the chest open. Immediately, the trapped air inside escaped, carrying with it a stale, musty fragrance.

The interior was full of thick, brocade curtains: a top layer of neatly folded squares and beneath these a second layer of densely compressed bundles. There was also a third layer of folded squares at the bottom. I could remember packing the chest myself, and how I had endeavoured to arrange the cloth in order to diminish the destructive effects of any knocks or collisions. Any damage – if I found any – must have arisen, not because of mishandling, but because of internal violence.

I removed the folded squares and considered how best to proceed. It would be madness to unravel the bundles. Even a glimpse of what lay underneath might result in a weakening of my mental powers. I imagined a distorted, reptilian eye – seen through the convexity of the glass, magnified, bulging – and shuddered. A supreme act of will was required to fight a sudden urge to slam the lid down and flee. Looking away, I saw the bracelet of flowers that Annette had given me and was able to draw strength from the memory of her little act of kindness. I slipped my hands beneath the brocade and, bracing myself, extended the tips of my fingers. Like the sensory apparatus of an insect, they made trembling contact with the curved crystal. I knew, instantly, that my misgivings were justified. The glass was warm. I caressed the sphere and explored its surface. My hands began to hurt, and tendrils of pain crept up my arms. And then it occurred to me that to undertake a proper inspection I should surely push the curtains aside and take a look at what I was doing. It was not my thought, of course. The very substances of my brain were being tampered with. I was in dreadful peril and had to accomplish my task quickly. The pain worsened, I felt sick, and my vision blurred. *Just pull the material aside . . .* The thought had acquired the qualities of a command. *Go on. It's quite safe.* I closed my eyes. A momentary lapse of concentration and I might have found myself yanking the curtains away.

'You will not have control of my mind,' I said aloud. My denial was followed by a retaliatory wave of nausea. 'And you will leave the girl's mind alone too.'

I pressed on with my examination and discovered an irregularity on the otherwise smooth surface. It was just as I had imagined – a crack – like Doriac's egg. I moved the soft flesh of my fingertip along the fracture to gauge its length, felt a stinging sharpness, and quickly drew my hand away. I opened my eyes and saw blood welling up from a cut. With great care, I put the curtains back in the chest, shut the lid and fixed the padlock.

20

I placed the heavy volume in front of Du Bris and opened it up.

'The first of twelve library registers,' I said. 'This one was compiled by your ancestor, Roland Du Bris. The handwriting might even be his.' Du Bris peered blankly at the faded ink. 'The first eleven registers are complete; however, it would seem that towards the end of the last century, interest in the library waned. Thereafter, not all the acquisitions were catalogued.' Du Bris poured himself a brandy and indicated, without speaking, that he was prepared to fill a second glass. I declined and continued: 'The final register is very inferior. Hardly any of the nineteenth-century publications have an entry. Would you permit me to make the necessary emendations?'

Du Bris shrugged. 'It sounds like an awful lot of work.'

'I would not find the task onerous.'

'Well, Clément, if it makes you happy, then please feel at liberty to do so. I have no objection.' He paused and added, 'Do you mean to say, you've looked at every book in the library?'

'I have.'

'And have you found anything . . . valuable?'

'There are many valuable books in the library.'

'Yes, I know. But have you found anything of exceptional value?'

'I am sure that there are dealers in Paris who would be anxious to acquire many of these books.' I passed my hand over the register. 'Even so, it would be a tragedy if such a unique collection was broken up.'

Du Bris took a sip of his brandy and said, 'We're not great readers.'

'But future generations, perhaps . . .'

'My grandfather used to take me into the library and read me stories. I never really liked him – or the stories. I much preferred playing outside.' He looked towards one of the windows.

'May I ask: have any of the books been removed from the library?'

'I beg your pardon?'

'Are there, for example, any library books in your private apartment?'

'No. Why do you ask?'

'See here.' I pointed to a particular entry, *Malleus Daemonum* – The Hammer of Demons – by Alexandro Albertinus, published in 1620: a treatise on exorcism. Now, just below, see, it says once again, *Malleus Daemonum*.'

'A second copy?'

'No, another Hammer of Demons, but this time one

written several hundred years earlier, by the great alchemist Nicolas Flamel.' I tapped the page. 'Unfortunately, it is missing.' Du Bris thrust out his lower jaw but said nothing. 'I believe that it may be the only copy in existence.'

'Which would make it very valuable?'

'Valuable and of incalculable interest to scholars. I have examined all the standard reference works, and nowhere is there mention of Flamel's Hammer.'

'Then perhaps old Roland made a mistake. Perhaps there was no such book.'

'I very much doubt that a man as fastidious as your ancestor would have made such a blunder.'

Du Bris raised his hands, as if to say, 'Well, what am I supposed to do about it?'

I closed the register and continued, 'I do not feel that it is for me to ask Madame Odile to look through her effects. I fear that she would consider such a request improper.'

'Oh, I see,' said Du Bris, laughing. 'That's what all this is about. No, I quite understand, Clément, of course. I'll explain the situation and get her maid to have a look. Her wardrobe is a veritable treasure trove – you never know what might turn up!'

'Thank you, monsieur.'

He stood, stretched out his arms and yawned. 'Did you go to the village yesterday?'

'Yes, I did.'

'I thought I saw the grey mare. I was there too – some

business.' He smiled and then asked, 'How is my daughter?'

'Mademoiselle Drouart brought a small matter to my attention, a disturbance of vision; however, I am not unduly worried.'

'Good. Good.' He shook my hand. 'And Raboulet?'

'In excellent health.'

'We are all greatly indebted, monsieur.'

I went straight to the library, where I immersed myself in magical writings: I read of ointments, philtres and potions, the consecration of lamps, wax, oil and water; of precious stones, secret seals and celestial correspondences – the twenty eight mansions of the moon – the preparation of amulets and talismans, incense and powders; and the characters that should be engraved on a protective ring. I applied myself to the *The Devil's Scourge*, *The Sworn Book of Honorius*, *The Key of Solomon* – all the time amending the notes that I had been keeping for well over a year. Oblivious to the passage of time, I only registered the lateness of the hour when the fading light made it difficult for me to continue reading.

There was a knock on the door.

I gathered my papers together and stuffed them into a drawer before calling out, 'Come in.'

Hélène entered. 'Good heavens, monsieur, I can hardly see a thing. Where are you?'

I stood and lit some candles. 'I am sorry, madame, I must have dozed off.'

She made her way to my table and I pulled out a chair. 'Thank you, monsieur.' She pinched her dress and raised the hem a little before she sat. 'The books you were reading couldn't have been very engaging.'

'No,' I said, returning to my own chair. 'They weren't. I was refreshing my Latin.'

She smiled somewhat nervously and made a few unconnected remarks about her own reading habits. As she spoke, I noticed that her hands were in constant motion, one revolving around the other. Eventually, she looked at me directly and said, 'Monsieur Clément, I wondered if I might discuss something with you in confidence.'

'Of course.'

'I am worried about my brother. He is talking of Paris.'

'Oh?'

'When he was younger he was always talking of Paris. He wanted to live there. In reality, he could never have made such a move because of his condition. He always knew that. But now, things are different. Your medicines have been very helpful and, once again, he is dreaming of theatres and the company of fashionable young men. He imagines that, very soon, he will be able to take Sophie and Elektra to the capital – that he will rent some rooms and support all three of them by writing articles.'

'The life of a man of letters is notoriously insecure.'

'He says that he is bored. I am sympathetic, of course, but he can't go to Paris, can he?' Her voice had acquired a pleading tone.

'No,' I answered. Hélène let out a sigh of relief. 'But

in the fullness of time, if he continues to enjoy better health . . .'

Her face fell. 'I would miss him.'

'I am sure you would.'

'Without Tristan's amusing conversation, life here at Chambault will be very . . .' her sentence trailed off and after a beat of silence she added, 'I fear I am about to embarrass myself again.'

I feigned ignorance. 'Again? I don't know what you are referring to, madame.'

In the candlelight, her eyes looked particularly large. She bit her lower lip. 'I haven't been sleeping well lately. Is there something you could make up for me? An infusion, perhaps?'

'Certainly.'

As I began to rise she said, 'No, monsieur. You do not have to prepare one now.'

'But it is no trouble at all.' I went into my study and mixed some camomile and lavender oil. When I returned, Hélène was standing by one of the shelves, examining the titles. I handed her the glass.

'Thank you, monsieur.'

'A very mild sedative. If you need something a little stronger, then let me know.'

She looked around the library. 'So many books.'

We stood together, surveying our surroundings. It felt to me as if she was delaying her departure because she had something more to say and was struggling to overcome a scruple. I never discovered if my presumption was correct, because at that moment the silence was broken by a strange, plaintive cry. It had come from the antechamber. We both hurried in that direction but slowed as we neared the interior doorway. Something was standing in the shadows – small and pale. I felt Hélène's fingers close around my arm and her grip tightening. Then, we heard a child's voice: 'Are you real?'

Hélène stepped forward and whispered, 'Annette?'

'Are you real, Mother?'

'Of course I am real. What is the matter, my dear?'

The child was obviously confused and I said, 'She has been sleepwalking.'

'Monsieur Clément?' said Annette, 'Is that you?'

'Yes, Annette.'

'I heard a voice, telling me that I should get out of bed and go to your room. It was peculiar, like my own voice, but different. I didn't want to get up, but the voice was very stubborn. I climbed the stairs . . . but then I woke up – and found myself here – and I couldn't tell whether I was still dreaming or not.'

'You have been walking in your sleep, Annette. It happens sometimes.' I turned to address Hélène. 'I think you had better take her back to bed. I'll get you a candle. It is quite dark now.'

On my return, Hélène glanced from the flame to the other side of the antechamber and the black emptiness of the entrance. 'I don't know how she managed to find her way here in the dark. She could have fallen and injured herself.'

'No,' said Annette. 'I was quite safe. The voice told me which way to go. It can see in the dark.'

Hélène shook her head and wrapped a gentle arm around the child's shoulders. 'Come on, my dear. Let's get you to bed.' Hélène looked at me and delivered a mute request for reassurance.

'Really, madame,' I said calmly. 'There is nothing to worry about.'

When they had both gone I went back to my table in the library. Hélène had left her infusion. I picked up the glass and drained it without pausing to take breath.

21

The following morning I received a note from the curé. One of the villagers had been involved in an accident. The man was in great pain and the curé begged me to come quickly. I dashed to the stables, saddled the grey mare and set off at a gallop. The address I had been given was not far from the market square and easy to find: a low building with a yard full of clucking hens. As I arrived, a door opened and the curé emerged. 'Oh, monsieur,' he cried, pressing his hands together and shaking them backwards and forwards. 'Thank you, thank you. Thank you so much.'

I dismounted and said, 'Where is Monsieur Jourdain?'

The curé sighed. 'He was not at home.'

'You mean that he didn't come to the door when you knocked.'

'That is a possibility.'

'Father Lestoumel,' I said sharply, 'something must be done!'

'Yes,' said the curé, 'you are right and I am sorry.'

We entered the building and I was immediately confronted by a curious sight. A woman was comforting two small children, but this charming little group – this artist's impression of a domestic ideal – was mitigated by the presence of a bullock. The beast was poking its head through a hole in the wall, and behind it, I could see the low roof of a thatched barn. I was momentarily stupefied.

'Please,' said Father Lestoumel, tugging gently at my sleeve, 'This way, monsieur.' He led me into the next room, where I discovered my patient lying on bed sheets soaked through with blood. 'Monsieur Ragot,' said the curé, indicating the poor wretch. Another woman, considerably younger than the first and whom I supposed to be the man's wife, was seated on a stool, mumbling prayers.

'What happened to him?' I asked.

'Some barrels fell off a cart,' whispered the curé. 'His legs were crushed.'

The man struck the mattress with a clenched fist and called out, 'Saints preserve us! The pain is unbearable!'

I opened my bag, took out a pair of scissors and cut away the sopping wet fabric of his trousers. The lacerations I exposed were ragged and deep – so deep, in fact, that one could see down to the bone. 'Madame,' I said to the woman. 'I will need some warm water and towels.'

'Will I lose my legs?' asked Ragot.

'No,' I replied. 'I don't think so. Providing the injured parts are kept clean.'

'Thank the Lord,' said Ragot, tracing a cross in the air above his chest.

I filled a syringe with morphine, pushed the needle

into Ragot's arm and, before the plunger was fully depressed, watched his jaw go slack and his eyes glaze over. When his wife returned with the water, I bathed Ragot's wounds, dressed them with lint soaked in carbolic and finally wrapped both of his legs in bandages. Turning to address Madame Ragot, I asked her for some wine. She blushed and answered, 'Forgive me. I'll get you some.'

'It isn't for me, madame,' I said, anxious to correct her mistake. 'I need wine to make a preparation for your husband, something for him to drink later – to ease the pain.' She excused herself and came back with a bottle that had already been opened. I poured the dark liquid into a glass and added a teaspoon of morphine. 'Give this to Monsieur Ragot when he wakes. By the time its effect wears off, I am sure Monsieur Jourdain will be able to assist.' I glanced at the curé and he shifted his weight uncomfortably from one foot to the other.

As we were leaving, Madame Ragot thanked me and said she would remember me in her prayers. I replied, 'You would do better, perhaps, to pray for the swift recovery of your husband.' It was an ungracious remark and I instantly regretted it.

I untethered the horse and strode off towards the market square. The curé caught up with me and said, a little breathlessly, 'Monsieur, I will make sure that you are fully compensated for your services. There is a small charity fund that I manage and . . .'

'That won't be necessary,' I said brusquely.

'But I insist,' said the curé. 'It is only right that you should be paid.' He paused, before adding, 'Especially so, given your other good offices.'

'Oh? And what might they be?'

'You have been seen up in the hills, monsieur.'

'I enjoy the views.'

'Entering the caves and carrying your bag.'

'Who told you this?'

'Fleuriot.'

'Perhaps your informant was mistaken.'

'On the whole, experience has taught me to trust his sources. Well? Is it true?'

'Some of the children were very ill.'

'I imagine some of the medicines you require are very expensive, and I would be happy to . . .'

Again I cut in: 'With respect, Father, there are better ways of dispersing your funds – better causes than my remuneration.'

The curé raised a placatory hand. 'You are very kind, monsieur.'

We walked on in silence, and a woman appeared at the end of the road. As she drew closer, I recognized her face. It was the same woman I had seen talking to Du Bris. She was young, pretty and dressed rather well for a villager. When she saw the curé she crossed to the opposite side of the road and, as we passed each other, she looked away, dramatically straining her slender neck and raising her chin in haughty defiance. I sensed Father Lestoumel bristling.

'Who is that?' I asked.

'Mademoiselle Anceau.' I could see that he was undecided as to whether he should say more. After a few
moments, he glanced back and added, 'She has something of a reputation.' He underscored his disapproval by
tutting loudly.

We reached the market square and I tied the mare to
a post. I was about to bid Father Lestoumel adieu, when
his face lit up and he exclaimed, 'I know! Why don't I
show you the church.' Before I could voice an objection,
he added, 'I am sure you will find the interior very interesting.'

He seemed eager to please, and I was conscious of the
fact that during our time together my manner had been
somewhat surly. I remembered the discourteous remark
I had made earlier to Madame Ragot, felt ashamed, and
suddenly found myself consenting to Father Lestoumel's
suggestion. The curé clapped his hands together and
cried, 'Excellent! Excellent!'

We marched across the square, entered the church,
and Father Lestoumel began a summary of the building's history. It was much as I had expected: a medieval
structure built on earlier foundations, destruction by fire
and subsequent restorations. Features were pointed out
to me, such as the carvings on the baptismal font, some
ornate candle-stands and a faded remnant of a twelfth-
century fresco – none of which excited my curiosity.
However, in due course we came to a stump of stone
mounted on a pedestal. It was evidently a religious effigy,

but almost all of its surface detail had been worn away. Only the petrified folds of a gown were now visible.

'That looks very old,' I said.

'Not as old as you might think,' replied Father Lestoumel. 'It is a statue of Saint Clotilde at prayer and believed to possess healing powers. For over a century, villagers have been scraping the stone and mixing the powder in their food as a kind of medicine.'

'Do you approve?'

'It was reputed to have been a very fine piece of sculpture. No, I do not approve. I do not want the entire church to be scraped away and used as a cough remedy.' His eyes sparkled and he ventured a wry smile. Crossing the transept, he continued: 'Joan of Arc may have stopped here once. Or so they say. In actual fact, many of the local churches have been linked with her legend. She couldn't have visited all of them!'

We came to a stained-glass window, the central lancet of which showed a priest reading from a large red book. This hefty volume, fitted with gold hasps, was held up by a demon that had evidently been forced into an attitude of servile compliance. Diagonal shafts of sunlight passed through the colourful illuminations, creating a submerged, watery effect, dappling the floor with patches of luminosity.

'That gentleman,' said Father Lestoumel, pointing up at the window, 'was one of my predecessors. His name was Gilbert de Gandelus. When the Ursuline convent at Séry-des-Fontaines was plagued with demons in 1612 it was Gandelus who cast them out. His fame spread far and wide, and he was subsequently called upon to conduct exorcisms all over the country. I believe he was once summoned by the Bishop of Paris.'

I noticed that the demon did not have claws, but human hands, with long fingers and tapering nails.

The curé moved on, indicating a fifteenth-century likeness of the Virgin and the fragment of a Roman tomb embedded in one of the walls. We had completed a circular tour of the church and had arrived back at the font. The curé pushed the door open and we stepped out into the square. I thanked him for showing me the church and made some comments preparatory to our parting. Just as I was about to say goodbye, he said, 'You are an intellectual, monsieur. Educated. Well read. And I am but a simple country priest. I daresay, you cannot conceive of any benefit arising from associating with a man like me.' I was about to make a polite rebuttal, but he raised his finger and shook it. 'No, monsieur. It is true – and I make no judgement. All that I ask is that, should you find yourself requiring assistance, you will at least remember that I am here. I am not foolish enough to believe that you will ever want my counsel. But I have much local knowledge and perhaps one day this may be of some use to you.'

'Indeed.'

He smiled. 'And do not fear, I will not try to convert you: you are a doctor, a man of science. Reason is your religion and I will respect that.'

'You think me an atheist?'

'Well? Aren't you?'

'No,' I said. 'Far from it.' I turned and walked away, leaving Father Lestoumel standing outside the church with his frown deepening. The door of the inn was wide open so I went inside and sat at a table.

'Will Monsieur Ragot keep his legs?' asked Fleuriot.

'Yes,' I replied. 'He will.'

'Good.' Fleuriot poured me a beer and began a story about an amputee he had known as a child, who was so fast on his crutches that he could race against able-bodied men and beat them.

On returning to the chateau, I went to the library and found a work on witchcraft that contained an account of the Séry-des-Fontaines possessions. The mother superior had been the first to succumb. She had fallen to the ground, shouted blasphemies and lifted her petticoats without shame. Others followed her example, and within a few weeks the convent had descended into chaos. Nuns were running around the cloisters naked and the chapel was despoiled. Several attempts at exorcism failed and the Church authorities became desperate. It was at this point that Gandelus appeared. The demons were vanquished and order was quickly restored. Nothing is recorded of Gandelus's life prior to the Séry-des-Fontaines possessions, and his sudden transformation from parish priest to 'God's hammer' was identified by some as miraculous.

I shut the book and walked to my study. Sitting at my

desk, I smoked until a paring of moon peeped through the window. I then crossed to the chest and tested the lid with the palm of my hand. It was warm. I spat out the words 'Damn you!' and went to bed.

The next day, I was once again invited to sit with the family beneath the cherry tree. Everyone was present except for Du Bris, who had gone shooting with Louis, and we could hear the intermittent crack of his gunshots coming from the woods. It was a humid afternoon and our indifferent conversation was punctuated by long silences. Victor was speaking. His words intruded upon my thoughts, but not enough for me to register their meaning. Even so, a note of shrill excitement jolted me out of my reverie. The boy was pointing and squealing, 'Look at Annette! She has seen something!'

Annette was standing in the middle of the lawn, her head tilted back, looking up into the sky. She raised her hand, fingers pressed together, and shaded her eyes from the sun. Very slowly, shifting one foot, then the other, she began to rotate.

'Can you see anything, Monsieur Clément?' asked Hélène.

The sky was blue and cloudless.

'No,' I replied.

It was as if the child had become fascinated by something circling overhead.

'Is she dancing?' asked Victor.

'I don't think so,' Mademoiselle Drouart replied.

Annette gathered momentum, extending her arms, revolving faster and faster, until her skirt fanned out and she began to resemble a ballerina performing a pirouette.

'It is not right,' said Odile. 'A girl of her age!'

'Annette!' Hélène called out, 'Stop it! You'll get dizzy.'

'Yes,' shouted Victor. 'You'll make yourself sick.'

But Annette did not stop.

I jumped up from my chair and started off towards her, quickening my pace with each step. Her hair was whipping through the air, her feet barely touching the ground.

'Annette?' I said, 'Annette? What is the matter?'

I reached out to grab her shoulders, and when I did so she became tense and toppled to the ground. She lay there for a few seconds, before her limbs started to jerk. The movements were violent and uncontrolled. I stuffed a handkerchief in her mouth and raised her head. When I looked up again, I saw Hélène, Raboulet, and Mademoiselle Drouart gathered around me, staring down at Annette with worried expressions.

'Is it a seizure?' said Hélène, kneeling down beside me.

'Yes,' I replied. 'I am sorry.'

Mademoiselle Drouart's expression was transparent. I could see that she was thinking about the day when she had shown me Annette's drawings, and I had told her that I was not unduly concerned about the child's health.

She was not judging me unkindly, but rather exhibiting surprise that I had been so badly mistaken.

'Was it the spinning that brought it on?' asked Raboulet.

I rested my hand on Annette's forehead: 'That is a possibility.'

The jerking gradually subsided.

'Shall I take her inside, monsieur?' said Raboulet.

'No,' I responded. 'Not just yet.'

Annette had bitten her lower lip and I removed some spots of blood from her chin with the handkerchief. As I was doing this, her eyes flicked open.

'Monsieur Clément?' She tried to get up but I did not permit her to move.

'You have had a seizure, Annette. You must rest here for a few minutes.'

'My head hurts.'

'I know. I will give you something to relieve the pain.'

'I saw a bird – a great bird flying in the sky.'

'No, my darling,' said Hélène. 'It was something you imagined.'

'With enormous wings,' Annette continued, 'going round and round.'

'Hush now,' said Hélène.

I stroked the child's brow and she closed her eyes again. Mademoiselle Drouart returned to the cherry tree to tell the others what had happened, and in due course Raboulet picked Annette up and carried her to the chateau, accompanied by Hélène and myself. The poor child was changed into her nightclothes and put to bed, where she slept for most of the afternoon. I sat by her side, with Hélène.

At six thirty, Du Bris arrived.

'Where have you been?' asked Hélène.

'I had to go into the village,' he replied.

'Again?' Her voice was tart.

'Yes.' He turned to address me and said, 'How is she, Monsieur Clément?'

'As well as can be expected.'

'My mother tells me that before she collapsed she was spinning like a top.'

'It was most peculiar.'

'Does it signify anything?'

My cheeks burned as I lied: 'I don't think so, and there is nothing unusual about her current condition. She is exhausted and has complained of headaches. That is all.'

'She thought she could see something in the sky,' Hélène interjected.

'A bird,' I said.

'That is why she was spinning,' Hélène continued.

Du Bris shrugged and came forward. He crooked his index finger and brushed the knuckle against his daughter's lips. Her eyes opened and she smiled. Du Bris returned the smile and said, 'Well? How are you?'

'Tired,' she replied.

'Yes,' he went on. 'You would be.'

There was something curiously touching about this

little exchange, the light of recognition in Annette's eyes and the unsentimental affection of her father.

'Do not look so worried,' said Annette. 'Monsieur Clément is looking after me, and nothing very bad can happen when he is here.'

It was at that point that I decided to leave Chambault. Annette's faith in me, her innocent trust, was breaking my heart. Travel arrangements could be made by the end of the week and I might be gone within a fortnight. I stood up and said, 'The crisis has passed and you will no doubt wish to be alone with your daughter. I will be in the library if I am required.'

'Thank you,' said Du Bris, inclining his head.

I spent the rest of the day reviewing my notes, particularly the material I had collected on protective charms. The Seal of Shabako caught my attention, an all-purpose amulet of very ancient provenance favoured by the inhabitants of Abydos. It was sometimes carved on Egyptian stone coffins and supposed to help the dead negotiate their perilous journey through the underworld. I took a square of parchment from the drawer of my table and, using a compass, drew a perfect circle, within which I then copied a precise arrangement of hieroglyphs. I repeated the procedure and placed both amulets in my pocket. When the opportunity arose, I would give one to Annette and tell her to keep it about her person at all times. It would be our little secret.

Just before sunset, Madame Boustagnier had some chicken stew sent up to my study. It was fortified with the red wine of the estate, and the pale meat was saturated with its spicy bouquet. When I had finished eating, I smoked a cigar and walked around my apartment, making an itinerary. Transporting my possessions to Paris would be straightforward enough. But then what would I do? I saw my life stretching out ahead of me: a pitiful, lonely existence, wandering from place to place, unable to settle, always fearful of the demon exerting its wicked influence on those to whom I might become attached. There was much I would miss: Annette's sweet smile, idle conversations with Hélène beneath the cherry tree, card games with Raboulet, and of course the library. I had always hoped that I would find the answer to my predicament somewhere in Roland Du Bris's remarkable collection. But there were thousands of books, and, the longer I chose to stay, the more likely it was that Annette or some other member of the household would be placed in mortal danger.

It was past eleven when I heard someone crossing the library. There was a knock on the door, and when I opened it, I found Hélène standing before me, holding up a candle.

'You are awake,' she exclaimed. 'Thank God!'

'Is Annette all right?'

'Forgive me. I did not mean to alarm you. Yes, Annette is well. We put a truckle bed in her room and one of the maids, Monique, is spending the night with her.' Hélène stepped over the threshold. 'I am sorry to trouble you at this late hour, monsieur, but last week you were kind enough to make me a sleeping draught – although I never drank it. I think I must have left it in the library when I took Annette back to her room.' The skin around her eyes was swollen and I suspected that she might have been crying. 'Again,' she continued, 'I am finding it difficult to sleep; perhaps I am worrying too much about Annette. The attack was horrible – one forgets.'

'Yes. It was most distressing.' I paused for a moment and felt some strange compulsion to invite harsh judgement. 'I fear that I may have been complacent, too willing to believe that I had developed a cure, when in fact my achievement was much less impressive.'

'Do not talk like that, monsieur! Annette and Tristan are so much better than they were.' She reached out and somewhat awkwardly took my hand and pressed my fingers. I had not been touched like that for a very long time and I was disturbed by a sudden frisson of desire.

'I will make up the infusion,' I said, pulling away from Hélène, although my withdrawal was delayed by a slight tightening of her grip. It was as if she didn't want to let go. I went to the cupboard, took out some bottles and set about mixing the ingredients. Outside, the dogs began to howl.

We looked at each other and Hélène said, 'What a noise! I hope they don't wake Annette.' She sat down on the divan and I saw that she wasn't wearing any shoes. Through the thin silk of her red stockings I could see her ankles and toes. I tried to stop myself from stealing glances but found it almost impossible. She did not notice this liberty because she had turned away from me and was gazing directly at the chest. After a few moments, she started and said, 'I beg your pardon?'

'I said nothing, madame.'

She seemed a little disorientated and when she noticed that she wasn't wearing any shoes, she stood up abruptly and shook her skirt to ensure that her feet were properly covered. I pretended not to see what she was doing and kept my head bowed. When I had finished, I handed Hélène the infusion.

'Thank you,' she said, 'I will drink it before I retire.' She picked up her candle and walked to the door. The howling of the dogs had grown louder and she tutted before saying, 'What is the matter with them?'

'I don't know, madame.'

'They often bark, but I have never heard them howl like this.'

She stepped into the library and glided through the darkness like a ghost. When she had gone I marched over to the chest, slammed my hand down on the lid, and hissed 'Stop it! Stop it! Leave them alone!' An image flashed into my mind: Hélène Du Bris lying with her legs spread apart, naked but for a pair of red stockings. I withdrew my hand so quickly the lid might have been a hotplate.

22

The following morning I went to see Annette. She was in fine spirits and seemed almost recovered. I had wanted to give her the amulet, but Monique was hovering, and I decided that it would be wise to leave it until we were alone. Although I was hungry, I wanted to clear my head, so I went for a short walk around the gardens before returning for breakfast. As I entered the courtyard, I saw Louis and Monsieur Boustagnier lifting one of two large trunks on to the back of the trap. Du Bris came out of one of the rear doors; he was smartly dressed and propelled himself forward with a cane. There was something about his confident swagger that reminded me of Charcot.

'Good morning, Monsieur Clément.'

'Good morning,' I replied. 'Are you leaving us?'

'Yes, just for a few days. Tours.' He paused, deliberating whether to say any more, then added, 'I have to sign some documents.' The smell of his cologne was somewhat overpowering. It occurred to me that he had taken more care over his appearance than was customary for an appointment with a notary. Du Bris straightened the carnation in his buttonhole and asked, 'How is Annette?'

'Very well. There are no complications.'

'Good. Good.' He then looked at me as if to say, 'Anything else?'

'I was wondering,' I began, affecting a casual manner, 'did you get a chance to talk to Madame Odile?'

'What about?' A trace of impatience had hardened his voice.

'The book I mentioned.'

'Oh that! No. I'm sorry, I didn't. I'll ask her when I get back. Now, if you don't mind, Clément, I really must go. I need to catch the diligence.' He climbed up onto the box and Louis tugged the reins. The trap rolled off and Monsieur Boustagnier threw me an amused glance.

After eating breakfast in the kitchen, I went to Annette's room, meaning to give her the amulet, but when I arrived she was not there. I discovered from Mademoiselle Drouart that Annette was feeling much stronger and that she had gone for a walk with her mother. On returning to my study I wrote to a hotel in Paris, before sifting through my belongings, separating those things I must take with me from those that I might leave behind.

Louis had returned from the village with some letters, and among them was one addressed to me from Valdestin. We had maintained a very occasional correspondence since my departure from the Salpêtrière. This opportune communication would add legitimacy to the story I was concocting in my head, concerning the receipt of bad news of a personal nature and the regretful necessity of my return to Paris. I had resolved to make my announcement the next day, and for that reason found it impossible to dine with the family. Once again, I ate in my rooms alone and, as the sun was setting, ventured out for what I imagined would be my very last walk in the gardens of the chateau. As I was making my way through the Garden of the Senses, I heard the dogs starting to howl, just as they had howled the previous night. A few minutes later I entered the courtyard and saw Louis standing by the kennel. The dogs were kept in an enclosure consisting of a low square wall, on top of which were high iron railings.

'I don't know what's wrong with them,' said Louis, removing a cigarette from between his lips. 'I've never seen them like this before.' Two of the dogs were standing on their hind legs, making a plaintive wailing noise, while the other three were crawling in circles, crouched low and whimpering. I shrugged, said, 'Goodnight,' and entered the chateau through the kitchen door. After passing through the dining room and parlour, I ascended the stairs and entered the library, where I took my seat at the table. I then went through my notes, checking my early transcriptions for accuracy – particularly those passages concerned with the construction of magical weapons. This was a demanding task, and the verification of hieroglyphs and symbols occupied me until the early hours of the morning.

It was only when I paused to smoke a cigar that I registered the silence. The dogs had stopped howling.

I should have been glad, because they had been making a frightful din, but instead the silence made me feel uneasy, as if every living thing had departed from the world and I was totally alone. The landscape beyond the library walls had become, in my imagination, a desolate, empty expanse. Opening my mouth, I released a cloud of smoke and watched it roll over the cracked pages of an illuminated manuscript. The minute hand dropped on the clock face and I noted the time: ten minutes past two. A faint pattering sound broke the silence, and I assumed that it had started to rain, but when I looked up at the window I saw no trails or droplets, and as I listened more closely, the sound became louder and clearer. Someone was running up the stairs. A moment later, I saw the glow of a candle and a figure wearing nightclothes entering the antechamber.

'Monsieur?' It was a young female voice, and belonged to Monique. She was obviously surprised to find me sitting up in the library.

I stood and marched towards her, 'What is it? Not another seizure, I hope!'

'No. The little mistress is well.' The maid's hair was uncombed and stuck out horizontally in matted bunches. 'Madame Du Bris sent me.'

'Why? What is wrong with her?'

'I don't know. Annie wanted me to sleep in her room again tonight – and I did – and I was asleep, but Madame Du Bris woke me up and told me to get you at once. She looked . . .' the girl hesitated, 'not herself.'

This was a peculiar turn of phrase and she seemed a little uncomfortable. She looked past me into the library, and I could see that she thought it most irregular for a gentleman to be reading in the middle of the night.

We rushed down the stairs and Monique led me through a series of connected rooms until we came to an elongated chamber that served as a kind of hallway, with doors running along either side. The maid indicated one to our left, and glanced, rather anxiously, down an adjoining corridor. I gathered that she was worried about Annette.

'It's all right,' I said. 'You can go now, if you wish.' She thanked me and scuttled off.

I was standing outside a room that I had never been in before. It was not where Hélène and her husband usually slept. I was familiar with the marital apartment because Du Bris had come down with a chest infection the previous winter, and naturally I had spent some time at his bedside. I straightened my neck tie, combed my fingers through my hair and knocked on the door. There was a lengthy pause, and I was about to strike again, when Hélène called out, 'Come in.' I turned the handle and entered. The room was lit by a single oil lamp and smelled of lavender. Medieval tapestries hung from the walls, and the furniture – a large wardrobe, a dressing table and a chest of drawers – was solidly built. I could not see Hélène because she was concealed behind the drapes of a four-poster bed.

'Madame?' I said tentatively. One of the heavy brocade

curtains moved aside and I saw her, sitting up and supported by a mountain of embroidered pillows. 'Madame?' I enquired. 'What is the matter?' I stepped forward and peered through the opening in the drapes. Hélène's eyes were half closed, the lids drooping, her hair a tangle of loose curls. She was wearing a nightdress, the neckline of which was low and revealing.

'I could not sleep,' she said. Her speech was slurred, as if she had been drinking, but I could not smell alcohol on her breath.

'Do you want another infusion, madame?'

Hélène continued as if I had said nothing. 'And I have a pain . . .' She touched her sternum and traced circles on her chest. 'Here.' Her legs became restless and her body seemed to twist and contort; her writhing did not suggest discomfort, however, but rather sensual abandon. Her other hand toyed with her curls before it disappeared beneath the counterpane, producing a wave in the crochet that rolled over her belly and subsided between her thighs. The small movements that followed were exploratory, and my head filled with images: a risen hem, an index finger curling between folds of flesh. I fancied that I could hear the whisper of silk and for no good reason supposed her to be wearing the same red stockings she had worn the night before. Desire ignited in the pit of my stomach and my loins burned.

'Come closer,' Hélène spoke softly. She reached out and pressed the palm of her hand against my tumescence and I gasped with astonishment. I knew that by submitting to her caresses I was acting dishonourably, but my admiration for her had always been complicated by deeper feelings. To be touched in this way, after so long, made her invitation to transgress almost irresistible. Yet, even as I stood there, trembling with expectation, I was also uneasy, and not only because of my guilty conscience. Since the dogs had stopped howling, everything that had happened had seemed unreal, like the disturbing events of a bad dream, and particularly so with respect to Hélène's extraordinary behaviour. 'Come closer,' she repeated, the words carried on a falling sigh.

She looked up at me and I recoiled in horror. There was nothing behind her eyes, only a terrible, submissive vacancy: a submissive vacancy that I recognized. I shook her shoulders, hoping to rouse her from the trance. 'Madame, wake up – wake up!' But it was no use, she simply fell back onto her pillow, moistened her lips with her tongue, and continued her sinuous movements. Once again, she touched her chest. 'It hurts,' she said. 'It hurts.'

I drew back, both fascinated and frightened by the spectacle of her sensual delirium. Her hand travelled through the air, the fingers making little grasping movements, as if she was hoping to attach herself to my person. Stepping backwards, I tripped on the rug and fell against the wardrobe. I did not know what to do and raced to the door, which I opened and slammed behind me. Before I had had a chance to compose myself, candlelight preceded the reappearance of Monique.

She gave a little cry when she discovered me standing in the dark.

'Monsieur!' She placed her hand over her heart. 'You made me jump!'

'Forgive me. I didn't mean to startle you.'

'Have you seen Annie? Did she come this way?'

'No.'

'She isn't in her room. I've been looking for her.'

'Was she gone when you returned?'

'Yes. I looked in the nursery, the chapel and the schoolroom. I couldn't find her anywhere.'

The door behind me opened, and Hélène stepped out. She had put on a night-coat and tied her hair up with a ribbon, but she still looked dishevelled and dazed. 'Monsieur?' she croaked, rubbing the sleep from her eyes, 'What is happening?'

'Annette is missing,' I replied.

'Missing . . .' she repeated.

It seemed that she had no recollection of what had just transpired between us.

'Yes,' I continued, 'however, I think I know where she might be.' Hélène allowed me to take her lamp without protest and I marched off towards the stairs. 'Monique,' I called back. 'Please carry on searching for the little mistress down here.' I retraced my footsteps through the connected rooms, my soul full of dread. When I reached the bottom of the stairs, I heard Hélène calling out, 'Monsieur Clément. Wait!' She had followed me and I turned to see her emerging from the gloom.

'This way,' I said, beginning my ascent.

'Where are you going?' she asked.

'To my rooms.'

'But why? Why would Annette go to your rooms. And at this time!'

'She is sleep-walking — as before. Forgive me, madame, we must hurry.'

When we reached the antechamber my pace quickened, and on entering the library I started to run. As I passed the terrestrial and celestial globes, the door to my apartment came into view. It was, as I had expected, wide open. The child had made her way through the chateau in total darkness. 'Annette?' I shouted. 'Annette?'

I burst into my study and what I saw brought me to an abrupt halt. My heart seemed to rise up and stop in my throat.

The lid of the chest had been raised and the neatly folded squares of fabric strewn across the floor. I saw a jar on its side, an upturned cash box and the glimmer of discarded keys. Annette was standing next to the chest, arms outstretched, the crystal in her hands. She was staring into its core, entranced by the thing inside — her features lit by a red luminescence that shone out from the crack on its surface. A distorted yellow eye looked at me from within the glass, and the sickening force of the demon's malice made me stagger. The eye blinked and vanished as Hélène caught up with me. I gestured for her to stand back.

'Annette,' I spoke gently. 'Annette, put it down.' She

did not hear me and continued to stare into the crystal. 'Annette,' I pleaded. 'Listen to me. It is very important that you listen to me.'

'What is she holding?' asked Hélène.

'Madame – please,' I pressed a rigid finger against my lips and took a cautious step towards the child. 'Annette? It is Monsieur Clément speaking – your friend, Monsieur Clément. It is so very important that you listen to me, so very important – Annette?'

I took another step.

'Annette!' Hélène called out. 'Listen to Monsieur Clément, he is talking to you!'

She was only trying to help, but it was enough to startle the child. Annette dropped the crystal and when it hit the floor the glass shattered. There was a flash of red light, a whiff of sulphur and a sudden rearrangement of the darkness – as if all the shadows in the room had rushed towards Annette. The child's legs gave way under her and she fell to the floor, unconscious.

I set the lamp aside, scooped her up and laid her out on the divan. Her breathing was shallow, her pulse fast, and when I lifted her eyelids I saw that her pupils had contracted to two pinpoints. I tried to rouse her, but she did not respond.

Hélène was standing by my side. 'Monsieur, what is wrong with her?'

My answer was redundant and evasive: 'She has lost consciousness.'

'Yes,' said Hélène. 'But has she had another seizure?'

'No.'

'Then what . . .' her sentence stopped abruptly and her brow furrowed.

'Madame,' I replied. 'Perhaps you should sit down.' Hélène withdrew a little and I continued with my examination, but a worried mother is never silent for very long.

'Monsieur? What was Annette holding when we entered this room?'

'A glass receptacle.'

'Yes, but what was it? I recall you once said that you kept dangerous chemicals in your chest. But . . .'

Annette began to mutter something and Hélène fell silent. When I listened closely, I detected snatches of Latin and Greek.

'Is she all right?' asked Hélène.

'Yes, for the moment.' I stood up. 'Madame, you must excuse me.'

'Where are you going?'

'Just next door. I won't be long.'

I went into my bedroom, sat on the mattress and buried my head in my hands. It had succeeded once again. It had taken me to hell.

Rage boiled up inside me. I clenched my fists, looked up at the ceiling and directed a stream of abuse towards heaven. But such was my despair I then fell on my knees and joined my hands together in prayer. I was prepared to try anything for Annette. I was even prepared to entertain the slender hope that Bazile's theology was true, and that ultimately there was no other choice but to abandon reason and place one's trust in an incomprehensibly higher authority.

'Please, God,' I prayed. 'Do not let her suffer more than she must. I beg You.'

'Monsieur Clément?' Hélène's muffled voice came from behind the door. I got up and re-entered the study, where I saw Hélène standing over Annette. The child was mumbling louder than before.

'Listen,' said Hélène. 'Listen to what she is saying.' I crouched down and heard a string of obscenities. 'Why is she talking like that? I did not think she knew such words.' Hélène glanced across the room and stared at the splinters of glass that sparkled in the lamplight. 'What did Annette take from your chest?'

'It is difficult to explain.'

'When she dropped the . . . receptacle, I thought I saw things.'

I opened my mouth but seemed to lose all powers of expression.

Hélène continued, 'What is happening, monsieur? Please tell me.'

'What did you see?' I asked.

'There was a flash of light and then the shadows seemed to gather around Annette.' She shook her head and I surmised that she had seen something more, something even stranger. Even so, she clearly doubted the evidence of her own senses and did not continue. The sound of footsteps made us both turn towards the library.

Monique came through the doorway and when she saw Annette lying on the divan she clapped a hand over her mouth in shock.

'She collapsed,' I said to the maid. 'It sometimes happens when sleepwalkers are surprised. I am looking after her now. Go back to bed, Monique; there is nothing you can do to help.' I was anxious for her to leave before she realized what Annette was mumbling. The two women looked at each other, and Monique's raised eyebrows betrayed her thoughts. It was not acceptable for the mistress of the house to be in the doctor's study wearing only her nightclothes. Hélène understood the meaning of the maid's stony expression and said, 'Monsieur, I will return after I have attended to my toilet.'

'As you wish, madame.'

The two women departed and I was left alone with Annette. I placed my hand on her forehead and discovered that it was hot. 'You think that you have won,' I whispered under my breath. 'But I will fight you.'

As if in response, the dogs began to howl.

When Hélène returned, Annette was quite delirious. The pitch of her voice had descended several octaves and she was growling blasphemies. It was disturbing to hear such deep tones issuing from the mouth of a child and the language she employed was exceedingly crude. Occasionally, her features would contort into a lascivious leer and she would clutch at her genitals. I had to prise her fingers away and hold her arms down, until a shudder passed through her body and the agitation abated.

Hélène had positioned herself behind my desk and looked on in horrified silence. As I recovered from my exertions, Hélène stepped forward and stood behind me. 'Monsieur,' she said, 'is my daughter possessed?'

'Yes,' I replied directly. I heard a small gasp. She had been hoping, no doubt, that I would say something different, that I would chastise her, perhaps, for being absurd and offer her a rational, scientific explanation. But I could give her no such solace. I remembered the curé and his suggestion that if ever the need arose, I should call on him for help. He was, by his own admission, only a country priest, but I badly needed someone to confide in. I found myself saying, 'We must send for the curé at daybreak,' and when I turned, Hélène was looking at me intensely. The dogs were making a noise that sounded uncannily like grief-stricken human beings.

'Monsieur Clément, you must tell me what is happening. And what was that thing . . .' She swept her hand over the broken crystal. 'The thing that Annette dropped?'

'Please sit down, madame.' I stood up, indicated a chair, and crossed the room. Shards of glass cracked and splintered beneath the leather of my shoes. I then opened the cupboard, took out a bottle of rum and poured myself a large measure. Staring into the dark transparency of the liquid, I set about answering her questions, although with little reference to my actual history. The prospect of a full confession was simply too daunting. Instead, I improvised an episode of biography only loosely related to real life, which served the purpose of communicating some essential facts – but nothing more. I told Hélène that while living in Paris I had mixed with students of the occult and that among their number was a scholarly priest who had given me the crystal to look after. It was his claim that the glass contained a captive demon. The priest had gone travelling, had never returned, and I had become its custodian. I explained that I had only recently discovered a flaw in the glass, and that this discovery had coincided with Annette's deterioration and the occurrence of strange phenomena such as the howling of the dogs. 'As soon as I realized that the crystal was dangerous,' I concluded, 'I began making plans to leave Chambault. But it was already too late, madame. I am so very sorry.'

Hélène squeezed her lower lip between her thumb and forefinger. It seemed to me that she had accepted what I had said as true. Or perhaps she was simply too stunned – too bewildered – to think of any more questions. Eventually, she shook her head and glanced over at Annette, who was beginning to grumble obscenities once again. 'Demonic possession,' said Hélène. 'It is difficult to believe.'

'But you saw something,' I responded. 'Is that not so? When the glass broke?' She nodded and shivered as if a draught of cold air had chilled her to the marrow. Yet she did not elaborate and I did not press her. 'It – the demon – took control of Annette's mind,' I continued. 'That is how it managed to escape from its prison; and you too, were, for a time, in its power.' She looked at me quizzically. 'Do you remember waking Monique?'

'When?'

'Tonight. You went to Annette's room, woke Monique, and asked her to fetch me.'

'No,' she brushed a strand of hair away from her face. 'It was a dream! I dreamed that I was unwell, and . . .' After a few moments of discomfiting reflection, her neck and face reddened and she turned away. The embarrassment both of us felt made it hard for us to look at each other and an awkward silence ensued. In due course, Hélène sat up straight, and, trying hard to recover her dignity, said, 'What shall I tell the others? Tristan, Sophie?'

'Tell them that Annette was discovered walking in her sleep. Tell them that she collapsed when we tried to wake her, and that shortly after Monique left us, Annette had another seizure.'

'Why not tell them the truth?'

'Your brother will not accept the truth. He will dismiss whatever it was that you saw as an illusion and he will question my judgement.'

'Could it have been . . . an illusion?'

'No, madame. You saw a demon, and I do not want to argue with Monsieur Raboulet. If you have any doubts,' I gestured towards Annette, 'consider what your daughter is saying.'

'But what if Tristan wants to see Annette?'

'Tell him that I have given strict instructions that

Annette is not to be disturbed. Tell him that her condition is critical and I have forbidden visitors.'

'We have always been honest with each other – Tristan and I.'

'These are exceptional circumstances, madame.'

Hélène rose from her chair and walked over to the divan. She looked down at her daughter and said, 'When will she recover from this . . . state?'

'I do not know.'

'Then how will she eat? Or drink?'

'While she is like this, eating and drinking will not be possible.'

'So what is to be done, monsieur?'

'We must consult the curé.'

'And what will he do?'

'Advise us with respect to the ritual of exorcism.'

'And once Annette has been exorcized: will she be well again?' Hélène observed my hesitation and said, 'Monsieur?'

'I hope that she will be well again, yes.'

'Hope?' Hélène's eyes were suddenly bright with anger. 'Monsieur, whatever made you bring such an object into our home!'

I could not justify myself and made another apology, but this time my voice quavered with emotion. Hélène registered my distress and her expression changed. I did not need further confirmation of her fine qualities, her kindness, her generosity of spirit, but that is what she gave me. Her anger seemed to melt away and her face exuded pity, as luminous as the aura surrounding a saint in a religious painting. 'Forgive me, monsieur,' she said, 'I spoke too harshly.'

'No more than I deserve, madame,' I replied, bowing my head.

Annette's body suddenly convulsed, her hips thrusting upwards, her torso and limbs describing a perfect arch. Her head was hanging down from her neck and I saw only the whites of her eyes. She opened her mouth wide and a jet of vomit hit the wall with remarkable force. It seemed to sustain itself beyond the point at which her stomach should have been emptied.

'Wake Louis,' I barked at Hélène. 'Send him to the village. The curé must come as soon as he is able!'

By the time I reached Annette she had become limp again and she was lying flat on her back. She licked the vomit from her lips, the corners of which curled upwards to form a hideous, leering smile.

23

Louis returned with the curé shortly after the sun had risen. The dogs had stopped howling, but they started to bark as soon as they heard the trap approaching. Hélène received the curé in the courtyard and conducted him directly to my study. She had evidently advised him of Annette's condition, because as soon as he came through the door, he barely acknowledged my presence and marched straight over to the divan.

Annette had been relatively peaceful since the break of day. Even so, she looked pale, drawn and exhausted. Her cheeks were hollow, her hair lank and her skin had turned a sickly grey-green colour. The air around her smelled faintly of ordure. Father Lestoumel gazed down at the child for several minutes. Finally, he turned and said, 'Monsieur Clément, I have been informed by Madame Du Bris that you believe this child to be possessed. Would you care to explain?'

We sat at my desk and I described how the drama of the previous night had unfolded, although for Hélène's sake, I omitted any mention of what had transpired in her bedchamber. I then informed the curé of how I had come to own the crystal, repeating the same half-truths. Father Lestoumel listened, showing increasing signs of discomfort, and when I had finished he asked Hélène a number of questions, quite clearly testing the accuracy of my report. As I listened to his gentle inquisition, I noticed two flies revolving around each other just beneath the ceiling. A third joined them, introducing an element of eccentricity into their orbits. I was mesmerized by their movements, the complexity of their mutual influence, and was startled when I felt Father Lestoumel's hand on my shoulder. 'You will excuse me a moment,' he said, tightening his grip. 'I am going to the chapel and will return shortly.'

Hélène and I waited for him in silence, and when he reappeared he was holding a small silver box in his hand. He lifted the lid and removed a communion wafer. Then, looking at Hélène, he said, 'Madame, what I am about to do may cause you some distress.' He brushed Annette's hair off her face and pressed the wafer down on her forehead. The child immediately screamed, as if in pain, and her limbs flailed around wildly. Father Lestoumel tried to restrain her without success and called out, 'Quick! Clément! Help me!' and I jumped to his assistance. Together, we managed to hold her down, but only with great difficulty. We were both surprised by her enormous strength, and, if she had continued kicking and punching for very much longer, our efforts to contain her movements would have failed. Fortunately, the attack subsided and Father Lestoumel silently drew my attention to the communion wafer, which had fallen to the floor. A red weal had risen up on Annette's forehead, its circularity and size corresponding exactly with the host.

Hélène was standing on the other side of the room, her hands crossed over her bosom. She seemed on the brink of tears. A fly landed on the child's cheek and I brushed it away.

'Madame,' said the curé, 'you must be very tired. Go and rest. In due course our needs will be better served if you are refreshed.'

'What are you going to do, Father?' asked Hélène.

'Nothing, for the moment; however, I would be most grateful if you would permit me to speak privately with Monsieur Clément. There are some matters concerning the provenance of the crystal that I wish to clarify. I will then decide how we shall proceed.'

Hélène did not want to leave, so I made a show of examining Annette, checking her pulse and temperature. 'Her condition is stable,' I said reassuringly. 'Perhaps you should do as Father Lestoumel suggests. Take the opportunity to rest while you can.' She nodded and went to the door, where, before leaving us, she glanced back at her daughter with tears spilling down her cheeks. The sight of Hélène in so much anguish made me feel utterly wretched.

'Thank you, monsieur,' said the curé, and we both sat down again at my desk. Father Lestoumel created a steeple with his hands and let it bounce against his pursed lips. After a long thoughtful silence, he said, 'I would like to begin by asking you one or two questions about these occultists you met in Paris. Were they members of—'

'Father Lestoumel,' I interjected. 'I regret to say that the story I told of how the crystal came into my possession was largely untrue.' The curé tilted his head to one side and eyed me quizzically. 'I did not wish to frighten Madame Du Bris with my true history.'

'You were not acquainted with any magical sects?'

'No.'

'And there was no scholarly priest?'

'Well, in that respect, I was telling a partial truth. His name was Father Ranvier. But he did not give me the crystal to safeguard in his absence. Nor did he fail to return from his travels.'

'What happened to him?'

'The demon . . .' I shuddered at the recollection of Father Ranvier's grisly end.

'Monsieur Clément,' said the curé, making the sign of the cross. 'Perhaps the time has come for you to unburden yourself.'

For a very long time, I stared at the surface of the desk, trying to order my thoughts. It was difficult to determine where I should begin, but eventually, I found myself saying, 'After the great siege, I travelled to the Antilles to work at the Poor Sisters of the Precious Blood mission hospital on the island of Saint-Sébastien.' And once I had begun, I continued, the words coming more easily, the momentum of the narrative demanding an ever-faster delivery. I told the curé everything: I told him of Duchenne, the experiment and my subsequent descent into depravity. I told him of Courbertin, the exorcism in the crypt of Saint-Sulpice and of Father Ranvier's horrible demise. It was only when I tried to describe my trip to Chinon that a lump in my throat made it impossible for me to go on. I extended my arm, as if I could push the memories away, and rushed to the cupboard to pour myself more rum. When I sat down again, Father Lestoumel rested his hand on mine and said, 'My son, how you have suffered.' I had not expected such a response and I was deeply moved by his sympathy.

Lifting the glass to my lips, I took a sip of rum and said, 'If it is God's will that I should suffer, then so be it; however, I cannot understand why Annette must suffer too. It is incomprehensible. Why does He allow such things to happen?'

'Wiser men than I have attempted to answer that question with less than satisfactory results. But our inability to penetrate God's mysteries does not mean that He is indifferent to our suffering.'

'I wish that I could believe that.'

'Our Lord was assailed by doubts, monsieur. When he was being crucified, did he not cry out, "My God, my God, why hast Thou forsaken me?" No one is without doubts.'

I looked across the room at Annette. 'She is such a sweet child. I cannot bear to think of what torments she is being subjected to, even now – as we speak. I cannot bear to think of what the demon is doing to her.'

Father Lestoumel withdrew his hand. 'Consider this, my friend: if an evil man were possessed, how would we know it? Both he and the entity that had taken control of his mind would share the same objectives. Consequently, the man's behaviour would not change. Now, look at Annette! Her soul is not yielding. The demon is unable to manipulate her. In spirit, she is not a helpless child, but a power to be reckoned with.'

'That may be so. But she cannot be roused and she cannot eat or drink. We must act promptly, Father, or she will die.'

'Of course.' He took off his biretta and used it to swat at one of the flies. 'The demon must be cast out, and soon.'

'Have you ever performed an exorcism before, Father?'

'No.'

'Are you sure that . . .'

'I am equal to the task? All priests are Christ's foot soldiers. All priests are exorcists.'

There was little point in observing small courtesies at this juncture and I pursued my theme, 'Father Ranvier was a distinguished scholar. He had made a lifelong study of the cathedral in Paris and its lore. Yet he was no match for the demon.'

'Do not worry, monsieur,' my companion replied, 'I will not underestimate our adversary.'

I took one of the parchment seals from my pocket and handed it to the curé. His eyes narrowed as he examined the hieroglyphs. 'It is an amulet. I made it for Annette, but unfortunately I did not give it to her in time. For over a year now, I have been studying the books in the library.'

'An intriguing collection.'

'And I have good reason to believe that this seal will give you some protection.' The curé turned the parchment over and held it up to the light. I thought I detected a certain wariness in his manner. 'Father Lestoumel,' I continued, 'some believe that Joseph, the son of Jacob – who interpreted dreams – was a practitioner of Egyptian magic. Moses too. You will recall that the lawgiver carried a staff. It could also be described as a wand. Not all magic is bad, Father. And some spells have been used against the forces of evil from the earliest times. Please keep the amulet.'

The curé inclined his head and tucked the amulet into his pocket.

'Thank you,' he said. 'But I am already protected.'

'By your faith?'

'Indeed.' His conviction did not strengthen my confidence. On the contrary: if anything, it weakened it. 'Do you think the child can travel?' he asked.

'Yes, I suppose so. Why? Do you want her brought to Saint-Catherine?'

'No. I was thinking of somewhere further afield.'

'Where?'

'Paris.'

I was so stunned that I could only respond by making inarticulate noises.

'It may surprise you to learn,' the curé continued, 'that I am not entirely ignorant of the occult sciences. Indeed, I would go so far as to say that, for a country priest, I am quite well read. Before your appointment, after celebrating Mass in the chapel on special Saint's days for Madame Odile, I would very occasionally spend a few hours in the library. I may not be a scholar, but I have a reasonable understanding of what might be termed the elementary principles. And in my opinion the exorcism should take place in the cathedral. That is where this began, and that is where this must end.' I stuttered an objection but the curé dismissed my utterances with a wave of his biretta. 'Now, I wonder whether your friend Monsieur Bazile would be willing to help us? We will need to be in the cathedral at dawn, and we must have access to a secluded area where we will not be disturbed.'

'I have not corresponded with Monsieur Bazile since my departure from Paris.'

'Then we must hope that he still occupies the same position.'

The curé stood up and circled the desk, pulling at his chin and talking very quickly. He was not addressing me, but rather thinking aloud. 'We must leave as soon as possible to make use of the daylight. Louis will drive us. If we set off soon, we may be able to make the capital shortly after sunset.' I wanted to know why, precisely, he had determined that the exorcism should take place in the cathedral, but he was not very forthcoming. He offered me some vague generalizations and, when pressed, spoke only of symmetries, sympathies and correspondences. Eventually, he dismissed my requests for clarification with an impatient gesture and his monologue resumed. 'After my departure, you must inform Madame Du Bris of our plan. She will, of course, want to travel with us. I would suggest we assemble outside Saint-Catherine at one o'clock.'

As Father Lestoumel aired his thoughts, I became increasingly unsure whether I had made the right decision concerning his involvement. I was not convinced that he fully appreciated the terrible dangers we would face; however, I had no alternative but to follow his lead. He was a priest, and a priest was needed to conduct the exorcism. Our eyes met on one of his turns around the desk, and he must have seen my uncertainty, because he paused and gave me a strange little smile. 'Faith,' he said, before starting up again, 'have faith.' But I did not find this exhortation in any way reassuring.

When the curé finally ceased talking, he stood by the divan and removed the wooden cross that hung from his neck. He looped the leather lanyard over Annette's head and placed the sacred object on her chest. Then, touching the red weal on the child's forehead, he said, 'Be strong. May God protect you.' We shook hands. 'One o'clock, monsieur. Outside Saint-Catherine.' He pulled his biretta back on and vanished into the library.

I sat next to Annette and gazed down at her face. Her expression was serene and the colour had returned to her cheeks. She seemed calm and her breathing was regular. Outside, the birds were singing and the sun was high. A mechanical whirring filled the air before the clocks in the library and study began to chime. It was noon. Before the last note had faded, Annette's eyes flicked open. I was startled and gasped. Her head rolled to the side and she said, 'Monsieur Clément.' The voice was her own.

'Annette!'

'Monsieur, I am thirsty. May I have something to drink?'

'Yes, of course, of course.' I leaped off the chair and emptied a jug of water into a cup. Returning to the divan, I helped Annette to sit up and placed some cushions behind her back. I held the cup to her lips and she gulped the contents.

'I have had such bad dreams, monsieur.'

'Have you?'

'A foul creature, like the one on the church spire, came to me and would not leave me alone. It teased me and hurt me and called me names.'

'Annette, I am so sorry,' I took her hand in mine and held it tightly. I noticed that her nails had thickened.

'And there were fires and people screaming and monsters that came out of the earth.'

'Do not think about it.'

She frowned: 'Am I unwell again?'

'Yes.'

'Am I dying, monsieur?'

'No.'

'The creature said that I would die soon.'

'It was only a dream, Annette.' Her eyes glazed over and her head fell forward. 'Annette?' I cried, 'Annette?' But she was insensible. I heard a low growl, coming from the back of her throat, which was sustained and then inflected to produce obscenities. 'Annette?' She was gone. I removed the pillows, one by one, and ensured that she was lying comfortably. 'Take me!' I shouted in anger. 'Take me! Not her. I won't resist. Take me now!' But the demon did not accept my invitation. The hell that I occupied was far worse than the hell of fire and brimstone, and it wanted me to stay there for as long as possible.

I wiped away my tears and rang for a servant. It was Monique who came, and I told her to go and wake Madame Du Bris immediately. 'But do not alarm your mistress,' I called after her as she descended the stairs. 'Tell her that Annie is well.' A few minutes later, Hélène stepped into my study. She anticipated my apology and said, 'I was not asleep.' Looking about the room, she added, 'Where is Father Lestoumel?'

'He has gone back to the village.'

'And when will he be returning?'

'He won't be.' I gestured for her to sit and told her of the curé's plan.

'But why must we go to Paris? To Notre-Dame?' Hélène asked.

'It is a very holy place,' I replied. She did not appear very satisfied with my answer and I felt obliged to add, 'We must place our trust in Father Lestoumel.'

While Hélène sat with Annette, I searched for Louis and found him in the kitchen. I told him to pack a small travelling bag and to prepare the two-horse carriage for Paris. Years of service had accustomed him to obeying orders and he hardly blinked when I added that we intended to leave in half an hour. On my way back to the study I encountered Raboulet. He was wearing a dressing gown, a pair of oriental slippers, and held Elektra in his arms.

'Clément, what is going on? I can't find Hélène any where and Madame Boustagnier tells me that Annette is very ill.'

'Yes, I'm afraid that what you have heard is correct. Multiple seizures . . . through the night.'

'How dreadful.'

'I have done all that I can, but it is not enough. I have decided to take her to Paris, to see Charcot.'

'Charcot?'

'If anyone can help her, it will be the chief of services of the Salpêtrière.'

'Do you want me to come with you?'

'No, that won't be necessary. Madame Du Bris will be accompanying me on the journey.'

'Can I see Annette?

'Now? I'd rather you didn't – she's sleeping. The poor child is exhausted.' Elektra insinuated a tiny finger into her father's mouth and laughed. 'Forgive me, but . . .' I indicated that I needed to get past and Raboulet stepped aside. Thanking him, I hurried through the connected rooms and ascended the stairs to my study.

Hélène was still sitting beside the divan and she informed me that Annette had been silent and calm. In turn, I recounted what I had said to Raboulet concerning the pretext for our imminent departure. Hélène then left to make her own preparations for travel and I washed and shaved. Even though the windows were closed, there were flies everywhere, and I supposed that there must be some connection between their increase and the demon. Anger welled up in me and I slapped one hard against the mirror. As I removed my hand, the squashed insect fell into my shaving bowl and sank beneath the suds.

When I heard the horses neighing and the rattle of the carriage, I picked up Annette and carried her down to the courtyard. In the bright benevolent sunlight she looked much the same as she always looked: a beautiful child, sleeping. It was fortunate that the hour of the day favoured the forces of light over the forces of darkness, because Raboulet was waiting to see us off and I did not want him to see his niece speaking in tongues or mouthing obscenities. Hélène got into the carriage and Raboulet helped me to lift Annette onto the seat. We settled her head on her mother's lap and covered her body with a blanket. Raboulet stroked her hair and noticed the red mark that Father Lestoumel had made with the host.

'What's that?' he asked.

'A rash,' I replied. He looked a little perplexed but made nothing of it. He then jumped down from the carriage and handed me my medical bag and a battery I had sent down earlier. I was already thinking the unthinkable.

Louis mounted the box and as soon as we were beyond the gardens I instructed him to stop outside Saint-Catherine. We arrived at the village shortly before one o'clock, but Father Lestoumel was not waiting for us. I entered the church and found the curé kneeling before the altar and praying. By his side was a large leather satchel. It was unfastened and appeared to contain a Bible, several candles and a rolled-up stole. He heard my approach, made the sign of the cross and rose to greet me. 'Is it one o'clock already?'

'Yes,' I replied. What little confidence I had in him suddenly evaporated. He looked small and slightly befuddled. 'Father,' I continued, 'are you sure you want to proceed?'

'Of course'

'If you had decided otherwise, I would not think ill of you.'

'The child's life is in danger.'

'Yes, and so is yours, Father.'

'Indeed, but I am not frightened.'

'You should be.'

'I do not want to die. But if God wills it . . .' He shrugged and repeated the same empty injunction that I had heard so many times before, and now served only to deepen my despondency: 'Faith, my friend. Have faith.' He smiled and added, 'Come over here. I want to show you something.' I followed him down a side aisle and we stopped beneath the stained-glass window of Gilbert de Gandelus and the demon. The image was so arresting

337

and colourful it was easy to overlook the rusted metal plate in the wall below it. Plunging his hand into the deep pocket of his cassock, the curé produced a key, and it was at this point that I realized what I was looking at: not a plate, but a door. Father Lestoumel pushed the key into the lock and, when he turned it, the sound of the bolt's release echoed through the church. He pressed his finger into the small gap between the metal and the stone wall and pulled the door open. Then, he reached into the dim compartment and removed a large book which he held out for me to examine. It was bound in red leather and the hasps were made from gold. My eyes oscillated between the book and the glowing image of its double in the stained glass. The curé showed me the spine and indicated the title: *Malleus Daemonum* – the Hammer of Demons.

'This, my friend,' said Father Lestoumel, 'was the secret of Gilbert de Gandelus's remarkable success. It was given to him by Roland Du Bris, an ancestor of the family you serve, at the time of the Séry-des-Fontaines possessions. The author of this volume is none other than the great alchemist Nicolas Flamel, who lived not very far from the cathedral in Paris. You will already know, of course, that he is reputed to have made a philosopher's stone and to have discovered the elixir of life. This remarkable tome, which has, for obvious reasons, escaped the notice of scholars through the centuries, contains a ritual of restitution – a ritual that can send demons back to hell. Flamel suggests that, where an exorcist can identify the portal through which a demon came into the world, that is where the ritual is most likely to be effective. I have long wondered why it has fallen upon me, a simple country priest, to be the custodian of this hidden treasure. But now I think I know. The Almighty has a plan, you see? I have my small part to play – just as you do, monsieur.' He handed me the book. 'Come now,' he concluded. 'We must make haste. It is past one o'clock and the road to Paris is long.'

24

Little was said in the carriage. The curé closed his eyes, sat very still and only the occasional movement of his lips, accompanied by a whispered invocation, indicated that he was at prayer. Hélène rested her head on the woodwork and gazed out of the window at the rolling countryside. I studied her reflection in the glass and watched the clouds passing behind her image. The situation in which she found herself was so far removed from the gentle routines of the chateau: her expression was blank and her jaw tensely set. Apart from the occasional grumble, Annette was relatively quiet. At regular intervals I took her pulse and found no change. Consequently, I was able to spend much of the first half of our journey perusing the *Malleus Daemonum*.

It was a remarkable piece of scholarship and contained chapters on a wide range of subjects: the provenance of demons, the demonic hierarchy and the names of the princes of hell; words of power; summoning demons and commanding them to do one's bidding; the making of pacts; capturing demons in glass, precious stones and rings; the demons of the Middle East, or djinni; the classification of demons according to Raban the Moor; incubi and succubi; magical weapons; exorcism; and finally, sending demons back to the inferno. I was astonished when I discovered a map of Paris, showing the location of what Flamel called 'openings' between our world and the 'infernal region'. Each was represented by a black circle, and the largest of these was located on the Île de la Cité, next to a miniature illustration of Notre-Dame. The ritual of restitution was decorated with figures representing the exorcist in various attitudes, and superimposed on mathematical diagrams. An explanatory footnote suggested that Flamel's geometry was originally developed by Daedalus, the engineer who designed the labyrinth in which the legendary minotaur was imprisoned.

We made good progress, stopping only twice to water the horses; however, I was conscious of the sun's steady descent, and as the shadows lengthened, Annette became more restless. There were bursts of obscene language and her fingers toyed with the hem of her smock. An hour or so before sunset, I noticed another curious phenomenon: Annette's skin seemed to become unnaturally smooth, making her face look like a tight-fitting mask. I did not want to worry Hélène, and said nothing, but eventually the effect was so pronounced that she also noticed and said, 'Monsieur? What is happening to Annette's face? She looks like a doll.'

'Dehydration,' I replied.

The curé caught my eye and continued his prayers.

He knew perfectly well that the phenomenon was supernatural, but, like me, he did not want to alarm Hélène unnecessarily.

And so the day passed, and we arrived at the southern tip of the capital in darkness. I got out of the carriage, joined Louis on the box, and directed him through the streets. Louis had only been to Paris once before, as a young man, and he could not believe how impatient the other drivers were. 'They are all lunatics, monsieur!' he cried, as a cab carelessly swerved in front of us and a crude imprecation resonated in the air. The old retainer gawped at the advertisements, shop windows and painted whores, who showed us their ankles and blew us kisses. After the peace and sleepy charm of Chambault, Paris was indeed like a madhouse.

As we came to a halt outside Saint-Sulpice, the bells started ringing. I prayed that it was Bazile, and not one of his assistants – or even worse, a new bell-ringer. The door to the north tower was unlocked and I climbed the stairs. Only a glimmer of light filtered down from above. Eventually, I came to Bazile's apartment. I knocked on the door, which was immediately opened by Madame Bazile.

'Monsieur Clément!' She cried. 'Good heavens! Monsieur Clément! Do come in, do come in!' I stepped into the parlour and my head filled with recollections of talk and sweet cider. 'Let me take your coat,' said Madame Bazile, fussing around me. 'Édouard has just rung the hour. He will be down in a moment.'

'How is he?' I asked.

'Well,' she replied. 'And you, Monsiuer Clément? How have you been?'

Before I could answer, the door opened and Bazile stepped into the room. He started and looked at me as if I were a ghost. 'Paul?' he said, a note of doubt creeping into his voice. The sight of my old friend touched me deeply and my eyes became hot and moist. He came forward, extending his arm, but when I took his hand, I drew him towards me and we embraced.

'It isn't over, then,' he said.

'No,' I replied.

'I knew you would come back, one day,' said Bazile, slapping my back. 'What took you so long?'

We carried Annette up the stairs of the north tower and put her to bed, after which I dismissed Louis, telling him to return with the carriage an hour before dawn. Up until that point he had accepted all of his instructions without question; however, before making his departure, he hesitated and said, 'Does the master know we are in Paris?'

'Yes,' I replied. 'Monsieur Raboulet promised to send a note.'

Louis gave a curt nod and began his descent of the stairs, but a trace of mistrust lingered in his eyes.

On returning to the parlour I found Bazile poring over the Hammer of Demons, with Father Lestoumel sitting at his side relating its history. Hélène and Madame Bazile were in the bedroom, watching over Annette. I was surprised to discover that Bazile was acquainted with the name of Gilbert de Gandelus. He even knew of the holy man's victory over evil at Séry-des-Fontaines. The curé was most impressed. When I showed Bazile the map of Paris with its many circular 'openings', his face shone with excitement. 'There it is!' he cried, pointing at the illustration of the cathedral. 'Proof that Father Ranvier was right!'

I tried, as best I could, to summarize what had transpired at Chambault – the cracking of the glass and the sequence of events leading to Annette's possession – although, once again, I felt obliged to protect Hélène's modesty and did not mention what had occurred in her bedchamber. Nor did I say anything about Thérèse Courbertin.

Bazile listened in his customary fashion, smoking his pipe and frowning. When my story was concluded he shook his head and said, 'We are up against a fearful adversary!'

'Indeed,' said the curé, 'it is a member of the hellish aristocracy, a grand duke of the infernal kingdom.' He drew Bazile's attention to the final chapter of the Hammer of Demons. 'What we must do,' said Father Lestoumel, 'must be done in the cathedral. That is what Flamel advises. Can you help us?'

Bazile bit on his pipe stem. 'The bell-ringers of Paris are – as it were – a brotherhood, and if the need arises, we can call upon each other for favours. I will consult with Quenardel, the chief bell-ringer of Notre-Dame.' Bazile stood up and lifted his coat off a peg on the wall. 'There is a room in the north tower of the cathedral that will suit our purposes. I will return with the key as soon as possible.' And the next instant, he was gone.

After ten minutes or so Hélène appeared in the doorway that connected the parlour to the rest of the apartment. She leaned against the jamb and seemed so frail and weak, I feared she might be about to faint. 'Father Lestoumel, Monsieur Clément,' she said, her voice quavering. 'Please come quickly.'

She led us to the bedroom, where Madame Bazile was placing pieces of incense in small dishes. It was cold and the air was tainted with the smell of ordure. Annette was very still, but the skin of her face seemed to have shrunk even more tightly around her skull: it had a glazed quality, like porcelain, and seemed just as likely to shatter. Although her mouth was closed, I could hear a steady stream of obscenities, articulated in the unnaturally low register I had heard the previous night.

The curé knelt by the bedside, took Annette's hand in his own and began to pray: 'Soul of Christ, sanctify me. Body of Christ, save me. Blood of Christ, exalt me.' Madame Bazile held a lit match against the incense and the room soon filled with the fragrance of sandalwood. 'Water from the side of Christ, wash me. My good Jesus, hear me. Within your wounds hide me. Never permit me to be separated from you. At the hour of death, call me.' The demonic voice faded, but it was still present – a persistent growling. I listened to Father Lestoumel, his gentle delivery, and found some comfort in the rhythm and cadence of prayer. But I was still incapable of accepting such sentiments. I was still paralysed by reason: if God is love, then He would not permit a demon to torment an innocent child. Therefore, God cannot be love. I could not think beyond the logic of this proposition. Father Lestoumel continued, 'To you do we send up our sighs, mourning and weeping in this valley of tears.'

I watched the smoke rising from the incense dishes and noticed a strange discrepancy. Above one, the smoke was dissipating in the usual manner, whereas above the other the smoke seemed to be accumulating. Grey wisps and filaments collected in the air, becoming more and more condensed as the sandalwood burned. For a fraction of a second, the play of lamp light on the cloud made it look like a head with projecting horns, and then, a moment later, there was nothing to see except a haze of expanding tendrils. I threw glances at the others, Father Lestoumel, Hélène and Madame Bazile, but none of them had observed this sudden transformation.

What I had witnessed was no phantasm of the brain, but a demonstration of power. I was being mocked, taunted. Although the room resounded with prayer, the demon was showing me how it could easily reach out and manipulate the material world. I sensed that something very terrible was about to happen.

Annette's hand moved so fast, all that I could detect was a blur. Father Lestoumel cried out and fell backwards, gagging on the wooden cross that had been jammed into his mouth. I heard Hélène scream, and then, Annette's body, as rigid as a plank, levitated. She rose up off the bed and began to spin. I was dimly aware of Madame Bazile kneeling beside Father Lestoumel and leaped over the priest's body. Grasping Annette's smock, I pulled on the material, but my efforts met with strong resistance and my feet almost left the ground. As soon as her back touched the eiderdown she began to thrash about and I had to use all of my weight to restrain her movements. The voice started up again, close to my ear, and embedded within a continuous stream of ugly babblings I detected a single intelligible sentence: 'For her soul I shall defile and her flesh shall I use for my satisfaction.' I was sickened and hoped that Hélène had not heard this. Annette's limbs started to jerk. She was no longer trying to break free, but in the throes of another seizure. Her spasms were so violent that I began to fear that her spine might snap. When the bucking stopped I wiped the foam from her chin and checked her pulse, which I found to be slow and weak.

I turned round and saw Hélène standing in the middle of the room, eyes wide open and biting her knuckles. She looked like a woman teetering on the edge of derangement. Madam Bazile was squatting next to the curé dabbing blood from his lips. I hurried over to examine his injuries. Two of his teeth had been knocked out and the roof of his mouth was deeply scored.

'Do you want something for the pain?' I asked.

He shook his head, and for the first time I saw self-doubt in his eyes: recognition of his own limitations and the fact that good does not always triumph over evil. Although we were armed with Flamel's Hammer of Demons, our victory was by no means certain.

'Don't worry about me,' Father Lestoumel replied, 'Take care of the girl.'

I returned to Annette, who was now still and quiet, and with Hélène's assistance washed away some soiling and changed her clothes. Hélène worked quickly and efficiently, but her hands were unsteady and her eyes unnaturally bright.

'Madame,' I said, 'you do not have to watch with us. You are exhausted. Please, go next door.'

She did not reply and gave me a hard look: a look that pierced my heart, because her eyes were accusing me. 'This is your fault,' they said, 'this is all your fault.' I pulled a chair from beneath the dressing table and added, 'At least sit down.' She did as I asked, but did not thank me.

Annette's breathing had become very shallow and her skin was completely drained of colour – a terrible, inanimate white: the white of chalk or alabaster, as if all the vessels in her body had been sucked dry. Sitting by her bedside, I heard an abrasive noise and noticed dust on my sleeve. I looked up at the ceiling, warily, but said nothing to the others.

An hour passed and Bazile came back, brandishing the key to the north tower of the cathedral. He had, no doubt, been expecting a warmer reception – handshakes and congratulations. But his smile disintegrated when he saw our grim expressions.

'What has happened?' he asked.

Father Lestoumel took his arm. 'Let us go into the parlour. I will explain everything there.' The curé did not want Hélène to hear his account. He, too, was worried about her mental state.

Annette's pulse was weakening, and by the time Father Lestoumel and Bazile returned, I could hardly find it. The curé resumed his prayers: 'Glory be to the Father, and the Son, and the Holy Spirit. As it was in the beginning, is now, and shall be, for ever and ever. Amen.'

Bazile appeared at my side.

'Are you all right?' he whispered.

'Yes,' I replied.

But his dark eyes registered my apprehension.

Annette gave a little sigh, and when the exhalation was complete, her pulse faltered and stopped. She was dead.

I did not move. Time halted with the cessation of her life. The moment I inhabited was infinite, and it seemed that I had an eternity in which to commune with Annette's impassive features. But then a tremor passed through my body and I was seized by rage, 'No, no!' I shouted. 'You shall not have her!' The emotion that animated me was exceptionally pure: complexities could not survive its fierce intensity. Suddenly, the world was a simpler place, my mind was emptied of redundant philosophy, I was not a player in some preordained drama in which the forces of good were pitched against the forces of evil. God and his mysterious intentions were completely irrelevant. What mattered now was this: the demon should not be victorious. Excepting myself and my enemy, the universe was now void.

I opened my medical bag, removed a scalpel, and cut down the front of Annette's smock.

'What are you doing, monsieur?' cried Hélène.

I did not reply and heaved the battery onto the bed. I raised the lid, adjusted the coil and the machine began to buzz. Placing the electrodes over Annette's heart, I delivered the maximum charge. Her body convulsed, but when I laid my ear against her chest, there was no heartbeat. 'Damn you!' I shouted, and again I applied the electrodes. Two threads of brilliant blue light dropped from the rods and scorched her skin. A second convulsion: but still nothing. Cold flesh and silence. I brought my clenched fist down on her sternum with such force that Annette's body bounced several times on the mattress. A pocket of trapped air stimulated her vocal cords and she emitted a pathetic whimper. 'Come back!' I yelled. 'You cannot die, you must not die!' Again, I placed the electrodes over her heart and – ignoring the smell of cooked flesh – did not remove them until her third convulsion came to an end. The pitch of the buzzing ascended and there was a loud report. A flame danced around the blackened coil and then went out. I threw the rods aside and pressed my hand against the side of Annette's neck. 'She's alive,' I cried. 'She's alive. Her heart is beating again.' Then, addressing Father Lestoumel, I added, 'We cannot wait until dawn. We must go to the cathedral now.'

'But the demon is at its most powerful at night,' said the curé. 'That would be most unwise.'

'The battery is broken,' I continued, 'and if Annette's heart stops again, I will not be able to revive her. Father Lestoumel, we must go to the cathedral now or she will die!'

Hélène swooned and Madame Bazile rushed to her assistance.

'Very well,' said the curé, 'let us go.'

I did not stop to examine Hélène. Instead, I picked up the child and strode towards the door.

'But what about Madame Du Bris?' asked Madame Bazile.

'The ritual we are about to perform is extremely dangerous,' I replied. 'It is just as well she will not be present.'

The bell-ringer's wife looked up at her husband. 'Are you going with them, Édouard?'

'Yes,' said Bazile, nodding his head vigorously.

'It is not necessary,' I said. 'Father Lestoumel and I can perform the ritual on our own.'

'I am afraid,' said Bazile, 'that my mind is made up. Come now, my friend, this is no time to quibble.'

We did not have to wait very long outside Saint-Sulpice before the lamps of a cab emerged from the gloom. The driver looked alarmed when he saw the girl in my arms.

'I am a doctor,' I said. 'This child has had a seizure and is close to death. She has already received extreme unction,' I nodded towards the curé. 'Please, take us to the Hôtel Dieu.'

'Put her inside,' said the driver. 'I'll get you there in five minutes.'

25

The cathedral loomed over us, its communities of saints, angels and demons ascending in energetic elevations towards a low vault of heavy cloud. Bazile unlocked the door of the north tower and, when he pulled it open, light spilled out from within. The interior had been hung with oil lamps. 'Quenardel,' said the bell-ringer. 'He is most thoughtful.'

We ascended the spiral staircase and came to a cavernous room littered with pieces of masonry and the decayed parts of statues. I had passed through this space before – it seemed a lifetime ago – when I had climbed up to the viewing platform and observed dawn breaking over Paris in the company of the chimeras.

'Is this the place?' asked the curé.

'Yes,' said Bazile.

Father Lestoumel looked around and smiled. 'You have chosen well, my friend.' He then produced some candles, which he lit and fixed to the floor with melted wax. I made myself as comfortable as possible, sitting with my legs crossed and cradling Annette's head in my lap. Her breathing was barely perceptible. 'Please hurry, Father,' I said.

'Monsieur Bazile,' said the curé, 'would you be so kind as to hold the book for me?'

The bell-ringer positioned himself in front of Father Lestoumel, holding the Hammer of Demons open so that the curé could read the text. There were no preparatory remarks. Father Lestoumel simply cleared his throat and began to chant. Some of the words were familiar, being either Latin or Greek; others, however, were in a language I did not recognize. As Father Lestoumel chanted, he moved his hands through the air, tracing the outlines of figures. At first, the shapes were simple – squares, triangles, circles – but then the movements became more complex, and it was no longer possible to identify specific forms.

Annette's face was now like a death's head. She had become a strange ceramic effigy. Her thin blue lips were pulled back to reveal two rows of even teeth and a blackened, swollen tongue protruding between them. The fetid exhalations that rose up from her mouth smelled like rotting fish. She rolled her head and spat out words that sounded like an Arabic curse.

'Hurry, Father!' I cried, fearful that we might lose Annette at any moment.

The curé did not acknowledge my appeal. Instead, he maintained the steady metre of his chant and continued to divide the air with graceful, sweeping gestures.

When I returned my attention to Annette, her eyelids

rolled back revealing only white, bloodshot membranes. 'End this now,' she growled. 'If you send me back, you know who I will seek.' I felt as if I had been splashed with acid. 'I will befoul your strumpet and violate her – rip her belly and make a garland of her bowels. I will undo her and feast on her yielding parts.'

'Do not listen to it!' shouted Bazile.

I looked into Annette's empty eyes, fighting to overcome a wave of nausea and terror, and said, 'Your time in this world is over.'

The demon responded with a horrible, grating laugh: 'Have you found faith?'

'No,' I replied. 'I have found hate, and with it, singularity of purpose.'

'You make my work so easy,' the fiend replied, before producing a series of harsh barks that managed to express merriment.

'Do not speak to it!' screamed Bazile, making frantic gestures. 'Do not let it into your mind! Nothing can be gained by engaging with the deceiver!'

'You think it is over?' said the demon, a note of amusement animating its gravelly monotone. 'Think again, fool. It is only the beginning.'

Bazile was right. Even though our exchange had been brief, it was enough to empower the demon. With each sentence, it seemed to find communicating easier. Moreover, its parting remark, delivered with such supreme confidence, weakened my resolve. As I swayed on the edge of some inner precipice, confused, shocked, enfeebled, I was startled by an electrical crackling; a short distance from where I sat, beyond Annette's feet, the darkness was infiltrated by a soft red glow. Veils of luminosity folded and dissolved into shimmering sprays of light. The portal was opening.

Father Lestoumel's hands fell by his side and he began to recite the ritual of exorcism. Not the Rituale Romanum, but a translation of an eighth-century Galician manuscript favoured by Flamel: 'I accost you, damned and most impure spirit, cause of malice, essence of crimes, origin of sins, you revel in deceit, sacrilege, adultery and murder! I adjure you in Christ's name that, in whatsoever part of the body you are hiding, you declare yourself, that you flee the body you are occupying and from which we drive you with spiritual whips and invisible torments. I demand that you leave this body which has been cleansed by the Lord. Let it be enough for you that in earlier ages you dominated almost the entire world through your action on the hearts of human beings.'

Annette's limbs began to jerk.

'Father!' I called out. 'She's having another seizure. It's trying to kill her. Please hurry.'

The curé and Bazile came forward and the two men knelt beside me. Annette's jaw snapped shut and a stripe of bright blood appeared on her lip. I clasped her mouth and made sure that it remained closed.

'Now, day by day,' declaimed Father Lestoumel, 'your kingdom is being destroyed, your arms weakening.

Your punishment has been prefigured of old. Through the power of all the saints you are tormented, crushed and sent down to eternal flames.'

The candles began to flicker. We felt the flow of chill air against our cheeks, and a moment later the curé's biretta blew off his head and rolled across the floor towards the portal. Air was being sucked from our world into some empty vastness.

Father Lestoumel looked around anxiously before laying both of his hands on Annette's forehead. 'Depart, depart!' he cried, 'Whencesoever you lurk, and nevermore seek out bodies dedicated to God.' I could hardly hear his voice above the rushing wind. All the candles had blown out, but we could still see each other, our faces bathed in the radiance of the portal. Bazile lifted the Hammer of Demons higher so that the curé could read the text more easily. 'Let them be forbidden to you forever, in the name of the Father, the Son, and the Holy Spirit.'

This final affirmation of the trinity was like the last chord of a great symphony. Father Lestoumel allowed himself a small, triumphal smile. There was nothing more to do. He took the book from Bazile, closed its covers and held it against his chest.

Almost immediately, Annette stopped kicking. Her skin seemed to loosen around her skull – the hardened, smooth-textured contours became less reflective and softened as her features filled out. I watched, astonished, as the frozen thing she had become, thawed with the returning warmth of her humanity. Her face was so tranquil, calm and harmonious that I was suddenly fearful that she might be dead. I pressed my fingers against her neck. 'Dear God,' I cried. 'Please. I beg you . . .' And there it was – a faint perturbation, buried deep in the flesh. The movement of blood: life. I let out a sigh of relief, kissed her hair and thanked the Lord for His protection.

When I looked up again, I saw that something had interposed itself between our small, huddled group and the portal – a dark, nebulous mass. Against the glittering red light, I glimpsed the scalloped edge of an enormous wing, claws, two horns, the glint of polished scales. Each of these parts appeared momentarily before disappearing. The demon was clearly attempting to materialize. Was this supposed to happen? Fear gripped my throat and I could barely breathe. Then, quite suddenly, the demon was drifting backwards, its efforts frustrated by energies of unimaginable magnitude.

I was overcome by a kind of inebriate madness. Shaking my fist, I shouted, 'Go back to hell! You have been defeated! Go back to hell and never return! It is over! Do you hear me? Over!' The wind was still whistling above the crackling accompaniment of electrical activity. 'Go back to hell!' I yelled above the noise. 'You foul, pathetic creature! This child is free – and you will never have possession of her again!'

There were no more materializations, and the formless darkness receded through the twinkling veils.

I had always been the weaker party. But now, as the balance of power shifted, I became drunk with excitement. I wanted to taunt, mock and gloat, to revel in my victory. I let go of Annette, stood up and screamed abuse into the void. 'You have been defeated and I have won!'

Bazile and Father Lestoumel were scrambling at my feet. Then, I saw Annette's supine body sliding away. She was travelling fast, her legs slightly raised, her hair trailing, as if being dragged. I choked on my own words as she passed through the shimmering divide. My adversary was no longer visible. But neither was Annette.

The despair that I felt is impossible to describe. It fell upon me like a weight of marble: a devastating, crippling despair that I knew I could never live with. Bazile guessed my intention and grabbed my arm. He hauled himself up and hollered into my ear. 'No. Don't do it, Paul!'

'Let me go,' I protested.

'The portal will close and you will be trapped there forever.'

'Let me go, I say!'

'For the love of God, Paul. You can do nothing now.'

I prised his fingers from my arm, pushed him away and ran towards the threshold. The wind was at my back and I almost took off as I passed through the undulating waves of luminescence. I ran and ran, through glowing nebulae and cobwebby threads of light, and kept on running, beyond where the wall of the tower should have stopped my progress. The strength of the wind lessened and I found myself charging blindly through a sulphurous mist. I could feel pumice breaking beneath my feet, and the surface over which I travelled became uneven. 'Annette?' I called out. 'Annette?' The atmosphere thinned and I recognized an all too familiar landscape: a black sky riven by crimson lightning, an expanse of cinders giving way to a massive staircase of congealed lava, crags and smoking vents, belching pools of molten rock.

There was a loud detonation, and a tower of flame climbed to a great height. The blast sent me sprawling onto a carpet of hot ash. I quickly jumped up and waved my scorched hands in the air.

Unlike the occasion of my first descent into the pit, when I had arrived naked, this time I was still wearing clothes – the same clothes that I had put on in my rooms at the chateau two days earlier. They had travelled with me between worlds; however, the blisters that were already rising on my palms confirmed that, in one other respect, my circumstance was very much the same. I was fully embodied, with blood and organs and nerves that had the capacity to thrill with pain.

The smell of burning leather made me leap off the ash and I proceeded between two boulders, both of which bristled with large, flat-headed nails. Manacles hung down from rusty hooks and medieval instruments of torture lay abandoned and half buried in dunes of volcanic dust.

'Annette?' I cried. 'Annette? Where are you?'

I emerged into a shallow depression of shattered stone,

and saw a tiny crumpled figure lying on the ground a short distance ahead. I hastened down the incline and slid to a halt, falling on my knees at the child's side.

'Annette?' I whispered, lifting her face off a pillow of cracked granite. The blood on her lip had dried, but there were fresh lacerations on her cheeks. Her smock was torn and parts of her hair had been singed. I touched her lips and said, 'Annette? Can you hear me?'

Her eyes opened. 'Monsieur Clément?'

'Yes, Annette.'

'Have I been unwell again?'

'Yes. I'm afraid so.'

'Why is the sky black? Why is the sky on fire?'

I tucked a loose lock of hair behind her ear. 'Hush. We are going home.'

'Home?'

'Yes. Can you stand?'

'I think so. Where are we?'

'Annette. Take my hand. We must go now.'

But I did not move. There was a trickling of scree and a shadow fell across Annette's smock. My heart was hammering against my ribcage, and my courage drained into the earth. I was paralysed, unable to even turn round. Instead, I watched with weird fascination, as Annette's pupils dilated and her mouth opened wide. There was a beat of silence, before the scream came.

The demon had positioned itself on the boundary of the depression. It looked immense, silhouetted against a delta of blazing reticulations. Its great wings unfolded and it stood, legs set apart, proudly surveying its domain. I was in no doubt that we were in the presence of a true prince of hell, and my instinct was to prostrate myself and beg for mercy. I withered in its sight. The demon threw its head back and roared. A clap of thunder shook the ground, new vents opened, and the horizon burst into flames.

Annette's fingernails were digging into my skin.

'Monsieur Clément, Monsieur Clément . . .' she repeated my name, again and again.

'Run, child,' I said. 'Quick. This way.' I tugged her upright and we bounded up the incline, back towards the portal, but the loose stone was treacherous and we kept on slipping. I looked over my shoulder and saw the demon loping after us, horns thrust forward. 'Quick, Annette, you must run faster.'

'I can't, monsieur. I can't.' She had already fallen several times and blood was streaming from the cuts on her knees.

'You must!' I hauled her over the top. We ran between the boulders and out, into the open space beyond. I paused to get my bearings. The wide flat steps of lava were clearly visible, as were the bubbling pools of liquid rock. In the distance, I could see the coruscating mists of the portal. 'Not far now,' I said to Annette. 'Just over there.'

We set off again, giving the hot ash a wide berth. A meteor landed close by and we were showered with debris. Annette yelped with pain. 'We cannot stop,' I said. 'We must go on.' It was then that the air filled with a harsh barracking and a flock of demons soared into view. They glided over the lava steps and circled above us. One by one, they dropped to the ground, forming a ring that made our escape impossible. My old adversary appeared between the boulders and snarled some commands. The horde stamped their feet and waved their pitchforks, shrieking and grunting in their infernal language.

'What will they do to us?' asked Annette. I could not give her an answer. The thought of how these devils would abuse her made me feel quite sick. I could feel Annette trembling beneath the thin and filthy material of her smock. 'Is this a dream, monsieur?' she continued. 'A nightmare? Tell me that I am dreaming.'

The demon fixed its venomous eyes on Annette; its lower jaw sagged and its tongue slithered out. It tasted the air and the cast of its expression became eager and lascivious. Then it raised its arm, and a single talon sprang up, its curvature suggestive of beckoning without the necessity of movement.

'No,' I cried. 'You shall not have her!' A pitchfork hissed through the air and pinned my foot to the ground. I wrenched it away and enfolded Annette in my arms. The troop flapped their wings and jeered. More demons were landing on the lava steps; one of them was carrying a decapitated head which it tossed in the air and kicked. The head flew through space and descended into a pool of magma, where it sizzled and evaporated.

Annette was sobbing into my shirt. I held her close and said, 'Dear child. Know this. Whatever happens, you were loved.' She would be tortured for all of eternity and it was my fault. I was to blame! It was only right that I should burn, that I should be skewered and roasted. But I could not countenance the suffering of a stainless innocent. 'I am so sorry,' I said, tightening my embrace. 'So very, very sorry.' Tears streamed down her face and, out of habit, I searched my pockets for a handkerchief. How curious, that this reflex, this vestige of normality, should find expression, even in the depths of hell. My fingers made contact with something papery. It was the amulet: the amulet that I had copied in the library – the Seal of Shabako.

The demon lunged forward, and as it did so, I removed the parchment from my pocket. As soon as the charm came into view, the creature drew back. Its thick brows came together and it produced a lengthy sibilance. The amulet was emitting a bright, golden light. I whirled round, brandishing it like a torch, and our tormentors were thrown into disarray. Some opened their wings and took off, while others covered their eyes.

Here was old magic: power that required no faith or belief in an all-knowing God to have its effect; a power as morally neutral as magnetism.

'Get back!' I commanded as the monsters fled. 'Get back!' The ruddy luminescence of the portal was fading. 'Come,' I said to Annette. 'We are running out of time.' At that moment, my adversary chose to pounce. It leaped high and was almost upon us, its fangs bared and claws extended. Without thinking, I raised the amulet and shouted, 'Away!' A bolt of lightning streaked from my fist and exploded against its chest. The demon spun backwards and crashed into the hot ash, raising a column of grey cloud. I did not stop to enjoy the spectacle, but simply clutched Annette's hand and shouted, 'Run!'

I held the amulet high, and its radiance repelled the swooping demons. Pitchforks rained down and thrummed after impact, producing a strange, metallic counterpoint. The glittering mists of the portal lay just ahead of us. We ran, faster and faster, until we were swallowed up, and could see nothing but a wall of dense fog. There was no way of determining direction in this featureless expanse, and I wondered if it were possible to get lost in the spaces between worlds. Would we be there forever, trapped in a state of eternal transition? The lights were dimmer and it occurred to me that the portal might already be closed.

The acoustic changed and the ground became level.

'Keep going,' I said to Annette. 'We are almost home!'

I could hear the skittering of pebbles on flagstones. The fog parted, and its dissipation revealed a solitary shimmering veil. Through this ghostly partition, I saw two flames – oil lamps – the welcoming light of our own world.

'This way,' I said to Annette.

Although we were now sprinting, the distance between ourselves and the veil was not diminishing as fast as it should. The very fabric of space seemed to be stretching, denying us progress proportionate to our effort.

My lungs were aching and I was overcome by a terrible feeling of tiredness and fatigue.

'It cannot end here!' I cried out, and miraculously my anger released some last reserve of strength. Pulling Annette along behind me, I accelerated. It felt like running up an impossibly steep hill. Soon, the veil was floating in front of me – but its edges were contracting. I yanked Annette forward and pushed her through. Her body seemed to meet some resistance, and the child let out a cry. I pushed harder and saw her fall to the ground on the other side. Two figures rushed out of the darkness: Bazile and Father Lestoumel.

The bell-ringer was peering through the glare, as if trying to make out something distant or indistinct. 'Édouard!' I yelled, but he could not hear me. I saw him reaching out and his fingers penetrated the veil. Each digit became elongated and moved slowly, like the tentacles of a sea anemone. Concentric rings of light rippled outwards from the rupture as I leaned forward with my right arm extended, straining until we touched. Our fingers found mutual purchase and interlocked. Bazile pulled hard, and I was drawn closer to the veil; however, I could not make the transition. Then, dismayed, I realized that it was no longer Bazile who was dragging me through to his side, but it was I who was dragging him through to mine. His attenuated wrist and forearm were now clearly visible.

'Let go!' I cried. My friend held fast. 'Let go!' I struggled to free myself, but Bazile was strong and determined. He did not give up. I felt a sharp pain in my shoulder and imagined the tearing of ligaments, the ball of the joint being torn from its socket. An old memory surfaced: climbing a mountain of rubble during the siege and seeing a pale arm sticking up from the wreckage – tugging at the hand – feeling the whole limb come away. Had I been offered a cruel presentiment of my own end? A foreshadowing of my own dismemberment and demise? Had my doom been decided upon before the stars were scattered across the void?

'No!' I screamed – and jumped.

When my feet left the ground, there was a subtle change in the interplay of forces. Bazile's grip tightened and I seemed to be passing through a medium much thicker than air. Enormous pressures built up around me and I feared that I might be crushed. There was one more burst of red lightning – then nothing.

I must have lost consciousness, because the next thing I remember is Bazile's head, eclipsing the high Gothic ceiling.

'Paul,' he said. 'Are you all right?'

'Yes,' I replied. 'Where is Annette?'

'Just here.'

I sat up. Annette was lying close by, Father Lestoumel beside her.

'Is she alive?'

'Yes,' he replied.

I let myself fall back. 'Is it over now – do you think?'

'Yes,' said Bazile, making the sign of the cross. 'It is over.'

26

Annette slept for several days and I did not leave her bedside. When she awoke, she talked of 'bad dreams'. It was obvious to me that she was not speaking freely. Gentle coaxing had little effect: she remained reticent, and I could not persuade her to unburden herself. In the end, I was forced to recognize my limitations and cede authority to a superior healer: time. Father Lestoumel took me aside and offered me some consolation. 'Do not underestimate goodness,' he said. 'The child is more resilient than you think.'

I did not return to Chambault. When I spoke to Hélène of my intention to remain in Paris, she said, 'If that is what you want, monsieur.'

'Would you be so kind,' I asked, 'as to arrange the transfer of my possessions to the Hôtel Saint-Jacques?' I gave her a card. 'Much of what I own has already been packed.'

'Of course,' she replied.

I scribbled some prescriptions: 'Give these to Monsieur Jourdain. I am confident that Monsieur Raboulet and Annette will continue to benefit from my preparations; however, I would strongly recommend that you appoint another house physician. As you are probably already aware, Monsieur Jourdain is frequently indisposed.'

On the morning of her departure, I asked Hélène what she was going to tell her family. She replied that she had discussed the matter with Father Lestoumel and he had agreed to talk to Du Bris, Raboulet and Madame Odile on her behalf. He must have also told her much of what had transpired in the north tower of the cathedral, because she added, 'Monsieur: what you did for Annette – it was a very brave thing. We will be forever in your debt.' The directness of her gaze was unnerving.

'No.' I did not expect, or even wish to be forgiven. 'You owe me nothing.'

Hélène sighed and offered me her hand. I raised it to my lips and did not look up again until she was gone. A beam of sunlight slanted through a gap in the curtains, and I stood alone, breathing the lingering scent of her perfume.

The following week I wrote a letter to Charcot, requesting – with due humility – that he consider me as a prospective employee, should any suitable positions become vacant at the Salpêtrière. I was summoned to his office by return of post. He was perfectly civil. 'So, country life didn't suit you, eh? I didn't think it would. And yes, Clément, of course you can come back. There have been some very exciting developments.' The hysteria project was still Charcot's principal preoccupation and much progress had been made in my absence. It had been discovered that the symptoms of hysteria could be reproduced using hypnosis: a phenomenon of great theoretical and practical significance.

I had imagined that returning to work at the Salpêtrière would feel strange. But I was quite wrong. In fact, it felt very natural and I soon settled into a routine of ward rounds and research activities.

With the exception of Charcot's soirées, I did not see very much of my colleagues outside the hospital. Even so, I did not crave company, and there was always Bazile. I often found myself walking to Saint-Sulpice with a joint of lamb clamped under my arm, which Madame Bazile would later cook. And after we had dined, Madame Bazile would retire, and Bazile and I would smoke, drink and talk.

It was just like old times.

We revisited the same theological problems, the same arguments: 'I cannot believe in a perfect, all-knowing God, because a perfect God would not have created hell. Nor would He, by virtue of foreknowledge, have condemned so many souls to such a dreadful fate. The best we can hope for, I fear, is a good but flawed deity: a creator unable to exercise control over His creation, who battles with the forces of evil, much the same as we do.'

Bazile would listen patiently, and when I had finished he would doggedly reaffirm his faith. 'We are like insects, crawling over an edition of Montaigne's essays. With our limited sensory organs and minuscule brain, what do we perceive? A flat surface? Perhaps not even that. Montaigne's wisdom is right there, beneath our feet. But it is not accessible. And no matter how hard we try, we will never understand the great man's thoughts on virtue, indolence and cruelty – or benefit from his opinions concerning Cicero, Democritus and Heraclitus! Montaigne, and the complexities of human life, are utterly beyond us. Yet Montaigne's wisdom exists! The human world exists! And that flat surface is very misleading. One should never confuse evidence with reality, or facts with the truth.'

Our exchanges were always good-humoured. Bazile was no longer offended by my provocative remarks and I was no longer frustrated by his intransigence.

There were other pleasures: the smell of freshly cut grass, sunsets, bright stars on a cold night. Naive delights. But none of these pure, cleansing experiences ever dispelled completely the darkness I carried within my heart. My thoughts always returned to Thérèse Courbertin, regret and sadness.

Occasionally, I would receive a letter from Father Lestoumel. My replacement at Chambault, a young doctor from Orléans, did not stay for very long. Both Raboulet and Annette had stopped having seizures and there was very little for him to do there. He became bored and resigned his post.

I missed the gardens: the blossoms and the pergolas, the lawns and the box hedges, the statues and the forest. And I wondered whether Hélène Du Bris had realized her ambition of building a maze on the empty field behind the Garden of Silence. I imagined her wandering alone through its intricate avenues.

Years passed. I published many articles in international journals and wrote a well-received book on the diminution of the will in hysteria. In due course, I was promoted and became an associate professor. Ostensibly, life was good: a top-floor apartment on the Rue de Medicis, holidays in Italy, invitations to society gatherings on the Boulevard Malesherbes. I was even more comfortable in Charcot's company.

Then, one Sunday afternoon, late in the spring, I was strolling around the Luxembourg Gardens when I saw two women emerging from the crowd ahead. Their arms were linked and there was something about them that made me stop and stare.

'It can't be,' I whispered aloud.

Hélène looked much the same, but Annette was utterly transformed. She was no longer a child, but an elegant young woman of striking appearance. Mother and daughter paused to watch a little boy launch a boat on the octagonal pool. They were both dressed in fashionable red velvet and did not look at all like visitors from the provinces. Hélène made a humorous remark and Annette laughed. The toy boat sailed across the glittering water, listing in the breeze.

I felt curiously light-headed.

Hélène and Annette turned to face me, and I observed my own disbelief reflected in their changed expressions. The world fell silent and it seemed as if we were separated from the hubbub. I saw Hélène mouthing my name, the double pursing of her lips.

There they were! Occupying the foreground of a perfectly judged composition. Behind them, I could see the Luxembourg Palace, flowers in bloom and an immaculate sky. I might have been having a vision.

Annette rushed forward and, demonstrating a comprehensive disregard for convention, threw her arms around me.

'Monsieur Clément, it is you! I knew it!'

Something caught in my chest and I fought hard to overcome my emotions.

Annette stepped back and I shook my head in defenceless admiration. 'My dear child. How . . . extraordinary!'

I took Hélène's hand and kissed it.

'Madame Du Bris. What brings you to Paris?'

'We live here now,' she replied.

'You have left Chambault?'

'Yes. And our circumstances are somewhat altered.'

She spoke without a trace of self-consciousness. Du Bris had behaved dishonourably and their marriage had been dissolved. Subsequently, she had brought the children to Paris at the invitation of their uncle. Raboulet had pursued his writing ambitions and was now a successful journalist. So successful, in fact, that he had been able to afford spacious accommodation near the observatory.

'And you, monsieur?' asked Hélène. 'What is your news?'

I told them a little of my situation, but did not want to talk about myself.

'We still take your medicine,' said Annette, resting a hand on my arm. 'And it still works.'

'I am very glad,' I replied.

'Mother,' said Annette, 'can we invite Monsieur Clément to dinner?'

I glanced at Hélène. 'Really, madame, I would not want to impose . . .'

'What a good idea!' Hélène cut in.

Annette's expression intensified. 'There are some things I would like to talk to you about, monsieur.'

'Things?' I enquired.

'Yes, things that I remember – from when I was very ill.'

'And I am sure,' continued Hélène, 'that Tristan would be delighted to see you again, Monsieur Clément. It is you who have made his dreams possible.'

We exchanged addresses, said goodbye and I watched Hélène and Annette ascend a staircase and disappear from view.

The Greeks inform us that Pandora's box contained all the evils of the world, and that when she opened it these evils were released. There was, however, something left at the very bottom: Hope. Standing there, in the Luxembourg Gardens, among the bank managers and their wives, the lawyers and the seamstresses, the nurses and the children, I recognized that myths survive because they express the deepest of truths. And, miraculously, I found that I could hope for meaning and purpose once again.

Concerning Influences, Historical Figures and Sources

The Forbidden began as a homage to J.-K. Huysmans, whose *Là-Bas* is a firm favourite of mine; however, as the plot developed, other French novels began exerting an influence, most notably *Justine*, by the Marquis de Sade, and *Bel Ami*, by Guy de Maupassant. Saint-Sébastien is fictional, but owes an inestimable debt to another literary island – Saint-Jacques – as described by Patrick Leigh Fermor in *The Violins of Saint-Jacques*. As an adolescent, I consumed the black magic novels of Dennis Wheatley; readers conversant with his work – now a guilty pleasure for ladies and gentlemen of a certain age – might hear his voice echoed occasionally (although I have stopped short of the Imperial Tokay wine and Hoyo de Monterrey cigars). Wheatley was also a great fan of J.-K. Huysmans: in fact, *Là-Bas* was one of the volumes included in a series published as the Dennis Wheatley Library of the Occult, from 1974 to 1977.

Historical Figures

Many of the characters who appear (or are mentioned) in *The Forbidden* are real:

CÉCILE CHAMINADE (1857–1944) was a composer and pianist who achieved considerable fame in her day. The recital described in *The Forbidden* took place at the residence of Le Coupey on 25 April 1878. She was greatly interested in spiritualism.

JEAN-MARTIN CHARCOT (1825–1893) was a pupil of Duchenne and is now regarded as the father of modern neurology. He was chief of services at the Salpêtrière and became known as the 'Napoleon of the Neuroses'. His reputation spread worldwide and his soirées attracted many of the scientific, political and artistic elite of the late nineteenth century. Many of the descriptions of Charcot and the Salpêtrière in *The Forbidden* were based on material that can be found in *Charcot: Constructing Neurology*, by Goetz, Bonduelle and Gelfand.

GUILLAUME DUCHENNE DE BOULOGNE (1806–1875) was a pioneer of electrical resuscitation techniques and was an experimental physiologist. The resuscitation cases described in *The Forbidden* are authentic and taken from *Localized Electrization and its Application to Pathology and Therapeutics*. Duchenne's most celebrated work, *The Mechanisms of Human Facial Expression* – ostensibly an experimental study of facial musculature – reflects his preoccupation with the soul as the origin of human emotions.

JUSTINE ETCHEVERY – a notorious 'case study' – was admitted to the Salpêtrière in June 1869.

CHARLES MÉRYON (1821–1868) was an artist who produced an atmospheric etching (which he titled *Le Stryge/The Strix*) of the winged gargoyle on the cathedral of Notre-Dame. He died young in the Charenton asylum. Baudelaire wrote of him: 'a cruel demon has touched M. Méryon's brain.'

Other Influences and Sources

The neurotoxin TTX (tetrodox) is found in the skin of the puffer fish, certain fungi and other creatures indigenous to the French Antilles. It can induce a death-like state and is thought to be the means by which bokors create zombies.

Near-death experiences (NDEs) are a relatively common phenomenon. Today, one in ten resuscitated patients – if asked – report core elements such as the tunnel and the light.

Chambault is loosely based on the small but magical chateau of Chatonnière and its exquisite formal gardens (37190 Azay le Rideau). It is one of the Loire's best-kept secrets.

The relationship between the cathedral of Notre-Dame and all things demonic is long and curious. The Celtic tribe who worshipped on the present site produced an uncommon number of demonic figures, and in 1711 workmen digging beneath the choir discovered four altars, one of which bears the image of a horned god. The north portal of the cathedral shows the legend of Théophile, and it is perhaps the earliest representation of a Faustian narrative. Some of the stone used to construct the cathedral came from beneath the Rue d'Enfer – Hell Street (which an old prophecy identified as the site of an infernal abyss). The cathedral is most famous, however, for its gargoyles and in particular the winged demon now known as Le Stryge. The carving is notable for its long nails – a sign that the creature drinks blood. Before the nineteenth century, a vampire was 'a devil' equipped with the means to rip open flesh to satisfy its thirst. Fangs were a late nineteenth-century contribution to vampire mythology and not very practical. Only a small amount of blood can escape from puncture wounds.

In the Renaissance, capturing demons in glass was a relatively common practice among magicians of renown. The Holy Roman Emperor Rudolf II (1552–1612) is reputed to have obtained a 'demon in glass' for his extensive collection of oddities. Father Ranvier's exorcism employs two forms of the Roman Ritual, the first for exorcizing those possessed by evil spirits and the second for exorcizing Satan and apostate angels. Father Lestoumel's exorcism uses the text of an eighth-century Galician manuscript. The Seal of Shabako is an all-purpose protective amulet once very popular among the inhabitants of Abydos – the site of many ancient temples. Amulets and spells were essential for the dead to negotiate their way through the perilous Egyptian underworld.

F. R. TALLIS
London 2011

Kapitänleutnant Siegfried Lorenz looked back at the foaming wake. Pale green strands of froth separated from the churning trail and dispersed on the waves like tattered ribbons. The sea surrounding U-330 had become a gently undulating expanse of floating white pavements and the mist was becoming thicker. He had only been on the bridge for a few minutes, but already his hands and feet were frozen and his beard was streaked with tiny glittering crystals. Diesel fumes rose up from the gratings and lingered in the air like a congregation of ghosts. As he turned, his face was lashed by spray and his mouth filled with the taste of salt.

Below the conning tower sailors were hammering at shards of ice that hung from the 8.8 cm gun. Glassy spikes shattered and transparent fragments skittered across the deck. Others were engaged in the arduous task of scraping encrustations of rime from the safety rails.

'Hurry up,' Lorenz called down. 'Get a move on.'

Excess weight made the boat unstable. It rolled, even in the absence of a heavy swell.

Juhl – the second watch officer – moved stiffly towards Lorenz; he was wearing oilskins that had become as inflexible as armour. Icicles had formed around the rim of his sou'wester. 'I hope they don't do any damage,' he muttered.

'It'll be all right,' Lorenz responded. 'They're not using axes.' One of the men swore as he slipped and dropped his hammer. 'I'm more concerned about the state of the deck. It's like a skating rink. If one of them slides off the edge there'll be trouble. We'd never get him out in time.'

'Perhaps we should dive?'

Lorenz considered the suggestion. 'The water temperature will be a little warmer, I agree. But I'm not confident the vents will open.'

Juhl peered into the fog and grumbled, 'And all for a weather report!'

Lorenz pulled his battered cap down low and pushed his gloved hands into the deep pockets of his leather jacket. 'What are your plans – after we return?'

'Plans?' Juhl was puzzled by the question.

'Yes. Where are you off to?'

'Home, I suppose.'

'I've been thinking about Paris again. There's a very fine restaurant near the cathedral. A little place on the Isle Saint Louis – only a few tables – but the food is exquisite.'

Stein and Keller (one fixedly monitoring the south quadrant, the other gazing east) stole a quick, smirking glance at each other.

An iceberg came into view. Even though the sky was overcast the tip seemed to glow from within, emitting a strange, eldritch light.

'I didn't expect the temperature to drop like this,' said Juhl.

'Surprisingly sudden,' Lorenz agreed.

Veils of mist drifted over the bow and the men below became indistinct and shapeless. The gun rapidly faded until only its outline remained and within seconds they were moving through a featureless void, a white nothingness – empty, blind.

'This is ridiculous, Kaleun,' said Juhl. 'Can you see anything: anything at all?'

Lorenz leaned over the open hatch and ordered both engines to be stopped. He then called over the bulwark, 'Enough! Down tools!' The men on the deck were hidden beneath a blanket of vapour. Voigt, the bosun's mate who was supervising the work party, acknowledged the command.

The boat heaved and the collision of ice floes created a curious, knocking accompaniment.

'What are we doing, Kaleun?' asked Juhl.

Lorenz didn't reply. Paris, Brest, Berlin – the steamed-up windows of a coffee house, fragrant waitresses, billboards, cobbled streets and tram lines – umbrellas, organ grinders, and barber shops. They were so far away from anything ordinary, familiar, apprehensible. Eventually Lorenz said: 'We should dive soon.'

'As soon as possible,' Juhl concurred.

'If the vents are stuck,' said Lorenz, 'we'll just have to get them open again – somehow.'

The rise and fall of the boat was hypnotic and encouraged mental vacancy. Lorenz inhaled and felt the cold conducting through his jaw, taunting the nerves in his teeth.

'Kaleun?' The speaker had adopted a peculiar stage whisper. 'Kaleun?'

Lorenz leaned over the bulwark and could barely make out Peters – one of the diesel hands – at the foot of the tower.

'What?'

'Herr Kaleun?' The man continued. 'I can see something . . .'

Juhl looked at Lorenz – tense and ready to react.

The commander simply shook his head and responded, 'Where?'

'Off the port bow, Kaleun. Forty-five degrees.'

'What can you see?'

'It's . . . I don't know what it is.'

Lorenz lifted his binoculars and aimed them into the mist. He was able to detect drifting filaments, a hint of depth, but nothing materialized below the shifting, restless textures. 'All right, I'm coming down.' He squeezed past the lookouts, descended the ladder, and walked with great care towards the bow, where he found Peters standing in front of the gun and gazing out to sea.

'Kaleun,' Peters raised his hand and pointed. The commander positioned himself beside the seaman. 'You can't see it now. But it was just there.'

'Debris, a container – what?'

'Not flotsam. Too high in the water.'

'An iceberg, then. You saw an iceberg, Peters.'

'No, Herr Kaleun.' The man was offended. 'With respect, sir. No. It wasn't an iceberg. I'm sure it wasn't an iceberg.'

They were joined by two others: Kruger, a torpedo mechanic, and a boyish seaman called Berger. All of them were boyish, but Berger looked obscenely young – like a child.

'Ah yes,' said Berger, 'I think . . . Yes, I see it.'

'There! There you are.' Peters jabbed his finger at the mist.

Shadows gathered and connected: a vertical line acquired definition. Like a theatrical effect, gauzy curtains were drawn back until a pale silhouette was revealed. The object was a makeshift raft with barrels attached to the sides. A figure was leaning against a central post – one arm raised, a hand gripping the upper extremity for support, his right cheek pressed against his own bicep. The man's attitude suggested exhaustion and imminent collapse. Another figure was sitting close by: knees bent, feet flat, head slumped forward.

Lorenz's fingers closed around the safety rail and he felt the intense cold through his gloves. He called out: 'You. Who are you? Identify yourselves.'

A blast of raw wind swept away more of the mist. The figures on the raft did not move. Lorenz tried hailing them in English – but this also had no effect. Above the horizon, the sun showed through the cloud, no more substantial than a faintly drawn circle.

Lorenz raised his binoculars again and focused his attention on the standing figure. The man had empty sockets where his eyes should have been and his nose had been eaten away. Much of the flesh on the exposed side of his face was missing, creating a macabre, lopsided grin. A fringe of icicles hung from his chin, which made him look like a character from a Russian fairytale, a winter goblin or some other supernatural inhabitant of the Siberian steppe. Lorenz shifted his attention to the seated man, whose trousers were torn. Ragged hems revealed the lower bones of his legs. The raft was drifting towards the stationary U-boat and Berger whispered, 'They're dead.'

The milky disc of the sun disappeared.

'But one of them's standing up,' said Peters.

'He must be frozen solid,' replied Kruger.

Lorenz settled the issue. 'They're dead all right.' He handed Peters the binoculars.

The diesel hand whistled. 'That's horrible. How did it happen?'

'Gulls,' said Lorenz. 'They must have pecked out their eyes and torn off strips of flesh as the raft was carried north.'

'Extraordinary,' Peters handed the binoculars to Kruger. 'I've never seen anything like it. And one still standing . . . poor bastard.'

'Who are they?' asked Berger.

'They're from a liner,' Lorenz replied. 'Look at those life jackets. They're ancient. A warship wouldn't carry life jackets like that.'

The commander and his men stood, captivated, watching the raft's steady approach. Waves slapped against the hull. Lorenz wondered how long this ghoulish pair had been floating around the arctic and he toyed with a fanciful notion that they might, perhaps, have been adrift for years, even decades.

Kruger handed the binoculars back to Lorenz, who raised them one last time. The lopsided grin of the standing figure was oddly communicative.

'Well,' said Lorenz, letting go of the binoculars and clapping his hands together, 'let's move on. We don't want the

Tommies catching us like this – enjoying the weather and mixing with the locals.'

One of the radio men, Ziegler, stepped out of his room and called out, 'Officer's signal.' Juhl squeezed past some petty officers, collected the message, and set up the decoding machine. He did this with a degree of studied ostentation, supplementing his actions with flourishes reminiscent of a concert artist. The machine looked like a complicated type-writer in a wooden case. In addition to the standard keys, there was a lamp-board, three protruding disc-shaped rotors, and a panel of sockets that could be connected with short lengths of cable. Lorenz handed Juhl a piece of paper on which he had already written the daily code setting. The second-watch officer configured the machine and proceeded to type. His brow furrowed and he turned to address Lorenz. Speaking in a confidential whisper he said, 'For the Commander only.' Lorenz nodded, picked up the machine and took it into his nook, where he readjusted the settings according to his own special instructions.

Receipt of a triply encrypted message was an unusual occurrence. Lorenz could hear the muffled whisper of hushed speculation. When he finally emerged from behind his green curtain, he handed the code machine back to Juhl and climbed through the circular hatchway that led to the control room. He stood by the chart table and studied a mildewed, crumbling map of the North Atlantic. Altering the angle of the lamp, he moved a circle of bright illumination across the grid squares. Above the table was a tangle of pipes and a black iron wheel.

There was a sense of expectation and men started to gather, all of them pretending to be engaged in some crucial task. Lorenz rolled up the sleeves of his jumper and pushed his cap back, exposing his high forehead and a lick of black hair. 'How confident are you – about our position?'

Müller, the navigator, cleared his throat: 'It's been a while since I've looked up into a clear sky.' He slapped his hand on the sextant box. 'So it would be difficult to . . .'

'You're always being over-cautious.'

Lorenz stepped forward and examined Müller's plot. He took a deep breath, turned to face the group of men that had assembled behind him, and called out an order to change course. The helmsman, seated at his station, acknowledged the command and adjusted the position of the rudder. 'Full speed ahead,' Lorenz added. The engine telegraph was reset and a red light began to flash.

Müller glanced down at the chart and said, 'Iceland?'

'Thereabouts . . .'

'Why?'

The red light stopped flashing and turned green.

Lorenz shrugged. 'They didn't say. Well, not exactly.' The diesels roared and the boat lurched forward, freeing itself from the grip of a tenacious wave.

picador.com

blog
videos
interviews
extracts